Genevieve Lyons was born and educated in Dublin, where she began her successful career as an actress. She became one of Ireland's leading ladies, and was one of the founders of the Dublin Globe Theatre. Ms Lyons gave up her acting career to bring up her daughter Michele and has also spent time teaching drama and writing original plays for school-children.

Genevieve Lyons lives in London, but spends much of the year travelling abroad. Her previous novels, SLIEVELEA and THE GREEN YEARS, are also available from Futura.

D0589593

Also by Genevieve Lyons

SLIEVELEA
THE GREEN YEARS

Dark Rosaleen

GENEVIEVE LYONS

Futura

A Futura Book

Reproduced, printed and bound in Great Britain by
BPCC Hazell Books Ltd
Member of BPCC Ltd
Aylesbury, Bucks, England

Futura Publications
A Division of
Macdonald & Co (Publishers) Ltd
66–73 Shoe Lane
London EC4P 4AB
A member of Maxwell Pergamon Publishing Corporation plc

This book is for Alan and Howard, whose kindness to me during the writing of this book was incalculable, and, of course, Michele.

PART ONE

PART ONE

Chapter

1

THE land was drowning under the rain, and the dogs, howling in the night, vied with the screaming wind. Trees were swept clean of the few leaves that remained to them.

The girl raised her eyes to the moon, a paring of silver, obscured every other moment by swollen, angry, speeding clouds. She walked and she walked through the dark wildness of the night, placing one foot ahead of the other with the regularity of a metronome. Even when the wind tore her hair back from her face with a violence that was like a knife across the soft skin of her scalp her legs never lost the rhythm of her stride. Through the darkness of the wild night she walked, her back straight as the stem of an elm, determination in her every sinew.

Her toes were long and slim, and splayed when she walked, becoming stained with the mud and mire she waded through barefoot, and the bangles on her ankles clinked as she toiled along. Her legs were sturdy and she had a full curved bottom on her. Her waist was narrow as a reed from the fen, her bosom deep and full, and on it rested a babby supported in her arms. Her shawl was wrapped about the babby so her head was bare in the wild weather. Indeed, it was a freezing night and the raw wind would slice a body in two. She wore only the fine green velvet dress embossed in gold thread that she had off a high Sassenach lady of fashion down Tipperary way. It smelled of sweet sweat, the perfume of jasmine and a faint remembrance of camphor to discourage moths. It was muddy and spoiled now, the rain turning the fresh mossy colour densely dark. Nevertheless it kept her body warm.

The stones cut her feet as she walked, and the hem of her

3

dress trailed in the dirt, but she never paused, never hesitated. Though the road was long and wearying she showed no signs of fatigue. Her curly hair was soaked and clung to her bare shoulders. Her face was white as a drift of snow and her eyes blue as the pebbles at the bottom of the pool in the Arcadian Grove where she had met and mated with Creagh Jeffries ten months ago. There was water on her coarse-fibred lashes waiting to fall in drops like tears on her white cheeks. Only her mouth was red as blood on the breast of a swan. There was a wicked swan that sat mirrored on the Grotto's pool. She bit you viciously if you tried to see her young. She had pricked her breast on a thorn, that swan, and when Creagh tried to help her, she screamed at him, flapped her giant wings and hissed like the fisherwomen in Galway when they conveyed their disapproval of the girl as she swayed past them on the Quays. To look at, though, the swan seemed serene as the white-robed Sisters of Charity in the convent near Wicklow town, and so did she. No one could see the savage will behind the lovely face.

And still she walked over the mountain, purposefully, a firm and steady pace, indifferent to the owl screeching and the wolf hound that tore the night apart with his yowls. Rosaleen, they called her; Dark Rosaleen, after the land, after Ireland. She held her babby fiercely, possessively, but now and then she would move it a fraction apart fom her as if she had given it away already.

She covered the babby's face with the shawl against the wind. She remembered her father saying that the March wind drove men mad. Well, be that as it may, she had a journey to make, a task to accomplish, and if the weather decided to hamper her it would not succeed. March winds could blow, gulls cry out, a high lonely sound, dogs could vie with each other, lightning could rend the floor of heaven and darkness cover the face of the earth: nevertheless, she would march the Wicklow hills till she reached Usher Castle, and she would get there before the night was out. She was near her goal. Usher Castle lay before her and it was not dawn yet. She could see the turrets and towers piercing the gaunt skyline where the trees were beaten low by the storm. High up on its mountain Usher cast a gloom-heavy shadow.

Then she heard the noise. It made her falter. For the first time her footsteps were unsteady and tentative. It was a high

4

keening sound, as that made by a woman lamenting over the deep grave of her man. This sound, though, was unearthly. It came from the Elsewhere and it did not come from the Bri Léith, the fairy earth-mounds inhabited, as everyone knew, by the people of the god Dagda who had fled there when the Gaels came to Ireland. They could sometimes be heard singing in high sweet voices like the music of the harp deep in the night. But they were benign. This was a harbinger of death, a dark spirit, and though she had no religion she crossed herself.

She heard the cry again. It made her hair stand up and prickles shudder all down her back. Three times she heard it.

'Yerra it's the banshee,' she said to herself. 'An' it howling in the night. Tis a death in the Dun (Castle) an' no mistake. Ah God, it's as Lothar said. I wonder if it'll make the difference?'

She walked and she walked and she walked, and she heard the banshee, and she saw the great towers of Usher loom before her and the great bronze door closed against her. But her heart was triumphant.

Chapter

2

DARK Rosaleen was a metaphor for Ireland, for Erin:

'Oh my dark Rosaleen, do not sigh do not weep,
The priests are on the ocean green,
They march along the deep,
There's wine from the Royal Pope
Upon the ocean green,
And Spanish ale shall give you hope
My Dark Rosaleen,
My own Rosaleen,
Shall glad your heart, shall give you hope,
Shall give you health and help and hope
My Dark Rosaleen.'

Yes, the song was sung metaphorically, for the time had been, and still was to a certain extent, when patriotism was a crime punishable by death. For the Gaels to talk of help from overseas was to court the hangman or the executioner's bullet. 'Dark Rosaleen' was forever hopeful that her powerful Catholic neighbours would help her persecuted people to freedom, but she continually wept with frustration and disappointment for she was always let down. England sat between them and her, and England's navy brooded watchfully in the narrow Channel. The French and the Spanish did not want to flirt with that.

Rosaleen's father had named her after Ireland because she had been born there. Her father, Hagar, and her mother, Melba, were royalty of a sort in the Romany clans they belonged to, but neither of them knew where they hailed from. Swarthy-skinned, dark as Turks, though whether from grime or naturally no one knew, their ancestry seemed on evidence more Eastern than Northern. They were more like the Egypty men that came sometimes to the gatherings on their way across the world. Time and again Hagar pondered idly how Rosaleen had come by her pearly skin and wondered about Melba's fidelity, of which, deep down, he was entirely confident. He was sure of her slavish adoration and fear of him. All the tribe, including Melba, were mightily afeared of him, so he did not seriously doubt his parenthood, but the occasional thought of magic, of spells or enchantment, crossed his mind, only to be discarded. And sure, what did it matter anyway? Nevertheless, pure snow-white skin was rare among the caravan people, and Rosaleen's skin was white as the milk from the black Kerry cows, and you couldn't get much whiter than that.

Hagar was a leader and had been taught many things by Lothar the *filid* or seer, who was a Druid, a teacher and counsellor. As well as magic, Lothar had instructed Hagar in the ancient language of the Gaels which was near as old as the source of their Romany tongue, which came from the Egypt of the Pharaohs.

Their parents or their grandparents, it's as maybe, had come to this land after one of the European purges. At times, different nations, different cultures took exception to the gypsies and the inevitable persecution began. The gypsies simply moved. They were not settlers. They needed no fixed abode. And so, many moons ago, the family had come here to Ireland, after which Hagar and Melba had named their beloved white-skinned daughter; Dark Rosaleen. They had stayed, for the Irish were good to the travelling people. The British, who sat on the Gaels, sat on them as well and smothered them. They were scared of the Romanies, who were too much outside the law for their taste, and indifferent to it. The British did not understand this lawlessness. They could comfortably ignore the conquered people of Ireland, for they thought they had them cowed. The Irish wanted them to believe they accepted their conquerers and they suceeded. They are the greatest actors in the world. But the British kept away from Hagar and his like.

Sometimes Hagar took his family west with the caravan and they took a currach to the outer Isles. He would sit with Melba and Rosaleen in a scrumpy one-roomed cottage and in the light from the turf-fire they would listen to the official story-teller of the district who waited for '*Inis scéal dom*' ('Tell me a story') so he could begin. Then he would tell tales more marvellous than any others: The Ulster Cycle of Cú Chulain, King Conor MacNessa and Queen Maeve of Connaught and the White Bull of Cooley; the tales of Tir na nÓg and the Irish Otherworld. He would tell of the mythological Cycle about the Earliest Time, before the coming of the Gaels and the Goddess Danu, the God Dagda, and his son Oengus and Niamh of the Golden Hair. And lastly, the Fenian Cycle. The Fenian time was later: Tara in the third century, the reign of Cormac Mac Airt.

The ould fellow with the clay pipe, his hair wild and white as the crests on the waves, his eyes fervent, his gnarled brown hands active with beautiful gestures, would describe the stories of Fionn and Oisín and Caolte, of Cónan Marel and the great love of Diarmuit and Gráinne, and of the valour of the Gael. Fian is the Gaelic word for warrior and now some of the secret societies meeting through the land called themselves Fenians. That is how it came about.

Rosaleen had thought of those things as she walked along. She had tried not to think of the other thing, of Creagh and Arcadia, but it would come back.

The sweet sad memories of the previous May. May of the apple-blossom and the lark singing in the clear soft air. May of the clouds of bluebells that cloaked the earth beneath the fresh-leaved trees in the wood. It was a time for new things, soft colours — and love. Of course it was the drowsy time for love.

The Arcadian Grove lay deep in the Wicklow mountains. It was an enclosed spot, except for a footbridge over a mountainy stream that descended in waterfall and formed a blue pool in the hollow of the place. All manner of flowers grew there. Like a garden it was, albeit wild, with clumps of crocus, wild violets and hyacinth and scarlet campion, yellow buttercups and prim-roses, cowslips and narcissi, honeysuckle and sweetbriar. There were sea-pinks on the cliffs, sprouting from the verdant slopes that circled the pool and gave way suddenly to the craggy mountain sides. It was like a little oasis, the Egypty men said, and parked their caravans nearby. You couldn't get a dog-cart down there, or a horse even, for when you crossed the foot-bridge the mirrored lake with its pair of white swans was reached by a steep flight of steps carved out of the rock and descending almost vertically to the beautious spot below.

There was an ivy-covered ruin, though of what it was hard to say. The stumps of some pillars lay there and beside the columns cow-parsley and celandine blew in the breeze. The stones were warm, for the place was a sun-trap and retained the heat. It was totally protected from the wild wind by its circle of mountains. Perhaps it had been a Druid's lair in the old days, for the requisite oak was there, fat, squat and aged. Yet Rosaleen knew the Druids preferred high sites, near to heaven, the all-powerful sun, the magic moon and the stars.

Rosaleen loved the place. The gypsies roamed the length and breath of the land: the wild Mayo shores, chalk-stoned, stump-walled and cottaged, lush Kerry lakes, mist-veiled, purple, shadowed and fuchsia-decorated. They travelled the Druid lands in Galway and the Burren in Co. Clare, that vast bleached plateau of limestone, treeless, a series of mighty terraces and escarpments, a place to put the heart across the bravest man, yet starred with exquisite flowers found only in Alpine and Mediterranean climates — small brilliant gentians, pale yellow and magenta Dryas. They went in their wanderings to the edges of the towns of Limerick and Tipperary, Galway and Listowel when the cattle fairs were in full swing, to grand Dublin itself for the races, but this, this little spot, was the place she liked best.

Last year she had lingered there every day all summer long. At first she had been alone. It was May and she idled there letting time slip past. She drowsed, she drifted, and in some subconscious way she waited. She decorated her hair with flowers, studding her dark curls with daisies and buttercups, wild pink roses and pansies. She made wreaths of ivy and wove them through her jetty waves until the coronets nestled in the blue-black tresses as if they grew there. She bathed in the pool and tried to avoid the swans' reedy nest; they respected her privacy as long as she did theirs.

She studied her reflection in the still waters and stained her lips with early berries. She sang to herself as she idled, for the gypsies saw no intrinsic value in work for its own sake, a conviction they shared with the Irish. Work was done for a purpose and only when necessary. For who would want to waste such days as these?

Then one day of pale gold he came across the footbridge,

drawn to the magic place by the sweetness of her song. He sat on his horse, a dark shadow against the sun, reflected in the lake, casting a frown over the Arcadian Grove as her song faded to a halt.

He dismounted and tethered his big chestnut mare and climbed nimbly down the steps, never faltering. He wore riding garb and had a white stock at his throat. He strode across the grass to her and stopped a little away, quite amazed.

She saw he was only a wee bit taller than she and that his hair was soft hazel-nut brown, exactly matching his eyes. His skin was white as his teeth, and his mouth, she decided, was tender and ardent as a woman's.

'Your name?' he queried.

She shook her black hair and cried out, suddenly alarmed, for she had seen no man but the Romany men close-to before, 'An' you go from here now, me lad, or my Da'll tan your hide.'

He burst out laughing, hands on hips, head back, and she blushed, mortified.

She wore the green velvet dress embossed with gold thread. She had only just acquired it. The Tipperary woman had rejected it when April closed its doors and May had come. The dress then was the colour of the moss, and it left her white shoulders bare. She wore her petticoat under it and had draped a fichu of lace over her bosom for modesty's sake. She looked a wild and wanton thing, but like most gypsy girls was virtuous though unafraid.

'No. No,' he said. 'I mean you no harm. I took a wrong turning and heard your voice on the wind beyond this place. I had to follow it. I could not do otherwise. And look what I found. A princess in a fairy tale.' He paused, looking at her intently, not moving. Then he said, 'What is this place?'

'People call it the Arcadian Grove. Them that know of it, that is. But I think it's more a Druid place, a place of legend like Emain Macha. It would be in a place like this that Conor Mac Nessa hid Deirdre of the Sorrows, she who, was the most beautiful woman in the world, and that ...' she said, pointing to the ruin that slept, ivy-covered in the sun, 'that the place she lived with Lavarcham her bond woman until Naisi and the Sons of Usna came and they fell in love ...'

'Over the footbridge he came one day, "A fair-haired man coming at sun-rise to light the place. He rode over the bright

10

land against which the ocean murmurs. He stirred the sea to blood,'' he paraphrased the text to please her. 'Like me,' he added and his eyes smiled at her. She caught her breath and blushed, looking down, then up at him through her lashes, revealing to him her interest.

'You're wrong anyhow,' she said, teasing, pleased to show off her knowledge, ''Twas Bran the son of Febal that that referred to. But you're right too. For the woman said to Bran of the place, "The island is supported by pillars of gold" . . . that's the sun,' she pointed to the pale shimmering disc in the washed blue sky, '"Lovely colours shine on every side" . . . that's the flowers.' Her arm swept in an open-handed gesture that encompassed all sides of the valley and its covering of blossom. He interrupted her. '"Music sounds always in the air." That's your singing.'

They laughed together and he sat on a mossy stone saying in wonder, 'How do you know all this? You were well taught.'

'Ach, my father is a pupil of the great descendant pupil of a Druid, a *filid* himself who has taught him many things both dark and light.'

The young man sucked in his breath and nodded. 'He has luck,' he said, 'But you're a gypsy.'

'Yes I am. But I'm an Irishwoman too. An' what about you? You're a gentleman'.

He had removed his stock and opened the neck of his fine cambric shirt in the heat. Now he took off his jacket.

'It's hot in this place.' he said, 'I'm Creagh Jeffries of Usher Castle.' He said it matter-of-factly. She knew the imposing building not far away. 'How do they call you?' he asked.

'Rosaleen. Dark Rosaleen — after Ireland,' she said, and he smiled at her in a way that made her blush and then turn away.

They talked until the sun moved from them, never coming too close to each other. She marvelled that he and his sisters were called Jeffries yet his brother was Lord Usher. They talked of Erin and the old names and the old stories and both were surprised at the extent of the other's knowledge. And then he left, saying he would be back next day.

She waited, not really expecting him but hoping, pressing her hands against the wild beating of her heart. For the first time in her life she could not sleep and when she did his face haunted her dreams. She waited and he came. He came over the foot-bridge swiftly and sped down the steps to her, but they stopped a little apart from each other, fearful, expectant.

And so it went, day by day, meeting. Each day they drew closer till they were but a breath apart. And on the next day the great hunger had to be appeased and there was no longer a breath between them but mouth consumed mouth, body drew into body and the two became, as the Gods had meant, one.

Hagar saw it all, knew what was happening, but what could he do? He could not stop his daughter's growing beauty, stifle her blooming into love, forbid her eager departure for the Grove each day for then he would lose her forever. Nor could he halt the young cavalier on horseback rushing to the love awaiting him. It was impossible. It was not his way for he was wise and he knew it would be easier to tell the sun not to rise, forbid the flowers to bloom, stop the incoming tide.

And so that May they practised on each other's bodies the discovery of pleasure, the perfecting of love. They thought not of the morrow, they lived for the day only. They played like children together, hide-and-seek, blind-man's-buff and races, always ending in the sunlight in each other's arms. She would remove her green velvet dress and sit in her petticoat and chemise in the golden day till she lost even those coverings and they were like the First People, naked and joyous.

They talked of those people, the Fomorians and the Tuatha De Dannan and the legendary lovers of Erin: Tristan and Iesult; Deirdre and Naisi; Diarmuit and Gráinne; and of course, themselves, comparing. He was surprised she spoke Gaelic. He knew little of gypsies and she knew nothing of the aristocracy.

'An' I thought you were all terrible monsters altogether an' your sort always gettin' the gamekeepers to set the dogs on us.'

He threw back his head and laughed. 'I never knew your sort loved the land and the tales and the stories like we did,' he replied, looking at her pure profile as she gazed up at the mountain peaks outlined in the sun, her eyes wrinkled up against the glare. 'James, my brother, had a dog, a runt of an animal. We never knew how we came by it. His head was big and heavy and his back leg crooked, but he was a fierce fighter. James could not destroy him. He's soft like that. We tried to give him to the gypsies but they wouldn't have him. They jeered at James and called him an *amadán* which he didn't understand. Then they stole his donkey and left.'

She nodded appreciatively, 'Ah well, we wouldn't want a

crooked dog. That's maybe for the tinkers, *sin scéal eile*, you should have tried the tinkers.' There was withering scorn in her voice and with a dismissive gesture of her hand she continued, 'No. We are proud, and cruel maybe. We are brave and we are thieves ... to live and take what we need, that's all. They never took your horse?'

He shook his head, 'If they had James would have pursued them and caught them and given them to the hangman.'

She nodded sagely. 'You see? We are clever. They took your donkey knowing that.'

She was fascinated by his family, who lived in a fixed place, a house that they were tied to, a house that controlled their lives, that, it seemed to her, ruled them. And their home was a castle. He had had to describe the place to her, room by room: the great hall; the oak-panelled dining-room; the shooting gallery; and the minstrels' landing; the carved stone staircase covered in silk carpets from Samarkand. He had had to tell her of the priest's hole used in Cromwell's time when eventually the house was gutted by flames and the family went into hiding.

Now he said, 'We are five, and Dolly, my brother's wife. We don't count Fergal, the poor hunchback. My father is dead. He was a diplomat, and my brother and sisters were with him in the East. He left me at home with my Uncle, Old Gentleman, who hardly ever spoke to me. He still doesn't. I spent most of my time with the Widow Boann.'

Rosaleen nodded. She knew the Widow Boann slightly but she did not tell Creagh that.

'She taught me all the Irish tales and stories,' he continued, 'the legends and mythology. She spoke to me in Gaelic. Then my father was killed and my mother near lost her reason. She shipped the body home. It took ages and she spent all the time at sea lying on the coffin. Can you imagine? All the time it was in transit in the hold. The sailors thought her mad. Sometimes I do. There was a stench from the coffin, James said, but she didn't seem to notice. They had the funeral at Usher and my mother threw herself into the grave on top of the coffin. She did not want to leave my father. James and I and Old Gentleman and the priest had to pull Mother up. Oh it was a horror and a farce.' He shook his head, his soft brown hair falling over his milk-white brow. 'My mother behaved like a native woman on a funeral pyre. Must have rubbed off on her in India. James

13

thought she might go into purdah. I found it all very embarrassing. I had not seen her for so long, so very long, and I hardly knew my father. They came back to Usher every so often, but I'd always forgotten what she looked like. Now they are home for good. James and Sophie and Bella tease me horribly and call me a little Irish peasant. I adore Sophie. She is a darling. But I hate Bella. She is a cat. I really hate the British. All the British bastards in this country I hate them.'

'But a lot of them are Irish now.'

'No they are not. When did the British ever become integrated in a country, in its culture? They call it "going native". Not like the Romans, who utilized the best in every country they colonized. Sophie says that in the terrible Indian heat in the middle of the day, when all the natives from peasants to Maharajahs went to sleep, Mother and Father and all their friends were on the lawn drinking tea! Can you imagine? What fools they must have looked, and no wonder they became unhinged. Mother is certainly unhinged. They came here to Ireland, the British, and they took, took, and are taking. They are not putting anything back. Nothing at all. They are trying to strangle the Irish language, the Irish culture. Well, we are going to stop all that. There are many who feel the way I do. We meet ... we talk ... we plan.'

She took a sharp breath. 'The Fenians,' she said and he clapped his hand over her mouth though there was no one within earshot. Butterflies danced about the pale mauve buddleia and a fat bee droned.

'Hush ... never say that. It means death or prison or both. Never say ...' Her eyes were wide and her shoulders pale under her jetty hair that softly fell on the marble slopes. You could see the blue veins beneath her milky skin. 'Oh never, never, never, *a grá.*' she said, and he touched the white broderie anglaise at her bosom and ran his fingers over her breasts till they reached the cherry-red nipples and he buried his face in her body. She clung to him, arching herself to his desire and crying out her gratification.

Hagar sat by his caravan behind the curve of the mountain and wondered how it would end. Melba was quite sure: a babby. Ach, then, that would not matter. What was another babby in the tribe? Melba would have liked a whole batch of babbies to mother and bully and gently love, but it never happened though

14

Hagar was a virile man. It was as if it had taken all the essences of the best in her and Hagar to make her beautiful daughter, and there had been nothing left for another.

Creagh had gone with the wild geese and the swallow. Rosaleen knew he went to meetings the length and breadth of the land and the Fenians meant more to him than anything, even her. He was a man with ideals, with fevered ideas, intoxicating dreams in his head. Men so consumed, she knew, belong to no woman. She also knew that he could never marry her. She accepted that, too, without question. Socially they were divided, irrevocably, forever. He came sometimes after the enchanted month of May had given way to June's soft colours and July's flaunting, he came sometimes to her again in the Grove. And later with August's heat he followed the gaudy caravan she lived in with Melba and Hagar.

It was painted all the colours of the rainbow; green, orange, purple and blue, pink and yellow and red. There were flowers and magic designs both outside and in and garlic hung everywhere. There were rushes on the floor. Pictures, beads and bangles, bright shawls and shining knives with carved handles hung on the walls. There were other strange little pouches that held the ingredients for spells and magic and the weed to give you the gift of prophecy and deep sleep. Bronze pans rattled and pewter mugs clanked against each other as they rode through the land, Rosaleen and her mother leaning over the half-door at the back, Hagar in front clicking his tongue at the nag Sissy as she took her time on the way. The family smelled ripely of body-sweat and garlic, for they rarely washed and Rosaleen bathed only in the spring and summer, in the cold streams they passed on the way, or she waded into the lakes in Killarney and douched herself, gasping in their icy waters. Autumn and winter meant wrapping up in layer after layer of brilliant shawls and petticoats and overskirts and sleeping beneath the dressed skins of sheep.

Creagh had come to the Fair in Limerick and on the road to Mayo and then in the winter he disappeared and she had not seen him again. Commonsense told her that he had gone to ground in the damp dark days and she was content, for she felt her destiny.

When she knew she was pregnant she wished she could tell Creagh, but Hagar said not to.

15

'It's better, *alanna*. Those people litter the country with their childer an' no thought taken or given.'

Rosaleen felt as if she had fallen into a dream where everything had slowed up and nothing mattered much except the workings of her body.

Hagar and Melba were pleased, but if the child were lost, and it was common enough, then that would be fate too. Acceptance was all. Whatever life dealt out they accepted with grace. Any resistance wasted effort and emotion and like as not soured the life they loved and spoiled its flavour.

Rosaleen filled herself with fruit and goat's-milk, fresh bread and cheese, nuts and berries, and her body swelled and her face held a sheen of beauty that was radiant.

The birth, when it came, was easy.

Rosaleen was certain that the child would be special. A child selected by God, she said, a child with a great future. How she had come to this conclusion was beyond Melba's imagining. In the last weeks of her pregnancy Rosaleen had gone to see Lothar, who had confirmed her convictions, and she knew she must serve the interests of her child all the days of her life, and he would be called Cormac after the Fenian King.

That journey to Lothar had been hazardous, frought with danger for the lone gypsy on the dark roads. It was early February and the time of year when Dagda was dead and therefore all the good things of the earth, the beautiful things like flowers and trees, and sustenance for humans, fruit and vegetables, were not available. The god Dagda that gave them bountifully at the other times of the year was asleep now, so the land lay unguarded and unfruitful, left open to the gods of darkness, the evil ones that dwelt in the Halls of Death. It was the time when death stalked the land, a tall hooded and cloaked figure with a scythe in his right hand and a skull in the other and gathered the old, the despairing and the weak young in his harvest. Nevertheless, she had travelled miles through the dark of the day and the wildness of the blizzard to Lothar's tigeen at the edge of the plains of Meath, her body swollen with the coming child.

Lothar looked like any other. There was nothing to set him apart from the common run of men who lived their lives in the open off the fertile land. He was thin as a hound, he was ancient and gnarled as the old oak in the Arcadian Grove. His face was brown as the peat from the bog and he lived in a cottage that backed onto a cave that was dark with smoke and foul to the nostrils. It was chock-a-block with boxes, jars and leather bags all about the shelves on the cobweb-decorated walls. Herbs, agarics, and the carcases of animals and insects and their parts, sometimes pickled, sometimes not, lay mouldering in the dense gloom-laden interior of the cavern. Unguents and ointments, whose ingredients Rosaleen knew were too horrible to contemplate, were packed and stored tightly in phials. Rosaleen had heard Hagar talk of the contents of those small jars: entrails of cocks; dead men's nails, the brains of boys buried without baptism. She had always pleaded for him to keep quiet when he spoke of the arts of magic, and he had laughed at her squeamishness. Lothar had incorporated much of mediaeval warlock skill into his ancient Celtic practises. He had wild white hair on him. Only his eyes, the eyes of a seer, were exceptional, but he kept them mainly lowered.

He cast the runes and told the story and Rosaleen's heart beat fast and the babby within her leapt. It was a boy, the Druid told her, a child of grace and beauty as befitted the son of the most beautiful gypsy woman in Erin and the handsomest young strap in County Wicklow. How did he know all these things? she wondered.

'He will be tall and handsome and many will love him, but he will have danger attached to him like an amulet. To fulfil his destiny, which is to bring great joy through great pain, he must be taken to Usher Castle and left there so that that great family might acknowledge him,' the old seer intoned. 'For they will. No matter how strange it sounds, they will.'

Rosaleen felt faint, partly from fatigue and the pressure of the child within her, and partly from the smells and the smoke that overpowered her in this dark foul-aired place. The fire in the cave smoked and stung her eyes and the flames cast monstrous shadows on the walls. The old man rocked back and forth on his heels, squatting before the fire uttering strange sounds in a dialect she was not familiar with. Then he would lapse into the Gaelic she understood. There were specks of spittle on his beard and his eyes turned back in his head. But she listened intently to what he said even though she did not understand all of it. 'Take the child to Usher Castle. There is another there who is not fit to be master, who is not fair of visage or sound of wind and limb. He cannot be the Knight of Usher. And there is yet another who will be born dead. Your child, who will be called Cormac, must take that place, for it is vacant and he is next in line. It is his destiny.'

Rosaleen groaned and squeezed the tears from her eyes. 'I will not want to give my babby up,' she said softly.

The old man seized her wrist. 'Would ye be so cruel, then? To cheat yer boy of a grand castle, a position in the world an' the money to prosper?'

She pushed back her black hair from her face. Tendrils of it clung wetly to her pale brow. 'Is that the best, old man?'

He shook his head and his face seemed to her suddenly very sad. He had the look of innocence about him. 'I don't know,' he replied.

'You are supposed to be wise,' she insisted. 'Is that the greatest gift I can give him? What about the roads and the freedom in walking them?'

Lothar shook his white head again. His eyes seemed sunken, black holes in his head. 'The roads are a great place, to be sure, on a night like this, aren't they?' he asked sarcastically.

From outside they could hear the wind moaning and Rosaleen shivered in her damp green dress.

The *filid* shrugged. 'Ach! Ye may do as ye please. I'm not concerned. But his destiny is Usher Castle an' ye defy the fates at yer peril.'

So on that wild night the following March, Cormac in her arms, obedient to Lothar, she had come to Usher Castle.

Chapter

3

USHER Castle lay between Slievelea and Mount Rivers, the former being nearest Dublin, sitting as she did regally in front of the mountains and dipping her feet in the sea. The latter was further south, deeper into the heart of Wicklow, over the hills and in the lea of the valley at the confluence of the waters, rivers and streams. There Mount Rivers, home of the Vestries, sat proudly on her hill. Between the two, the homes of the Rennetts and the Vestries, lay Usher Castle. She clung to her mountain fastness, higher than the other buildings. Usher raised her turrets close to where the eagle flew and where the peregrine falcon cast hungry glances down in to the valley below. Originally a bleak Norman fortress, it was destroyed, and subsequently rebuilt, added to and changed as the years passed. Ponderous and heavy, it was not picturesque as Mount Rivers, or exquisite as the pearl-grey Slievelea but it was older than any building in that part of the country. The stone battlements had ringed the mountainside when Slievelea was fields and virgin country leading to the sea, and Mount Rivers an empty sward near the Meeting of the Waters.

The house had been radically changed, particularly since the seventeenth century when it had been sacked and burned down in Oliver Cromwell's reign of terror. It had been rebuilt and two wings added. Efforts had been made to landscape the garden but most of the land developed its own wayward beauty over the years. However, the terraced gardens that hung at the edge of the mountain were now rightly famous for their delightful style. Usher was easier to reach than it had been before, for the

Jeffries had had roads cut in the mountain and surfaced to make access less hazardous.

Edward III of England had bestowed the title and lands of Usher on the Jeffries, and with it went the title of Knight of Usher, an honorary position that called on their House and the Silver Knight himself, the male head of the House of Usher, to do great deeds of honour for their King.

It was written: 'The Head of the House, the Silver Knight, will be fair of visage and sound of wind and limb, and in his sacred capacity as Knight shall be defender of the Faith and of the King.' Many of the early Knights had fulfilled and even surpassed expectation, but lately their loyalties had become divided, their deeds more in pursuit of personal advancement than for the glory of Queen and Country: the Queen being Victoria; the Country, naturally, England.

Creagh's uncle was the oldest member of the family. He gave himself up to a joyful pursuit of kitchen wenches, any passing colleen and the nubile daughters of the tenant farmers and labourers. A lusty sixty-five-year-old, he still rode to hounds, drank immoderately, played cards and gambled, carousing the night away in the company of cronies with similar tastes and giving his family scant attention. He had been dubbed Old Gentleman by everyone, and succeeded mostly in avoiding responsibility.

Jeffry Jeffries, Creagh's father, could have been said to have been cast from an older, more responsible, mould and he certainly died for Queen and Country, albeit, witnesses said, a trifle unnecessarily. A monosyllabic man, incapable of sharing his feelings, he seemed to have a vocabulary of no more than six words. He nevertheless inspired great devotion in his wife Angela, who happily bore him four children: James, Arabella, Sophie and Creagh.

They travelled through the East, from trouble spot to trouble spot, where Jeffry was sent, people said, because he was incapable of stringing a statement together to say, 'I have been to Singapore, India, Burma and I have a wife and four children, estates that need my attention in Ireland. Don't you think I have done my duty?' But being unable to plead his cause, perhaps not even wanting to, he got stuck with the toughest jobs in the most unpopular places at the most difficult times.

They came home on furlough rarely. Angela kept her daughters with her. Sophie grew spirited and independent, beautiful and graced with a sunny disposition, whilst her elder sister Arabella learned to depend on the services of a multitude of Ayahs and Amahs and servants who were in reality slaves and who allowed her to order them about. She hated the heat, the mosquitoes, the humidity, and whined and whimpered and complained her way through life. Her father adored her and spoiled her completely, and since his death she had been very difficult.

Sophie, Angela said, was born optimistic, hopeful and with an inclination to be happy. Sadly her sister was quite the opposite. Bella's disposition was pessimistic; she had unrealistic expectations so was constantly disappointed. This was aggravated as she became aware that her little sister Sophie attracted people like a jar of honey attracts flies. She did not understand that a lot of Sophie's attractions, both physical and mental, lay in Sophie's great good humour and happy face. Whereas Sophie's cornflower-blue eyes sparkled with a love of life and a joy in living, Bella's glittered with suspicion and distrust. Sophie's rose-pink mouth turned upwards in dimples and smiles whilst Bella's drooped downwards in discontent. The girls, the Widow Boann said when she met them, had made their own faces and each one was indicative of their personalities.

Why they were so different was widely speculated upon. Most agreed that Angela, their mother, was a hard task-master when her husband was alive and that she had brought James and Sophie up with a rule of iron, teaching them manners, discipline and consideration for others and the sense of honour that comes with the bearing of a great and ancient name. She had dinned it into James how important that name was. But she had no control over her eldest daughter. Arabella was her father's pet. Cossetted and spoiled by him, she never received the benefits of being deprived of her slightest wish, and she was incapable of adapting to the change brought about by his death. Up till then she had had her own way in all things. Now suddenly she was thwarted at every turn. She had developed a great mistrust of life and a resentment that fate had been so cruel to her. At the age of twenty she was terrified of becoming an old maid.

Her sister was a year younger, and Creagh eighteen. James at twenty-four was now head of the family and on the death of his father was Earl Usher. He had expected to play the bachelor, sow his wild oats for at least another decade before donning the heavy mantle of responsibility. He had been precipitated into the assumption of his dual titles Earl and Knight of Usher, by the death of his father. Lord Usher was a kindly man, but unbending. He was proud of the fact that when he made a decision he never changed his mind. It was a habit that would cause him much unhappiness. 'Once I've made up my mind,' he'd say, 'there's no going back.' He was intensely proud of the family name and honours and full of fear that he might be the first Jeffries not to produce a healthy heir for Usher, a son who could live up to the titles and heritage of the house.

In London on their way home James had met Dolly Cranson-James. He had fallen in love for the first time in his life. They had married in London and on returning to Usher their great happiness was increased by the fact that Dolly was pregnant.

Dolly was superstitious. She worried about the fact that she was too happy, that happiness of such magnitude would have to be paid for. Their son Fergal was born tragically malformed, a hunchback; no fit contender for the title of Knight of Usher, 'fair of visage and strong in wind and limb'. Heartbroken and shocked, afraid and ashamed, for he obscurely blamed himself for the child's deformity, James banished the baby to the High Tower at Usher, refusing to look upon his son, putting him out of his life by removing him from his sight. The child lived with the Widow Boann, the redoubtable woman who had reared James' little brother Creagh, and the household was instructed to leave the boy Fergal to the care of the Widow.

Creagh hardly knew his brother and sisters, brought up as he was so far away from them and in a completely different culture. When he was four years old he had become ill and the doctors advised a hot climate unsuited to him. So it was decided to leave him at Usher in the care of the Widow Boann, to guide, discipline and rear him. Most of the people about Usher thought she had done a remarkable job. He was a gentle charming fellow, brave to a foolhardy degree. He was the only member of the family who began to consider himself an Irishman. He knew the history of the land; the tales, the sagas and the legends had been so much a part of his education that they had become in adulthood a part of his life. He had no love for the British. After all, they had deprived him of his father and mother all the years of his childhood and had eventually taken his father's life and driven his mother near mad in her loss.

As they grew older James had been sent to school, then to Oxford, from whence he had been sent down for nothing more dramatic than never opening his books at all or even making a pretence of doing so. Creagh was supposed to follow him there, but his father's death saved him in the nick of time, and nothing was done about his education after that, for which he was profoundly grateful.

Despite changes, the castle had retained its imposing Norman structure. Arches and fireplaces were decorated with mediaeval carving, mullioned windows winked from a hundred embrasures. The height of the doorways was low, the ceilings high, and the doors so thick it was difficult for Angela, Dolly, Sophie or Arabella to open them. It was a cold vast pile of stone, where friendliness and love and comfort were concentrated around the huge log fires the servants kept burning in all the rooms, and the beds. The latter were curtained four-posters, made of polished oak ornately carved. The furnishings were as heavy and ponderous as the building and as grandly ornate.

Usher Castle was a repository of the most remarkable art-treasures brought back from the Orient by Jeffry Jeffries, his father and grandfather before him. They had been bought for a song, and shipped back to Wicklow by the East India Company. Chinese porcelain Buddhas and priests, jade horses and figurines, marble and stone statues, marvellous Chinese and Arabian carpets, paintings on silk from China depicting the daily life of the Mandarins, and from Japan watercolours portraying mediaeval actors in the Noh plays.

The Jeffries displayed their treasures proudly, never asking if they fitted into the decor or whether they sat side-by-side comfortably with the house's baroque grandeur. But the Asian works of art gradually became part of Usher, and in time achieved a curious harmony with the place. Buddhas squatted everywhere and at the top of the stairs the God Shiva stood in glory, three-eyed and four-armed, wearing snakes as ornaments and a string of skulls around the neck. The Irish servants did not take kindly to the Indian diety, which, they said, gave them nightmares.

The west wing incorporated the High Tower and was inhabited by Sophie and Arabella. They shared a bedroom, but each had a separate dressing room and drawing room. Above their apartments, at the extreme top of the High Tower, high up where the eagles flew, Fergal lived with the Widow Boann.

The central part of the building housed James, who was now the Knight of Usher, his wife Dolly and Creagh, as well as the shooting-gallery, the library on the ground floor, the music room and the breakfast and dining room as well as the banqueting hall.

The east wing was the domain of the older folk: Angela who lived in mourning and retirement; and Old Gentleman, reduced now to drinking brandy by the quart and dreaming of past conquests. There was also deep under the castle a priest's hole. The servants' quarters were at the back and in the basement, near the kitchens, the pantry and the accounting rooms.

On this dark night as Rosaleen made her inexorable way to their door, the girls were in their room preparing for bed. Sophie, undisturbed by the storm outside, the banging of the shutters, the wailing of the wind and the blood-curdling tales repeated by their maid Molly, was driven to distraction by Bella. The latter had been in a constant state of hysterics since Dolly had gone into labour. Her sister-in-law had kept Arabella awake all last night and seemed set on doing exactly the same tonight.

'Oh, Bella do hush,' Sophie cried impatiently. She was extremely pretty in her oyster velvet *robe-de-chambre* trimmed with swansdown. She sat at her dressing table brushing her long pale-gold hair. She was as delicate as a Dresden figurine, with pastel cheeks and a tiny determined chin. 'You give me a headache, Bella, you really do. Poor, poor Dolly is having such a terribly painful time. Truly you would think she cried out on purpose to upset you and I'm sure nothing is further from her mind just at this moment. Molly, dear Molly, make me a tisane … of camomile, please. I am undone and I do want to sleep tonight. Oh shut up, Bella, do!'

Molly, their maid, dipped a bob and went to the corner of the bedroom, where, on a little paraffin stove she was used to brewing for her ladies the herbal teas that Lady Angela and the Widow Boann mixed. She made a ceremony of it, and Sophie stopped brushing her golden locks and Arabella ceased her wailing as both girls looked at her. It calmed them to watch her boil the water in the copper jug, rinse the delicate Meissen china cups, pour the water out of them into a silver bowl, then,

24

with an ivory scoop, carefully measure the leaves into a little strainer and pour over the water.

When she handed Sophie the gold-rimmed cup and the girl curled her hands around it, leaving the saucer on her dressing-table Arabella started up her whine again. There was a great moan issuing from the other side of their rooms and Bella cried, 'I hate it! I hate it! It makes me ill. Oh I shall never have a baby, never!'

The sound of Dolly's moans echoed through the room again and Bella continued, 'It's horrible, horrible.' She put her hands over her ears. 'Make me a tisane too, Molly please. Make me Mother's special one ... you know.'

Molly's startled eyes met Sophie's in the mirror and the latter imperceptibly shook her head, so Molly made her a cup of camomile, the same as her sister's.

'It was wonderful, that one,' Bella continued.' Mother gave it to me when Father died. You know how upset I was. I had strange dreams after drinking it and I felt so happy, even though my heart was broken. I didn't feel any pain when I burned myself on the candle, did I, Molly? Anyhow, I can't stand Dolly's perpetual screaming and moaning, I really can't.'

A shrill scream had pierced the air and Sophie and Molly's glances met again over Bella's head and they sighed simultaneously. Although Arabella was a year older than Sophie she often seemed to her sister to be still in the nursery. The bed-curtains were open and she sat in her lawn nightgown, frills at neck and wrist, rocking herself to and fro. She was pretty, her sister thought, but in a petulant spoiled way. Her rosy bottom lip was perpetually stuck out and her forehead was constantly creased.

'I don't think Dolly means to irritate you, Bella, and she can hardly help herself, now can she?' Sophie remarked reasonably.

'It wasn't like that before ... last time ... you know.' Bella said.

'Never talk about that,' she cried vehemently. 'Never, do you hear? You've been warned and warned. We must obey James' wishes, you know that'.

'I don't see why. Everyone knows Dolly produced a monstrosity of a child, and unless James has a son Usher will go to a hunchback and the next Knight of Usher will be an idiot.'

Sophie smacked her sister hard across the cheek with the flat of her hand. The hand was tiny so the blow was not strong, but wiped the vicious expression off Arabella's face and she burst into tears.

'Don't you speak like that, Miss Bella,' Molly said firmly.

Arabella turned on the maid. 'Don't you dare speak to *me* like that, Molly Broderick. You're our maid, for pity's sake, and you must not get above yourself.'

'Hush, Bella. You are not in India now, you know.' Sophie said with asperity.

'Hush. Don't speak. That's right. All of you nag me and nag me and it's Dolly who should hush. Oh, tell her to stop. I cannot bear the sound.'

'I think it's time we went to bed, Miss Bella,' Molly suggested, trying to calm the situation.

But Bella was not to be molified. 'Indeed? I declare, Molly, you are in a pet because you cannot sneak off and see your boyfriend, now can you? The storm's too bad.'

Molly looked at the girl, aghast. It was forbidden to have romantic entanglements within the staff, and if she were found out she could lose her job. 'Oh my lady, how can you suggest such a thing. Indeed an' you are mistaken.'

Bella looked at the maid through narrowed eyes. 'I can and I do. Now if you don't stop nagging me I'll tell Maitland all I know about you and Cronin, or if you're not *very* nice to me I'll tell my brother James. So there!'

Molly burst into tears and Sophie turned on her sister in exasperation. 'Oh, you are horrid, horrid, horrid, Bella. God will punish you, you'll see, for being so beastly. Please don't take on so, Molly. I'll swear it's all one of Bella's made-up stories.'

As she spoke a horrifying cry came borne on the night wind from outside the castle.

Bella jumped in fear. 'You see? It's awful, terrible. How can I be blamed for ...'

Molly had stopped crying abruptly. Tears still wet on her cheeks, she interrupted Arabella sharply. 'That's not my lady Dolly. It's not her at all. It's the banshee. Listen. Oh Jasus, Mary and Joseph, the child is dead for sure.'

She crossed herself, and dropping to her knees on the floor started to pray, chanting the prayers under her breath. 'Hail Mary, Mother of God. Hail our life, our sweetness and our hope. To Thee do we cry, poor banished children of Eve. To Thee do we send up our sighs, mourning and weeping . . .'

The cry came twice more. Arabella dived beneath the covers but Sophie stood rooted to the spot, frozen by the awfulness of the sound. It was like the screaming of the damned, she thought, the wailing of a soul in torment, the keening of the lost in hell. Then she went to the window and drew back the curtain. She looked out into the wild bleak night as the sound echoed away into the valleys.

Something caught her eye. The moon came out from behind the swollen purple clouds and drenched the land in its silver sheen for a moment. In that time she saw a barefoot girl, dark hair, wild in the wind, streaming out behind her like a banner. She held a bundle in her arms and she was climbing the hill to Usher. She raised her face, white as the moon, to the Castle, then turned and disappeared behind a thicket of birch and rowan.

After a while Sophie thought she must have dreamed it. She let the curtain fall, shutting out the night, and went back to the warmth of the fire, its soft marigold glow consoling her, obliterating the vision she had just seen. She sat on her vanity-stool and began to brush her hair again till her arm grew tired and Molly took the brush away from her.

The maid half-carried the drowsy girl to her bed, helped her remove her peignoir, and pulling aside the stiff, starched, verbena-scented sheets she tucked the exhausted girl up and kissed her pale forehead.

She looked at the hump in the other bed where Arabella had burrowed down, not a particle of her visible, and shook her head. She looked to the window, shuddered at the remembrance of the cry, turned down the lamps and tiptoed out of the room.

Chapter

4

THE light in the room was dim; it had been dark all day. The lamps flickered, casting gigantic shadows on the wall, and the fire was leaping in the grate. Lady Jeffries, blonde curls dark with sweat, sank into the soft mattress which dipped with time in the curve under her back. That dip made her hotter and accentuated the pain she was in. The room was stifling, air trapped, windows hermetically sealed. It was full of the reek of exhausted human sweat.

Agony ripped her apart as she tried to give birth. She was floating in a half-dream. The pain continued and she heard voices in a haze, the sounds advancing and receding. She felt the warm slippery sweat running in rivers down her throbbing body. She felt her pulses hammer in her ears and head, as blackness came and went and the hours ticked by on leaden feet.

The doctor, Hegarty, was a friend of her father. He was assisted by the Widow Boann. It consoled Dolly that the Widow was at her side in the hour of her agony. The Widow radiated authority. She and most of her family had been in the service of the Jeffries at Usher for generations. The rest of them, Hegarty most of all, were afraid of James and the trouble they would be in, if, through no fault of their own, they failed this time in the task he seemed to feel they were completely responsible for. As if they could guarantee the outcome! As if anyone could!

Dana, a scullery maid, scared out of the few wits she had, ran back and forth with ewers of hot water and towels. They were not helping her at all, Dolly thought. Dr Hegarty was becoming more nervous, and not without reason. He had arrived two days ago when she had gone into labour. James was desperate for a son and heir. Not another mistake, he cajoled, threatened, bribed the poor doctor, as if the man had any control over things of that nature. He had not allowed Dr Hegarty or the Widow Boann to leave his wife's room, except to attend to the call of nature, and they had been with her now for two days, this being the second night. She had grown to hate them, grown to loath the smell of them, the foul smell of stale perspiration and the smell of her own sweat in labour. Earlier she had begged for a window to be opened, but Hegarty had refused to countenance it. He was terrified to take the chance. He was a rural physician, devoted to a more primitive code of practice and he would have no truck with the new fangled hygienic modern ways of delivering babies. He had introduced hundreds of bairns safely into the world in his thirty years of practising medicine and he was not about to change his tried and true method now, no matter what the younger men were saying.

'Stuff and nonsense,' was his bristling reply when challenged. 'Stuff and nonsense. Sure the Good God himself,' making the sign of the cross. 'Devised the means a chisler entered the world, and if it was good enough for the Virgin Mary herself, sure it was good enough for the likes of the Rennetts, the Vestries and the Jeffries.'

He was fond of making this kind of *pronunciamento* at the local inn as he quaffed his evening libation with Peggy Callaghan, and she would nod, yes indeed. He told them, and they had to believe him, for wasn't he a professional man? That stood for the voice of authority in the community.

Nevertheless, James had scared him when he had delivered Fergal three years ago. James' fury had known no bounds when he had been told his first born was a hunchback. He had laid hands on the doctor and thrown him out of the house into the snow, screaming at him about the malformed thing he had delivered and saying he was not satisfied, as if, Dr Hegarty said, he could send it back like an ill-fitting suit to the tailor.

Hegarty needed the county families. He had no real practice without them, and they clung together, they did, a clannish lot, and if you were out with one you were out with all. He had had to ingratiate himself again with Lord James who had toyed with the idea of employing the new young doctor who was

29

practising in Arklow. By a persistent show of self-confidence, an unswerving and tenacious determination and veiled threats about it 'being on his own head' if he trusted the inexperienced young medic, he eventually won the day.

He was devoted to his rich society patients and the living they enabled him to make, and he was a good doctor and mainly successful in his treatments. However Lord James Usher, had put him in an untenable position this time. He had insisted, on the doctor's arrival two days ago, that he would have Hegarty thrown out of the county if this baby was not a perfectly formed son. So naturally he had been frightened. How could he guarantee that? How could he promise such a thing? Only God could, but he was too scared to tell James that. And James had flattered him, calling him the best doctor this side of London.

Then, in his room, the old familiar scene, the memories flooded back: three years ago, the malformed child crying lustily, loudly proclaiming his strength to the waiting world. How could they blame him? But they had, and now he was faced with the fear, the terror that it might happen again.

Time was passing on leaden feet and Dolly, Countess of Usher, tiny, fragile, blonde hair plastered to her skull, was in deep trouble again. The child inside her was too large, too hefty for her narrow pelvis. The fight she put up was worthy of an Amazon, but Hegarty could see no sign of success and reluctantly made up his mind to operate, otherwise he might lose them both. The anxious eyes of the Widow Boann met his over the writhing body of the Lady Dolly, wide with apprehension. They would have to cut to allow exit at all, and he realized that he had the tacit agreement of the Widow, who nodded imperceptibly at him. He was glad she was there, for she was a tower of strength.

Dolly lay as still as she could. She had fought and fought and now after her struggles the raw pain tore through her and she felt she was beyond caring. Her hands plucked at the sheet and she thought that perhaps if she lay very quiet, very very still not moving a muscle, perhaps if she remained immobile, it would go away. Please, God, let it go, for she could not bear it. But she knew it would not remove itself that easily. The child was pushing out, tearing her apart, pressing unbearably on every nerve in her body. The pain was excruciating, it spread through her legs, pierced her chest and thrust its fiery darts through all her body.

She dimly saw through the film of agony the Widow and the doctor look at each other.

'Please,' she whispered feebly. 'Please.'

She smelled a sweet, sweet smell and heard the doctor murmur consolingly and she lost consciousness.

The mess was bloody and the child was dead, strangled, the cord tight about its tiny neck. The doctor was beyond caring. He had tried so very hard, and to have failed was unbearable. They stood around the bed, heart-sore in defeat. Then the Widow Boann heard the crying in the night outside the castle and knew it was the banshee.

Dolly lay drugged, at peace at last, unknowing and unaware yet of her plight and the heart-break and disappointment in store.

'I kept my promise,' the doctor thought. 'He said a boy and perfect and so it was.' And he shook his head sorrowfully, tears drenching his cheeks. His sadness was not only for himself and his failure. The little corpse was a pathetic sight, perfect in all parts. Perhaps, the doctor consoled himself, Lord James could be persuaded to rejoice that he was capable of siring a well-formed male. But not his wife. She could never risk pregnancy again. He looked at the pale face on the pillow and sighed. She was such a sweet lady and she had wanted this son so much. It was her gift to her husband. She would be distraught when she realized she had failed. He hoped she would sleep long so that the inevitable moment of realization was delayed.

He took a deep breath and said sharply, 'Go to the kitchen and tell the maids to come and change Lady Dolly's sheets and bathe her. Open the window a crack, it can't hurt now, and let in the clean air to sweeten the room a little, but leave it open only five minutes. And tell them I'll be down for some coffee, hot and strong, as soon as I've finished here.'

The Widow, hurrying to see his instructions were obeyed, found Sophie outside Dolly's room. She had crept down, anxious about her sister-in-law, and had fallen asleep in a chair in the corridor. The Widow shook her gently. Sophie started up, drawing her robe about her. Her hair was tousled and her blue eyes were worried.

'How is she, Widow? And the baby?'

'Everything is all right, Lady Sophie. Go back to bed, *alanna*.'

'But I'm so anxious. Tell me if I can help.'

'This is no place for a maiden lady,' the Widow tutted. 'No, no. You can help best by going to your room and sleeping till a reasonable hour. Then you'll be rested and more than able to keep my lady company, for she'll like a visit tomorrow, I'll be bound.'

And with that Sophie had to be satisfied. Obediently she tip-toed back to the tower where her sister snored gently in a deep sleep.

When the maids came, hushed and scared, they told Dr Hegarty that the Dowager Lady Jeffries and her daughters were asleep and that Creagh was absent in the night as he so often was. Lord James, they said, was drowsing in front of the fire in the Great Hall. The doctor begged them to be gentle with my lady and they promised, wide-eyed and concerned, and set to to obey his orders and care for their poor mistress and make her comfortable and sweet-smelling again.

Dr Hegarty left the room and went below by the servants' staircase. He did not want to face James yet, not until he had half a pint of coffee under his belt.

The kitchen was a huge room with glazed brick walls and flagged floor and gleaming pots and pans, coppers and pewter everywhere. There were vast ranges, sinks and a spit, a huge dresser, numerous shelves and milk urns, and a large table down the middle of the room. The seductive smell of coffee filled the air and the cook, Bessie Broderick, had poured him a breakfast cup full and gave him thick yellow cream to cool it and white sugar for sweetening.

She was a buxom woman, and she ruled the kitchen staff with a rod of iron. Mother of five girls, Annie, Clarie, Molly, Jenny — and little Sylvie, who had run away with a farming boy, earning her mother's rejection by her precipitate action; her name was forbidden on the premises. Her other daughters were all in the service of the Jeffries. Bessie was sister to the Widow Boann, whom she kept at a wary distance, ever protective of her realm of authority. They had another sister who lived in the valley below Usher, Craw Kilty by name.

Bessie's usual vitality was subdued. The sad news had

reached them in the kitchen ahead of the doctor, and her face was stained with tears. Only the kitchen staff had remained up so late, available to help if necessary. Maitland and Mrs Maitland, the butler and housekeeper, were abed this long time. It was more reasonable, they felt, to be alert and on call early in the morning, and Bessie Broderick had shooed them off, saying she and her sister were perfectly capable of giving the good doctor all the help he needed. The Brodericks loved Countess Dolly and wanted to assist her in any way possible in her dark hours of torment. All had felt for her in the last two days and now a great melancholy had fallen over them at the news that the baby was dead.

The Widow Boann had followed the doctor into the kitchen and they both sat at the table sipping their hot drinks. There was no sound there save the gentle sighing of the Widow and the ticking of the grandfather clock as the doctor drank his second cup of coffee.

The stillness was suddenly broken. James shouted from the hall above, 'What news?' and simultaneously there were three sharp knocks on the back door that led to the yard.

The Widow Boann and Dr Hegarty looked at each other. The moment they had both been dreading had arrived. James was unpredictable, and they dreaded his response to the news. Dr Hegarty felt unable to move, a wave of inertia settling over him, pinning him to his chair. The last two days had utterly drained him.

Bessie Broderick rose heavily to her feet and waddled across the flagged floor. She was followed by the Widow, alertly curious as usual to know who was knocking on the door in such a night and at such a time. They reached the door as James came barging through the entrance from upstairs. He glared at them all, his eyes red with lack of sleep.

'What has happened?'

There was silence in the kitchen. Then the knocking came again. Everyone stared at James. At last Hegarty sighed and said, 'He's dead. Your son is dead. I'm so terribly sorry, my lord. He was, God have mercy, quite perfect. But dead.'

For a moment James stared at the doctor as if he couldn't believe his ears. Then he seemed to grow in stature. He looked as if he might explode, as if he would kill the doctor, and the women at the door shrank back from him. Then he let out a

33

cry, torn from his heart, and the doctor was, for a moment, terrified. But there was nothing frightening about the grief that overwhelmed James Jeffries, sending sobs coursing through his great frame, bowing it over and rending it asunder, causing him to shudder and shake like a man with the palsy.

At the kitchen door the knocking continued. The Widow Boann opened it. A sharp wind tore in from the inclement night, chilling the air in the kitchen. There, under the lintel, silhouetted by the moon which had escaped once more her cloudy prison, stood a girl, a slip of a lass, beautiful, black-haired, bare-foot, her velvet dress clinging wetly to her, and in her arms, a babe.

They stared at her as if she were a goddess from the moon, or a witch from the Island of Mona. They stared at her dumb-founded, the cook, the Widow, the doctor and the Master, when the baby set up a delicate wailing, fragile but demanding.

Still they stood transfixed, and the girl wrapped around in moonlight spoke as she held the baby out to them.

'Take him, please. Lothar commanded me to bring him to you here. He said you would have great need of him. His name is Cormac and he is Creagh's child and mine. But I must give him to you. Guard him with your life. I charge you.'

She placed the infant in the Widow's arms, though she had been speaking directly to James. The shadows veiled the moon, darkness flooded the doorway, and she was gone.

Chapter

5

THE tall man stood on the edge of the cliff and peered into the darkness below. He was shrouded from shoulder to boot in a black cloak, and the driving rain had soaked the collar he had turned up to protect his neck and chin against the storm.

The wild wind lifted his black hair away from his white forehead and his cloak billowed out around him. Rain ran in rivulets down his strongly-boned face, and he bit his lips in exasperation as he tried to penetrate the darkness. He could see nothing, his view obscured by the torrential downpour. He could hear the sea crashing far below. It was tempestuous tonight, great breakers as high as a house thundering onto the black and slippery rocks.

'There'll be no boat tonight,' he said to the lad who accompanied him, but his words were torn away on the wind.

'No sir, Mister Rafferty, sir. It's too wild by half. Merciful hour, ye'd want to be an eejit to try to get to shore on a night like this.' The lad shivered. 'Ach, we'll have to give up. The divil save us, it's an evil storm. There's no point in waitin' around for the soljers.'

The man narrowed his eyes, peering around him trying to pierce the blackness of the night and the sleeting rain. The moon struggled to escape the tempest-tossed clouds.

'Let us go. We are sitting targets here, Fogey, ye're right. We can do no good tonight. If the ship is out there, then all I can say is God help her, for she's doomed.'

He strode away from the cliff edge, pulling his hat further over his forehead. Fogey Mulcahy scuttled after him, sniffing, shaking the water out of his hair. He had to run, for the man in front of him had long legs. Away from the cliff, hiding in a clump of trees a group of men waited. They watched the tall man stride up to them.

'No luck?' Creagh Jeffries tossed the reigns of the chestnut mare he held to the dark man. 'I knew it was a fool's errand. Damn it, Red, they promised delivery. It'll take weeks if not months to rearrange it all. Damn, damn, damn.'

The tall man laughed at the boy's impetuosity. 'It was impossible,' he said. 'The sea is like a witch's cauldron. The night itself is good for neither man, nor beast, nor, for that matter, ships, to be abroad. The waves are as high as the cliff. I've never seen the like, Creagh. I hope to God they put in somewhere safe if they were fool enough to set out at all. I pray they are not there battling with the elements, for if they are, they'll lose for sure.'

Creagh turned his horse and yelled over the wailing wind, 'Let's not linger here. Not that I think any of Her Majesty's military are abroad in such a night. Still, better we're off. We'll rendezvous in a week at Usher, Red,' he continued, 'Try to be there. I have John O'Grady coming from America. He'll put fire in the lads, that's for sure. See if you can get news of the cargo we were to receive this night.'

He grinned at the tall man and leaned over to grasp his hand. Their greeting was firm and conveyed a warmth and trust beyond mere words.

'Slán leat a cairde. Take care, Red,' he said, spurred his black mare, and galloped away to the west.

'Dia's Muire duit,' Red Rafferty shouted after him but his words were lost on the wind.

He watched the group of men, some on horseback, some on foot, disappear into the night. He sat on his horse, a solitary figure etched against the charcoal-coloured sky. He was saturated, but not heeding the storm, indifferent to it, his hair plastered to his skull, his blue eyes full of pain and longing, looking out to where the waves with mighty strength crashed against the shore.

'Damn, damn, damn.' he cried, echoing Creagh Jeffries, and shook his fist at the sky. Then he too spurred his horse and galloped into the night.

Chapter

6

WHEN James entered their bedroom next morning at break of dawn he was carrying Cormac in his arms. He found the air sweet and his wife lying on fresh pillows in their giant curtained bed. It was big enough to house a family, Dolly had said, wishing in her heart that it was as full of romping children as the basket at the foot was overbrimming with golden retrievers, Angel's latest litter.

The maids had plaited Dolly's hair and it fell over her shoulders, and her delicate-boned face was in the deep repose of sleep, lips parted, eyes bruised. She seemed almost corpse-like in her exhaustion. A huge log fire crackled and hummed in the fireplace. Annie had scattered pine cones on it to purify the air and scent the room.

Dolly's eyes fluttered open, flaxen lashes quivering against her apricot cheek. Her sleep had been deep for she had been completely spent. Awakening to find James ungroomed at her bedside, she felt a moment of fear and apprehension. She looked at him anxiously, and he put the child in her arms.

'Listen, Dolly. You must listen,' he said.

Her face had become dissolved in love and she was crooning over the babe, tears, gentle as rain, splashing on her cheeks.

'Listen, Dolly,' he cried in a panic. 'It's not your child.' She looked at him, eyes full of alarm. 'Our son died,' he continued rapidly, seeing her total confusion. 'He died. 'Twas no fault of yours. No one's fault. 'Twas meant. This is Creagh's son. By a gypsy girl. It came last night like a miracle, like an answer to a prayer. As if it was meant to be. The doctor said you can have no more children, my darling. You'll die if you do.' He took her

37

hand in his and raised it to his lips. 'I couldn't bear that,' he said. 'Nor could I bear that that poor hunchback upstairs should inherit. But there. It's not necessary now. Everything is going to be all right.'

He looked at his wife. He was worried, she could see. She took her hand gently from his and turned back the fold of the soft cobweb-spun shawl that the Widow had wrapped the baby in. She looked at the round pink face, scrunched up against the sudden light. He was not new-born, she saw. He had had time to smooth out, become defined and he was beautiful. The bright blue eyes blinked, the rose-bud mouth was mobile, little lips smacking together to grasp something to suck, china-fragile hands were waving about aimlessly. He smelled so seductive and new, and she was totally enchanted by his helplessness.

She gave up thinking. She gave up reason. She was too worn out, had been through so much, and she wanted a baby more than life itself. She avoided the dilemma. She let her instincts take over. Her body cried out to welcome this little bundle in her arms. Every natural emotion yearned for the child. She had given birth and after her labour it was essential that she have a result. She craved to hold the infant to her bosom. She would think about it all later, reason it out, weigh up pros and cons. For now, for this moment in the warm illumination of the leaping flames of the fire, in the smile of endearment on her husband's face as he looked on the mother with the babe in her arms, she accepted it, and by accepting it even for a moment she was lost.

James' feelings were in a more unruly state than his wife's. She was still drugged after her ordeal, her body weighted by lassitude, her mind in a euphoric half-dream. He, after his long tension-wracked night, was taut and quivering with nerves. He had run the gamut of emotions in the last few days, and felt now that he had walked in a nightmare. Sleeplessness had made him light-headed and curiously divorced from reality. He looked at his wife. She glowed with that bemused expression all new mothers wore when they looked upon their offspring. Bathed in the firelight, the dawn stealing through the curtains, she was the image of his ideal woman, a madonna with a child in her arms. He had dreamed of this moment for so long that he could not bear to let it go. He pushed all uncomfortable thoughts aside and kissed Dolly lovingly, reverently.

'Let it be,' he whispered. 'Let it be.'

Annie brought in some hot chocolate for her mistress and exhorted her to rest, so James left the room, having once more kissed his wife on the lips, and the top of the baby's head.

He went to his dressing-room where he was sleeping for the moment and ringing for Maitland and his son Nern gave the first instructions about the household, and allowed the second to help him as he bathed and changed and dressed in his riding habit. He then went below for breakfast.

Sophie and Arabella were already in the breakfast room. It faced east, the better to catch the early sun, but there was no light today. The aftermath of the storm had left the land wind-swept and dun. Mole-grey clouds obscured everything and the trees' branches drooped, exhausted after their battle with the elements. Wisps of pearly fog drifted across the valley below and hung on the air like fine silk banners.

The breakfast room was relatively small. A large wood fire crackled merrily and silver dishes stood on the heavy mahogany sideboard. A chafing-dish held kidneys and fat slices of bacon. Barley cakes and breakfast bannocks warm from the range lay under a linen cloth, and round brown eggs were piled up in a silver dish. James helped himself to some porridge and cream. He did not want to explain everything to either of his sisters. He simply did not feel up to it, and there were some things he did not want to put into words. Arabella irritated him, though he welcomed her presence this morning as it prevented him from being tête-à-tête with Sophie. To meet those clear cornflower blue eyes was more than he was capable of at present. She, however, in her pale blue gown, a light wool India shawl over her shoulders, was not to be so easily avoided.

Arabella was moaning as usual. 'Molly was late this morning and I didn't sleep last night, James, with all that screaming. Dolly is an awful ninny.'

'Really, Bella, you are the silliest miss I have ever had the misfortune to come across. You have absolutely no idea of the pains of child-birth or you wouldn't say such stupid things.' James voice dripped contempt and Arabella covered her cheeks with her hands.

'Don't you dare say such shocking things, James. It is not per-mitted and you know it. I shall tell Mama, I shall complain to her ...'

'Oh be quiet, Arabella,' her sister said. 'You are a veritable whinge, you know.' Sophie tossed her curls and turned her back on her sister. 'So, James, what is the news?'

Arabella was not to be stopped. 'Don't you dare speak to me like that, Sophie. You don't know how my head hurts. You would never have dared to talk to me like that if Papa were alive. But he's dead and I . . . oh, I . . .'

James knew Bella had been her father's favourite and he suddenly felt sorry for her. She must miss him a lot. 'There, there, Bella. Don't take on so,' he said, but Sophie interrupted.

'Oh, leave her, James and let's get down to the really important thing. Any news?' Her voice was carefully neutral, her face only sympathetic.

He met her eyes squarely. 'There is a boy. Cormac,' he said, but before he could continue Sophie shrieked in a most unlady-like manner, and knocking down her chair rushed around to her brother and enveloped him in her arms.

'Oh James, James, how wonderful. A boy? Just what you wanted. Cormac? Where did you get that name? Sounds more like Creagh than you. But it is nice. Oh James, James, I'm so happy for you.'

Arabella smiled. 'A baby. A boy. Then it was worth it — all the screaming, I mean. Oh, I'm sorry, James. I have been horrid, I know, but I have this beastly headache. Forgive me. Oh, I must see it and Dolly. You must be so proud.'

James smiled at his sisters, though he still felt uneasy. He was relieved. A burden had been lifted, a huge problem removed, and now he had to adjust to face the newer problems the solution had presented. Sophie and Arabella were making it very easy for him, and once something had been said, he thought, it was well on the way to becoming a fact.

'Dolly's resting. Cormac is with the Widow. Leave it till a little later,' he said, rising. 'Now you must excuse me. I'm going for a ride. I haven't left the house for two whole days.'

He needed the air. It seemed such a long time since Dolly had gone into labour, it felt as if a year had passed.

Cronin the stableboy brought the glossy dark-brown mare, Pixie, ready for him to mount.

'Come on, me darlin',' James whispered and urged her forward with whip and spur. They sped away, horse and rider, into the grey morning and the sharp piercing March wind, leaving behind his problems and the reverberating thud of the horse's hoofs.

Chapter

7

WHEN Rosaleen left Usher in the darkness of the night she had no intention of going back to the caravan trail. Not yet, not yet at all. She wanted to see what would happen to her son, wanted to stay near enough to know of him. Gone for her were the days of unthinkable freedom, travelling the highways and byways at whim. Hagar and Melba knew her wishes. They did not mind. They were Romany and free of ties, self-reliant and independent, and they had brought her up to be like them.

Turning from the kitchen entrance, she shivered suddenly, her arms empty, the warmth gone from her breast. She knew a moment of devastating pain, and she moaned at the extent of her loss. But she would not allow herself to be self-indulgent. There was no time for that.

She went out into the courtyard and through it to the stables. She made a noise deep in her throat and got an answer from the little donkey who carried the faggots for the fire and the twigs for the brooms made by the scullery maid Dana. She whispered to the donkey in the old language and led him out noiselessly. She smiled a little sadly to herself as she thought of Creagh and what his reaction would be if he knew. 'Yerra, girl, can't your lot leave us even one donkey?' she could hear him say.

She knew exactly where to go. She left the confines of the castle and journeyed through the edges of the wood. The wind tore at her and she felt cold and lonely as she battled with the elements. The rain blinded her and she could not tell if she was crying. She crossed the footbridge. It was a dizzying link, a short-cut from mountain to mountain not often used. It swung now, fragile in the storm. Leading the donkey, she took the pathway down the other side to the valley below. The dark clouds raced across the face of the moon and the wind pierced her. Nevertheless, she made fair progress. Her arms were lighter now without their precious burden, but her heart was heavy within her and her steps were slow. She felt as cold as a stone at the bottom of a well.

Her destination was a place well known to her and others of her kind: Craw Kilty's cottage in the valley. She lived there with her son Ronan, the Minstrel. He was the singer of the hills, the minstrel of the dales and valleys of Wicklow, the lad she had often planned to lie with until she met Creagh. It was a sad thing that, she thought, for he would have been more suited to the likes of her than the lord in his castle she had fallen for. But she was realistic and she shrugged her shoulders and tried to put a brake on her feet for it was steep down the last bit of pathway and the donkey slipped and slid with her.

Craw Kilty, they said in these parts, was a witch but a kindly class of a one. She was sister to the Widow Boann and Bessie Broderick above at the castle. The Minstrel, her son, was gifted with second sight. It was a fearful thing to see him, as she had once done, fall writhing to the floor and come to, pale and handsome as he was, mouthing the future. She had been a child then, and Hagar and Melba had taken a sailing boat to France because of his prophesy of a famine. They went to their tribes in Brittany, then south to the sunny lands of Spain and the caves of Scaramouche. Their brethren had given them a fine welcome everywhere and they ate and drank off the best in the land, food filched from castle and farmer alike. Meanwhile across the sea the Irish starved in millions. They fell, they died, while typhoid and plague stalked the country. The grim reaper with his glittering scythe carved a swathe across the land and had a fine harvest those times, spring, summer and autumn as well as winter.

They stayed away a long time. Then Hagar and Melba got restless eventually for the grey crashing seas, the dark hills, the purple mists and the wild light that breeds magics and enchantments. When the news was good they sailed from Valparaiso on a sea placated by spells and came again to Erin.

That had been long ago and the boy who had seen it all had grown to a man. He still fell, and prophesied when he came back from the Dark Place, and he played like an angel: the fiddle, the flute and the knee harp.

42

At the bottom of the mountain Rosaleen mounted the donkey and as she turned its head into the valley she felt tired and old as an ancient. Her feet scalded her and she was weary unto death.

At last she could see the little cottage in the valley through the grey dawn. The mists drifted, wispy, hovering low and curling around the trees, hanging from their branches and reaching up from the bed of the valley like pale ghosts aimlessly floating in the morning chill. She reached the cottage, and tethering the donkey, rapped on the door. After a while the top half of the door opened and Craw Kilty put her face out. Garlic and herbs hung down from the lintel in ropes and she had to part the hanging garlands to peer through, her black eyes bright in the brown of her face. Her skin was the texture and colour of a walnut and her hair sparse on her head, yet she was not that old. She had little tufts on her chin, and growing from her nostrils like bracken. Prematurely old, incredibly ugly, she nevertheless had a good-humoured and kindly expression. She wore a homespun gown of grey and had a red shawl over her shoulders.

'Ah *Dia's Muire duit, Rosaleen Dubh, tar istigh agus glac do shuaimhneas. Cad e már atá tú?*' she welcomed Rosaleen in Gaelic. ('God and Mary be with you. Come inside and take your ease. How are you?')

'*Tá go maith, go raibh maith agat.*' ('I am very well, thank you.') Rosaleen replied automatically.

'The milch goat is ready an', I'll get you some milk foaming like the curling of the sea, but warmer. Sit you down by the hearth and hug the fire. Ate yer fill of the bannocks and the *cáis* (cheese).'

The fireplace was a hollow in the wall with a funnel in the ceiling for the smoke to exit, not that much of it escaped. It depended on the way the wind blew. A sharp breeze from the east and the smoke turned back on itself and filled the room so you couldn't see across it. The cottage was thatched and made of stone painted white with a bright yellow door on it. There was a kettle on the hob and in the embrasure in the window sat a fat pottery jug of ale and a yellow round of cheese on a platter. A basket of brown eggs, two fresh-baked loaves of bread, powdery on top, sat on the table with a candle. The quivering flame of it flickered until it was quenched in the draught from the open half-door. Craw Kilty took the tin tray of bannocks from the cinders and pulled them out, sucking her fingers against them burning her. 'Sit you there. You'll not wink before I'm back,' she said and left the room.

Rosaleen sat on the bench before the fire, drooping with her weariness. She toasted her feet. They were wet with the dew that had bathed them clean. She tried to bring life back to them, but they were numb. In the darkness of the room, lit only by the turf fire, she saw the Minstrel laid out on his pallet under the other window. He was motionless beneath the thick quilt that lay on him. It was a present to him from her mother Melba from Spain in gratitude for the warning about the famine. It had the colours of Spain, poppy-red, brilliant yellow and black.

Craw Kilty returned, a foaming mug and a pail in her hands. The mug she thrust at Rosaleen. 'Drink it, *alanna*, yer half dead be the looks of ye.' She went to where the Minstrel lay beneath his quilt and kicked the mound his body made. 'Get up wi' ye, Ronan ... up an' out, now,' she yelled, kicking again with her rag-bound foot.

A groan came from beneath the covering and it moved and shifted, and the dark curly head of the Minstrel appeared.

'Ach, Mam, leave it. It's still the dark o' dawn an' last night the fit was on me. I need my sleep after the prophesy. You know that.'

He rubbed the sleep from his eyes and when he took his knuckles away he saw Rosaleen, who turned aside and blushed as he rose, naked as the statue in Usher Castle and just as beautiful. His body was white and the skin on it soft, for he never worked in the fields or on the sea. His head was a cap of tight black curls like the coat of a ram and his eyes were wide and blue as the wild iris near the lake and had the same fleck of yellow in the centre.

He was unembarrassed in his nakedness and he yawned and scratched and drew his trews on. They ended above his long slim ankles and he pulled some brown socks over the ends.

'An' how are ye, Dark Rosaleen?' he asked sleepily.

'There is no sun in this day, Ronan *astore*,' she replied wearily, 'It's a black one for me.'

He laid a warm hand on her dark head. 'Ye know where to come until it shines again, don't ye? You know where you'll get rest?'

She nodded. Her cobalt-blue eyes held his steadfastly. He bent and kissed her hair.

'Me Mam will put you at your ease,' he whispered, and taking his white shirt and jerkin he left the cottage. The women could hear him pump the water and yell out as the cold liquid drenched him in its icy shower.

'Ah, Craw, 'tis a sad day for me, an' I need you.' Rosaleen's eyes were full of tears, exhaustion in every line of her body.

Craw Kilty gave the girl a fierce hug. 'Ye heard Ronan. Yer safe now. Yer home.'

'Next to Melba and Hagar you're the one I come to, Craw,' Rosaleen murmured, her head drooping.

'Me an' the Widow an' Bessie Broderick, me sisters above in the castle, we've gypsy blood. We're your own kind. And we're Irish. We know, love. We understand.' And, as Rosaleen slowly slipped to the flagged floor, 'Ná tit, a stóirin.' ('don't fall, darling.')

Craw Kilty removed the girl's soggy finery from her unresisting body. The green velvet would never be the same after last night, it was ruined entirely. As she untied the girl's petticoat, Rosaleen heard the Minstrel relieve himself outside against the wall. It reminded her of the caravan and Hagar and Melba and she felt lost and lonely. Her breasts were sore and heavy with unsucked milk and she missed her babby with a fierce empty ache.

The ould wan pulled her gently to her feet and walked her across the room. Rosaleen acquiesced like a sleep-walker. Craw Kilty pushed her beneath the quilt still warm from the Minstrel's body. She snuggled down, feeling the fatigue take over, her senses float away and blessed sleep lull her into unconsciousness.

Chapter

8

WHEN James returned from his ride that morning the mist had lifted and the sun had lit up the world in a pale buttercup glow. He threw the reigns to Cronin, who had heard his master's approach, and giving the mare an absentminded pat on her steaming haunches he ran into the great hall, calling for coffee and Creagh.

The morning winds had cleared his brain and blown the dark clouds from his mind. He felt much more optimistic and sure of himself now, decided in his plan of action.

James was the first of the Earls of Usher to eschew the Army or the Diplomatic Service. The heir to the titles settled for his position at home. He deplored the absentee landlords, too long away, whose homes and lands degenerated into ruins and unproductive fields. Not that Usher was fruitful farming land, but he owned the surrounding forest and wood was always in demand. It was good sheep country.

Besides, he was fed up with travel. Racketing around the world in his father's wake had soured him and decided him to try, as he put it, to 'make a go of things at Usher'.

He could afford to; the Ushers were rich: Not fabulously wealthy as the Rennetts at Slievelea, whose money, old, had been added to over the years by good investment, mainly in gold; but certainly outstripping the profligate Vestries to their south and the Blackwaters to the west. Besides, James was a home-loving man who liked a fixity in life, a hearth and wife to return to each evening, a settled existence. He was staunchly loyal to his Queen and England, but he loved the house and lands of Usher with a passion, and took his position as head of the family, although it had been a premature inheritance, very seriously indeed.

He was a big man with a ruddy complexion tanned by the Eastern sun, which had left his skin heavily wrinkled about the eyes and mouth. He had bright red hair, a volatile temperament, and implacable determination to do what, in his judgement, was the right thing. He was, in the main, sweet-tempered, a cheerful and fair-minded man. He had a soft heart which he tried hard to conceal and his ill-humours were short-lived.

He had his meeting with Creagh in his study. His young brother exasperated him. He felt him alien in thought and manner, opposite in ideas and cultural loyalties and therefore anathema to him. But he loved him dearly, perhaps more fiercely than if he had understood him. He, like Sophie, was utterly charming and it was impossible not to fall under Creagh's spell.

The boy looked at him now, his eyes serious. 'How is Dolly, James?' he asked.

'We'll talk of that in a minute, Creagh,' James replied.

He sat in front of the blazing fire fondling Angel, the beige-haired golden retriever, praying he would find the right words.

'What is it that takes you from your home so much, Creagh?'

Creagh, opposite him warming his hands, looked discomfited. 'Is that why you wished to see me, James? If so you should have spared yourself the trouble, for the reasons are trivial.'

James cleared his throat. He knew he was hedging but felt he could broach the burning topic better if he pursued another line of conversation first. 'Answer me, Creagh,' he said. He saw his young brother shift uncomfortably about in his chair. 'We searched for you last night, high and low, Creagh, and you could not be found.'

Creagh shrugged.

James could see he looked as tense as a young deer scenting danger in a thicket, uncatchable, constantly slipping out of reach, out of contact, eyes wide and brown darting away from a meeting with James'.

'I spend my time, my dear brother, as I have told you repeatedly, with my friends. They are far and wide in the land. I love to see them. Love to travel, though I have not had your opportunities, James.'

Creagh did not mean this resentfully, but he found it politic to turn the screw on his brother. James' guilt at having had the

47

company of his mother and father on their travels had got Creagh off the hook many a time.

'I'm restless,' he continued. 'Call it what you will. Also I am young and carefree.'

'Being young and carefree does not give you permission to come and go as you please, Creagh. You are not so juvenile as to think that.'

'Indeed, James, you do me wrong.' The boy had blushed, James saw, though whether through anger or embarrassment he could not tell. 'You forget I've never had to ask permission before in my life. It is too late to ask me to change now. You forget too, James, that I was left here whilst Mother and Father and all my family went gallivanting in foreign parts.'

'That's unfair, little brother,' James protested. 'You know I could do nothing about that. You were not fit enough to travel with us. You were ill.'

Creagh shrugged. 'Be that as it may, I was left behind and have learned a different way. The Widow Boann was not so strict as you.' He smiled up at James, his brilliant disarming smile and James gave up. He changed course.

'I want to talk of other things,' he said, and bent over Angel to scratch behind her ear. The room was dark. A large mahogany desk in the corner had an oil lamp upon it and on either side of the fireplace were brackets of ornately gilt bunches of grapes with branching candles flickering in their holders. The room was alive with leaping shadows and the sound of the clock ticking. Books lined the walls, and James turned his attention from the dog, picked up the book he had been reading before Creagh had come in and held it loosely between his large freckled fingers.

After a pause, he asked, 'Do you know Deirdre Rennett?'

Creagh shook his head. 'I hear she's been in Europe finishing, and that she's come home,' he replied.

'We all went to Slievelea at Christmas for her coming-out party,' James said. 'But you, Creagh, were from home and did not come. You avoid your social duty too often, my boy.'

'Oh James, you sound exactly like a father and you are but my brother.' And as James was about to admonish him he continued, 'She's very beautiful, Deirdre Rennett. Ulrick Vestry says so. But then so is his sister Aurora'

'She is exceedingly beautiful and extremely rich. She's

48

heiress to Slievelea, unless Lord and Lady Rennett produce a son.' James sighed, thinking of his own quandary. Then, drawing himself together, he continued, 'And that, I hear from Hegarty, is very unlikely, not to say impossible.'

He glanced at the young face before him. The glossy brown wing of Creagh's hair had fallen over his brow.

'I have a mind to wed you to the Lady Deirdre,' James said.

Creagh shrugged. It was his habit to agree until he saw fit to disagree and then he simply held his whist and disappeared, removing himself entirely from the arena until the problem had solved itself, as was often the case.

'I can have no cause to quarrel with that,' he said. An alliance with that great family could only do him good and benefit the Cause immeasurably. 'She and Aurora are great friends of Sophie's,' he added.

'Or,' continued James, 'Aurora Vestry, now that you mention her, is another good choice. The Vestries of Mount Rivers are an old and noble family, quite impeccable. Although the men in that clan are fearful gamblers, still Aurora would suit nicely. I would have no objection if you chose there.' James paused and frowned. 'You have no other ties?' he asked, then added, 'I hear you lay with a gypsy girl some moons ago?'

Creagh smiled into his brother's eyes. Here they understood each other well.

'Yes. 'Twas the lusty time; spring. I loved her, too. Such wanton hips she had on her, James. And she would be a sore temptation to me this day were I to clap eyes on her again. But that's not likely and there would be no possibility of an alliance. So . . .' He spread his hands in a gesture of finality.

There was a pause, then James sighed and said, 'Last night Dolly gave birth to a son. Who was dead.'

Quick sympathy sprang to the young man's eyes as tears stung the back of James'.

'Oh James, I'm sorry.'

James shook his head, then pulling himself together continued, 'The seed you planted last spring bore fruit that was handed to us by your young wanton last night.'

Creagh looked uncertainly at James. He pushed back his hair and James saw a frown had creased his brow.

'It was a boy your gipsy wench bore. I want to keep him as our own. Dolly and I, our heir. Dr Hegarty says she can have no

49

more children.' His voice broke and Creagh saw there were tears in his brother's eyes. He had never known James to show weakness before and he was concerned for him.

'Creagh, this place cannot be left to ... to ... Fergal.' He spat the words out as if he had bitten into a wormy apple. 'You understand? You can have many a child by your wife, Deirdre Rennet, if you marry her as I sincerely hope you will see your way to doing. If you allow us to keep this baby Usher will be kept in the family and your son will inherit all.'

Creagh nodded. It was all one to him. He had no feeling for a child conceived in the heat of love he had felt through spring and summer, the great flood of passion that had come with the sun and vanished with the cold and rain, leaving only tender memories. It suited him too to have a hold over his brother James, for his dearest love, his over-riding obsession, the Fenians, might have need of a loaded gun some day. Besides, he was moved by James' situation and was only too glad of the opportunity to help.

He rose and held his hand out to his brother. No words were said. It was understood. Their clasp was firm.

'The less said of this the better. The Brodericks know, and the Maitlands of course. However it will be a seven-day wonder bruited about by servants and provided we make no fuss it will all blow over. People will talk, but the lad is a Jeffries and we are big enough to rise above it,' James said, then added as Creagh reached the door, 'You'll need to move as fast as you can with Deirdre Rennett. Young Anthony Tandy-Cullaine and Darcy Blackwater are hot contenders for the lady's hand.'

The brothers smiled at each other and Creagh left.

Chapter

9

WHEN Creagh left his brother he had meant to ride out and deliver some secret messages to a few rebels who lived scattered in far-flung mountain cabins and tell them about the meeting to be held in Usher. However, he was way-laid by his sister Sophie, who pulled him, willy-nilly, into the Red Drawing-room. The room was small. Crimson silk covered the walls and it was used mostly by the females of the household for their embroidery and needlework.

'What do you want, Sophie?' Creagh asked, trying to control his impatience, for he longed to be away. His sister shut the door behind her. He was thinking how pretty she looked when he caught sight of Arabella and he groaned.

'No, no. Let me out of here. Whatever it is you want, you'll have to ask James about it.'

Sophie giggled merrily. 'Did he order you to marry, Creagh?' she teased. 'He is quite mad on the subject at the moment. You know how James is when he gets an idea into his head. He never lets up. Oh dear, oh dear, poor Creagh. Will it spoil all your fun? You won't be able to gallivant over the country any more and ... and ...' Her little face was flushed as she tried in vain to imagine her brother up to all sorts of naughtiness outside the scope of her imagination.

Creagh laughed. 'And what, little sister? What terrible behaviour do you imagine I get up to?'

Sophie stamped her foot. 'Oh, how should I know?' Then she smiled and pulled her brother onto the scarlet and gilt *chaise-longue*. She settled her skirts about her and cast a quick glance at Arabella who was sitting on a high-backed chair in the

51

corner of the room doggedly embroidering her sampler, very badly.

'Now, Creagh, tell us what James' business with you was all about?'

'Hussy!' Creagh cried. 'You are a monster, Soph. That is absolutely none of your business.'

Sophie pinned him with the full azure glow of her eyes. Coaxingly she smiled at him, an irresistible smile. 'Oh please, Creagh. Do tell us. Was James being heavy-handed? Remember, he is very young for such a responsibility as Usher.'

Creagh sighed. He knew when he was beaten. 'Well, he did ask me to court either Lady Deirdre Rennett or Lady Aurora Vestry. I assured him I would give the matter my most serious attention. And I might add, I am not in the least averse to either lady.'

'Oh Creagh, how awful,' Sophie burst out. 'What about love?'

Creagh shrugged. 'So? What about love?'

'Well ... well ... people fall in love, you know. Oh Creagh, don't smile in that horrid way. They do, and people say it is most agreeable.' She faltered and blushed, lowering her eyes.

'Oh Sophie, you are such a romantic.' Bella paused in her stitchwork. She looked at Creagh. 'She is always deep in the poems of Mr Keats.' Casting her eyes up to heaven, she quoted, '"Oh what can ail thee, Knight-at-arms, Alone and palely loitering".' Then, seeing Creagh's look of incomprehension, she explained patiently, 'La Belle Dame sans Merci,' and as she realized he still did not know what she was talking about, she shrugged and returned to her work.

'People do fall in love, Creagh,' Sophie said stubbornly.

'Of course they do, Soph. Look at Mama and Papa. But it is to be hoped that no lady will fall in love with any other than her chosen husband. There are only a few families around here with which a suitable alliance could be formed; the Rennetts, the Vestries, the Gormans, the Blackwaters, the Tandy-Cullaines.' He ticked them off on his fingers. 'You must know that. Unless we go to London. That, after all, is how James met Dolly. I wish it was not so, but it is.'

'Oh Creagh, you don't understand Sophie at all.' Bella once more paused in her work.

'How could I?' Creagh asked reasonably. 'You have only

52

been back a few years. I spent many years growing up without you. You had each other. You got to know each other. I was alone.'

'Dearest Creagh, you have us now.' Sophie smiled at her brother and squeezed his hand.

'But you do not make it any easier by hardly ever being at home,' Bella stated bluntly.

'Oh Lord, Bella. Must you?' Creagh said irritably.

'Well. All I am trying to say is that Sophie is waiting for her dream love to gallop across the countryside on his white horse and in his shining armour and carry her away, who knows where? I'm sure she does not. I declare she has not thought further than the romantic gallop.'

Sophie looked at her sister crossly, 'You *are* a horrid tease Bella. I'm sure you have exactly the same dreams for the future as I do.'

'There you are quite wrong.' Bella looked across the room to where the fire gleamed and crackled, casting a red glow into the red room. 'I will be quite content to wed the man of my brother's choice, and escape from here, from Usher. I hate this cold, cold house.'

Creagh hooted. 'Bella! Even I know you well enough not to believe that. About you obeying James, I mean. You have never obeyed any one in your life. And how can you hate this house? It is the most beautiful place in the world. This is the most beautiful land.'

'You have never been out of it.' Bella said simply.

There was a pause as each of them reconsidered.

Then as Creagh started to rise, Sophie stopped him by saying, 'What we really wanted to know, Creagh, was about the baby? The Widow or Bessie Broderick won't talk. But Molly said Dolly had ... her baby was ...' She floundered to a halt and Creagh, despite a strong desire to parry the question and escape, faced up to his responsibility.

'Oh, you had better be told now, and not blunder about in front of Dolly, and perhaps upset her,' he said.

He looked at the two faces turned to him, one so innocently concerned, the other avid for information, with the look on her face of Tabitha, the kitchen cat, as she waited to pounce.

'Dolly's baby died. I fathered a child, a boy, on a gypsy girl, and James has given him to Dolly. He is to be the next Knight of Usher, for Dolly can have no more children.'

Bella snorted. 'A hunchback or a bastard for the next Knight of Usher. How wonderful!'

Sophie sprang to her feet. 'Oh, how can you be so cruel, Bella? How? Poor little lad upstairs. Fergal. He cannot help his handicap.'

'Then ask him down to join us,' Bella said. The others looked at her, horrified. Such a thought had never occurred to them.

'Oh I'm sure he's better off away from us. It is James' order. He is more comfortable away from normal people, for, I am told, he is not.'

'More comfortable, too, for us,' Bella answered Sophie coldly.

Creagh looked at her in astonishment. 'How can you think like you do, Bella?' he asked.

'Well,' she said, 'it's the truth, isn't it?'

'What you say is usually the truth,' Creagh said thoughtfully, 'but you have a very cruel way of saying it. Beware, Bella, or it will recoil one day and bite you.'

'How can you expect me to like the fact that one day this noble house, as you call it, and all its lands, will go to the bastard son of a gypsy?'

Creagh rose slowly and put his arm around Sophie's shoulder. She had been watching them, her face turned now to the right, now to the left in the ruby glow that enveloped the room.

'You forget, Bella, it matters little whether you like it or not. It has nothing whatsoever to do with you. You have no say in the matter. It is my business, and James'. And Cormac is my son. Never forget that. His mother may be a gypsy but she was of royal Romany blood. Not that that matters one whit to me. But I will not have you cause any trouble. Do you understand me?'

Bella raised one shoulder and then let it fall in a curiously vulgar gesture. 'I'm sure I don't care,' she said.

'Oh yes you do, Bella.' Sophie cried. 'It's wonderful, wonderful news. I know you'll think that when you have had time to consider. James has what he most wants, and Dolly, dearest Dolly, would have gone out of her mind if . . .'

Her brother hugged her. 'What a dear you are, Sophie,' he said, kissing the flaxen curls on her temples. 'I hope some really handsome, suitable suitor comes riding over the mountain for you, dearest, I really do.'

54

Sophie laughed. 'Oh, I'm not in that much of a hurry, Creagh,' she said. Her brother kissed her again and turned and left the room.

'But *I* am. Oh, I am,' Bella thought to herself as she picked up the beastly sampler and went back to the stitching she hated.

10

Chapter

10

WHEN Rosaleen finally awakened, the day was at its height. Craw Kilty eased her breasts for her and gave her a red flannel skirt, a white cambric chemise and a shawl that Melba had given her long ago and which she had used to decorate the table on grand days, or wore across her shoulders when she went to the Fair. It was black with huge red cabbage roses on it and it had a silken fringe.

Rosaleen looked and felt more like herself after she had eaten some barley-cakes with yellow salt-butter and sipped some warm ale. Her hair she washed and dried out in the sun, for the day, after the anger of the night and the mists of the morning, was mellow and mild. The March winds were still worn out by last night's violence. The storm clouds had blown away and the pale azure sky was full of fat little cirrus clouds and the sun was pale primrose yellow.

Craw Kilty, skirts hitched up under her waistband revealing her rag-covered feet and fat mottled legs, was scattering some grain for the hens. Rosaleen spread her wet black hair out over her shoulders and turned herself, eyes closed, to the sunlight.

There was a stream running through the valley and a flock of geese were grazing at the reedy banks. Matty the shepherd was toiling up the hills that led to the mountains and she could hear the low baa-baa of the sheep in the distance. The mountains, like a patchwork quilt of amber and olive, purple and maroon, rose steeply on either side, and you could see Usher up yonder on the farther reaches, dramatic, dark against the soft spring day. The sun was warm on her cheeks and she felt content in herself, her belly full, her body rested, her mission fulfilled, her child in good hands. She would bear the pain of her loss in order that he might grow up a gentleman in a castle. It was a better fate altogether than to be a gypsy in a caravan. For though the life was wild and free, the winter was cold and the stones cut your feet. Nor were you welcome many places; you were reviled in most and the dogs barked at you as you went by.

Craw Kilty was spinning now in the cottage doorway and a deep peace lay in the valley. Rosaleen kilted her scarlet skirt and spread her naked legs to the warmth of the sun.

The old woman came and squatted by her. 'The Minstrel was at it again last night before you came,' she said. 'That's why I half expected ye. Tell us the tale.'

Rosaleen did. She told the truth, though it was not her nature. She was a gypsy and did not easily trust people. But she knew Craw Kilty would know whether she was lying or not and anyhow the Minstrel had surely seen some of it. Hadn't the ould wan as much as said so just now? So she told her tale.

When she had finished Craw grunted, satisfied. 'Now you've been straight wi' me, so I'll tell ye what I know.' As Rosaleen opened her mouth to speak she said sharply, 'Shut yer gob an' listen. The Minstrel talked rubbish, I thought as ought to know better. But not so, I see now. Now some of it at least makes a groundling of sense, a smattering anyhow.' She scratched at the earth with a twig as she sought the right words.

'He raved on about two bairns an' one of them dead. That musta been in the castle, for I heard the banshee.'

Rosaleen nodded, and she continued, 'He said your name an' talked of a friend ... a man, Redmond Rafferty, and a blacksmith. Do you know him?'

Rosaleen shook her head. 'I know no Rafferty, but I know the blacksmith.' He was a friend to her race. He lived and worked on the Dublin Road and was another link in the chain of sympathetic folk that stretched the length of the land.

Craw Kilty continued, 'He said help would come from there, soon, but not yet, not yet. He talked of danger and escape from Usher. Does that mean anything to you?'

Rosaleen shook her head again. She could not think what the danger, if danger there was, could be. 'No, nothing at all' she replied.

'He talked about an heir, who was not an heir, come to Usher. Just like you said. "The new heir will come and the real heir will go," he said. Ach well, it will all come out, deary, in the fullness of time. In the end everything does. So. What will ye do now? Now the babby's in his rightful place?'

'I don't know, old mother. I don't know. Listen. I'd like to keep my eye on Cormac. See that all is well.'

The old crone nodded in agreement. 'It would be wise. The grand folks up there are fickle.' She gestured to the mountain shoulder where Usher, fiery-stoned in the sun, grew out of the rock pointing to the sky, proudly stalwart and impenetrable. 'You'd do well to keep your eye on your bairn, *alanna*, so you would'.

'But how?'

'You could go as a servant, maybe?'

Rosaleen answered vehemently, 'No. No. That would never do. Creagh would be there, you see, an' how could we keep from each other, I ask you, the hot way we feel? And the child there, and me the real mother? Ach no. It would be a hornets' nest I'd create an' I'd do that.' The ould wan thought a while and a rook flew overhead. Then she whooped and nearly over-toppled. 'Ach, I know. I'm an eejit of the worst order. Me sisters. Whyn't I think of it afore. Shoulda thought long since. The Widow Boann must mind the lambkin. An' she worships the ground Master Creagh walks on. She brought him up.'

Rosaleen felt unexpected tears spring to her eyes and the Arcadian Grove came to her memory instantly. She could smell the fragrance of the place, see its beauty as if she were transported there on the instant. What lovely days they had been. She remembered Creagh telling her of his childhood and the part the Widow had played in it.

'I'd say Bessie Broderick, the other sister, but her hands are full with those straps of hers. No, the Widow is the perfect choice an' there's nothing she would not do for Creagh, an' so I reckon there's nothin' she'll not do fer his babby.'

Rosaleen, quite recovered from her memories, clapped her hands together joyously. 'That's it. That's it. Oh mother, you are right. Sure Creagh told me all about her an' wasn't she the one I gave my angel to last night? I'm sure I'd know her anywhere, though I've never clapped eyes on her in me life. That's the thing. I'll speak to her when she comes here; old mother, an' if I'm not around you'll store the good news an' let me know the bad quick as the wind.'

58

Craw nodded and looked intently at Rosaleen. 'And you? What will you do?'

'Well, I don't know yet.' Rosaleen frowned. 'I'll go to Hagar and Melba for a wee while maybe and . . .'

But the ould wan was shaking her head. 'They're gone. Over the seas to Valparaiso. And after that the caves of Scaramouche I'll be bound. Ah, lovie, 'twas for you they came back here. For love of you only. They knew how you loved this land, and they loved you. They are getting old and the mists of Ireland don't suit ageing bones. They passed through here on their way to Waterford and the ships. 'Twas scarce a day ago. Said you were going to Usher with the babby and how they'd leave for sunnier climes. If you hurry you can still catch them.'

Rosaleen shook her head. She sighed. 'No. I could not go that far from Cormac.'

'But if Melba knew you'd stay with them she'd never go. If Hagar knew you needed them . . .'

'No. No, old mother. It would be wrong and selfish of me.' She looked at the old woman with tears in her eyes. She felt suddenly bereft, doubly lonely, as if she had been deserted. She had needed all her courage to give up her baby. She had had to bury her feelings and try to be realistic about her lover. Now to find that the people who loved her most had gone out of her life shattered her. She had not expected to feel like this, but the desolation swept over her and she bowed her head. Craw Kilty had a shrewd idea of what was passing through the girl's mind. She got up and went into the cottage. There she poured a stiff two inches of poteen into a mug and brought it out to the girl.

'Here, *alanna*, drink this. 'Twill take the dark hand away.'

Rosaleen took it and drank it in one gulp, wiping her mouth with the back of her hand when she had finished. 'I'm sorry, Craw. I felt sad suddenly. Yerra, it's not like me. Oh I'm selfish woman there's no doubt, but I'd never stop my parents going into the sun. You are right and I'm no longer a chick to be cared for and babied. I must make my own way over the land. Take my own path, find my own destiny.'

Craw Kilty sighed and rose and patted the girl on the shoulder. 'Well, bide with me awhile. You would be good company an' I a lone woman in the long evenings. We could talk of the great tales and the legends together an' have a grand time.'

Rosaleen sucked in her breath. 'Ach no. I'll bide with you a wee while, but not for long. I can't stay sat here waiting, watching.' She pointed to the dark bulk of the castle.' I'd go mad. I'm young, old mother. I've a life to lead, yes, an' money to make too.'

'Gypsies don't need money,' Craw Kilty said.

'Everyone needs money. It's the thing that brings power, so it is, an' now I've a mind to protect myself.'

'Where will ye go to get it, *alanna*? There's many a feisty farmer, red-necked and strong in his loins, wid bags full of gold under the mattress that'd be droolin' over the chance to wed ye.'

'What farmer has gold in this land, I ask ye? An' what would I want with a great red farmer at all in the name of God and the Virgin? I can't be dependent on any man an' be safe, now can I? An' I've no mind to lie beneath a fat hairy man o' the land an' him pushin' into me an' gruntin' like a pig an' giving me no pleasure at all when I'm used to a refined sort of lovemaking that plays my body like a violin and gives a colleen such thrilling trembles as to make the other a horror and a revulsion.'

'Oh law-de-dah, how fine and uppity ye sound. Holy Mother of God. Take care, my pretty, ye don't come a cropper on yer pride.'

'Ach, shut yer gob, ould wan, an' listen. In a wee while I'll go to Dublin town itself an' there I'll find a way ... you'll see. An' in time I'll come to you, maybe at the fullness of the moon, maybe at the wane. I dunno yet. But come I will to see how my son does above in the castle. Make no mistake about it, ould wan, I'll want to know. An' if summit goes wrong, then send the Minstrel to me, or a message. Let nothing interfere or stop word of his welfare reaching me if aught is out of kilter. I will reward you well.'

'Yerra, sure, why should I want your money, for God's sake? Hasn't Melba been that good to me? It'll be a pleasure, lovie, an' don't you fret.'

She believed Dark Rosaleen when she said she would get money. The Minstrel had promised strange things for Rosaleen and she knew better than to query his prophesies. Craw sighed and went to the half-door of the cottage and sat down. She picked up the threads of her spinning. The wool had coarsened the skin on the fingers of her left hand and she rubbed the callouses and looked to where the mountains breathed beneath the green covering of fields and tufted grass. She could still see Matty the shepherd in his short trews and thick sweater, his stave in his hand. She watched him, eyes narrowed. His whole life was his flock, he loved his sheep, lived with them, was uncomfortable in any other company. She knew he carried his lunch of bread and cheese, and strong onions from the loamy patch behind his cottage, in the pouch at his waist. He reached the high-land path as she watched, and disappeared behind the curve of the mountain's cheek.

'I'll do it, *alanna*. I can always leave a message at the forge you mentioned on the Dublin Road. Who do I ask for?'

'Riley is the name. He'll give ye every co-operation.'

'Riley then. But only in an emergency. Don't you fret about it no more. Don't tease yer mind. Let it rest. You have my word.'

Rosaleen nodded, well satisfied. The sun felt warm on her bare legs and she wriggled her toes in the heat. Her feet were used to cold and the harsh ground under their tread, yet they were pretty and she smiled at them, admiring them, moving them this way and that, stretching her legs out before her.

Ronan must have come silently behind her for she did not hear him at all until he caught her foot in his slim musician's hands and held it between his palms as he sat on the ground in front of her. Rosaleen's wide eyes flew to the cottage door, but Craw Kilty was nowhere to be seen. Instantly she was ashamed of herself, then amused, then excited, for she realized why she had cast the look and felt a qualm of guilt. She had held the thought, a tiny seed at first when she had spoken of the red-necked farmer and thought of Creagh and his white skin, soft as silk under her hands, and that thought had been followed by a vision of the only other man she knew with the same satin sheen on him like the gloss on a pearl. The Minstrel, taking her foot between his hands, instantly revealed to her her desire for him, which was why she had looked for Craw Kilty with the panic of the already guilty. What was to happen now was an inevitability.

'Old mother is gone,' the Minstrel said, caressing her foot, knowing her thoughts. He bent his head and kissed the arch, then the instep. His kisses scorched her skin and he smiled up at her. 'I think she knows. She's gone over yonder on the pathway to the castle. She's off to her sisters at Usher, a place she never goes, but I reckon she wants to get news of the babby for you.'

His fingers were on her ankle, touching gently. Then they travelled to her knee and she felt the tingling of the nerves high in her thighs. It was a pleasurable exciting feeling that made her open her legs, and the Minstrel, on his knees, put his arms around her waist and let his curly head rest on her full breasts. She opened the tiny buttons of the camisole top she wore and with a gasp Ronan felt them near his lips and he suckled the hard rose tips, the feeling of his teeth sending a wanton excitement down her body in surges.

He looked up at her, mouth damp, eyes clouded with desire. 'I've never . . . I dunno how . . .' he said feverishly.

'Ah, lovey, hush . . . I'll guide you, *astore*.'

They lay on the grass, buttercups close to their faces, crushing the daisies, and she guided him to the centre of her being and to the rhythm of her pleasure. He was hard and strong and eager to fulfil her and she was excited and ready and their consummation was mutual, a wild cry that reached Craw Kilty on the wind.

She shook her head as she plodded up the mountainy path. 'He'll lose the gift, now, for sure,' she muttered and could not make up her mind whether it was a good or a bad thing should he do so.

Ronan lay spent, his eyes darkened with love. 'Oh Rosaleen. My Dark Rosaleen,' he said, but she laid her fingers on his lips.

'Hush now. 'Twas good. So good. But I must go, Ronan. An' I want your promise to help me. When I need you.'

'You've got it,' he said, nodding gravely.

'You come to me when I call? Come with the wind at your heels?'

'I promise.'

She gently kissed his lips and ran her fingers through the crisp curls. She stood and shook down the scarlet skirt and petticoats. She buttoned her bodice and pulled the shawl on her shoulders, crossing it over her breasts and tying it around her waist, neatly tucking the ends under the tight fold. She shook out her curls, dry now, and went into the cottage.

Ronan hovered, head still clouded from his experience, uncertain, not quite knowing what to do.

'I'm on a sudden determined to leave,' she said to him over her shoulder, packing a loaf of bread and a hunk of cheese in a red kerchief and slipping it over her wrist.

'I know,' the Minstrel replied.

She looked at him sharply, scrutinizing his fine-boned face and sensitive mouth. 'I reckon you do at that,' she said.

''Tis the itch to go,' he said. 'You never lose it.'

She crossed the room to where he stood — two steps it took — and laid her hands on his shoulders.

'You know it?' she asked, 'That feeling?'

He smiled at her. 'I don't know where she got me,' he replied, jerking his head towards the hills where his mother had gone. 'Mebbe she lay with a gypsy herself. But, oh yes, I know it. Amn't I away over the hills and dales, singing and journeying most of the time God gives me? Times my feet will not be still an' the urge is overpowerin' and the land spreads out before me, calling, seductive as a woman.'

She laid her forehead on his shoulder. 'I know. I know. It's a siren call,' she said, her voice dreamy. 'An' I'm never so happy as when I obey it an' I'm on my way. Free. Free.' Then she looked up at him and shook her dark locks. 'But I canna go too far, an' that takes the freedom away. It changes everything. I canna go far. That life is over for me now.'

'Only for the moment,' he said. 'We don't know what's in store, do we?'

'That's true enough.' She smiled, then kissed him softly on the mouth.

'I'll come to you whenever you call,' he whispered.

She nodded. 'I know,' she said. Then with sudden energy, 'I must go now.'

She took her sharp knife from the window-sill where she had left it last night and concealed it at her waist. 'Goodbye, Minstrel,' she said and smiled at him.

He stood helplessly by watching her. Then she had gone and it was as if the sun had gone down. There had been a bright light and now it was dark.

He went to the half-door. He saw her crossing the field and moving to the grey stone hump-backed bridge over the stream. Her back was straight and her hips swayed as she walked. He would have done anything to keep her there but he was helpless in the face of her determination.

When she has reached the centre of the bridge she turned and waved. He returned her salutation and watched her until she was out of sight.

Chapter

11

THE Widow Boann lived high in the tower apartments of Usher. Green ivy wrapped it around and the windows were small and barred, mullioned. The look-out sentry in the old days used to keep guard there, pacing the walls outside and coming here to the keep for a welcome drink at the end of a watch. The rooms were comfortable enough, two floors set aside for herself and the child Fergal. There she took Cormac on the night of his dramatic arrival in Usher. He would bide with them both, the Widow and Fergal. She kept him there in the hours he did not spend with Dolly.

She was a taciturn woman who related best to children. They sensed the quiet strength and love beneath her rather formidable appearance. She was a Gaelic speaker whose brains had been addled by a father who was the official story-teller to the Wicklow gatherings. Kevin Kilty made his way from fair to fair, from racecourse to racecourse, from the parties of the rich folk whom he held in thrall, to the shebeens and inns, the taverns and hostelries on the way, dragging his three girl-children behind him. He told his marvellous stories in Gaelic or English as the need arose and could quote long heroic poems by Sophocles and Aeschylus in Greek. He had learnt fluent Greek and Latin from the hedge-priests when he was a boy. He had the tigeen in the valley where Craw Kilty and the Widow and Bessie Broderick had grown up. They dwelt with their mother, the daughter of a labouring man from Arklow, until the Widow married Boann, the head gamekeeper at Usher. She had gone there as a girl in service, as had her sister Bessie. Bessie had married the gardener and eventually become cook to the family, a position of responsibility. Only Craw Kilty had never been to Usher, though the castle loomed over the shoulder of the mountain and its shadow was omnipresent as she hurried about her tasks in her little cottage in the valley. Their mother had died and their father answered the lure of the open road and they had not set eyes on him again. The Widow's and Bessie's husbands had died and they had soldiered on, not missing their mates too much.

In the castle they had found the Widow was best with children, though she had never had any of her own. She had been nurse-maid and mother-substitute to Creagh all his life and then to the hunchback baby Fergal. Like her sister Craw Kilty she had aged prematurely.

The Widow loved Fergal dearly, as if he were her own, as indeed he might be, for he saw no one but her and received no other love. She tended him well and played with him every chance she could. As she bathed his little body her heart would be filled with tenderness at the sight of the purple hummock on his shoulder that near touched his ear. He was a bright little thing no matter what the rest might think, and his face held the beauty of the unexpected. She taught him words in Gaelic and he learned quick enough. He touched her lips with his pink fingers as he tried out new sounds she murmured over and over to him in the dawn of the day or the shimmering twilight.

He had a sweet temperament and she thanked God daily that he was not a howler or a bawler like Miss Arabella. If he created too much noise it could perhaps bring him unwanted attention from the household downstairs, which preferred to pretend he did not exist. She had planned, though, what to do if ever they decided to get rid of him or otherwise dispose of what they thought of as their deep shame.

She had nursed Creagh, and she just out of school, become his mother, for the Lady Angela was wandering far over the face of the earth in wild foreign places with queer sounding names like Burma, Calcutta, Singapore and Ceylon. The fact that she traipsed Sophie, Arabella and James with her caused the Widow a deal of contempt, for how could they grow in the serene crook of her arms, a mother's duty surely, unless she was static? Unless she rested in her home as was natural, instead of journeying under hot suns that drew the juices from the brain and killed any dreaming at birth, how could a child's imagination develop and expand? So she mused as she nursed the little

Creagh in the tranquillity of Usher Castle.

She had shown Creagh how to dream, to loiter through the slow days of childhood with time and to spare. He learned to tickle a trout, poke about in the rock-pools down by the sounding sea. There he learned to examine the undulations of the sea-anemone, pop the pods on the seaweed and discover the bitter smell of iodine, prize open the pink grooved shells and listen to the sea. The Widow hitched up her black alpaca skirt at both sides and tucked it into her belt where the keys hung, keys that clinked and jangled when she walked, and took him through the woods and the hedgerows. There she revealed to him the secret flowers. There were soft yellow cowslips, lupins and ragwort, cornflowers, black briony and cow-parsley whose stems had a pile like velvet. She taught him how to avoid poison ivy that lurked in the forest, and stinging nettles that made your legs itch. They explored the willow islands set in the shimmering waters of the rivers and lakes near Mount Rivers, at the Meeting of the Waters. She showed him blue shadows and golden lights and the deer leaping. They wandered through Glenascaul, the valley of shadows where her sister Craw Kilty lived. They spent many an afternoon casting the runes together in the bright cottage while Creagh played on the hearth with the Minstrel, Craw's magic child — some said the spawn of angels while some said the Devil was his father.

They would talk, the sisters, like two witches. They were closer than twins and they would nod and leave sentences unfinished for they knew each other's thoughts and acted always as one. They drank dark sweet tea and smoked leaves that they rolled and dried in the cottage. They ate sweets made of honey and hazelnuts gathered from the thicket behind the cottage. Creagh heard them talk in Gaelic of the ships carrying cargoes of illegal weapons for the secret struggle against England. He learned the ways of the magpies, the larks, the thrushes and the blackbirds. He knew the sounds of the hounds in the slips, and the horses in the stables and could decipher their needs and messages at a distance. In the grey dawns and the purple twilights, before the fire in Craw Kilty's cottage, he heard the tales of Erin and he absorbed them all.

Fergal had not been so lucky, but now, with this child in her arms, the Widow Boann hoped she would be able to repeat that education. The little mite Cormac would know, like his father,

66

the magic of wood, water and earth. She had loved his father and now she would love the son. It would not interfere with her love for Fergal nor her championship of him. She felt a fierce protective urge towards Fergal that sometimes shook her to the core so that her whole body trembled when his lordship spoke of his son with contempt, or Old Gentleman refused to talk of him at all, or the Dowager Lady Angela had the vapours at the mere mention of his name.

She busied herself in her tower stirring the pap she fed Fergal with, lamb and yellow carrots, green cabbage and sliced potatoes, stewed until mushy, a thick concoction that he gobbled, mopping up the juice with hunks of bread and looking up at her with enormous blue eyes, Lady Dolly's eyes, thick lashed and guileless. She was his world, the only one in it, for he saw no one else.

The infant slept in her arms and the moonlight filtered through the pattern of ivy that veiled the window in the circular room. It was peaceful there; the child had settled well since his arrival a week ago. In any event no sound reached them this high up except the hoot of the night-owl odd times, or the wind in the high-top trees above. The valley lay below, and far in the distance the Widow could see her sister's cottage there, a dot, a plume of smoke rising from the chimney. She felt peaceful, as she always did with a babe in her arms. There was only one thing to disturb her peace, an anxiety that gnawed at her constantly; her beloved Creagh and his secret pursuits. Her sharp eyes raked the valley, peering into all the shadows, trying to penetrate the purple darkness until her eyes could decipher what they sought.

Yes, at last, there it was. The lights. One by one. Isolated. Each from a different place, a different direction, each secretive. There were flares that were suddenly extinguished, lanterns to guide over rocky passes, lighting the way through the shadows of the valley or the black denseness of the forest. She could see the outlines of the travellers on horseback and donkey, and she could see the men arriving on foot. They would be invisible or unremarkable at the least to anyone not as high up as she, but from her eyrie the whole world spread before her and she could see it all. She prayed no one else could. Her heart stopped with terror at the thought of what would happen if anyone else could see as she did.

Creagh and his meetings. He was getting careless. Here they were, the conspirators, coming across the land to Usher to meet below in the priest's hole, a criminal offense that sometimes carried the death penalty. She had begged him not to have them here in Usher, these fervent men intent on freedom. She cared not about his meetings in other shebeens, halls, inns or caves. She knew Creagh's slipperiness, his ability to speedily vanish. He had always been good at it, from the time he was a little *buachaill* and she wanted to bath him. He had had the ability to slither away like a shadow and she never managed to catch him. In those days she had been much quicker on her feet. She had had to be pretty nifty at evading the clutches of the young gentlemen who wanted and were entitled to lay her if they caught her. They never did catch her, just as she never did catch Master Creagh. So she did not worry about his meetings elsewhere in the country. She knew he attended them, from the Mountains of Mourne to Queenstown, from Skibbereen to Galway, but anxiety gnawed like a rat at her heart here in Usher. If someone saw the lights and travellers journeying here they could realize what was happening. That would not be hard, she thought, sure any *amadán* could put two and two together. Why in the name of God would the likes of farmers and cattle-men, peasants and landowners, publicans and town workers, artists and journalists be creeping the highways and byways in the dead of night, if they were not going to a forbidden secret meeting? She wondered would it not be better if they came in broad daylight, fearlessly? Maybe then they would not cast suspicion. But this way? God help him if they suspected him, if he was betrayed. Heaven knew there were enough informers about. If they came for him here he could not run. He had nowhere to flee to from Usher. It was his own home. In those circumstances it would be either him or James for the high jump and no one would suspect James, although he too would suffer. Creagh had always been hot-headed and outspoken. Many knew his feelings. But that was all right. It was not a punishable offence for a member of a prominent Anglo-Irish family to be liberal, have humanistic views. It was quite another kettle of fish to have a meeting in your cellars. That was a crime punishable by death. It was treason.

The Widow blessed herself. She was not overtly religious but liked to be on the safe side. 'Protect him, Lord,' she muttered.

'The fool,' she added.

She watched till dawn and the last torch, the last horse, the last shadow had slipped into the misty morning. Then as the baby started its mewling cry she sighed, flattened her hair with the palm of her hand, splashed icy water from the ewer into the pink porcelain basin and onto her face, put on a fresh apron, ankle-length, pinning the bib across her ample bosom. She picked up the baby Cormac, left the sleeping Fergal in his bed and went down to Dolly with her surrogate son.

Chapter

12

THE walls were slimy, wet with the constant dripping of water seeping through the rock-face. This passage was deep under the little river that ran beside the church at Usher. It was covered in soft verdure, sweating mosses and lichen, curling fronds of fern, and the leprous night-time fungi that flourishes only in dark places. They came, two by two or singly, over the hills and the mountains, across the swaying rope-bridge and over the grey stone humpbacked one, using narrow pathways where the horse grazed his side against the jagged rock and had to have sure feet to arrive in safety. They crossed the valley and journeyed in from the villages to keep their tryst. They came secretly and as noiselessly as they could to the sleeping castle, and disappeared into the cave-mouth concealed by trailing ivy, waist-high bracken and swaying fern. They crept down the slimy dripping passage to where the caves divided. They took the branch to the left that led beneath the castle foundations and opened the well-oiled gateway. They crept up the oozing steps, being careful and placing their feet firmly on the slippery stairs, holding tightly to the iron bar that was worn thin by the grip of a thousand secret conspirators. They had come here year in year out over the ages, stretching back to the reign of Henry VIII, plotting freedom, escape from oppression. Priests had come here and rebels, Earls in flight, men interested in revolution and a safe place to whisper treason.

Now it was the turn of the Fenians, and this time without the knowledge or consent of the inmates of the castle. Except one: only Creagh knew. The little band of conspirators and plotters had to be careful, mistakes could end in death.

They had no fear of discovery once they were below ground. The getting there and the leaving were the dangerous times and the making sure they were not followed. Once below in the underground caves they were as safe as they could be, for the passages were deep and naturally soundproof and the priest's hole built for secrecy and safety.

There were thirty to forty of them and no women. In Dublin and Galway the women came and in other large towns, but not here. The men were an excitable bunch, they needed strict control, and tempers flared, sometimes dangerously at the gatherings. Feelings ran high, yet they were united by a passionate belief in Ireland's freedom and ultimate independence.

Their leaders had originally followed the great Daniel O'Connell's aims; repeal of the Union, a common and separate nationality which would embrace Protestant and Catholic alike. But as time went by the Fenians became desperate and more and more impolitic.

They held meetings, drilled in the hills and mountains, becoming reckless and foolhardy. Many were arrested. One was a young lieutenant in the movement, James Stephens, a Protestant from Kilkenny. He barely escaped and made his way to France. In Paris he became involved with radical and revolutionary secret societies that were a blue-print on his return to Ireland for the Fenians. He became leader and broke the brotherhood up into hundreds of secret and organized cadres of picked men bound by oath for revolutionary action. Because of splits of opinion, rewards and sometimes agrarian problems, secret movements in Ireland had been riddled with informers. Stephens was determined this would no longer happen. He took precautions, with an elaborate system of security. The secret society, spread throughout Ireland, was split into 'circles'. Only one member knew the one member of any other circle and contact could only be made through this member.

It was to work well, for when the government discovered a meeting-place and arrested the leaders they did not realize there was a connection with any other group and completely underestimated the scope of their discovery.

In America the Fenian Brotherhood functioned in the open. Led by John O'Mahony it flourished in spite of the Civil War there, and Dublin crawled with ex-Confederacy soldiers. The Fenians infiltrated even the British Army, a good number of its forces being, in any event, Irishmen.

Fenian drilling had become more blatant, and mysterious bodies of men were seen moving through the countryside, and the words of a new song rang on the air:

'Pay them back woe for woe,
Give them back blow for blow,
Out and make way for the bold Fenian men!'

One of the most active and reckless of these men was Redmond Rafferty. Tall, handsome, a student of history, wild and magnetic, he was one of Stephens' closest aides. An Irish Catholic landowner's son, he was both invaluable to the Fenian leader and a thorn in his side. Stephens was an egotist and jealous of his leadership. He was incredibly hardworking, and a brilliant organizer. Red Rafferty was a wild man, frantically devoted to the cause. Stephens feared his ardent impulsive nature, and was jealous of his good looks and charismatic personality. Yet he admired the man. The British knew about him and there was a price on his head, yet he took dangerous chances. Although he led a pleasant existence in exile in Paris, he insisted on returning to his native land and risking his life for the Cause. He was here tonight with Creagh Jeffries. He had come to talk to them of insurrection, of rebellion, of uprising and the establishment of a United and Free Ireland.

The men crowded into the priest's hole. It was dry there, less damp than the passageways outside. They huddled together, squatting on the seats cut out of jutting rock, standing uneasily in the cold vaulted place, nervous of betrayal, fearful of being trapped yet fired with eagerness. The Cause was their passion, the burning flame at the core of their hearts. *Erin go brách* was their cry. Erin free, Erin forever. They had sworn an oath of fealty and they did not take it lightly.

The flames flickered on their faces. They were mostly middle-aged or young. It was not a place for the old. Where once had been the altar and an escape trap-door for the priests, there was a high stage jutting out from the rock wall, and on it stood Creagh, Red and two other men. One was a tall bearded giant of a man with an American accent. He wore a soft hat with the tattered grey coat of the Confederate soldier. His face was tanned, his teeth big and brilliantly white. He was flanked on his right by a middle-aged, dapper-suited, white-faced individual with spectacles concealing eyes that burned like coals in his head, and on the left by Creagh and beside him Redmond Rafferty.

Creagh stood forward and the murmurs that filled the place were hushed in expectation. This was what they had come here to do: listen. 'A *cairde gradh* (loved friends),' he said, speaking in Gaelic. 'We are honoured tonight to have our illustrious brother from America with us. He has crossed a great ocean to be here and he will journey back taking news to our brethren in that great land. He will tell how no Irishman is free in his own country. He will tell how we cannot use our own liquid language, the language I use to you today and for the preservation of which I am prepared to die. I give you John O'Grady.'

There was applause. O'Grady spoke well. He talked of freedom. He talked of the Constitution of America where every man has a right to speak his own mind.

'I am pledged to tell you that we will send you arms and men. We will send you money, and most of all, we will give you our word that we will help you in any way we can in your heroic and historic struggle.' There was clapping of hands and a stamping of feet and a yelling that ceased only when Creagh got to his feet again and held up his hand.

'Listen, men. Quiet, please. I now present to you a man who needs no introduction. Redmond Rafferty.'

The clapping and stomping was renewed with even more fervour. Red Rafferty was a favourite. He inspired them. He stood tall, his black hair tousled, his blue eyes full of fire and fervour.

He started quietly. 'It's been a long time. A very long time. They came here, the Sassenacht, in the reign of Henry VIII and they are still here. Do you know why they came? I'll tell you why. They came because the English they had sent before became assimilated into Irish culture. They started to speak our language! They copied our hairstyles! They married into our families. The kings of England tried to put a stop to it. They banned in 1366 the wearing of Irish clothes, they banned the copying of Irish hairstyles and they forbade the use of the Irish language. But it was no use. The House of Fitzgerald, Earls of Kildare, the House supposed to represent Royal Authority in Ireland, was in open rebellion against the Crown. So King Henry laid down his charge.'

There was an murmur sullen as an angry sea.

'You all know it here. That all lands in Ireland, whether owned by Gaelic Irish or Gaelicized English, were to be surrendered to the Crown.'

The murmur grew, but Red's voice over-rode the sound.

'They said then, "A barbarous country must first be broken by war." Our land has been occupied since. That was 1534. This is 1865. Three hundred odd years. Years of exhausting fighting, years of losing battles, years of neglect and torture from the "severing of the heads from the bodies of our people *ad terroram* (to terrorize)" — their words, my friends, their words. And it went on, from Cromwell's butchery to the incomprehensible failure to help during the famine less than twenty years ago. Charles Trevelyan said, when Irish lay dead and dying, starving, in a pitiable state — you remember, most of you were here — Charles Trevelyan said, "Too much had been done for these people ... Ireland must be left to the operation of natural causes." That man has now been knighted for his labours by a grateful Queen and Government.'

There was a roar, a great tidal-wave of anger. His voice rose once more effortlessly above the noise.

'I have come to tell you that we will not tolerate it any longer. We want to be a nation once again.'

The roar changed to a cheer.

'James Stephens has made a vow. He has promised, on oath, and I quote, "In the presence of God, to renounce all allegiance to the Queen of England and to take arms and fight at a moment's warning to make Ireland an Independent Democratic Republic, and to yield implicit obedience to the commanders and superiors of this secret society." My brothers, can we be deaf to this call? I ask you tonight, can we?'

The concerted cry was unanimous. '*No!*'

'Will you join us in our fight for freedom?'

Again the thunderous response. '*Yes.*'

'We have 85,000 men organized in Ireland alone. We hope to get arms from America.'

The large American cried out, 'Guaranteed, sir. I give you my word.'

'And reinforcements of trained soldiers?'

'My promise, sir.'

'Then, brothers, this year, and let there be no mistake about it, this year must be a year of action. The flag of Ireland, of the Irish Republic, must this year be raised.'

The cheering reverberated through the vaulted room. Creagh thanked God that the rocks made it soundproof. The men's faces were filled with the fervour of the moment. Creagh sighed. How long would it last? There were forever desertions. After so many years of subjection there was a great inertia in the people of Ireland. Apathy was ingrained in their souls, a soporofic acceptance had been ground into their very bones, and after three hundred years he marvelled that they had any fight left at all. But now was not the time to ponder on this dangerous thought. Fired by Redmond Rafferty's speech they felt warmed and hopeful as if they had drunk brandy. They left silently, their heads filled with impossible dreams, slipping away one by one out into the darkness of the night.

In the wood outside, Creagh and Red Rafferty embraced the American, who clapped them on the shoulders and quickly left them.

Red put his arm around Creagh affectionately.

'That was good for the soul,' he said, and moved to where his chestnut mare was tethered.

''Twas well done, Red,' Creagh whispered. Red stared at the trees, his eyes remote.

'If only ...' he sighed.

'What?'

'Oh nothing, Creagh. I get discouraged. I sometimes think there's only you and I and Stephens, and a handful really. Who are really dedicated, I mean. The others are full of,' he shrugged, 'good intentions. They've learned to accept over the years. Accept humiliation and defeat.'

'How can you say that, Red? You saw them tonight. You set them on fire.'

'But how long will it last?'

Red looked at the younger man. He saw the light in his eyes and he felt ashamed. He did not want to disillusion the lad.

But Creagh said, 'I know what you mean. One cannot keep them at fever pitch all the time. But Red, Red, we've got to hope, pray. We've got to believe.'

'There now, Creagh,' Redmond Rafferty said, 'pay no attention to me. I'm a fool, and there really are many like us. When the time comes there'll be legions. For the moment ... I'll send word. I'm grateful, we all are, for your help, Creagh.' The boy's face glowed under the unexpected praise. 'Now I must be off.' He mounted his horse. '*Slán leat a cairde.*' He clasped Creagh's hand firmly in his own.

'*Slán leat*, Red, *Go n'éirí an bóthar leat.* (May the road rise to meet you)'

Red raised his hand in a last farewell and galloped away from Usher.

Chapter

13

IT was a day full of birdsong in late April. The apple-blossom cast drifts of white petals which carpeted the grass like lace. The sun sent silver shimmers through the lime trees and the lilac's mauve and white clusters scented the air. Sophie Jeffries, driven from the house by her sister Bella's ill-humour, had slipped quietly from their room to the arbour at the base of the high tower. It was a small paved garden enclosed and shaded by lime trees and hedges of privet hung and entwined with clematis. There were camellias in tubs there and an arch looped by wisteria which when in bloom draped itself in heavy azure bunches over the frame. And there were roses everywhere. A mossy statue of Flora, the flower girl, stood on a heavy pedestal at one end, and a stone bench with dragon supports at the other.

Here Sophie liked to come to be alone. It was not a popular place, for the trees permitted only the slanting rays of the sun to edge through their leafy branches and it could be chilly there sitting on the stone. It was out of the way too of the terraced gardens more usually used by the family.

Arabella had been particularly irritating after lunch and had moaned on and on about her lack of a suitor, as if there was anything anyone could do, Sophie thought.

So she had crept out and come to the arbour for a respite. She held her blue cashmere shawl tightly around her, for it was chilly. It had been raining earlier in the day and the grass in the arbour still held moisture which dampened the hem of her sprigged muslin dress. She had brought a small cushion with her and she placed it on the bench and sat on it and sighed. There was no sound in the vicinity except the plop of the drops of rain as they fell from the leaves. Far away she could hear the whinnying of the horses in their stalls and the barking of the dogs. Geese hooted from the valley and the birds sang overhead, but Sophie felt cut off from those sounds here in the arbour, surrounded by trees.

As she sat and tried to compose herself for serious thought she heard a slight rustle behind the statue. It was probably a bird, she thought, a baby fallen from the nest in one of the trees above. She glanced towards the statue. Flora stood there on her pedestal draped in her stone tunic holding her basket of stone flowers over her arm as she gazed sightlessly out through the trees to the mountains beyond the valley. Sophie looked up towards their purple peaks touched in grey mist, a pearly luminous light about their tops, and sighed again. As she did so she could have sworn she heard her sigh echoed by another. The faint sound came once more from the cold grey statue. She felt a thrill of fear and pressed her hand to her heart, then shook her blonde curls and said aloud, 'Nonsense. Nonsense. Nonsense,' three times.

But the sound came again, this time tinged with a groan, and with a cry she ran to the statue, coming face to face with a tall man wrapped in a dark cloak. He was leaning against the stone, his pale brow beaded with sweat. When she appeared before him he was so startled that he let out the moan he had been trying to stifle.

'What ...' she started to say, when her attention was caught by the drops of blood that were spattering the flagstones at her feet.

'You're ...' she began again, but he forestalled her.

'Shush. I beg of you, m'lady, oh hush.'

Sophie looked at the stranger again. His hair was wild and raven-black and clung to his saturated forehead. The eyes that looked at her pleadingly were dark with pain. His teeth were clenched and she could see the muscles and bones of his jaw move under his skin. His wide mouth was closed to stop the sounds escaping.

'For God's sake, m'lady,' he whispered. She looked back to the blood so darkly crimson it was almost black. It dripped in large drops onto the flagstones, and she saw the hem of her dress dip into the puddle it made there. A pinkish stain had already appeared where the material had absorbed it.

'What's that?' she breathed, although she knew.

'Oh, a scratch. A bullet winged me.'

Her wide eyes met his again. 'A ... a ... bullet?' she whispered fearfully.

He nodded and moved his cloak and held out his arm. He wore a white shirt, frilled at the wrist, and one arm was red and moist and dripping with blood.

'How? ... But why? ... How?' she stammered. She was bewildered. Here in the peace of a spring day, the only sounds domestic and tranquil, the violence of the scarlet stain seemed at odds and out of place.

'Just leave me here, m'lady,' he urged her. 'Go. Pretend you have not seen me. Go. Go. I'll be all right.'

She shook her head. 'Why do you hide?' she asked. 'Come inside with me. Molly my maid will bind your wound ...'

'You do not understand, do you?' He sounded impatient now, and still the blood dripped on the mossy stones where they stood. 'The soldiers are after me. They'll be looking. They know they hit me. They know I've been wounded. I don't want to drag you into this, m'lady, so please, please go.'

She stared at him again. 'I am in it already,' she said. She paused in thought, then made up her mind. 'Come with me. This is the tower of the house I live in and there is a door here ...' She dimpled at him, smiling in spite of the seriousness of the situation, for there was a gleam in his eyes too. 'It is a secret door. Isn't that droll? It leads to the priest's hole in the cellars.'

'I know but ...'

Nonplussed, she echoed him. 'You *know* ...?'

'Hell, I shouldn't have said that. Beg pardon, m'lady.' He smiled at her through his pain, then bit his bottom lip with his fine white teeth. In the distance she suddenly heard the hoofbeats of a troop of horses and simultaneously Bella's voice called from a window high in the tower.

'Sophie. Sophie. There are soldiers coming. Oh, how exciting. They seem to be coming here. Oh Sophie, Sophie, where are you?'

The stranger's eyes met her in query. Sophie put her finger to her lips. 'She cannot see us,' she said. 'Quickly. Follow me.'

She ran towards the back of the arbour and parted the foliage clinging to the wall of the tower. A small door, thick as two fists, was hidden there behind the ivy, the tall grasses and the ferns.

'I haven't done this for ages,' Sophie whispered. 'I expect it's very stiff.'

To her surprise it wasn't. The door sprang open to her touch and closed smoothly behind them. They were in a long corridor. The walls cut from the rock were dry and as they tip-toed along they could see the passage which led to the kitchens and the wine-cellar. As they progressed they could hear Bessie Broderick's voice scolding her youngest.

'Yerra, how many times do I have to tell ye? Don't dip yer fingers in the puddin'.'

The stranger drew his cloak closer around him and Sophie led him on, puzzled, for it seemed to her he was not unfamiliar with the place. Indeed, when she hesitated at the spot where the passages divided and went two different ways, he unhesitatingly chose the one that veered right. She followed him, for she was not at all sure of the way from here on in. They had played here as children on their odd visits home and the only one that knew the underground corridors and all their many entrances like the back of his hand was Creagh.

Creagh. Her mind suddenly became alert. Creagh. Murmurs of an Irish Rising. Whispers of treason. She shivered. She had picked up the tail of a conversation here and there and remembered Creagh's flushed face when, on many an occasion, he had railed at James about the 'freedom of the Celts', the 'oppression of the Irish nation', and such wild talk. She had paid no heed at the time, but now the bits and pieces began to take a shape of sorts. This stranger had been hiding behind the statue, not by accident, but by design, she was sure of it. He must have been shot in the woods or the forests on the mountains behind the house. No one wounded there would risk coming down to Usher, skirting the entrance, courting discovery at every turn. Then to deliberately choose the arbour as a place to hide was madness, and this man's face was nothing if not intelligent. It was a senseless way to behave and the man with her was no fool. Those eyes, though filled with pain, were shrewd. He had come there because there was someone at Usher he could trust. And it could only be Creagh.

The passage sloped deeper into the ground and they came to a door. Sophie was surprised.

'This is usually kept shut,' she said. 'How very odd.' She looked into the face of the stranger and saw he had become very pale and movement obviously hurt him. 'Oh, you're in pain. Let me help you.'

'It's all right,' he whispered and led the way down till they came to a small room. He opened the door and flung himself on the monk-like bed. It was made up with clean linen. A crucifix hung on the wall and on a table stood a ewer and basin. There was a single upright chair. Light seemed to come from above, an opening in the ceiling. There was a bowl of herbs to sweeten the air. It sat on the table, a candle and tinder-box beside it. Sophie caught her breath in amazement. She was about to exclaim that the room was obviously used, when her attention was caught by the stranger divesting himself of his cloak, and she saw that the blood-stain had darkened and spread. She poured some water into the basin and brought it to the bed.

The stranger seemed in a swoon so Sophie slapped him. He groaned, but opened his eyes.

'That was cruel,' he whispered and gave her a crooked smile.

'It was necessary,' she said tartly. 'You'll have to help me. I cannot manage otherwise. I'm not strong or big enough. Take off your shirt,' she ordered and was immediately startled at her own daring.

He groaned again but struggled to a sitting position, and between them they got the shirt off except for the blood-stained arm which was stuck to him. Sophie bathed the dried blood until it softened enough to allow her to pull it off. Even so, he bit his lip until it went white and the muscles in his jaw were taut.

Sophie was amazed at the way she was behaving. With what calm she had helped him remove his shirt. Yet though she appeared serene, inside she was in turmoil. She was stunned by the feelings that overwhelmed her. Each time she touched his flesh her fingers caught fire. Each finger tip, like a sensitive antenna, reacted to the feel of his skin with a tumultuous jumping of her nerves.

The bullet had pierced his arm well above the elbow and he swore it had not lodged, for Sophie worried that it had.

'I'm not afraid, you know,' she said to him.. 'I have a lot of commonsense.'

He smiled at her bravura but noticed that her cheeks paled

when she bathed the wound. She bandaged him with strips torn from his shirt. 'We'll get you another,' she said and as she bandaged him he glanced every now and then at her anxious little face.

She looked up and met his gaze. She blushed.

'Who are you?' she asked.

'I'm nobody you need bother with,' he answered and gave her a smile. The colour flooded her face again and she hated herself for betraying her feelings in such a namby-pamby manner.

'You must think me an idiot,' she said. 'You obviously knew this place. You were coming here to hide.' And as he began to shake his head she continued, 'You're a friend of Creagh, are you not?'

But he had become very pale and he lay back exhausted. She covered him with the blanket, staring down on the face relaxed in unconsciousness. It was a handsome face, dark hair sloping off his white brow, poetic and reckless. She felt suddenly embarrassed looking at him thus, as if she was invading his privacy yet at the same time she ached to touch him. She felt tearful and strangely elated all at once.

She did not know what to do with the basin of bloody water. She poured the last of the fresh water from the ewer over her hands into the basin. She would have to leave it there. She dried her hands in the clean part of his shirt. As she pressed the fine cambric on her damp palms she caught the scent from it and without thinking she brought it to her face for a moment. She could smell the warm male perfume of his body and she inhaled deeply, then horrified at what she had done she dropped the shirt on the floor and left the little cell, closing the door behind her.

Returning was easy. She followed the tunnel's uphill incline until she came to where the passage divided, then went in the direction from which she could hear the servants' voices.

'Yerra, I'll have yer guts fer garters if ye don't lay off the marzipan.' It was Bessie Broderick continuing her diatribe against one of her unfortunate children.

Sophie slipped past the larders and the wine cellar, then, finding the door, let herself out into the arbour again. She picked up her cushion and ran around the tower, coming into the castle through the door on the other side.

Unfortunately the entrance led into the great hall, and as she hurried in she realized that the place was full of soldiers. They stood in the hall with Bella, Creagh and James. There was a Dragoon officer in bright uniform standing beside James. Sophie could see a handful of men behind him. The officer and James were talking.

'I most certainly will inform you if I see or hear anything,' James was saying. The others looked at Sophie.

'Where did you come from, Sophie?' Bella asked. 'You missed all the fun.' Then she gasped as she lowered her eyes to the hem of Sophie's dress.

Creagh's eyes followed Bella's glance and he said hurriedly, 'Go to your room, Bella. This is man's business. It is most incorrect that you are here.'

James looked at Creagh in astonishment and Bella tossed her curls in a most flirtatious manner.

'Since when have you worried about correct or incorrect behaviour, Creagh, I should like to know?' But her attention was on the officer and Creagh noted with relief that her interest in Sophie's hemline had been deflected for the moment.

The officer was staring at Sophie, too enamoured by the excessive prettiness of her cornflower-blue eyes and the arrangement of the golden curls caressing her pink-tinted cheek to notice any disarray or irregularity in her apparel.

'Bella,' James said severely, 'Creagh is quite right. Go to your room. You too, Sophie. Perhaps the Lieutenant would like to take a little Madeira with me?'

He courteously bowed and gestured to the fireplace flanked by an armchair, where a table stood. There was a crystal decanter with glasses, and a plate of almond biscuits on it. In the fireplace great pine-logs burned with a bright blaze and a sweet scent.

The Lieutenant shook his head. He had lost interest when he saw Sophie turn her back and prepare to mount the stairs in the wake of her sister. It was back to business for him; duty called.

'I'm sorry for the intrusion, m'lord. Thank you for your offer of hospitality, but do not take it amiss if I refuse. We must, however, leave you and get on with our search.'

Bella had disappeared around the curve of the stairs. Creagh caught Sophie as she reached the first landing and turned towards the west wing and the tower. He took her arm and said,

83

'Shush,' as she opened her mouth to speak. He drew her after him into his apartment.

The room they found themselves in was very masculine. Winged chairs and a deep sofa sat before a cheery fire. Hunting-prints decorated the dark-pannelled walls. There was a walnut desk littered with papers in one corner, and shelves of books in Gaelic in the other. Blanche, Creagh's dog and sister to Angel, rose from her recumbent position in front of the fire and greeted her master affectionately, licking his hands and nuzzling up to him. Creagh bade her sit and indicated one of the chairs to Sophie, who obediently sat opposite her brother. She watched him pour a glass of Madeira, his face intent as the ruby liquid splashed into the cut-glass. She thought, as she often did, how sensitive a face her brother had. He was incapable of dissimulation with her, his brown eyes were candid and revealed every emotion. Now as she watched she could see his lips tighten and she knew he was tense.

'Dear brother, what troubles you?' she asked gently.

His eyes rested on her blood-stained skirt. Her brocade shoes, she saw to her horror, were also stained, muddy and spoiled.

'That troubles me,' he replied tersly, pointing to her hem. 'You cannot know how frightened I was for you, Sophie, for that is blood, as any fool could see, and when I saw you standing there before the soldiers ... Where is he?'

'Where is who, Creagh?'

'Don't play games with me, miss. You know very well who. Redmond Rafferty, that's who. Those soldiers were in hot pursuit of him, and in you come, the bottom of your gown stained with blood. You put the heart across me, so you did. I knew it could only have come from Red, for the captain said he was wounded.'

'You'll not give him to the captain, will you, Creagh? Not until he's better, at least?'

Creagh looked at his sister as if she had run mad. 'For God's sake, woman why would I do a thing like that? Redmond Rafferty is a great man, indeed he is, a man who is fighting for his country's freedom.'

'By that you mean he's a rebel, his face set against his Queen and civilization as we know it. So James says, Creagh.'

'And what, pray, does James know about it? He had not lived here year in year out as I have. He has not seen how it is with these people, who cannot work their own land or study or speak their own language. It is their land, Sophie, and we are the interlopers.'

Sophie remembered once in India her father becoming angry when someone — who, she could not remember — after a luncheon party had said the same thing about India. She remembered the day vividly, the heat of the sun, the still, humid air, the fans turning overhead. The Bengali servants were clearing away after the meal, serving coffee on the terrace. They surreptitiously chewed betel nuts, which was forbidden, and she remembered watching Bella's face, for she knew her sister was going to report them to Papa as soon as the guests had gone. There were vultures in the trees near the tennis court, and her dress was sticking to her in the most unladylike fashion. The white women in pale colours, floppy hats and parasols chatted to each other, while the men, also clad in white, stood about perspiring. There was the heavy scent of flowers and spices on the air.

The man's voice, louder than the heat-laden murmur, shocked them all into silence. 'We are interlopers here,' he had said. Her father had been very angry.

Now she heard Creagh ask her again, 'Where is he?'

'I'll have to tell James. He's head of the house and ...'

'Do you want him killed? Are you so unfair, Sophie? If you tell James, he'll hand him over to the soldiers and they'll execute him, or put him into prison, or both. Do you want that?'

'But it's treason, Creagh. Why did they shoot him? What had he done?'

'They caught him addressing a meeting last night. In his own language in his own country. But he escaped. Then today they caught up with him in the woods beyond and shot at him.'

'How do you know this?' Sophie looked at her brother aghast. 'You are in this too. Oh Blessed Virgin, are you mad? I guessed but I couldn't believe it. I thought he knew where he was going when I took him to the priest's hole. I thought of you. But it can't be true ...'

Creagh crossed to her and knelt before her. He took her little hands in his, rubbing his fingers on her pearly thumb nail.

'Well, Sophie, and why didn't you give him to the soldiers? Why did you keep quiet about him? Down there in the hall?

You could have easily told them about him but you did not. Why?'

'I didn't have a chance,' she said defensively.

'Oh come now, sister, all you needed to say was, "Officer ..."''

'All right. All right, Creagh. I don't *know* why I didn't ...'

'You won't tell James? Please.'

'No. Not yet, anyway.'

'Then where is he?'

'Safe enough in the priest's hole below.'

Creagh jumped up. 'Capital,' he said. 'Capital.'

He hugged his sister, who had also risen. 'Oh Sophie, you're a wonder. An angel. *An aingeal.*'

'I only said "not yet", Creagh'

He tweaked her golden ringlets. 'I know you, Sophie. You won't tell. You wouldn't give a man away to be shot maybe.'

Sophie sighed. She feared her brother was right. 'I'm coming with you to him now,' she said.

'Oh no, Sophie. I don't want anyone in the house to become suspicious. Females are such silly creatures and ...'

Sophie stamped her foot. 'I'm not silly,' she cried. 'If it wasn't for me your precious Rafferty ...'

'Red. He is called Red. Short for Redmond Rafferty.'

'Well, your precious Red Rafferty would be in prison now waiting to be executed. *If* it was not for this *silly* female.'

'All right, sister, you win. I admit you behaved most sensibly. However, you must change. You cannot go about in that stained garment or they'll ask questions and we'll all be shot. I'll go below. You change and when it is safe, and only then, follow me. It would be best to wait until tomorrow. Don't let Bella get wind of this, or we'll be in queer street an' no mistake.' He kissed his sister's cheek affectionately. '*Tá tú iontach* (you are wonderful),' he said.

'Oh that gibberish,' she replied, but she was glad of Creagh's surges of brotherly love. James had inherited some of their father's inability to express affection and Bella frankly was too selfish to respond to spontaneous hugs. Endearments always warmed Sophie.

She went quickly to her dressingroom and throwing open the door came face to face with her maid.

'I'll help you, m'lady.' Molly said, coming forward towards her, and Sophie felt a surge of confusion. Desperate that Molly should not see the stains she tried to get her to leave. Instead of being surprised Molly seemed impervious.

'No, I'll not go to Miss Bella. I'll help you first. Now stand still an' we'll get this offa you. There now. That's better. It's funny how the damp can spoil like that m'lady or cochineal. It looks like cochineal to me. Yes indeed.'

Sophie was too surprised to speak and Molly Broderick took the offending gown, her face impassive, and left the room quietly saying, 'I'll be back in a jiff, Miss Sophie, as soon as I've dealt with this.'

She left Sophie nonplussed but with a strong feeling that her maid knew quite a lot about the whole affair.

Bella burst in then and quizzed her unbearably about her stained dress. 'I saw it, Sophie, indeed I did. There was blood on the hem of your muslin. I felt quite faint with fear.'

'Oh nonsense, Bella. It was cochineal for my watercolours. Blood? How very melodramatic.'

Molly came back into the room. 'The cochineal stain *will* come out, Miss Sophie, Clarie swears, if taken in time, but I would not bank on it.' And when her mistress caught her eye she saw reassurance there and wondered what kind of conspiracy she had stumbled into. So many people in the castle seemed to be in the know.

Bella looked puzzled at Molly's information. She was obviously still doubtful, but was silenced when the gong sounded for dinner.

Sophie dined in a dream her thoughts full of the tall stranger. She was deaf to her mother's monologue about their father, and she simply did not hear Old Gentleman's long speech about the youth of today. He was glad he had been born into a more gracious age when the young cut up a merrier caper, bedded more wenches, quaffed more wine and in general had a vastly more entertaining social round than the young milk-sops of the present.

James replied to this long dissertation with the casual remark that he was not so certain. 'For,' he said, 'Creagh seems to absent himself from home quite a lot these days, and what you can be doing, brother, is beyond me. Really, I am honoured at your presence here tonight, though I am not sure what we have done to derserve it.'

Creagh smiled at the assembled company but vouchsafed no reply.

'What you get up to I cannot dare to imagine,' James said, exasperated. Still there was no reply from Creagh who fiddled with the stem of his wine-glass, watched by a petrified Sophie.

'If your father were alive today you would not be so casual in your comings and goings,' Angela said, then sniffed and dabbed her eyes. 'I wish he were here, indeed I do,' she added.

There was sudden burst of tears from Bella, who cried out, 'Oh, so do I. So do I,' and ran out of the room.

At last dinner was over but it was much later, after Bella had fallen asleep that Sophie, lying awake in the dark, made up her mind that she must see the stranger once again. Surely there could be no harm in checking to see that his wound was clean and healing? Surely it was her duty? She would be ever so careful and make sure no one saw her creeping down to see him. There could be nothing wrong in that. She resolutely put from her mind what her mother or the Widow Boann would think if they found out what she was doing. Red Rafferty might have a fever, she thought, down there all alone. On reflection, she realized that she had not emptied the basin of dirty water. Surely it was her duty to do that? Creagh was a man, and these niceties never occurred to men.

Sophie tiptoed in her nightdress from the bedroom to her dressingroom. She chose a dark wine-coloured velvet peignoir instead of the peach one laid out for her, for she feared discovery if she dirtied the hem of another garment.

It was dark, so she took the lamp. The shadows frightened her and with beating heart she crept downstairs making sure she was not followed, and through the secret door and down the stone stairs. All was silent from the direction of the kitchen. She scared herself by nearly taking the left fork of the passageway. She was terrified of getting lost down here in the dark and cold. A cobweb brushed her cheek and she gave a little shriek of fear and said aloud to herself, 'What am I doing here? Oh what?'

Her lamp guttered in the chilling breeze that rustled down the tunnel. She could hear the squeaking of mice, or, horror of horror, could it be rats? Her flesh crawled at the thought of that possibility and she hurried along, trembling, until she reached the door. She tapped and entered quickly, and nearly died of fright. Red Rafferty sat up on the pallet, his back to the wall, his black hair wild about him, his bright blue eyes wide with fear and tension. He was holding a gun pointing straight at her. She nearly dropped the lamp.

His face broke into smiles of relief when he saw who it was and he tossed the gun on the bed. 'Oh you frightened ...' She could not finish, for he had leapt from the bed and placed his hand over her mouth and with his other hand he held steady her lamp.

It was then that she heard the voices. They came from above, from the trapdoor in the ceiling she had noticed earlier in the day. She knew it led to the big vaulted room where they used to say the forbidden Mass in the bad old days.

Voices. Wildly she thought of the penalty if anyone found her here, of the fact that this must be a secret meeting above, of the type forbidden by law. Anger took over. How dared they use her home? How dared they come here to Usher and place her family in jeopardy? In a surge of fury she bit Red Rafferty's hand which still covered her mouth. She nearly laughed at the intake of his breath and the sight of him clamping his hand over his mouth to still his cry of agony, as he danced up and down in pain, soundlessly.

'This place is a ... is a den of iniquities,' she said, but she whispered, a fact not lost on Red, who grinned.

He took her hand and led her to the bed. Sitting her down on it he took the chair and stood on it to close the trapdoor overhead.

When it was shut and he had put the chair away he said to her sadly, 'It grieves me that you have been brought into this situation.'

There had been the sound of many men above and now all was silence. She noticed that Red Rafferty had on a clean shirt and his arm was freshly bandaged. Who had done it? It was not Creagh's work, of that she was certain. It had the neatness of a woman's touch. Were the Brodericks involved, then? They must be. She remembered Molly's impassive face when she handed her the stained dress. She shivered. She thought of James, ignorant of the powder-keg he sat a-top of. God help us all, she thought if they are discovered.

'How dare you do this to us? How dare you? You place us all in terrible danger, for who is to believe we know nought of it?' she cried angrily.

'Oh Lady Sophie, all you have to do is cry out an' you'll be rid of us all in a trice.' He smiled into her eyes, and her knees went weak.

Tears of rage stung her eyes. 'You know I can't do that. You know I won't betray my own brother.'

He smiled at her again and she saw with amazement how his lips curved and how beautiful his face was and how the sight of him melted her anger. He looked at her.

'An' maybe you don't want to hurt me either? Ah now, don't look at me with those eyes so full of innocence like the blue of the sky on a cloudless day.'

She tried to maintain her anger but she couldn't. She tried to remember all Lady Angela had told her, long ago when her father was alive and she had been a real mother to them, not as she was now, constantly in a dream of the past. 'It is not done to be alone with a man,' her mother had said. 'Make sure that Papa or I am with you my love for men are dangerous.'

There was no doubt in her mind now that her mother was right. The atmosphere that permeated the little room was full of danger. And excitement. Her heart beat fast and all she could see was Red's gentle mouth and his soft black curls and his white skin, so touchable. All she could feel was that unfamiliar weakness in her knees and her bones turned to water. And all the while he looked at her intently.

'You are like a moonbeam,' he said softly, 'come to light up my cell.'

'Ah, don't joke,' she cried, tears springing to her eyes.

'I've hurt you,' he said, aghast. 'Oh, I did not mean to hurt you. I mean it, you see. You are like a moonbeam.' He could not take his eyes off her. 'When I first saw you, peeping around the statue, I thought you were the most beautiful creature I had ever seen.' He tried to say it lightly but the words came out as a plea. She gazed at him and he saw in her face her bewilderment.

'You are beautiful,' she said in wonder, 'and I love you.' She hardly knew what she was saying. 'You love me too,' she added. 'I know. I can see it in your eyes.'

She was as surprised as he at what she had said. He groaned and took her in his arms and it seemed to both of them that she belonged there. He held he close to him, kissing the soft curls at her forehead, the dimples in her cheeks and the tip of her pink little nose. When his mouth met hers, though his lips were cool their touch was scorching. Her whole being welcomed him and she felt her mouth responding to his, her body clinging to his and she knew that what she did was wrong but she could not stop it if the Virgin Mary herself had appeared and asked her to.

He was as lost as she, and when they were spent they lay side by side, silent and strange with each other.

He was first to speak. 'Oh my darling, what have I done to you?'

She blinked the tears from her eyes. 'Nothing I did not want,' she said. 'I must go,' she added, and standing up she arranged her garments about her with a modesty that he found touching. She was exhausted and ached to sleep. Her confusion was total. How could she have behaved with such wantonness? She was bewildered by what had happened, at her capacity to behave as her mother said only servant girls and peasants did. But she was still overbrimming with tenderness for the man who had held her and guided her to a sensuous awakening, and she wanted now only to lose herself in sleep.

He kissed her, slowly and languidly, all passion spent.

'*Oíche mhaith.*' he said. 'Goodnight.'

'Goodnight,' she replied softly, and left him.

That night Red lay sleepless in the small dark room. The sheets retained the sweet smell of Sophie's flesh and he pressed the linen to his face and groaned aloud.

'I love her. Oh Lord, I love her, and we are doomed.'

He writhed on the little pallet and shook his head aghast at what he had done. He was a wanted man. There was a price upon his head. Yet he had fallen in love with his friend's innocent sister, and he had seduced her. He remembered her face pale in the lamplight. 'Nothing I did not want,' she had said.

He would go away. Leave here. It was the only honourable thing to do. To stay would be folly. He would not be sure that he would not try to see her again if he was near her. He was lost when she looked at him with her great blue eyes and dimpled smile. If he stayed he would place her and all she loved in danger. Her very life was at stake. He shivered. He would never forget those eyes wide in passion or the taste of that sweet mouth. How could he stay away? But he must. He was a marked man. If he was not, he would run now to her brother James and demand her hand in marriage. But that was impossible. He would be arrested forthwith.

He did not doubt, too, that she loved him, but if he disappeared now she would recover in time, and he would soon become a memory. He did not like the idea, but it was the best, the only, way for her. If he stayed he could only ruin her whole life.

The selfish part of him yearned to remain, to see her just once more, but he pulled himself upright on the bed and forced himself to face facts. He was a fugitive. He had no right to love. He was pledged to another: Ireland. His mistress was his country and she was a jealous lover.

He heard the voices above. Creagh was speaking. They would know where to find him. There was a chain of safe houses across Ireland and he was welcome in any one. If needs be, the inmates would send messages of his whereabouts to Creagh.

He sighed and drew his cloak around him, and silent as a shadow he slipped out of the chamber and left the place altogether.

Chapter

14

THE next morning was Sunday. Sophie stirred in her sleep, gradually becoming conscious of the intrusion of Bella's voice. Her body felt utterly relaxed. She was filled with a soporific lassitude that immobilized her from head to toe.

'... Oh *do* wake up, Sophie, do. You're not usually such a slowcoach. Come *on*. You'll be late for Mass and you know how James feels about that. He was beastly to me last week, absolutely beastly.'

Bella's voice droned on and on, pulling her from the safe cocoon of unconsciousness into dangerous reality. There was something she did not want to remember, something worrying, alarming. And there was something she did want to recall, something beautiful, exciting.

As her eyelids stirred, memory flooded back. The stranger, his eyes, his mouth on hers, the taste and smell and feel of him. Her eyes flew open wide and she put her hands to her cheeks. Red Rafferty. She remembered what she wanted to remember — and what she did not.

'Get up ... oh, Sophie, James will bark at me. He always does because I am the eldest. He'll kill me if I arrive in the chapel without you. I declare I do not want to get into trouble again, indeed I do not.'

Did it show? she wondered. She threw back the bedcovers and fled to the bathroom, Bella's voice washing over her unheeded. Molly was pouring hot water into the ceramic tub. Sophie silently divested herself of her nightgown and stepped into the steaming water, gasping as she did so. Molly soaped her with the sand-coloured sponge, briskly rubbing her back and shoulders, her breasts and arms, until with the rubbing and the heat of the water her skin turned salmon-pink.

She dressed with care. She put on an amethyst-coloured satin dress trimmed with lace and ribbons, with a shawl of silk bobbin lace and a silk parasol with an ivory handle. Her mind was quite made up. After Mass and breakfast she would go to the priest's hole. She would see him. What she would say to him she did not know. It was enough to know that she would see him. Her heart beat twice as fast as usual and she peered again into the mirror to scrutinize her face. There should be a sign, a scarlet cross on her forehead, something to show that yesterday she had lost herself in a tide of love, that she had behaved shamelessly and enjoyed every moment of it. She smiled at herself in the mirror. There was nothing. Nothing at all to show that she was a changed person. True, her eyes sparkled more than usual, the colour in her cheeks was heightened, and her mouth had a curiously vulnerable look, trembling as if she might weep. She did not feel like crying. She felt weightless and elated, suspended between her last sight of him and her next. She gave herself a little hug, then called to her sister as the warning bell sounded from the Usher chapel belfry a stone's throw from the house.

'I am ready, Bella. So there. Let's go.'

'My, my, my, Sophie, don't we look pretty this morning? It's still much too cool for your satin. The amethyst gown, I declare. Lordy, anyone would think you had an assignation with a suitor.'

Sophie tossed her curls. 'Nonsense,' she said. 'You are a ninny, Bella. And who, pray, is this suitor, do you imagine?' She would have to be very careful. Bella was as sharp as a sword and she loved poking her nose into everyone's affairs. She would have to be very careful indeed.

It was Lent and they were fasting. She looked through the window and saw the day was fine, a pastel-pale April day, a day of daffodils tossing in the breeze that ruffled the fields and set the leaves on the trees trembling. A fragile sun washed the hills in lemon and the river winked broadly in its dancing light. She could see the farm-hands and the shepherd, the tenant-cottage dwellers make their way over the hills and up from the valley. They wore stiff shirts, donned only on the Sabbath and holidays. Their faces were red and scrubbed and they were uncomfortable in their movements, restricted by the formal attire. The women in clean petticoats and shawls had a prouder tilt to their heads, their bodies unconsciously swanking in their Sunday best. The servants chatted as they walked over the gravel and down the boreen that led from the castle to the church.

Sophie watched, incapable of hurry or rush, as she saw Bessie Broderick, her vast frame resplendent in black bombazine, a fox tippet around her neck, a huge black bonnet firmly pinned on her head, sail down from the house, followed in single file by her daughters, Molly, Annie, Clarie and Nelly. Maitland and Mrs Maitland and their son Nern, Matt Dominic and Cronin, his son, who spent all his time trying to catch up with Molly Broderick, followed. Molly laughed over her shoulder at the groom and Sophie knew exactly how she felt, then was terrified at feeling so.

'Will you *come along*, Sophie? Why are you mooning about? James will be ...'

'Angry, I know.' Sophie sighed and left the window, pulling her silk shawl about her and fixing her bonnet on her golden curls. Taking her bible and rosary from the escritoire, a fresh cambric handkerchief edged with lace and a fan against the body-odours that sometimes became overpowering in the little church, she took her sister's arm and they left the house.

Sophie shivered. Bella was right. It was colder than she had thought. Usher, high on its mountain, caught every breeze. She could sense rather than see her sister's 'I told you so' expression. She did not look at Bella. She dipped her gloved forefinger in the holy-water font at the church entrance, bending her knee in genuflection and blessing herself.

The chapel was a little square Gothic building with a low arched ceiling. It had a beautiful stained-glass window over the altar depicting St Agnes dressed in mediaeval garb and carrying a lamb. The colours were jewel-bright and the early sun sent shafts of multi-coloured light onto the bent heads of the congregation.

The workers, peasants and tenants knelt at the back; the first six rows of velvet-padded pews were reserved for the gentry and their guests. Even if there were no visitors at Usher and there was only standing room at the back no one would dare to cross the invisible boundary that separated the upper orders from the lower.

The sisters walked arm-in-arm to the family pew, where James sat beside Dolly. Old Gentleman was there with their mother. He was full of brandy as usual, red-faced and rigid with drink. He never fell about or appeared inebriated. He just stood, knelt or sat ever so slowly and carefully, exuding fumes of alcohol and looking at the world with slightly unfocused eyes.

Lady Angela was draped from head to toe in deep mourning, heavily veiled in black, a form of dress she had adopted since the death of her husband. James thought it pretentious in the extreme, but deference to his mother prevented him from telling her so. 'She should have been a player on a stage,' he thought bitterly, but reminded himself that the staff and country-folk loved her outward display of grief. James thought it typical of the Irish that they should admire such histrionics. It took an English gentleman to show proper reticence and a modicum of reserve. Sophie, James thought as she took her place near him, looked uncommonly pretty that morning, her face flushed and her eyes sparkling. Bella, however, had her sly look, which meant that she was up to no good.

'*In nómine Patris et Filii et Spiritus Sancti, Amen.*' The priest intoned.

'*Ad Deum qui laetíficat juventútem meam,*' the congregation breathed in reply.

No sign of Creagh. He would have to speak to the boy. They hardly ever saw him these days, James thought, as he repeated the words absentmindedly. He really must be made to settle down and pull his weight. What James liked best about Mass was that it gave him time to think.

'*Kyrie eléison, Christe eléison.*' The chapel was filled with the murmur of the congregation, the odd cough or the cry of a babby and the heavy scent of the incense.

'*Gloris in excélsis Deo, Et in terra pax hominibus* ... The freckle-faced altar-boy swung the censor, clouds of incense billowing from it, then handed it to the priest.

James' mind wandered again. He had not bothered too much with Creagh because he had been preoccupied with Dolly. Her strength had never fully returned since the birth of Cormac — he thought of it like that. She adored the child, fussed and worried over him, insisted he be kept bound up against the cold, swaddled tightly lest he catch a chill. She herself succumbed to every cold and cough in an alarmingly vulnerable way and he worried himself silly about her. He loved her to distraction and prayed now, as the priest intoned the prayers of the faithful, for God to give her back her health and strength.

Dolly next to him was thinking too, not of health but of Cormac. True, she was very tired these days, she felt blanketed in fatigue all the time, her head ached and she felt feverish. But her major preoccupation was Cormac. She adored the baby, spent hours with him, staring into his eyes that had turned a light hazel exactly like Creagh's. And therein lay the problem. Creagh. James' little brother was mercurial and elusive and she feared he might suddenly change his mind. She knew she could not bear it if he did. She knew she would lose her mind if she lost Cormac. She fretted constantly about the slim hold she felt she had on the child and prayed that Creagh would give her some assurance, some little word of commitment, but he never did. He said nothing about the situation when they met, which was not often. He was rarely to be found at Usher and she consoled herself with the faint hope that the matter was beneath his notice.

Her pale fair face, eyelashes and hair almost silver in the sunlight, looked fervent in the light of the flickering candles.

'Dear God, let him not change his mind,' she prayed. 'Let me have Cormac for my own. I love him so. He is the light of my life. If you let me keep him, dear Lord Jesus, I'll never ask you for anything else as long as I live.'

Sophie beside her heard her sigh, and pressed her arm. They glanced at each other and smiled.

Sophie's prayer was a simple chant that throbbed in her brain in time to the beating of her heart. 'Red. Red. Red. I love you. How I love you.'

She smiled again, gazing at the stained-glass window, seeing not St Agnes carrying the lamb but Red's face leaning over her, his lips softly curved, his eyes, dark blue, looking at her full of love. She knew it was love. He had not said so, but she knew what she had seen in the depths of his eyes. He would tell her today. As soon as she could escape Bella she would hurry to him, to the strength of his arms and the passion of his body. A blush suffused her cheeks and she bent her head and buried her face in her hands.

Bella on her other side noticed her gesture. She noticed everything. She liked to watch and listen. She wondered what had caused Sophie to cover her face. It was unlike her. She had behaved oddly in the last twenty-four hours and Bella determined to find out why. 'And God, please listen to me. I want a husband,' she prayed. 'There don't seem to be any young gentlemen about. Any who are, are running after Deirdre Rennett at Slievelea, or Aurora Vestry. Or they are dangling after Sophie. Please make James listen to me and let me go to London to stay with some of our friends there. There are heaps of people I could visit but whenever I ask him he will not hear of it.'

She paused sullenly, remembering the last time she had suggested it. James had been adamant. 'D'ye think I'll let you off the leash to waltz about London and get up to the Lord knows what mischief? Oh no, Bella. Papa would turn in his grave.' Bella had tossed her ringlets, her eyes full of impotent rage. She closed them now and prayed more fervently, 'Send me a husband, a lovely man who is to my taste.'

Then there was the other prayer, but it was so difficult to say. She hated pain, did not like to be reminded of grief. She squeezed her eyes shut and held her breath so that she would not feel sad. 'God have mercy on the soul of my dearest Papa and grant him eternal rest. Amen.'

She tried to think quickly of something else, but found her mind dwelling on the tall quiet man she had adored and the pain of remembrance surged over her. It was a physical pain that she dreaded. She felt as if her heart would burst. She remembered him picking her up and carrying her to bed, the solace of his arms had been an infinite blessing and constant reassurance of his love. But God had taken him away and she knew it was her fault. In some way she had been to blame, for if she had shown him how she loved him surely he would never have died? She shut her eyes tightly to blink away the tears.

'I won't cry. I won't. I won't. But Papa, Papa, I miss you, oh how I miss you. Why did God take you away from me? What did I do? Oh what did I do?'

'Agnus Dei qui tollis peccate mundi: Miserére nobis ...' They filed up to the altar rail to receive Holy Communion. Eyes closed, tongue outstretched for the wafer, Christ's body, they knelt and prayed fervently. James for Dolly, Dolly for Cormac, Sophie for Red Rafferty and Bella for an unknown man who would marry her and take away the haunting memory of her father and the boredom of Usher, and would set her on a road to pleasure, enjoyment and sin.

98

Chapter

15

THE family had breakfast together, but each was locked in their own thoughts, and conversation was sparse and infrequent.

Afterwards, Bella was going to her room, and had just reached the Chinese Buddah that squatted under the first floor landing when she saw Sophie come out of the breakfast room, look furtively around the hall, then go to the left and disappear down the corridor that led to the servants' quarters. Intrigued, Bella followed at a safe distance. She saw Sophie get to the indoor entrance to the priest's hole, the little door that led to the cellars and passages that ran beneath the castle. Where on earth could she be going? Bella was perplexed. She could not understand why Sophie was making such a surreptitious journey below stairs. She passed a corridor that led to the kitchens, larders and cellars. Holding her skirts in her hand a little above her ankles, for she feared dirtying the hem, Bella crept after her sister. Where on earth was Sophie going? Her heart beat fast and she stopped with a start when she suddenly heard voices. She dropped her skirt and held her breath, trapped by the chatter of her maid Molly and Cronin the groom, who had come from the kitchen and who were giggling now in the passage just a little way from her.

She pressed herself to the wall, concealing herself as best she could in a niche created by a curve of the tunnel. Nevertheless she was scared silly as she waited there trying to make herself invisible.

But Molly and Cronin were not interested in their surroundings. The groom was hugging and cuddling the maid in a most unseemly way and Bella bit her lip in aggravation, for she would dearly have loved to reprimand the maid waspishly for her impertinence in carrying on thus under their roof. However, she could do nothing. In impotent anger she hid, watching the girl press herself against the groom's body and kiss his face as they murmured extravagant endearments to each other. Bella felt hot and oddly excited by what she saw and she wished she could escape but she had no choice. She had to remain where she was.

Molly laughed. 'Oh me darlin'. You'll have to help me get the wine. Come on.'

'Me Da'll be lookin' fer me in the stables ... Aw, Molly ...'

'He can wait five minutes.'

'Just five, then. God, yer a sore temptation to a man, Molly Broderick, so ye are.'

'Only this man, Cronin. Remember. Only this man here. 'Tis you I love.' And she gave him a kiss and pulled him into the wine cellar with her and Bella saw them disappearing behind the casks.

'Well, my mother is going to hear a bit about this, my fine serving girl.' Bella muttered.

Sophie had disappeared momentarily and Bella crept forward, listening. It was years since she had been down here and she was not sure of her ground. All was still. A faint odour of damp made her wrinkle her nose, but there was no sound unless you counted the far-off voices of the kithcen-maids and Bessie Broderick. Suddenly the air was rent by a cry and she nearly jumped out of her skin. It was a heartbreaking sob that echoed down the passageway. The sound was repeated, a wail charged with misery that hung on the air. Bella recognized her sister's voice. 'Ah no. Ah no. Dear God, no.'

She heard the words and the sound of Sophie's sobs. Then she heard the tread of running feet. The steps were heavy and obviously masculine. As she stood trembling something scuttled over her foot, making her jump again. Looking down she saw a rat, red eyes glittering in the gloom, staring up at her. Filled with panic she fled back the way she had come, closing the secret door behind her, subconsciously noting its ease of movement. Hurrying to her chamber, she flung herself on the bed and set herself to the task of calming her nerves so that she could ponder the mystery.

Chapter

16

IN the little chamber beneath the castle, Creagh held his sister in his arms, rocking her to and fro, trying to comfort her. Perplexed by her weeping, confused by the violence of her outburst, he soothed her as best he could, patting her soft hair and handing her his fine embroidered cambric handkerchief. She looked at him, her eyes swimming with tears.

'Where is he, Creagh? Oh where has he gone? You must know. Please tell me.'

'Sophie dearest, calm yourself. You must not take on so, really you must not. I did not know he had gone and I don't know where he is headed for. Red has simply flown the coop, most likely for his own safety. Sister dear, I beg you, dry your eyes and go to your room and rest. Females are the most senseless creatures.' he said, more to himself than to her, 'Throwing a pet just because a man you saw yesterday for five minutes has disappeared, for I swear to you , I know nothing of where he has gone. If I live to be a hundred, I'll never fathom what goes on in a girl's mind.'

Sophie held her brother's lapels in her fists as she shook him.

'I want you to find him for me, Creagh. You must promise.'

'Find him? Find him? That is utterly impossible, *alanna*. He'll have told no one where he's bound if he hasn't told me, you may be sure of that.'

Sophie sniffed and dried her eyes. She made a visible effort to pull herself together. She suddenly seemed very calm.

'Creagh, you must try,' she said. She knew she had to see him. She would die if she didn't. As he started to protest she continued, 'If you do not, I shall tell James what you do down here. Not that I know precisely, but a word to our brother that you are holding illegal meetings in the priest's hold will be enough, Creagh, to put you in a fix you'll not escape from lightly.'

Creagh groaned. 'Oh, I hope you'd not do that. You couldn't be such a — *ni leomhfainn* (you wouldn't dare).'

'Yes I will, Creagh, as God is my witness ... if you do not try to find him.' Sophie was desperate. 'Find him for me. But tell him to be careful,' Sophie cried, an edge of hysteria in her voice, 'you can do that can't you? Find him and bring him here, Creagh, promise. Otherwise ...' She thought for a moment then she said, 'I will give you a letter for him. Have it delivered to him, I beg you.'

He gave in and nodded. What could he do? If James ever found out what was happening in the cellars below his beloved Usher his fury would know no bounds and God knows what trouble it could cause the movement. People's lives were at risk but Sophie would be incapable of understanding the situation.

Where he could locate Red Rafferty was another question. The man was slippery as an eel, and like a shadow flitted from place to place. No one knew where he would be at any given time, it was a deliberate manoeuvre to thwart informers. But everyone knew that if he was needed Red Rafferty would be there. He had a charmed life. The man had nerves of steel and the luck of the devil. Few could resist his smile, Creagh knew, and damsels swooned before it and magistrates came to the conclusion that Red, his blue eyes confidently smiling into their's, dancing with intelligence and understanding, could not possibly have been party to the crime, the treason he was accused of. Creagh shuddered. He did not want to pursue the line of reasoning this inevitably led to. He pushed his forebodings firmly to the back of his mind, and looked at his lovely sister. Her face was splotched with tears, her big gentian eyes pink-edged from crying, her cheeks pale, her little hands, delicate as butterflies, tearing his handkerchief between tense fingers. Ah dear God, he thought, then brightening, he realized that Red would most certainly be able to deal with my lady Sophie very competently.

'I'll try,' he said, 'I'll only promise to try.'

She rushed over to him and hugged him ecstatically and he sighed. Heaven help her, she must think she had fallen in love with the reckless Red. Well, he would not think about it. Red

102

could deal with it. It could only lead to restless nights and he had neither the time nor the energy for that. All his strength was needed at the moment for other more important things.

He sat in the tiny room after Sophie had left, thinking about the Cause and the Brotherhood. There had been great activity lately. Guns had been promised from France and Spain, and America was on the move. Once upon a time in Ireland the people really believed that their Catholic neighbours across the water would help with battalions, even armies, with which to crush the Protestant enemy. Time had disillusioned them. Not since the Spanish Armada had foreign ships and soldiers in quantity, other than the British, set foot on the shores of Ireland. Politics, tangled power struggles, had intervened between good intentions and action. The Spanish, the French and the many states of Italy had answered the cries for help from the beleagured little island with empty promises. Most were afraid of the Protestant mistress of the seas and the greatest Navy in the world that stood between them and the country they wanted to help. Although sympathy was proffered, it remained politic to be on good terms with the British, and help was usually confined to secret dispatches of guns. In any event, all the Fenians could hope for now were guns and ammunition smuggled across the channel, around the toe of England into the Irish Sea. Sometimes they landed at Queenstown and sometimes at Waterford or the Dingle Peninsula. They had been known to land at Wicklow, but it was a tricky business and more often than not ended in failure and disappointment, capture and imprisonment.

It was in this business of smuggling guns into Ireland that Red Rafferty was involved up to his neck. While he led the life of a gentleman in Paris, he organized the procurement of ammunition and its secret delivery to his homeland, where he was a wanted man. The struggle was long and hard, but there was always the hope, always the ache, always the long dream of freedom which ultimately had to come. One day. Some day.

Creagh shook himself and pulled himself out of his reverie. He reminded himself of his promise to Sophie and he sighed. It was going to be very difficult finding Red. Creagh wished for the millionth time that his father was still alive and living with his exasperating family in some exotic-sounding Asian city. That they were not here at Usher interfering with his plans at every turn.

Chapter

17

SOPHIE found her sister on her bed stabbing her needle through a badly stitched sampler. She drove the needle through the cloth like a sword and looked at her sister with narrowed eyes. Sophie was a fool, she thought, so transparent. She allowed everything to show on her face, just like Creagh. Well, she, Bella, knew the virtue of concealment.

She wished that Sophie wasn't just that much prettier than she. Bella was quite realistic about it. She had to be. People had cooed over Sophie all her life, the sunny, shining little girl whose hair was just that bit blonder, whose eyes were just that bit bigger and deeper a blue, whose mouth was more perfectly formed and who had a hundred dimples beside her lips and in her cheeks. People doted on Bella until they saw Sophie. It was a cruel fate that had left Bella a pale copy of her sister and the only way Bella felt that she could defend herself was with guile.

'Well, sister? Where have you been? You seem distressed. Can it be you have been crying?'

Sophie turned to face her sister and Bella was amazed to see that her eyes were sparkling with excitement and her cheeks were glowing. She looked as she had in the chapel and Bella was confused.

'You must be dreaming, Bella, for I never felt less like crying, and why you should think I was I cannot comprehend. Indeed, I don't know what you are on about, truly I don't. I fear you are touched, quite touched.'

She shook her head in mock sadness and giggled. Bella leapt from her bed and grabbed her sister's hair in sudden fury and started to pull at it, shrieking in a high voice her true thoughts about Sophie. Sophie cried out in anger and pain and tried to escape her sister's clawing fingers, but Bella held on tenaciously as she pulled her sister to the floor in a flurry of petticoats.

'Ladies, ladies, please.' The voice of the Widow Boann brought the struggle to an abrupt end. Her authority was never questioned, for truth to tell both girls were a little frightened of her. Bella especially was nervous of the nurse and had the feeling that the Widow saw right through her.

'Yerra, what do ye think yer doin' spittin' at each other like a pair of Kilkenny cats an' ye supposed to be grown up.'

'It was Sophie, Widow. She is spiteful, spiteful. I was quietly doing my sampler when she ...' Bella's voice dwindled to a halt. The Widow had turned a dark and piercing gaze on her. The look, penetrating and contemptuous, made her feel that she, the Widow, had read correctly her innermost thoughts. She faltered and blushed as Molly came hurrying in.

'I could hear ye right down the corridor. Ye ought te be ashamed an' ye just out o' church an' poor Lady Dolly trying to rest. Is it any wonder Jesus wept for ye, is it? Ye've added to His crown of thorns this day, so ye have. Mother of God forgive ye both, though I've got it in me mind that the full blame rests more on you, Miss Bella, than on Miss Sophie. An' it's no use yer dartin' those looks at me, so it isn't. I'm going to ask Lord James te give ye separate rooms, so I am.' This would not suit Bella at all, but before she could say anything Molly continued, 'Anyhow, let me tidy the both of ye, for the gong is just about to go fer lunch, an' I can imagine, an' you too, what Lord James would say if ye went down in the mess yer in. Come here, the both of you an' behave.'

It was approximately a week later when Bella, sitting in the window of the room she and Sophie still shared, saw the horseman coming from the east. The window was bay, set in the tower and had a window-seat where Bella liked to sit and dream. You could see all over the countryside from there. The major road through the mountains that ran from Dublin to Wexford was quite visible with its ups and downs, its twists and turns. Coaches and horsemen, carriages and travellers passed that way. It had been the tower's original purpose, for soldiers, in the olden days, had kept watch here, sounding the alarm at the approach of the enemy from the nursery above and the

Widow Boann's room, from which you could see even further.

Bella sat quite still and watched. There was something remarkable about the horseman. She did not know what it was. He wore a broad-brimmed hat pulled low on his head. He looked tall and slim, and there was an odd furtiveness in his progress along the road.

As she looked, she saw him come off the main highway and take the turn that led to Usher and the valley on the other side of the castle. The sun shone through the pearl-grey high-flying clouds. There was a light wind and the traveller's cloak billowed sometimes when a breeze caught it, giving him the look of a mythological character from one of Creagh's books.

The horse and rider disappeared behind the cluster of yew trees that flanked the tiny graveyard behind the chapel. The graveyard with its slabs of stone which covered the bones of the deceased tenants and farmers, servants and estate workers from Usher, held the huge mausoleum where the corpses of dead Jeffries and Ushers were slotted in coffins in crevices down the sides of the walls. The path behind it led nowhere. Bella leaned forward. Where could he have gone? What was there of interest to a traveller in the graveyard at Usher? She could not understand. There was nowhere else he could have gone. There was the steep slope to the valley beyond, and he did not appear on that incline, and only the highway, and the driveway to Usher Castle, between.

Bella suddenly made up her mind that the rider had something to do with Sophie and her strange mercurial changes of mood over the past days. She did not know why she connected this man with Sophie but she trusted her instincts. She thought deeply, her sampler forgotten, the threads fallen to the floor in a multi-coloured heap that she would have a hard time untangling.

Then she had it: the cellars. She remembered the incident the other day, remembered trailing after her sister down the underground passage. She remembered the cry that had reverberated through the darkness from some secret chamber, and she instantly decided to go down there again. As she left the tower she became more and more certain that she would find her sister and the cloaked stranger together.

Creagh had told Sophie that Red Rafferty would wait for her in the chamber below the priest's hole. Red knew the many secret entrances to the passages that criss-crossed below Usher; he had gone to many meetings there. Creagh had urged him to come, but, Red noticed, Creagh did not ask any questions of him concerning his sister. For this Red was extremely grateful. He had had an awkward week, at odds with himself and everyone. There was a shipment of weapons hot from the armoury outside Paris expected any day now, yet he could not seem to keep his head clear to make the necessary plans. All he could think of was Sophie. He cursed himself for a fool every time he thought of her, and he thought of her constantly. He was tormented by the memory of her sweet young face, her trusting blue eyes, the passion of her kisses.

He read her letter and groaned. 'My darling man,' it said. 'I think of you night and day. I dream of seeing you. Why did you leave so abruptly? I do not understand. Is it because you do not love me? I have to know. Have you no heart? But I know you have. I felt it beating beneath mine. All I ask is a moment of your time to see you, to touch you, to know that you are real, that you breathe and exist in the world with me. But be careful, my love. Be careful.'

So he went to Usher. He was angry with himself, with fate. Yet at heart he was charged with excitement. Although he did not want to admit it, his whole being was filled with a passionate yearning to see her again.

And when he saw her, he was thrown into confusion. Instinctively he reached out for her, and she came into his arms and settled there like a bird flown home to roost.

'Oh my darling, my darling, my darling, I love you so,' he cried, and realized it was true. He buried his lips in the soft curls about her neck.

'Why did you leave me?' she asked him piteously when she got her breath back. 'Why?'

'I *had* to. Sophie, dearest Sophie, although I love you with all my heart and soul I'm going to have to leave you again.'

'No. No. No. I won't let you. I won't let you,' she cried and covered his face with kisses. Stooping to her smallness he gathered her to his heart and enveloped her in his arms with such a fierce hold that she gasped. She pressed her body to his, but he gently disentangled himself and held her at arm's length.

'No. We will not do that. We must keep our heads, *alanna*. No more loving.'

'Oh Red, I want you so. I need you so.'

'It is impossible. I am a fugitive. I have no right to your love. Do not make me lose my honour, Sophie, any more than I have already.'

'You talk of honour. It is too late for that. I love you more than truth or life or honour.'

'Please, my darling, never say that. It unmans me. Oh, my life's blood, you are the only woman in the world I have ever loved. But I must not see you, we cannot meet. It is too dangerous for you and for your family.'

'Red, we love each other. We will wed. Once married there will be no danger. My brother James is a tartar but he is not unreasonable. He will come round eventually ...'

Red took her arms gently from around his neck. 'Sophie, my dear lovely Sophie, you sweet child. How little you understand. Oh my darling, if only it was that easy.' He looked into the wide blue eyes gazing so hopefully and trustingly into his and he felt his heart twist within him. He took her hands between his.

'My dearest, listen to me. I am a rebel. I am a wanted man. They know me. There is a reward out for Redmond Rafferty. I believe it is one hundred guineas. Quite a fortune.'

She stared at him in disbelief.

'Listen. You are a fine lady and, oh yes, I am a gentleman, but I'm an outlaw too. Some would say a traitor. In years to come I'll be honoured as a patriot, no doubt, but that will not help us now. Sophie, this is not something you can use your influence to make disappear. Though my life be empty without you and my heart dead within me, I cannot take you from the safety of your home, the shelter of your loved ones and bring you into my world of forbidden midnight meetings, secrecy and subterfuge, even you must see that. I am on the road through weary winter nights and grey days. The sunlight is my enemy, and you were made for the sun and light and laughter, people and dancing and joy. Oh, you would be happy at first. Novelty and love would keep you content. But then you would begin to hate me. You would miss your family, your comforts, things you now take for granted. Worry would grate on your nerves and turn to resentment. The life of a rebel is not exciting, no matter what you think. It is squalid and frightening and exceedingly uncomfortable.'

'We could go away. We could leave Ireland.' Her little face was piteous and looking into her eyes he felt his heart beat hard and fast within him and he prayed silently for courage.

'I cannot do that, my dearest Sophie. I cannot betray the Cause.'

'Because you don't love me enough,' she cried sadly.

'No. Never say that. I love you with all my heart, and you know it. But I love my country more. You are in my heart, but this land is in the very fibre of my being. I can no more leave her to perish than I can stop breathing. This land is dying. The foreigners keep us in subjection. There is no freedom here. They are taking and taking and giving nothing back. They are bleeding us dry. The tenant farmers on your brother's land have to pay him exorbitantly for what is rightfully theirs. They owned the land long before he came.'

She was torn by his words, in a morass of divided loyalty.

''I don't understand. Oh I don't understand. You talk of James as if he were bad. He is a good, kind man, Red. Oh do not pain me so.'

'I do not think that James is bad. I believe him to be all you say and more. He does a lot for the land he holds in trust. Many do not. The majority are absentee landlords and our country is being bled by them. No, James is not like that, but he is ignorant. He will not listen. He sees nothing wrong in the situation. But be that as it may, I cannot desert my country. I would have no more peace. I could not do it for you, though I love you more than myself. Not for anyone could I do it even though I die for it.'

She shook her head hopelessly, tears streaming down her face. 'You do not really love me, then. How can you say you love me, yet do this?'

'Do you think it's easy? Do you know how you are tearing me apart, that I'll never again have a moment free of longing for you, aching for you? You have undone me, Sophie. No other woman in the world had ever done what you have.'

They clung together hopelessly. She could smell his skin and the soft leather of his jacket and she took deep breaths as if to inhale his scent and keep the memory forever. She kissed the soft lips, pressed her mouth against his until he yielded to the pressure and avidly returned kiss for kiss, his whole body crying out for her. But he found the courage somewhere and pulled away.

'I must leave you. I must. I have got to go.'

'Why? Oh why? I cannot see the reason. There is no country, no family, no home I would not leave for you and I would follow you to the ends of the earth if needs be, if you asked me. What has Ireland got to offer you more than my love? I give you my body, my soul, my heart, freely, freely. Take me. I am yours. What is Ireland to that?'

'Nothing and everything,' he cried, tormented, vulnerable, yet implacable. 'Ireland has not your generosity. Dark Rosaleen, Kathleen Mavourneen, Erin, Ireland — this country devours all her men in a mystic love that has no rationale. There is no basis in logic for the feelings, the reverence, she arouses. She holds her menfolk to ransom. It is all or nothing, and cast out from her, betraying her, I could not live with myself.'

'You speak as if she were a woman.'

'Ah, my love, she's more than that. She is my country.'

'Then I hate her. I hate Ireland. You have no right to kill our love. It is wicked and . . .' Sophie broke down, sobbing, looking at him uncomprehendingly. The lace of her blouse hugged her slim white throat and he saw it was fastened by five tiny pearl buttons. He wondered how anyone's fingers could be small enough to undo them. He bit his lip and felt an almost uncontrollable urge to unfasten the tiny pearls, to hold Sophie in his arms, to make love to her, to see her blue eyes darken in passion till they were the colour of the sky at midnight. He knew the colour they took on in moments of passion and how they widened in love, for he had seen the other night. But he pulled himself together.

He took her hand. He could feel the little bones in her wrist. 'I am death for you my love,' he said. 'I don't want you to weep for me,' he went on. 'I must go now. Every moment I am here puts your family in danger. I must leave you. I have no choice, you must see that. But remember always that I love you.'

She looked into his eyes, seeing the love in their depths. She looked at the strong line of his lips, tender and kissable, and she ached to cover them with hers. She looked at the soft darkness of his hair and restrained her instinct to caress it. He was a mystery to her. She shook her head then and let her shoulders rise and fall in a shrug of despair. She lowered her eyes and sat on the cot. She felt cold and empty. She sat like that for a few moments and when she looked up he had gone.

Very calmly she stood and smoothed down her skirt. She breathed deeply for a few minutes, the better to be in control of herself. Then she let herself out of the chamber, closing the door softly behind her.

As she walked up the passage she saw someone coming towards her from the place where the passages divided: A glimmer of pale skirt — Arabella. She felt a quiver of fear and hurried to catch up with her sister.

'Bella. Bella. What are you doing here?'

Her sister turned. 'Well you may ask. And what pray are you doing here, sister dearest? Assignations with men in dark passages no less. Suppose I tell brother James?'

Sophie's heart missed a beat. They were whispering, and to her right she could hear Bessie Broderick's voice complaining on and on. She felt sick with terror.

'Listen, Bella, we cannot talk here. Let us go upstairs and I will tell you all.'

She could not think what to do, how to wiggle out of her dilemma, and Bella smiled at her sister's discomfiture and pressed home her advantage.

'No. You'll have time to think of an excuse by the time we get upstairs. I saw a stranger, cloaked and booted, come out into the passage beyond, and then you followed. If that is not an assignation, then I don't know what is.'

'Sophie stood before her transfixed, wordless, and Bella smiled and added, 'Tell me now what you were doing, who it was, or I'll go straight up to James and lay the whole of it at his feet.'

Sophie thought ironically how the pressure she had used on Creagh to get Red Rafferty here was now being used against her.

'All right,' she said with a sigh. 'But will you promise, if I tell you the truth, will you swear you'll tell no one? Most of all James?'

Bella nodded briskly.

'Well then. It's all to do with the Irish Cause. Creagh and ... and ... I ...' she swallowed, wildly improvising, not really knowing what she was talking about, trying to deflect Bella's interest, 'Creagh and I are ... involved with ... the Cause.'

111

Bella looked bewildered, as well she might. 'Cause? What cause? What are you talking about?'

Sophie gave a bright little laugh and said airily, 'Oh, don't you know? It's political.' She knew that Bella hated even the mention of the word politics. 'We have meetings ... and discuss ... things ... about Ireland's freedom.' She watched the disappointment flood Bella's face. 'But please, please, Bella, don't tell James. Remember you promised.'

'Oh,' Bella said, rapidly losing interest. 'Is that all? Well, I see. Oh, this is a horrid place. Please let's get out. I cannot bear the darkness. How you can come down here to discuss ... I'm sure I do not know. Politics! Oh Soph, what a ninny you are. So is Creagh. It can only lead to trouble.'

'Not if you don't tell.'

'Well, I promised, didn't I? Come on, Soph. I'm going to pick some wild flowers to press in my journal. Do come with me.'

'I'll go upstairs, Bella. I've important things to think about. Remember, not a word.'

Bella nodded and hurried away, glad to be gone. Sophie went to their room and threw herself on the bed. She felt empty an drained. She had no tears just now. She lay and looked at the canopy over her head and sighed. A huge ache squeezed her heart and she thought it actually pained her, like a knife in a wound. She wondered if she would ever smile again.

Chapter

18

TWO months later, on a glorious June day, Dolly and James, the Earl and Countess of Usher, gave a christening party for their new son Cormac.

The countryside was invited and they came, grumbling at the terrible journey it was to Usher Castle on its perch half-way up a mountain, mumbling about how anyone expected a body to cross the awful roads and the dangerous mountain passes, narrow as Caitlin Mavourneen's waist, they did not know. But they came. The Vestries and the Rennetts, the Blackwaters and the Gormans, the O'Sheas and the Parnells arrived in carriages, gigs, and on horseback.

On one side of the house the land sloped down in a series of three terraced gardens. Three stone steps led from one level to the next. There were little stone balustrades marking off each level and red urns filled with geraniums squatted at the end of the pathways. There was a pink gravelled loggia at the far end, hanging at the edge of the mountain where it sloped into the valley below. There was a great stone statue of David, about to sling his ridiculous shot at the giant, in an alcove, with a water-fall at one end and at the other a very ancient weeping pear tree with a stone bench beneath it.

The dogs lay around the gardens and barked at the new arrivals, or slept in front of the fire in the great hall. Young girls looking virginal and very pretty in their white muslin dresses were chased down the stairs or the steps of the gardens by young dandies who pursued them with whoops of admiration, shredding them of their dignity. They giggled and skittered away, holding their wide straw picture hats on their heads against the whim of the gentle breezes. The children ran rings around their parents, bonnetted, full-flounced skirts, ribbons and laces, making their skin pearly with sweat in the warm sunshine. The little ones bounced balls which usually disappeared over the edge and down the mountainside. There were iron tables on the terraces and the view was spectacular. You could see across the purple mountains nearly to Dublin City itself and Wexford at the back and a glimmer of the sea in the distance.

It was usually a breezy spot, clouds so low you could touch them, but today was mild as a baby's smile, soft as a swallow's wing and warm as Italy. Banks of azalias and rhododendrons in full bloom flanked the neat squares of grass, red and pink, cerise and white in riotous colour.

Young mothers strolled about two by two under frilly parasols, gossiping and clucking at their offspring in an absent-minded way. They lifted their skirts with pale hands as they tripped up and down the stone steps, pausing on different levels to recover their breath, made short by the tight lacing of their stays. They leaned closer to each other every so often, the better to impart a piece of gossip or the recipe for a new herbal remedy for the curing of a toothache, a childish fever or the monthly indisposition they all suffered from but could not talk about directly in polite circles. The women whose hair was dressed in soft ringlets beneath their bonnets, pushed tendrils of hair stirred by the breeze back behind their ears and exclaimed at the wonder of the view. The men in their blazers and boaters also walked two by two and talked of politics and the state of their lands and estates, or sat in the smoking-room at Usher and puffed Havana cigars while they speculated, and sounded each other out, over money and investments.

At twelve noon the Angelus rang out over the hills, and the guests trooped into the tiny chapel beside the castle.

It was a simple ceremony, the christening of Cormac James Montague Jeffries, eventually to be twelfth Earl of Usher and Knight of same, a great burden for so small a mite, but sure, the servants said afterwards, he obviously was born with a sense of the fitness of things, for he was as sunny as the day until the priest poured the water over his scalp and then he let out such an outraged cry that the devil surely quit him at that very moment, which was just as it should be and a cause of great satisfaction to everyone present.

114

Creagh stood up as godfather and Sophie as godmother. Creagh wanted to get away as soon as civilly possible for there was a traveller he wanted to see down in the village inn. However, he was trapped by courtesy, good manner and James' and Dolly's happiness.

The irony did not strike him, neither did the fact that the baby was his seem to have any relevance. The thought hardly entered his head. He had a glancing moment of surprised affirmation; this was his son, but the thought, was quickly strangled, with no great difficulty let it be said, and there was real relief in his soul that Dolly and James had the baby firmly under their wing. The child was heir to Usher. Dolly was the perfect mother. It all seemed right and proper and very convenient. He did not want to be saddled by a child spawned on a gypsy witch, but neither would he want in all conscience to reject his own offspring as most of his contemporaries did in such circumstances. This situation provided the perfect answer, and Dolly so loved the babe.

Sometimes she looked at him, her childish blue eyes full of a pleading so sweet, so vulnerable that his heart shook within him. Today he went to her and taking her arm said softly. 'Ach, *alanna*, it's yours, never worry. It's my gift to you, Dolly darlin''

She smiled, her lips tremulous, her eyes full of relief.

'Oh thank you, Creagh. Thank you. I love him now, you see, as if he were my very own.'

'He is, Dolly. He is.'

She put a nervous hand on his sleeve. 'I worry so, Creagh, in case you change your mind. I couldn't bear to lose him now.'

With a fingertip, Creagh smoothed the lines of worry that furrowed her brow, and kissed it.

'I'd never do that. I give you my promise.'

She let out a great sigh of relief. 'Oh Creagh, thank you. You don't know how frightened I've been.'

Creagh patted her hand. 'Well, I assure you there is no need.'

She looked so fragile, Creagh thought, especially when she stood beside her large red-haired husband, for she barely reached his heart. She was very pale and her skin seemed transparent in the sunlight. Gold butter-coloured hair and lashes, and the innocent face of a child made her appear insubstantial, ethereal almost.

Sophie did not look well today either. She must have her woman's complaint, he thought, though she would die before she would tell him, even though he was her brother. As they walked back up the gravel pathway from the little church, followed by the guests, he caught up with her, worried by her vapourish looks.

The leaves above them fluttered in the breeze and Creagh watched the shifting patterns of light and shade on Sophie's face. She really is very lovely, he thought, but pale as a ghost.

'Are you all right, Sophie?' he asked. 'You don't look at all well to me.'

'Oh, how typical of a brother. Beast. Beast!'

'I didn't mean to unsettle you, Soph. You know I wouldn't hurt you for the world,' Creagh said defensively. 'But, God's truth, ye don't look well, and damnit, I can't think why I mustn't be honest.'

Sophie glared at him. 'It's just that ladies don't like to be told they are not in the pink, Creagh, and if you don't know that yet, why you are more of a dunderhead than I supposed.'

'Now I'm mortally offended, Sophie, truly I am. You have wounded me to the quick.'

Sophie cried, dismayed, 'Oh, you are laughing at me. You *are* a beast.'

'No, Sophie. I'm not really. I wish you'd confide in me, though. Ye know how fond I am of you. You and Dolly both. But ye look like ghosts, the two of you. Arabella is the one who usually has the vapours. Is she a vampire or what, that she's bouncing about full of life, which is not like her at all, and ye two are like little *plúirín sneacht.*'

'Ah, Creagh, don't talk to me in the Gaelic, please. You know I don't understand.'

Sophie tossed her curls angrily and he thought again how pretty she was. If Deirdre Rennett was the beauty of Co. Wicklow, then Sophie Jeffries was the prettiest.

'It means 'snowdrop', you pretty *amadán.* So you see it's a compliment really.'

Sophie stamped her foot on the gravel. There you go again.'

'Yes. Well, that one means fool, so it's not so good. Anyway, that does not answer my query, which you seem hell-bent on not answering. Are you not well?'

A flush rosy as dawn suffused his sister's face and her

116

eyelashes swooped down to veil her bright feverish eyes. 'I am a little unlike myself today, Creagh, and the sun is hot.'

She pushed up the parasol, trimmed with lace, that cast a shade over her face and dabbed her forehead with a tiny embroidered handkerchief sprinkled with Eau de Cologne. She shivered then and he put his hand under her elbow as they walked up the gravel pathway from the church. He looked about, remembering his conversation with James and his promise to court Deirdre Rennett or Aurora Vestry. He had done precious little about it. He had been too preoccupied with other and more important things, and James had been too busy with Dolly and Cormac to notice.

'Are the Rennets or the Vestries here? he asked Sophie, who shook her head.

'Not yet, Creagh. They will be here later. They promised Mamma to be in time for the cake.'

As they moved forward Sophie stumbled, and Creagh was just in time to catch her or she would have fallen. As he slipped his arm about the girl's body he realized she had fainted clean away and was alarmed and surprised, for it was not like his sister at all. Dolly rushed up quickly, thrusting the baby she had been carrying, against the Dowager's wishes, into the arms of the Widow Boann two paces behind her.

'Oh Sophie, Sophie, are you all right? Whatever is the matter?'

The Widow sighed and passed the soft-wrapped babby to Annie Broderick, Dolly's maid, who was also in attendance.

Sophie gave a little moan and leaned her head on Creagh's shoulder.

'*Cad é bhí sibh a dhéanamh, Creagh?* (What were you doing Creagh?) 'The widow asked.

And Annie piped up, '*Ní dhearna sé rud ar bith*, Widow. (He did nothing, Widow.)'

The Widow gave the servant a warning glance but the others were too busy hovering and speculating over poor Sophie.

The Widow said loudly, 'Will all of ye leave her a bit of space? With the crowd and the sun she'll suffocate.'

Dolly cried, 'She's right.'

The Widow paying no attention, continued, 'Untie her bonnet strings, m'lady. Master Creagh, carry her to her room. Give me the babby, Annie and go and fetch Molly and send her

117

to Miss Sophie's room. Tell her to unlace her stays and bathe her face in Eau de Cologne.

Dolly interrupted the Widow. 'Tell her to make a soothing tisane for Lady Sophie and keep her there resting in bed.'

'There'll be no party for the *máthair bhaistí* (godmother) to-day. Now hurry, hurry,' The Widow called after Creagh, who had already started for the house carrying his weak but protesting sister.

'Put me down, Creagh. I will *not* stay all day in my room, no matter what Dolly and that old witch say. I do feel awful, though.'

'Of course you do. Girls suffer horribly, they say, at these times.' Sophie was white with rage and shame at these words, yet she was obliged to admit to herself that her brother was correct. Girls did suffer horribly at those times. But her great fear was that she was suffering for quite another reason than her brother supposed. She had been sick every morning for weeks now, and to her horror she had felt faint a couple of times, which was totally unlike her. Luckily so far she had been able to hide her indisposition. She could not, would not, contemplate the obvious reason for this. Far from having her monthly liability she had missed two periods and was terrified to draw the fairly clear conclusion.

She gave in to the Widow Boann and her sister-in-law's instructions and let herself be carried upstairs by Creagh. Then she meekly submitted to Molly's administrations. The maid was full of sympathy, and applied compresses to her forehead, made a tisane of rose-hip and settled her comfortably on her bed.

Sophie could hear the voices of their guests below. The sounds floated in through her window. The little windows of her room were barred and ivy-covered, but to-day they were opened to the sun to let it filter through in shimmering bars across the room. She wished she could join them below; the shrieking children, the laughing parents, the flirtatious giggling of her friends, the exciting buzz of conversation engendered by the celebration. There would be feasting now, she knew. The food served *à la buffet* in the great hall; sides of pink ham; a rack of lamb — the lambs were new-killed, tender as butter, sweet as honey and with crispy skin on them, scorched by Bessie Broderick before serving. Sharp sauce made with fresh mint from the herb garden would garnish the lamb. There would be salmon, cold and pink with pale mayonnaise; fat Dublin Bay prawns lying on a bed of ice. There would be ice-cream later and cheeses and strawberries and whipped cream and a wonderful *mille-feuille* decorated with walnuts and angelica. Her mouth watered as she thought of it but then she started to feel nauseous again. Molly had offered to bring her a tray later but she doubted very much whether she would be capable of eating.

Later there would be dancing. She would hate to miss that. She would not see Deirdre Rennett, who had newly come back from abroad, or her best friend, Aurora Vestry. She so wanted to find out from Deirdre how Paris was and what the new fashion dictated, what Austria was like and if the cakes in Demel's were as melting as one had been led to believe, and were Italian boys the most handsome in the world. She had been to Deirdre's coming-out party at Slievelea at Christmas but there had not been time to have a long gossip, as Deirdre was hostess. She had no been to Mount Rivers and had not seen Aurora for an age, for Dolly had wanted her and she loved her sister-in-law and felt happy and privileged by Dolly's need of her during the last anxious days of her pregnancy and her subsequent recovery, which was not yet complete. She felt very disappointed that she could not see her friends today just when she most needed a heart-to-heart. It was too bad, really it was.

But could she tell her friends about her worry? Could she confide in Deirdre or Aurora what might have happened to her? She knew it was considered shameful, a complete disgrace, that she would be ostracized when the fact became known, as it surely would. She groaned, and twisted and turned on her bed, hot and cross, giving Molly a hard time until the tisane began to work and she fell into a deep sleep.

Meantime, below, James and Dolly and their guests celebrated. Little Cormac had been taken to the high tower by the Widow for his rest. Dolly, after her exchange with Creagh, felt more relaxed and began to believe that the baby could really belong to her. She had felt the awful pains of child-birth and she had not seen her dead son. James had placed Cormac in her arms, Cormac who was Creagh's. In her heart of hearts she believed Cormac was really hers. So if Creagh, who was like a dear little brother to her, could let go, give her this babe, then all was well.

It had bothered her, nagged her so much over the last

months, Creagh's position vis-á-vis Cormac. Today he had wiped her worries away, and she felt at peace.

James, she knew, had simply accepted Cormac as a God-given gift. He was deeply ashamed of himself, fearful that in some way his manhood was deficient, that he was somehow inferior, incapable of producing the essential heir. Dolly worried desperately about how to reassure him. She loved her husband deeply, had been happy with him in every way and, except for the birth of Fergal, which they thought at the time was an accident, a freak of nature, life had been perfect for her with James. She had worried about what they should do about the Hegarty's ban. She could not bear to forbid her husband her bed, her arms, and the warm places of her body she had so loved him to occupy. Some of her friends spoke with distaste and a kind of martyrdom of 'the marriage act', and she had often felt her cheeks grow hot with shame when she realized that unlike them she enjoyed her husband's embraces, enjoyed his cries of pleasure, enjoyed the throb of her own body's response to his. It was obviously not done, was *infra dig* and she was no better than Creagh's gypsy girl, but she could not help that.

Now it seemed that was all over. Her friends had said, and curiously they all seemed in agreement, that at first their husbands had consummated the marriage act most nights of the week. Afer a month or two it went down to a weekly event. In a year or so a clever wife could wangle it that the spouse's nights diminished to once a month. No one had reached this enviable target yet, except Verity Blackwater, who had constant head-aches, backaches and the vapours. All the others envied her, except Dolly. She trembled inwardly as they spoke, worrying in case they found out how wanton she was, how peasant in her instincts. 'She is no lady,' she could hear them say, if they ever got to know.

It was the Widow Boann who had helped her out. She had suggested the use of 'her time', as she put it. She was very help-ful and far more practical than her mother-in-law, her friends or Dr Hegarty who was all doom and gloom about any more physi-cal activity between husband and wife.

Hegarty was vastly relieved at the way things had turned out. His job was secure. He could count on treating the family at Usher and charging a healthy fee each time measles, mumps, colds, chills, hunting accidents, womanly indispositions, all or any of the hazards of life, threatened. He wanted no accidental pregnancy that was sure to end in death. He shuddered at the thought, and did not even hint at a safe way for husband and wife to make love.

Dolly had happened to remark to the Widow one morning when she brought Cormac in for his feed that the joys of motherhood would be forbidden her in the future, so she had best make the most of it whilst she could.

'I intend to enjoy every moment of his babyhood, Widow. At least I have that. So much else has gone.' And she added, hardly aware of what she was saying, 'I'm not even allowed the solace of my dearest husband's arms any more.'

The Widow had cleared her throat. 'Well now, m'lady, that's as maybe, but sure there is a way. Craw Kilty, my sister y'know, m'lady, an' she's never wrong, says sure you go on as usual, only except ye can't have out to do wi' each other for the week in between yer times ... I think that it. Ye must be careful But, there now, that's not too bad, is it?. Craw swears, m'lady. She's never wrong.'

Dolly smiled shyly at the large woman looming over her. She trusted the Widow, who gave her a great sense of reassurance.

'I love him, Widow, and I don't want to lose him. He's a normal man and I don't want him to find someone else,' she said.

'Yerra, now, where would he go for someone as lovely as you, *alanna*?' the Widow sighed but added, 'Ach, but men are funny animals. Ye never know, do ye? I must say meseln I don't understand it. A lot of fuss about an over-rated performance, I say. Me sister Craw would agree. On the other hand me other sister, Bessie Broderick, ye cook, she enjoyed it above everything. Wore her husband out, so she did. He weighed seven stone when he died, poor man an' he six foot three in his stockings. Well, you don't fuss. just do as Old Craw says an' I'm sure it'll be all right. My sister knows the secrets of the world, so she does.' Dolly believed her implicitly. A great flood of relief had swept over her.

So now, on this summer day of her son's christening, all shadows had vanished from her life. She hung on her husband's arm, looking up at him now and then, her eyes full of the great love she bore him. She chatted with their guests and gave instructions to the staff via Maitland the major-domo and the party ran smoothly, the guests visibly enjoying themselves.

Her mother-in-law, the Dowager Lady Angela, was, as usual, dressed in full black. She was sitting with a group of her contemporaries, looking older than they by at least a decade, and relating the oft-told story of her husband's exploits and death. Her friends clustered about her hid their boredom behind fluttering fans, their eyes darting here and there, picking out friends, relatives and neighbours and waiting eagerly for a lull in the Dowager's monologue to exchange the latest gossip and the juicy bits of tittle-tattle their hearts were set on. A jealous cantankerous group, they tended to hand down judgements on the young as if they were veritable Solomons.

Angela was a thin-lipped woman, cold-faced and nervy, but you could see her as the mother of Sophie and Arabella in the beauty of her eyes and the fine-planed sculpture of her bones.

Old Gentleman sat in a corner sipping wine. His soft white hair spilled over the collar of his cream blazer. He pecked at the children's cheeks and his kisses were distasteful to them, smelling as they did of his oldness and the alcohol. He pinched them too, which they hated, and his embraces were often followed by a tap on the cheek that was more painful than he intended. He loved to watch the pretty girls in their pastel dresses, but he would prefer it this evening at the ball, if he lasted that long and the wine didn't get to his head or his knees first. Then the maidens would have a low cleavage and he enjoyed nothing better than to peer down every available bosom, irrespective of the embarrassment it caused.

Arabella was having a wonderful day. All during the christening in the little chapel she had knelt watching the young men, so handsome, so young, the best-looking of whom, Darcy Blackwater and Conel Connelly, were drooling over Sophie. It was unbearable. Her heart filled with rage, her hands shaking as she turned the pages of her missal. Then Sophie had fainted on the gravel pathway and caused all that fuss. She had been put to bed with Molly the maid for company and Bella's day had suddenly brightened. With Sophie gone she had no rival. It seemed to her that her sister stood between her and every eligible boy in the country. She hated Creagh too because he could read her plots to get Sophie out of the way and try to entrap her sister's boy-friends and turn their interest towards herself. He always saw what she was doing and frustrated her whenever he could, with a malicious grin on his face which drove her wild. Now as she stood in her leaf-green and white organdie, swaying under her parasol, batting her lashes and flirting with Conel and Darcy, quite in her element, he whispered so that they could hear 'Who's glad to have her sister out of the way? Oh Bella, stop looking so smug and silly.'

They were standing at the top of the stone steps that led to the second garden level. They had their backs to the mountains and were facing the great entrance to Usher Castle. Arabella's eyes had clouded with tears of rage at her brother's cruelty when she saw the Rennetts and the Vestries arriving. The Rennetts had come in two Victorias, their horses sure-footed up the narrow road that led to the entrance. As Bella's eyes cleared and they all turned to watch the newcomers she saw Deirdre looking beautiful in white muslin with blue forget-me-nots and a bonnet and parasol trimmed with blue satin ribbons. As she stepped from the carriage and one of the two riders that had accompanied them dismounted, Bella saw to her relief that it was Anthony Tandy-Cullaine. She watched as Deirdre took the young man's arm and moved towards Dolly and James who had arrived from the house to greet them. Lord and Lady Rennett followed their daughter to the castle.

Next Lady Vestry and her daughter alighted from their brougham, Aurora delectable in pink, a flush of excitement on her cheeks. Her father, Lord Vestry, and her brother Morgan had ridden beside the carriage and were now dismounting. But Bella's attention was caught by a third rider who was with them a stranger. He was the most handsome man Arabella had ever seen. He was dressed slightly differently from the rest in dove-grey pantaloons and a high frilled shirt. He wore a short cloak and sat atop his roan, reigns loosely between his fingers. His hair was blonde, softly waving, his eyes were brown, teeth white, his features so romantic as to make any girl's heart beat fast. Arabella lost hers and her head in a moment.

He dismounted and threw his reigns to the waiting groom. As Anthony Tandy-Cullaine took Deirdre down the garden steps to join a group of their friends who idled on the loggia below, the romantic-looking stranger trailed after them. When he came level with Arabella she deliberately tripped on the stone step, tilting her weight towards the newcomer who, perforce, had to catch her lest she fall.

Half-swooning in hs arms, Bella gave him a dazzling smile, and opened wide her hazel eyes, looking up at him with an expression of heartbreaking innocence.

'Oh sir, I beg your pardon. My heel caught on the stone.' She lifted her petticoats, just revealing the dainty shoe and looked up at him in wide-eyed guilelessness. She wiggled her slim ankle about in its pink silk stocking, then dropped her skirt as the stranger spoke.

'*Mam'selle. Mille pardons. Je suis un barbarian . . .*'

He had had his arm about her waist seconds too long for good manners. Now he pressed her gently before letting her go, which surely, Arabella felt, meant he liked her, even though it was considered in the worst possible taste, except perhaps during the waltz. But then, he was French. She looked quickly about to see if anyone had noticed, but they were all engrossed in their several conversations. Except for Creagh, she noted, who looked at her ironically, one eyebrow raised. She glared at him, sent up a prayer of thanksgiving that Sophie was sick and turned back to the stranger.

'How do you do, Monsieur . . .?'

Catching sight of Creagh bearing down upon them she steered the stranger across the gravel to the house. It was no use, she thought despairingly. Creagh would catch them and say something to put the stranger off, spoiling things for her as he always did. Then the giant bronze gong in the hall, a trophy from a temple in Burma, loudly reverberated through the house and grounds and over the mountains, announcing that the buffet lunch was served. Bella thanked God again as everyone started to drift into the house, and she smiled up at the young Frenchman, pleased to use her school-room knowledge of his language.

'*Je m'appelle* Lady Arabella Jeffries. *Et vous?*'

'Ah, Arabella. *Enchanté. Le* Conte de Beauvillande, Fabrice, *á votre service.*' He bowed over her hand, kissed it, then said in English, 'Arabella. Enchanting. But please speak to me in English.'

'Come with me, sir. You must be hungry after your journey here. It's such a climb over the mountains . . .'

'Oh but I rode. It was the poor horse . . .'

'Oh, I know that, sir. I did not think you walked.' They both burst out laughing in comradeship. The excited undertone of

124

interest was there already and Arabella was relieved not to have to continue in French for her vocabulary was not very large. She was overwhelmed by an infatuation so intense that she could hardly breathe. All she knew was that Fabrice de Beauvillande was the most beautiful young man she had ever seen and she made up her mind there and then to marry him. There was nothing in her life that she had ever wanted so much so suddenly, and with such passion. He had in one glance totally bewitched her.

She guided him into the great hall.

'You must choose for me. Only the nicest meats,' she said, looking at him provocatively. 'The choicest cuts, and not too much. Only a little.'

She placed her hands on her tiny waist, drawing his attention to it, as if to illustrate why she ate minute quantities. Then she smiled at him, fully aware that her dimples were riotously in evidence about her mouth. All her sulks and ill-humour had vanished and now she resembled her sister much more than she usually did.

'Arabella. Excuse me. I will do as you say. Wait just here and do not move,' he said, smiling at her, playing her game. He had secured a seat for them both in the embrasure of the tall bay window overlooking the gardens, the valley and the mountains beyond. He bowed over her hand and left her. She waited for him in an agony of expectation. She could see him at the buffet table that ran down the whole side of the great echoing hall. Among the crowd he stood out, a tall handsome figure. He smiled across at her occasionally as he filled two plates and he mimed choice of meat and fish to her from the distance. She laughed back at him and felt her knees weak and her heart flutter.

'Please, God,' she prayed silently. 'Please, God. Let it be me. I'll never ask anything of you again if only I can have this man.'

He told her whilst they ate that he had been staying with the Rennetts at Slievelea. Although they were the most hospitable hosts in the world he did not wish to impose on them much longer. He had decided to move on to Dundalk.' Oh dear God, I'll never see him if he goes there,' she thought in panic. He had a second cousin living there, he said, who expressed a great wish to entertain him for a month or so. Arabella made up her mind instantly. The opportunity was too good to miss and she could not lose what she had so jubilantly found.

'But you must stay here first before you go to Dundalk. We have the most wonderful views, don't you think?'

She gestured and he nodded, looking through the open window towards the misty mauve mountains and the valley, sage green below them, glimmering in the sunlight.

'And we have the finest stables in this part of the world. People always stop over here after they have been to Slievelea.' It was true. 'I am sure your cousin will survive a little longer without your company, and my brother James would love to have you. It is not often we have the opportunity of such a charming guest from France, of all places. Oh you cannot disappoint us, for we pine to know all about the latest fashions in our remote part of the world, and all the gossip from such a metropolis as Paris.'

Fabrice de Beauvillande smiled brilliantly at her, using all his charms to bewitch the girl. But it was not difficult. Arabella responded with a flutter of her eyelashes and her fan. Fabrice thanked his stars, for here at last was a conquest. He had nearly given up hope, and he had been very depressed at his lack of success at Slievelea. Deirdre Rennett had seem impervious to the charm that had won him a hundred hearts, and Aurora Vestry had not given him a second look. He had had to leave France in disgrace, and as his mama had turned her back on him, he had come here to Ireland to find himself a rich wife. In London there were only Protestants and that would never do. What he needed was a well brought-up Catholic girl who had money. Deirdre Rennett was the richest heiress this side of France, their families had always been close, he had been sure of success. But he had failed miserably. Then he had looked optimistically to the lovely Aurora Vestry but failed again. The thought depressed him and he felt himself expand and glow under Bella's admiring glances. It had been such a blow to his pride when Deirdre and Aurora had pursued a round of parties, balls and soirées and Fabrice had looked helplessly on while they showed him no interest at all.

'Oh, you are not interested in *me*.' Aurora had remarked when he inquired if his interest bored her. 'No, *chèrie*, you are interested in a *wife*. It is quite a different thing.'

Well, the time had come for him to change his direction. He would concentrate on this very eligible Jeffries girl. He was a shrewd judge of character, for life's little emotional dramas had

126

taught him much. In fact, he considered himself an expert, for he had been involved in so many *affaires du coeur* and extra-curricular flirtations, scandals and dalliances that had ended in tears, and he had extricated himself from them all, except for that last appalling blunder.

At any rate, he was tired of wasting his time kicking his heels at Slievelea. It was time he changed his modus operandi. The Jeffries, he knew from enquiring, were nearly as rich as the Rennetts. Ireland was not that much further from Paris than London and the traffic between the capital of England and Dublin was constant. Social news spread fast. He did not want his reputation to catch up with him and spoil his chances here, for he dreaded having to journey across the wild Atlantic ocean to the barbarity of America to find himself a suitable bride. He did not have time on his side.

He would have liked to have fallen in love with the girl he chose but as he still thought himself in love with Ornella he realized this was not likely. It would be a bonus, but after all he was a practical Frenchman, and one did not expect to be in love with one's wife on the wedding-day. He was pretty sure he could grow to love any attractive woman who was suitable and had the necessary wealth to extricate him from his troubles. He was blessed with a philosophic acceptance of the *marriage de convenance* that helped so many of his race to connubial, if not bliss, then at least content. As long as she was pretty, well-bred and rich he believed he could manage very well to make her happy.

This one was delightful but too coquettish for his taste. She did not know how to do it. She lacked *finesse*. And there was something else, a curious ill-tempered look about her when she was off-guard, a sullenness he did not like. It was not the undertone of wickedness he was so drawn to in Ornella. More a bad-tempered quality that might be awkward and difficult to deal with. Nevertheless she was pretty, a definite candidate for pursuit.

He turned on his most magnetic smile. 'I will accept your invitation, but only if it comes from your brother and if the Rennetts are happy,' he said.

He thought briefly of Ornella, his love, his mistress, the oval-faced beauty whose great brown eyes could drive a man to larceny or worse. He shuddered. He had killed someone for her sake, and though it was accidental it was nevertheless shocking. He had nearly lost his mind when he had realized the magnitude of what he had done for Ornella.

He put such thoughts away. He would stay here at Usher. He would play his role of the penniless aristocrat in all honesty and he would pursue this willing victim who so obviously adored him, woo her, win her, marry her. He put his mind to finding a common interest with the girl's brother James in order that he had a firm invitation. The rest would follow.

Chapter

19

AFTER lunch the girls retired to the guest rooms to rest. The older generation followed suit and the married women settled their offspring for sleep and made their way to the music room or the drawing room where the curtains had been drawn for shade, and settled down for an uninterrupted gossip. Some of the maidens reclined in hammocks under the apple-trees near the chapel. They lazily plucked grasses and daisies and drowsed in the dappled light, fanning themselves with leaden arms. They rarely succeeded in keeping their eyes open, although they had cited their alertness as the reason not to retire to a chamber. They lay in inert billows of white muslin or organdie, petticoats in lacy flounces festooned about them like posies of flowers.

Aurora Vestry had been told about Sophie's indisposition, and longing to see her friend as much as Sophie wanted to see her, she crept away after lunch, found Molly and asked her to take her to Sophie's room. Molly was only too delighted to oblige.

Aurora peeped around the door, gave a little squeak at seeing Sophie propped up on her pillows, her face pink and healthy-looking, and rushed in and threw herself on the bed.

'Oh Soph, Soph, I missed you. Oh how have you been? Are you really ill or are you shamming?'

Sophie held out her arms and clasped her friend to her bosom, then set her free.

'I've missed you too, Aurora,' she said affectionately.' It's been so hectic since Christmas with Dolly's baby. She was so sick, you see, and I just couldn't leave her. Not that I wanted to.'

'Dearest Soph, I quite understand. She didn't look in the pink today, I thought. She's as pale as a nun and doesn't seem to have the strength of a fly.'

'Oh I hope she'll get stronger as time goes by, and she's so happy with Cormac. She has great faith in Dr Hegarty, who is insisting that she drink a pint of porter every day.'

Aurora laughed. 'I do not believe it. How *can* she? I'd die.'

'We are all so fond of her and she is so happy with the baby.' Sophie said.

Aurora sighed. 'The baby has been hard on her, though. It quite puts one off having children, doesn't it?'

She was amazed when Sophie burst into a sudden storm of tears. All her pent-up feelings overflowed and she was unable to contain herself any longer.

'Sophie darling, what's the matter?'

Sophie looked at her friend who sat beside her on the bed, her expression perplexed and anxious.

'Oh Aurora, Aurora, dare I tell you? Can I trust you?'

Aurora's face went bright pink and Sophie saw to her horror that she had seriously hurt her friend.

'Oh Aurora, I didn't mean. . . . It's so awful. I've been out of my mind with anxiety. You'll understand how careful I have to be when I tell you. If those cats down there caught one whisper . . . Of course I trust you. Oh Aurora I think . . . I think I'm going to have a baby. There! I've said it.'

She saw the pink vanish from her friend's face leaving it very pale.

'Sophie! Oh Sophie. Sophie!'

'Don't keep saying my name like that, and don't you go all moralistic on me, Aurora Vestry, and don't ask me the details either, for I cannot tell you.'

'But who . . . who? Who on earth . . . ?'

'It's no use casting about in your mind as I can see you are, for you don't know him. He is not a Vestry, Blackwater or a Gorman or any of those. He is a rebel and an outlaw and I love him, how I love him.'

'Well, you'll have to stop right now, Sophie Jeffries, or you'll be ruined entirely.' Aurora's face was clearing for she had thought of a perfect plan. 'Listen, Sophie, I know exactly what to do. I take it this gallant outlaw will not marry you?'

Sophie thought of Red and shook her head. 'He cannot.'

'Oh Sophie, how *reckless* and romantic you are, doing something like that. What was it like?'

'Aurora! How can you ask me? Oh, you should be ashamed.'

'It's you who should be ashamed, not me.' she cried tartly. 'Well then, if your rebel cannot marry you and I'm glad to see he has that much sense then you'll have to marry someone else.'

'Oh Aurora, don't be silly. There is no one I love or care for in the least. Who could I marry?'

'Fabrice de Beauvillande. Deirdre brought him here to meet you. He is as pretty a gentleman as ever you'll see. He comes from a noble family. He is here looking for a wife. Oh, he is not aware that I know all about him. He thinks Ireland is on the moon as regards gossip. Little he knows! Anyhow, he'll fall for you the moment he claps eyes on you ... that I'll wager.'

'Then what is the snag?' Sophie asked. 'If he's so perfect, why has he not been snapped up before? Why has he come to Ireland for a wife? Are the French girls not pretty enough?'

'The snag, dearest Sophie, is that he is penniless and in disgrace. His Mama cut him off and he is here because he *had* to leave France. He was involved in a duel. That is all I know. There was a scandal. But what do you care? It is an answer. It will suffice.'

'Oh I dare say, Aurora. It sounds perfect. But I love my outlaw. How can I in conscience marry this man when I love another?'

Aurora shrugged. 'Very easily. Your outlaw will not, cannot, marry you. In any event it would not suit. You simply would not be allowed. Can you see James? In a little while you will look like a whale. You will be disgraced. You will be ruined. No one will marry you after that. I am being sensible, Sophie, you must listen.'

Sophie had turned away. Her face was defeated but stubborn. 'I don't want to marry a man I do not know.'

'It is done in lots of families. I will probably marry Gareth Gorman because Mama and Papa want me to. They think I'll be happy with him. They are probably right. I would be like you and fall for ... for ... well, someone most unsuitable, if I was left to myself.' She shrugged. 'I don't know. But think, sweet Sophie, what you will be doing to your family. They'll share your disgrace. You will be a burden on them and you will have shamed them. James will put you in a convent.'

Sophie shrieked in horror. She knew Aurora was speaking the truth. She clasped the pillow over her head but her friend pulled it away.

'No, you must listen. You'll end up being a nun or an old maid helping Dolly with Cormac or,' she added wickedly, 'Bella with the babies she'll have when she weds.'

'Oh Aurora, you're cruel. Cruel. Don't.'

'Yes I am. Cruelly honest with you, for I love you, dearest Sophie, and I'll not see you ruin your life. You may not be in love with Fabrice but you soon will be. He is as handsome as sin, as charming as Don Juan himself, but I know he would be faithful and devoted. He really is a pretty fellow.'

Sophie giggled. She had spoken to no one during the previous months when she had been worried out of her mind. Aurora sounded so calm, was so practical, offered her a way out of a dilemma that, in the solitude of her dressing-room, or in the bedchamber accompanied by Bella's incessant chatter, had seemed insurmountable. She felt relieved and hopeful for the first time in weeks.

'Well, then, I'll have to meet this paragon.'

Aurora laughed. 'You two were made for each other. I'm quite set on being a match-maker, Sophie.'

The girls embraced and Aurora said, 'Now you must come down after our rest and dazzle him at the party tonight.'

'Oh Aurora, I don't think I'm up to that, really I don't.'

But Aurora was firm. 'My dearest Sophie, you have no time to waste.'

Sophie nodded sadly, her depression returning.

'Now don't be cast down. Chin up. Everything will be worked out satisfactorily, you'll see.'

Aurora kissed her, then crossed the room and looked out of the window. She could see through the lattice the panorama of the valley before her. The mountains lay sleeping in the sun, sharp-etched against the clear blue sky. There was a flock of sheep filing down one side, a dog nipping at their recalcitrant heels and yapping, the shepherd lad behind with his staff. A curl of smoke rose from the cottage in the valley and an old woman there shook out clothes and hung them on a tree to dry. A young man lay on the grass near her, playing the flute. You could hear the notes sweet as treacle hanging on the hazy air.

The stream danced through the valley, pin-points of light like diamond motes leaping in a twinkling ribbon. The world below swam in a shimmering end-of-day heat-haze. It seemed as if all the light in the world had concentrated there.

Aurora blinked at the radiance of it and turned back into the room. Sophie lay against her lace pillows in her peach velvet *robe de chambre*. Her glorious champagne-coloured hair, the colour of the dazzling light outside, lay spread out around her. Aurora thought how pretty she looked.

She said to her friend, 'Are you sleepy? Would you like to rest or shall we talk?

Sophie raised herself on her elbows. 'No. I'm wide awake now. I couldn't sleep if I tried. I wonder where Bella is. I do hope she doesn't disturb us.'

'And what is baby Cormac like? I should love to see him, for I adore babies. At least I think I do.' She clapped her hands together and laughed at Sophie's astonished face. 'You see, Soph, I've never seen one. Can you believe? Let me think. No, I don't believe I've ever really looked at a baby. Except of course the servants and they were never new-born.'

'Well, Cormac is hardly new-born. He's a very large five-month-old.'

Aurora grimaced. 'Oh, you know what I mean, Sophie. I've just thought. Could we go to the nursery now to see him?'

'I don't think he'll be with Dolly just at present as she's downstairs with the guests. He'll be having his nap. Better wait till later.'

Aurora looked surprised. 'Why on earth cannot we go now to the nursery, Soph, and see your baby nephew?'

Sophie looked embarrassed. She had taken it as normal in their household that Cormac should be with Widow Boann when not with her sister-in-law, and one did not intrude on the Widow.

'It's difficult, Aurora,' she said now, a delicate line creasing her forehead. 'You see, he's with the old nurse up in the tower, way above me.' She looked towards the ceiling. 'We never go up there. You see it's where ... it's where ... the other one is.'

Aurora left the embrasure and crossed the room. She sat herself on Sophie's bed, all interest.

'You mean your other nephew ... the one who is a hunchback?'

'Fergal. Yes. I mean . . .'

'Well, come on, Sophie. What's he like?'

'I don't *know*. We never go there. I've never seen him.'

'Oh Sophie, don't be feeble. You must have seen him. Curiosity must have got the better . . .'

But Sophie protested, 'I haven't. I've never even thought about it.'

'Well, I want to see the baby. I'm going up.

'Oh dear, no. No. We're not supposed to,' Sophie said in panic. 'James has forbidden it. We would get into the most *awful* trouble.'

'Honestly, Sophie, how you ever broke the rules enough to get pregnant I'll never know.' And as Sophie started to protest she added, 'Don't you ever do anything your brother forbids? What can he do *after* we've been?'

'I don't know . . . he'll be very angry, and no, I never disobey James.'

'Let him. It'll be too late then. Oh don't be such a ninny. Aren't you dying of curiosity? I am. Come on.'

She pulled Sophie off her bed. To her surprise Sophie felt fine and not faint as she had expected. She tied the tapes of her gown more tightly, and in a last-ditch attempt to escape an excursion she deplored, fell back on the bed saying, 'Oh. I'm going to swoon. Oh. Aurora! Oh.'

'Sophie Jeffries, that's the worst piece of play-acting I have ever seen in all my life. It would not fool anyone, even an idiot, for five minutes.'

Sophie opened one eye and sat up. 'Aurora do we have to? I've never really seen Fergal and I'm frightened. I shall probably be sick and it will be your fault. Anyhow, if you have an ounce of patience you'll see little Cormac when James brings him down after tea.'

'No, no, no.' Aurora cried as she dragged Sophie off her bed again. 'I've quite made up my mind, you lily-livered soppy thing. I'm going up even if you're not. I shall say I lost my way, so there. Then no one can be cross.'

Sophie groaned. 'Oh, all right. But don't say I didn't warn you. Don't say . . .'

'Come *on*. Let's go.'

The girls left the room, Aurora Vestry leading. They lifted their skirts and tiptoed down the corridor and across the landing. They turned into a alcove where there was a stone stairway winding upwards. The steps were uneven in the middle, worn down with time. The stairway led to the apartments high above them.

They came to the Widow Boann's room, tapped on the door and entered. It was a white-washed little place with a pallet bed, a crucifix on the wall, with a night-light beneath it on a wooden shelf. Beside the night-light was a little earthen jar containing a bunch of wild flowers. The place was spotless and smelled of carbolic.

They climbed another flight of the small twisting stairs and came to the next door. It was a big wooden one with a heavy ring of a handle. Sophie was half-dead with fear and Aurora Vestry's courage was swiftly vanishing. The girls leaned against the door, ears pressed to it, trying to hear what went on inside. Sophie's heart was pounding and Aurora began to wish she had not insisted on coming. There was a profound silence everywhere except for a faint singing from behind the door.

It seemed to the girls that they stood for an age listening. Then the singing stopped abruptly and there was a pause. The girls pressed closer, gazing at each other saucer-eyed, but there was only silence. Suddenly the door was wrenched open and the two young ladies fell to their knees in front of the Widow woman herself.

'Ach, my fine young mistresses, now what is this? An' why are you lurking and skulking outside my door when all ye have to do is knock and enter?' She laughed goodnaturedly. 'I'm mostly at home,' she added, 'though no one ever calls.' Her voice was sarcastic.

The girls scrambled to their feet with as much dignity as they could muster. The Widow looked at them, a twinkle in her black-currant eyes.

'Miss Sophie! Sure, I thought ye were dyin' in bed. That's what I heard. An' here ye are, up two flights in yer house-clothes an' not a thing wrong wi' you as I can see. Well come in, come in now yer here the both of you an' see my *babies*.'

She ushered them in to the large light circular room. It too was white-washed and spotless. Everything was bright and cheerful, and Sophie, who had not known what to expect, was certainly taken aback by what she saw. There was a heavy arm-chair, big enough to take the Widow's considerable weight. It stood before the fireplace. There were bowls of flowers on the two tables that stood in the room and the room was full of their scent.

Aurora had run to the crib that held the baby.

'Oh, he's an angel,' she cried, delighted with the pink mite all wrapped in shawls. 'The prettiest thing . . . oh, he's a darling. Delicious. Oh please, ma'm, may I hold him? Please? Please?'

'Sure an' why not.' the Widow said, smiling. She was watching Sophie with shrewd eyes. The girl's gaze darted about the room.

'There's what yer lookin' for,' she said and pointed to the far corner where there was a roughly-made play-pen. Wooden bars, knee-high in an unanchored square on the stone floor.

Sophie looked at it fearfully, now knowing what to expect. What she saw surprised her. True, the little shoulder was ear-high, but the hands reaching out for her were rosy-soft and beautiful; there were dimples in the cheeks; and the great china-blue eyes, so like her own, were full of wonder.

'Petty . . . petty,' he lisped. 'Look, Nana. Look. Petty lady.'

'He's never seen the likes of you, Miss Sophie. Only me.' The Widow's voice was brisk. 'An' I'm no oil-painting.'

Tears filled Sophie's eyes and she instinctively responded to the outstretched arms and picked the little boy up. He curled his legs about her like a little monkey and she held him tightly to her. There was a lump as hard as a cooking-apple in her throat, which dissolved and melted when she swallowed.

'I didn't know. I didn't know,' she sobbed, and the Widow said with some asperity. 'I won't have any bawlin' here. This is a happy room. There's no' a place for weepin' here. So if you don't mind, miss, and beggin' yer pardon, hush up, do.'

Sophie sniffed back her tears but the child saw them.

'Ah no,' he said 'Don't cry.'

Sophie held the little creature and looked into the calm blue eyes. They were brightly intelligent. How shameful, she thought, that he is shut up here without a chance to defend himself, without hope of understanding, all for an accident of birth, the hump on his shoulder. Dear God, it could have been me. He was malformed, true, but obviously there was nothing wrong with his brain. He smiled at her trustingly.

'It's not right,' she said to Aurora who had replaced the baby Cormac in his cradle.

'Indeed it's not.' Aurora looked at the little boy, whose legs were wound tight around her friend. 'That little fellow is the sweetest thing.'

'Ah, young mistress he won't be for long.' The child looked from one to the other. 'He's happy with me here. Aren't you, my precious? But now he's seen you he'll never be as happy again. He knows now there is a world out there. Sure, you've given him something. But you've taken something too. Are you willing to pay for your curiosity? Curiosity satisfied always carried a price, ye know.'

Sophie looked perplexed. The Widow continued, 'Will ye come to see the wee mite again? Now he's seen ye he'll ask. An' it's not fair if yer not consistent, my fine young colleen. Do ye understand?'

Sophie nodded, 'Oh I will. I will. I'd love to.' She kissed Fergal's cheek, and she smiled at the little boy and tickled him over his good shoulder in the nook of his fat little neck. He gurgled, the happiest sound, and wriggled delightedly in her arms.

She gave him reluctantly to the Widow, who set him on the floor, and he ran over to the crude play-pen, and stretching a plump little arm inside he retrieved a tattered book. He held it out to Sophie.

'Look. Look at dis. Pretty pictures. See?'

Sophie leaned over the tattered book. 'It's lovely,' she agreed.

He thumbed the pages clumsily, then pointed to the illustration of Cinderella getting into her coach. 'You,' he said, looking at her with shining eyes.

Her own eyes were full of tears and she was afraid she would cry, afraid she would upset the little fellow.

'Tell you what,' she said, 'I'll bring you another. The prettiest one there is in Dublin City. Would you like that?'

'He has no notion of "city", or town or village, come to that. All he has seen is my sister's cottage in the valley and the view from that window there. This room is his world.'

'I'll come back, Widow.' Sophie turned, 'Bye-bye,' Fergal. Say goodbye to me,' she called across the room and the child obediently said, 'Bye-bye. Bye, petty lady.'

'My name is Aunt Sophie, Fergal. You can call me that.'

The child nodded. 'Bye-bye, Aunt Sophie,' he said and the

137

Widow lifted him back into the play-pen.

Aurora was standing in the shadows crying. The Widow pushed her out of the room.

'I *won't* have the lad upset,' she said firmly, 'by silly girls in tears.'

She hustled Sophie out of the room too and closed the door, standing with her back to it and glowering at the girls.

'Now listen, the two of yiz,' she said a tigress defending her cubs. 'If you do anything to harm my lamb, I'll murder ye. Do you hear?'

Aurora was still in tears. 'Oh the poor little fellow,' she cried, hiccupping. 'The dear little mite.'

'Hush up,' the Widow hissed, stamping her foot in exasperation. 'Think of the wee mite himself and not yer own feelings. Stop yer silly sentimental balderdash. Fergal is quite content as he is.' She peered into the girl's large violet eyes. Aurora hiccupped again and nodded. 'Now go. Be on yer way,' she said.

She opened the door behind her and turned back to them, smiling.

'Ach, now, get on wi' ye, and come again do. Ye've made a friend inside, so ye have.' She went back into the room, closing the door behind her.

Chapter

20

JAMES, a perfect host, thought more of his guests' comfort than his own. Aware of his position as head of the most important family in the county, aware of the fact that the heads of the other great families were his senior by a couple of decades, he strove for a wisdom beyond his years and had succeeded in impressing everyone in Wicklow County.

The men went to the smoking-room after lunch, while the ladies were resting, and some of them played backgammon in the card-room.

Lord Vestry murmured to Lord Rennett, as their young host went to speak with Fabrice de Beauvillande, 'The fellow is a credit to Usher. He takes his position seriously indeed.'

Lord Rennett replied doubtfully, 'A mite too seriously for one so young.'

Puffing on his cigar, Lord Vestry gave his friend a quizzical look. 'Heavens, Rennett, don't quibble. Better that than a wild young buck like my Morgan. He'd squander away the inheritance in a trice. S'truth, I shudder to think of the consequences if I dropped dead suddenly and that young strap took over Mount Rivers.' He said it proudly, for truth to tell he admired his son's youth and recklessness and was quite proud of his wildness.

Lord Rennett, knowing this, smiled. 'You are right, old friend. One can be too old too young.' He glanced at James who stood talking to Fabrice. 'Still, James has a heavy load to carry,' he said, 'and I only hope he has the sense to go easy on himself and not expect too much. He takes life so seriously and sets such high standards for the House of Usher. I hope he is never let down.'

Lord Vestry scratched his head. 'Don't know what you mean, old boy. Really I don't.'

'I simply mean that I fear James will go to any lengths to keep this Knight of Usher title untarnished. I hope he is not let down. It would kill him.' Then seeing Vestry's uncomprehending look he called Maitland for another brandy and leaned down and scratched Angel behind her ear. 'I think James is bound by the black-and-white of youth,' he said. 'He cannot see that there are shades.'

The subject of their conversation was speaking to the stranger in their midst.

'My sister Arabella has told me of your desire to paint in the vicinity. I would deem it a privilege if you would stay with us here in Usher when you have tired of the beauties of Slievelea.'

'Indeed, sir, you are most kind and I make no bones about my wish to capture, as you say, on canvas the glories of this spot,' 'Fabrice replied in his charming accented voice. 'It is indeed more lovely than anything I have so far seen,' he continued. 'I would be grateful and honoured to accept your so kind invitation.'

'Then I open my house to you, sir, and hope you'll avail yourself of our hospitality.'

James bowed and was about to turn away when the stranger detained him. His voice was low.

'Sir, you have been so kind and I am grateful. But I would rather die than be your guest under false colours. He looked at James squarely. 'You must know that although my family is an illustrious one, I am, at the moment and entirely through my own fault, quite without funds. I say this because I would no more impose upon you ...'

But James interrupted, placing his hand on the young man's arm. 'Lord and Lady Rennett have told me of your situation, and I am grateful for your confidence and honesty in telling me about this. Your present circumstances are no concern of mine and I welcome you to my house with pleasure nonetheless. There will be no need for you to worry about, er, finances whilst under my roof. Sir.' They parted with a mutual bow.

James smiled to himself. He was looking for husbands for his sisters. He knew, and the young Frenchman knew, what was really behind that conversation. Thinly veiled, it was an inquiry if the Frenchman could woo Arabella and the answer James had given was yes. And the Frenchman's lack of funds was of no consequence. But the Frenchman had not seen Sophie for Sophie had been confined to her room. James frowned. 'I must not meet trouble before it comes,' he thought, and regretfully realized that it would be impolite to run up to see Dolly for five minutes. He sighed and returned to his guests.

Chapter 21

PARIS society had been rocked by the scandal of Fabrice de Beauvillande and Ornella Duvall. Fabrice's mother was the most deeply affected. Many said the trouble was all her own fault. Her husband the Conte had died just after her son Fabrice, her only child, had been born. She had loved her husband and with his untimely death she transferred all her passion to her son. He grew up a delightful, good-humoured dilettante. She spoiled him dreadfully, indulged him disgracefully, paying his debts when he gambled too deeply, covering for him when he was caught in some mishap, smoothing over his indiscretions involving the daughters of their friends. Many a payment was made to cover a spot of bother he had found himself in, many a misdemeanour was tactfully sorted out by the doting Contesse. And in the last extremity she had smuggled him out of Paris when he had killed the Duc de Mandeville's son Armand in a duel over the beautiful courtesan Ornella Duvall. She had, however, told him she would never speak to him ever again after that disgraceful episode, and he was heartbroken.

From his cradle everyone, both men and women, adored Fabrice. His charm conquered all. His tutors were beguiled into letting him have his own way. Older women were dazzled by him, young girls fell head-over-heels in love with him. He was extremely handsome but there were handsomer men, certainly. It was his charm and an extraordinarily sweet disposition that protected him from retribution, amendment or reparation. He never had had to pay for an escapade until now, and was optimistic even in these circumstances. Duelling had been banned: in the eyes of the law his crime was murder. For this crime he was wanted in Paris. Nevertheless he believed that some day the scandal would blow over, the Duc de Mandeville would forgive him for the slaying of his son for after all it had been a tragic accident — his mother would welcome him back to her arms and he could return to Paris. Then he would win Ornella back.

He had met her first at the Opéra Comique. She had been with her protector, the Duc de Mirabeau, whom he had first thought was her father. He had been quite blinded by her beauty and he had asked his best friend, his *cher-ami* Pierre Montaigne, to introduce them, for Pierre knew everyone in Paris. Pierre straightway took him to her box.

Fabrice was instantly smitten. He fell in and out of love easily and Ornella was very beautiful. She dazzled him with one of her famous smiles and, to her surprise, found herself melting to his charm. She was amused by his avowals of love whenever he got the opportunity and the Duc's back was turned. He entertained her and she was a little tired of the constant attention she had to lavish on her elderly protector.

The Duc was leaving the next day for the country in the company of his wife, which made Ornella a little cross. So she permitted Fabrice to coax her into letting him visit her in the Duc's absence.

Fabrice became her lover. He was young and ardent, a glorious change from the Duc, for she sometimes feared she would run out of ways to arouse his ageing body. Fabrice was so charming and delightful a companion that he became her play thing, and her rich protector had not minded him, any more than he had minded her lap-dog Frou-Frou, a fluffy little white Maltese terrier who sat all day at her feet.

The situation had been perfect. It left all of them quite free. The old Duc had entire right of entry at any time of the day or night to the luxurious apartment he had provided for her, and to her beautiful voluptuous white body. As he was in his seventies and as he had a country estate, a fabulous vineyard famous for its wine, houses in Paris and Monte Carlo to administer, a wife who liked him to spend time with her on the Côte d'Azur, three sons — one his heir, one a diplomat, one a banker — and two daughters, all of them married with numerous offspring, he was quite a busy man, though not as active as he once was. So his demands on Ornella's time were not as great as her beauty and his gifts to her would pre-suppose. He kept her more as a symbol of status, an ornament in the crown of his achievements, a possession that proved to the world how important he was.

He knew of Ornella's feelings for Fabrice, that she thought of him as a delightful companion, that she was a little contemptuous of his ardour, the seriousness with which he loved her. She simply did not understand his obsession with her. Typically Parisian, she was primarily practical, and wondered why he did not obey his Mama's entreaties and find a wife who could give him an heir, keeping Ornella as his mistress. It seemed to her the most eminently sensible thing to do.

She used Fabrice as she used the other luxuries the Duc provided in abundance for her; whenever the urge came she satisfied her pagan appetites. The Duc, knowing all this, was quite complaisant about the charming Fabrice.

Then Ornella, to everyone's surprise, not least her own, fell head-over-ears in love with Armand de Mandeville. The Duc watched in horror. With Fabrice he knew that her emotions were not seriously engaged. Armand was another matter entirely. He realized that Ornella, heartless, indifferent to the emotions of love as all good courtesans must be, greedy and materialistic, was uncharacteristically falling for the intense and passionate scion of the illustrious family of Mandeville. The Duc decided not to worry. His plan was to withdraw his protection from Ornella, leave her homeless, without a sou, take away her gowns, jewels, horses and servants, all of which were his property in any event, and leave her penniless as a beggar in the Boulevard du Crime. He thought that she would hardly sustain her romantic fervour in squalor, and he knew that the de Mandeville family would not lift a finger to help, no matter how piteously Armand pleaded. In fact, they would silently aid and abet the Duc, for they could have no desire for their son to be so seriously involved with the notorious scarlet woman.

The Duc had reckoned without Fabrice de Beauvillande, who had turned the little drama, that promised to be a farce, into a tragedy. Who could have foretold his idiotic reaction to the love affair? He had gone to de Mandeville's club and struck Armand, who was a hot-headed romantic fool and stupid enough to respond to the over-dramatic gesture by challenging Fabrice to a duel. Childish and entirely unnecessary, a gesture of folly, and even worse, a criminal one for duelling was banned. Yet what did these two young hot-heads do but take themselves off to the Bois de Boulogne at dawn. Armand, who was a lieutenant in the army and a prodigious shot, expected to fire a bullet harmlessly, perhaps grazing Fabrice's shoulder to teach him a lesson. Instead he got himself killed by a boy who had never handled a gun in his life. It was tragic and ridiculous.

Fabrice grew up that morning in the Bois de Boulogne. He was, for the first time in his life, overcome with grief. In his mind's eye he saw again and again the misty place, felt the early-morning chill on his face and the knot of fear in the pit of his stomach as he realized that they had met in this dark dawn to kill each other. The trees were tall, like sentinels, and Armand stood between them, his white shirt fluttering in the breeze. He remembered the anger on that young face. He remembered raising his gun and he heard again the explosion. He had aimed at one of the trees, but his bullet had gone clean through de Mandeville's heart. He could see the blood, the horror of the face of death. He knew, alas too late, that he had pulled the trigger for the first and last time.

He had been violently ill. At twenty-three he had never seen death before. Cossetted, pampered, never having known any real pain, he was cast now into the depths of despair. He had been protected by his mother all his life from the consequences of his acts, and now he turned confidently to her, trusting her to help. Coldly she had agreed to smuggle him to Ireland, to make the necessary arrangements, but she gave him no comfort. She turned from him because he had brought the family name into disrepute. It was this rejection that wounded him most.

The duel often came between him and his sleep, but eventually the practical streak in his make-up came to his aid. An Italian might die of love, an Englishman shoot himself, but he was a Frenchman and he would survive. He came to realize that depression and despair are great isolaters, that if he were to survive he would have to pull himself together and get on with his life.

He would marry. He was an easy-going gregarious fellow and he liked the company of women. He would find a rich wife, for his Mama allowed him only a pittance. He would marry and father a son. Then his Mama would forgive him. She could not, would not resist that. Then she would persuade the de Mandevilles to forgive him too. He never doubted that they would eventually, for they must see he had not meant to harm a hair of Armand's head. The wretched pistol had had a mind of its own and had exploded on him before he had even taken aim. He would return to Paris and cast his spell on everyone, and all would be well again.

No doubts troubled Fabrice's mind on this June evening. He was elated. Everything had gone smoothly. James had spoken to Lord Rennett, who was inclined to think Fabrice's behaviour was typical of a young blade-about-town and it was all arranged. His things would be sent to Usher from Slievelea. And he had made a conquest: Arabella. She had totally lost her head over him, anyone could see that. He was of the opinion that James, her brother and guardian, was aware of the situation and tacitly in its favour. His plan, as usual, was working. He would marry Arabella as soon as custom permitted, keep in touch with Paris, and when the clouds lifted he would bring his bride home to the chateau, and coax his Mama into forgiving and forgetting. Then perhaps he could put the whole dark business behind him and the nightmares would finally go away.

Chapter

22

WHEN Aurora and Sophie left the high room they returned at once to Sophie's bedroom two floors below. They threw themselves on the bed in a flurry of muslin and lace and lay there confused and exhausted by their adventures. They chatted awhile, yawning prodigiously between sentences.

'You will talk to James? Promise, Soph?' Aurora begged. 'He shouldn't be up there alone like that, the poor wee lamb.'

Sophie nodded vigorously. She knew her friend spoke of Fergal. 'I will. I had made up my mind already. You, know James is difficult, but he *must* see ...' her voice trailed into silence. There was no sound now save the far-away voices of the man gossiping under the trees and the drone of the bees buzzing around the bright flowers.

Sophie gazed at the canopy above her, her thoughts taking a different turn. 'I wonder where Arabella is? She should be here resting, but I'm so glad she's not. She's such a pest, Aurora. You've no idea how mean she can be.'

Sophie turned to her friend, her face flushed. She saw that Aurora had fallen asleep, her cheek on the palm of her hand. So she too gave in to the drowsiness that overwhelmed her and resting her head on Aurora's shoulder she let nature take its course.

They slept soundly for an hour until the maid awakened them. Molly had brought them China tea to drink in the fine bowls James had brought back from Siam. Arabella was still absent, curiously, but they were not inclined to bother about that now. They ate tiny almond biscuits and pieces of short-cake and when they were finished they bathed, giggling and laughing together. Molly helped them to dress for dinner and dancing. Sophie with the resilience of youth had recovered her good humour, and her spirits had lightened considerably. She had at last a plan of action, and though it was not the path she would have chosen, nevertheless she resolved to take her friend's advice. She had no choice. She knew she would love Redmond Rafferty until the end of time. However she knew she would not tell him about the baby; there was nothing he could do. She had been frightened, very frightened, until Aurora had come up with her plan. And now she decided to marry this stranger, if she could bear to as her friend had proposed she should. Provided, of course, he pleased her.

At the last moment Arabella came in. She seemed over-excited and not a little secretive and the girls teased her unmercifully. She, however, was in a merry mood and soon escaped, having insisted to Molly's fury, that the maid lace her and dress her and arrange her hair first.

'She's found a suitor, I'll be bound,' Molly whispered to herself.

Aurora, wearing her ivory satin ballgown, and Sophie, looking enchanting in pink silk organza, followed at a more leisurely pace. They went down the stairs arm-in-arm and made their way towards the long ballroom on the right, off the hall. It was also the banqueting hall, but it had been garlanded and decorated and was ready now for the dancers.

At the end of the hall an orchestra was playing and the music of the waltz flooded the room. As Aurora and Sophie entered they were immediately surrounded by a group of young blades. Darcy Blackwater, Conel Connelly, Barth Gorman and Anthony Tandy-Cullaine came up immediately, to greet them.

'Can we bring you a glass of Madeira?'

'Please let me have the honour?' This was Conel to Aurora who was paying him no attention but waving excitedly to a tall blonde stranger. The stranger's evening dress was of an exquisite cut and he was talking to Arabella. His eyes, however, were not engaged and he was glancing about the room, this way and that, so he soon saw Aurora's gestures. He bent and said something to Arabella, who looked angry and shook her head. He, however, left her with a bow and crossed the room, Arabella hurrying after him.

Aurora greeted him warmly. 'Dear Fabrice. Look who's here.

148

I told you she was the prettiest girl in Wicklow. No — I beg your pardon, Sophie, in Ireland. And she is my best friend. Sophie, may I introduce the Conte de Beauvillande? And Fabrice, this is my dearest Lady Sophie Jeffries.'

Sophie blushed deeply and curtsied with a graceful little bob as the stranger kissed her small pale hand.

Arabella stood in the background hardly concealing her fury. 'I thought you were indisposed, Sophie. Were you shamming?' She could not keep the asperity out of her voice.

'*Enchanté Mademoiselle* ...' The handsome young Frenchman put his arm around Sophie and they waltzed away. It had been automatic; he had not asked her to dance. He had held out his arms and she had slipped into them as if she belonged.

Fabrice was overwhelmed. The band played 'Tales From the Vienna Woods', and all about them couples whirled, skirts billowing, satins and silks, diamonds and rubies, emeralds and sapphires shimmering and glittering in the light from the chandeliers. Servants moved from group to group offering goblets of champagne. Mamas balanced on little gilt chairs and fanned themselves, keeping a protective eye on their offspring. papas ogled the pretty posies of *debutantes* who tried to hide the eagerness in their eyes as the young blades, full of wine and false confidence, asked them to dance.

Fabrice saw none of it. All he was aware of was the girl in his arms. He was oblivious of all else but the blue of her eyes, the shadows her lashes cast on the porcelain-pink of her cheeks, the rosy gleam of her lips, the scent of her breath on his cheek, and the diamond ear-bobs in her ears, bouncing and swinging as she danced, catching occasionally in the golden ringlets at her neck. He was enchanted. He was bewitched. He who had always chosen his love, decided on the woman he would pursue, was suddenly bereft of defences, was enslaved. He fell in love.

As for Sophie, she had been scared and frightened. She had been worried sick about her pregnancy, fearful of the shameful position she was in and fully aware of James' feelings about the family name and its honour. Aurora Vestry had pointed a way out of her dilemma and she had decided, full of the optimism of youth, to follow her advice. Aurora had told her Fabrice was a pretty fellow and she had hoped that he was attractive. She had not been prepared for just how delightful she found him. He was good-looking enough to satisfy the most fastidious taste. He was charming and obviously smitten with her. This was a stroke of good fortune that she had neither expected or hoped for. She felt relief flood her, for if this was to be her fate it was one she could welcome with open arms.

She smiled up at him, excited by the music and his admiration. She felt light-headed and bubbling over with a kind of exaltation. The dancers swam before her eyes, and she realized that she was very happy.

To Aurora it was clear that they were smitten with each other right away. She knew that Sophie was predisposed to like the Frenchman, and certainly Fabrice, who had an eye for beauty, must adore Sophie's delicate loveliness. But also Aurora knew, he would be drawn to the sweetness of her friend's expression, the gentleness in her face. She watched them as they waltzed, laughing into each other's eyes, oblivious of everyone in the room. Sophie was flushed, her eyes bright as stars, and Fabrice could not take his gaze off her.

Arabella watched too. She could not believe what she saw. The man she had decided upon, the man she was set on having for herself, held her sister in his arms as if he could never let her go. She narrowed her eyes and when Aurora turned around the expression on Arabella's face made her shiver.

'Are you all right, Bella?' she asked kindly.

The girl turned her blazing eyes on Aurora. 'Much you care how I am,' she cried. 'Much anyone cares.'

Aurora stared at the girl's white hate-filled face. She was just about to say something to comfort Bella when a tap on her shoulder made her turn.

'This is my dance, I think,' Conel Connelly said, then steered her onto the dance floor and she forgot all about Arabella Jeffries in the exhilaration of the waltz.

Everyone was having a good time. Old Gentleman was roaring drunk, chasing a couple of young blossoms from the Carey pack. Lady Angela sat with her friends, wonderfully mellow after a few glasses of champagne, and talked of her late lamented husband to her captive audience, who did not really listen any more. James danced with Dolly, holding her to his heart. Aurora sighed with happiness. Perhaps her plan for her friend would work out. She hoped so. She waved to Sophie, but her friend did not see her though she was only an arm's length away. She was too busy gazing into Fabrice's eyes.

Conel snorted. 'That French chap is certainly busy. First he casts a spell on Bella, but not content with that he must do the same with Sophie.' He was peeved with the stranger's success. 'Really, those Frenchies should stick to their own women. Do they think they can come over here and run rings round Irish girls? It's not on, you know. Bad form.'

Aurora giggled, 'Oh don't be ridiculous. You're a stodge, Conel, really you are. Do you wonder that I won't marry you?' she said it lightly but she was thinking, 'So that's what's wrong with Bella. Well, the fat's in the fire now and no mistake.'

She glanced over her shoulder to where Arabella stood motionless, staring at her sister in the arms of the man she loved. Aurora, knowing Bella's temperament, made a mental sign of the cross and sent up a silent prayer for Sophie. She foresaw troubled waters ahead.

Chapter

23

A week later James was in a towering rage. Speechless with anger he looked at the stubborn face of his beloved sister. Why he wondered, was he burdened with such a difficult family? Why had not his father lived to bear the responsibility of dealing with all the problems they now dumped on him?. His mother was worse than useless, locked as she was in her prison of self-indulgent grief. You could not deflect her mind for five seconds from the subject of her husband's past triumphs, most of which had become exaggerated out of all proportion, to James' intense irritation. She thought of nothing but the past. She was disinterested as a cod-fish in the present, the family and their lives. James found his patience, not his strongest virtue at the best of times, stretched beyond endurance. Old Gentleman was no help to him either, preferring to closet himself with his books and his brandy.

Much of the time James felt himself too young to bear the sole responsibility for the running of Usher Castle. He felt the burden cast upon him by his father's untimely death too heavy. Here he was carrying the full weight of the estate, with two troublesome sisters to take care of and a brother who seemed to spend most of his time away from home. He often came across Creagh gossiping with strangers in Gaelic. It irritated him mightily when he found his brother deep in conversation in a language he did not understand with people he had never properly been introduced to, who he thought were quite appalling and who often had ghastly Amercian accents. His brother was no help at all with the running of Usher or family problems and sometimes James longed to be rid of the whole lot of them and wished he were free to spend all his time with his darling wife and child. But he was a conscientious man, a man very well aware of his duties and he would not feel comfortable unless he was executing them to the best of his ability.

Arabella was as annoying as Creagh. She had been plaguing him for the last few days with demands that he prise Fabrice away from her sister Sophie. James was exasperated. How on earth did she expect him to accomplish that?

'I saw him first. I have first claim on him, you must see that, James. It was I who persuaded you to ask him to stay with us. *And* I am the elder sister. You must tell him I have to be married first, before Sophie. You *must* put your foot down, James as the eldest and the head of the family. Tell her to leave him alone. Send her away. You could have her visit the Rennetts at Slievelea, or her precious Aurora at Mount Rivers. She had shrilled this refrain at him non-stop, it seemed to James, since the day of the christening and he was heartily sick of it. He wished now that he had not invited the handsome young man to Usher Castle, he had caused such a furore since his arrival. Not that one could level any complaints about his behaviour. He had acted impeccably, even though he had changed horses in mid-stream. But in all honesty, James could not blame him for so doing. Sophie was irresistible and Arabella a heavy pill to swallow and in conscience he knew that if he were a suitor coming to this house he would have done exactly the same. No, Fabrice de Beauvillande was a delightful and charming guest, discreet and tactful, wonderful company and best of all, he made Dolly laugh.

That was another of his worries. He adored his tiny wife and was anxious over her assurances that her doctor had said it was all right to consummate his conjugal rights at certain times of the month. He hoped she was not fibbing to smooth away the problem for him and make life easier. He assured her, and he hoped she believed him, that he loved her so much that it was infinitely preferable to him to restrain his natural inclinations rather than risk her life. There was no way he would put her life in jeopardy. But she had told him there was no need.

He had been brooding about all these problems when Sophie had burst into his study and started off about the hunchback baby. She had reduced him to a rage such as he had never known before.

153

'Get out of here, Sophie,' he yelled at her, quivering with fury. 'Get out of here and never bring up that subject again. Do you hear?'

He sat down, trembling, while his sister stood near the door, her vivacious little face white with fear, yet standing her ground bravely. She had never seen her brother so angry before.

He made an effort to control himself and said coldly, 'I left strict instructions — no: ruled, forbade — *anyone* on *any* pretext whatsoever to go near those rooms in the high tower. You disobeyed my explicit orders. How dare you? Then to come to me here, issuing commands that that *cripple* be allowed out for all the world to see our shame ...'

Although Sophie had never been so terrified, she dredged up the courage to whisper, 'Oh James, he is not a shame. Really he is not. He is a sweet little ...'

James banged his hand on the desk. 'Silence! Silence, my lady. At once. Go to your room before I use words unfit for a lady's ears. I am master here. I have long thought that ill-begotten devil's child should be sent away from here and you have quite made up my mind for me. He will go to the orphanage forthwith, and I do not mind telling you that it will ease my mind to be rid of the unpleasant fact of him in our home.'

Sophie burst into tears. She ran around her brother's desk in great distress and fell on her knees before him.

'Oh no, no, no, James. Please, please, I beg you, do not do that. I pray you, upon my soul I do. Leave him be. Leave him here in peace.' She wrung her hands together in an agony of agitation.

James plucked at her arms which were trying to wind themselves around his neck. He firmly removed them.

'Rise to your feet, Sophie. It is of no avail to distress yourself. My mind is quite made up.'

Sophie rose. She looked at her brother's implacable face and saw he spoke the truth. She was devastated by the fact that she had precipitated a calamity. She knew her brother well enough to know that once he had come to a decision like this he was not likely to change his mind. It would be useles to argue.

She left the room and closed the door softly behind her. She knew that to speak to Dolly, asking her to intercede for her, was useless. To Dolly, her husband's word was law. No. Her only hope was to go to the Widow Boann directly and confess everything. Perhaps the redoubtable woman could think of some way of saving the poor little child whose only crime seemed to be the fact that he had been born malformed. Sophie sighed, dabbed her tear-stained face, stilled her beating heart and mounted the steps to the high tower.

To her great surprise the Widow was not there and the door was locked. Frustrated, she returned to her room and sat restlessly trying to embroider until it was time to dress for dinner.

Chapter

24

DINNER that night was a sorry affair. Fabrice tried to enliven the meal but to no avail. James was in a thoroughly bad mood though he did his best to hide it for the sake of their guest. Dolly was tired and seemed listless. Arabella was sulking and Sophie seemed in great distress, her eyes red from weeping. Fabrice was terribly concerned about her, whilst Arabella could not hide her satisfaction that things seemed to have gone wrong for her sister. Angela and Old Gentleman were both there at the table but in separate worlds of their own, and Creagh, appearing unexpectedly for his first meal with them since the party, caused James to remark with heavy sarcasm that it was nice to welcome a stranger in their midst, which Fabrice took to mean him and caused a slight *contretemps* and a lot of embarrassing apologizing and explaining.

Angela suddenly said, 'James I do hope you'll have the maids take better care of the Burmese Buddha in the Great Hall. They allow dust to collect *behind* it. Your father was always most specific on that point. Never, he would say, never allow dust to accumulate *behind* anything. It shows mental and spiritual slovenliness.'

'Yes, Mama,' James dutifully replied. He could not recall his father ever completing such a long sentence. It was far more likely that his mother had expressed herself so and his father had agreed.

'James, don't take that tone with me. You may be master here now, but you'll never be the man your father was.'

James bit his lip. The only sound in the room was the loud ticking of the grandfather clock and Old Gentleman sucking the bones of the fricassee of hare. It seemed an age before dessert was served, but even though it was chocolate pudding and James' favourite it did not lighten his mood. They had not eaten two spoons when Dolly excused herself.

'Dear. I feel a little tired. Will you all forgive me if I retire early?'

James looked worried. 'My dear, of course you must go. I'll be with you shortly. Ring for Annie.'

Then Angela and Old Gentleman rose together as if by signal, but before they could speak James waved his hand.

'Oh do go too, Mama. Uncle, go. I don't know what is happening in this house. Manners seem to have vanished. Everyone is behaving most oddly.'

As the older couple left the room Arabella said tartly to her brother, 'Not least of all you, James.'

There was another silence, then Sophie, who had spent the meal sniffing into her handkerchief, becoming increasingly restless, suddenly burst out, 'Oh James, James, I cannot bear it. Please, please reconsider, I beg of you.'

James smashed his hand so hard on the table that he caused the glasses as well as his brother and sisters to jump.

'I have told you, Sophie, never to broach that subject again. I forbid it, do you hear?'

'What subject?' Arabella asked avidly.

James looked at her coldly. His icy glance quelled her curiosity.

Although Sophie was frightened she was also very angry. She had enough of her brother's temperament to be equally stubborn. She rose to her feet and shook out her taffeta skirt.

'Well, James,' she said in a voice that shook but with an expression in her eyes that her brother recognized. He put up his hand in a gesture of silence and as Sophie began to protest he looked at Fabrice who had a spoon half-way to his mouth.

'Please, Monsieur le Conte. I am sure you will understand if I ask you to leave. This is a family matter and I apologize most humbly to you that it was so inappropriately brought up at dinner.'

Fabrice rose, bowed to the table in the most elegant way, kissed Sophie's hand and left the room without more ado.

'Now, Sophie. I cannot tell you how displeased I am with your atrocious behaviour.'

'Well, and James, so am I with you.' Creagh sucked in his breath at the frigidity of her tone. 'In the event that you will not reconsider, I have no option but to leave this house at once. I will not stay under this roof a moment longer than I have to.'

A flicker of surprise crossed James face. 'And where will you go, pray?' he asked sarcastically. He wondered briefly what he had done to deserve this day.

Sophie had not planned what she now heard herself saying. In fact she had not planned anything. She simply knew that she had to act. True, Fabrice had told her he wanted to take his bride to live with him in France. He had also, the day before in the conservatory, held her pink little hand in his and told her he had never seen a prettier girl and that he doted on her. He said that he intended to ask her brother for the privilege of marrying her. She thought Fabrice the nicest person in the world and if she could not have Red Rafferty, then she could not think of a man she would rather spend her life with than Fabrice de Beauvillande. And he adored her.

So now she said to James, 'I shall marry Fabrice and I shall go to France with him.'

There was a stunned pause. Creagh burst out joyfully, for he had been plagued with thoughts of his sister and Red, 'Oh capital, Sophie. Capital.'

'Shut up, Creagh, this instant. Try to act your age,' James said, then turned to Sophie. 'Has he asked you yet? For if he has, my girl, it's a sorry breach of etiquette.' He was white-lipped with anger.

Sophie said uncertainly, 'He is about to ask you, James. He only intimated to me ... You know there are certain things that a woman understands. He has not breached etiquette. He will approach you first, of course.'

'Well, he won't, for he has behaved in an intolerably under-hand way that is inexcusable.'

'You are quite wrong, James,' Arabella said, 'From the very first he had told *me* plainly that he wishes to marry *me*. It may have been a breach of the best manners but you remember how he begged you to allow him to stay here before he ever laid eyes on Sophie. My sister has embarrassed him ever since by throwing herself at him in the most wanton way.'

Creagh whistled beneath his breath and James stared at her in amazement.

'When did he ask you to marry him?'

'I don't believe it. He couldn't have. She's mad,' Sophie whispered.

'Today. On the terrace. After lunch and before he went riding with you, James. He asked me quite distinctly to marry him and go to France. So you see, he must keep his word. If he is a man of honour, and you are to do your duty as a brother, James as a gentleman, then he must marry me. It is a matter of honour.'

Arabella's heart was beating excitedly. It was a desperate gamble to prise the man she loved from her sister. It might come off. Men were notoriously tricky about honour especially James, and it was Sophie's word against her's. Sophie would tell the truth and she had said that Fabrice had not explicitly asked her. On the other hand, she Arabella, would go to any lengths to get him. She would lie, she would cheat, there was nothing she would not do to get Fabrice de Beauvillande.

A loud laugh shattered the amazed silence Arabella's words produced. It was Creagh, and he guffawed heartily.

'If that was a proposal, Bella, then I'm a Dutchman.' He slapped his thigh. 'Oh heavens, what a liar. I was standing just under the terrace and I heard every word of your conversation. "Oh Fabrice, the woman you choose will be so lucky",' Creagh simpered, clowning in an exaggerated version of Arabella's voice, something guaranted to infuriate her. '"I cannot think how you can dally after my sister Sophie, for she is a vain and silly creature and says you are a fool and worse, and that she despises you and is simply leading you along".'

Sophie let out a squeal of rage but Creagh continued, 'Then I heard Fabrice reply, for he is a gentleman, "Oh Bella, how you do run on. I'm sure I do not wish to discuss your sister Sophie with you. *Au revoir*." That was the entire conversation, I swear to you, James. You really are frightful, Arabella.'

Arabella turned to Creagh. He was startled by the naked hatred in her eyes.

'I'll pay you for this, Creagh, see if I don't.' She spat the words out, her face contorted with malice. 'I'll pay you back, you hateful cad.'

'Arabella ...' James thundered, but she flounced out of the room slamming the door behind her.

Sophie's lips were stiff, her face hurting in its rigidity, for she did not want to break down. She hated loud voices and unpleasantness and one of the things she loved most about Fabrice was how gentle his behaviour was.

'James, I meant what I said. Really I did,' she said with difficulty. Then she walked to the door and left the room.

Creagh jumped up, and still laughing, slapped James on the back.

'Really, brother, you take the girls too seriously. You should ignore their petty little female dramas. Ignore them, James, and leave them to their little intrigues and stratagems. You and I have man's work to do. Goodnight, brother.' And he too left.

James, left alone, could not imagine what Creagh's reference to 'man's work' meant in his case, seeing as he gave him no help whatsoever with the running of the castle, but he was too tired to puzzle it out.

He put his head in his hands, sitting at the head of the table with the debris of the dinner spread before him and sat for a long time weary unto death.

Sophie found Fabrice in the music room. He was lightly fingering the piano, playing snatches of a prélude by Frederick Chopin that Ornella had taught him in Paris. That lady had faded from his thoughts since the enchanting Sophie had entered his life and his urge to love and protect and cherish her had become paramount, whereas before, with Ornella, it had been his carnal desires that had been predominant. Sophie made him feel grown-up, manly and chivalrous, and now, as she entered the room, closing the door behind her, he could see she was in distress and he yearned to help her.

'What is the matter, *ma petite*? I noticed you were *triste* at dinner. May I help you? You must give me the honour to help you.'

She looked at him, her large blue eyes awash with tears, and his heart melted.

'Oh Fabrice, I have been awful. You cannot imagine what I have done.'

'Tell me, my sweet. Here. Sit down before the fire.' He felt full of such protective ardour that he knew that even if she had committed cold-blooded murder he would have defended her with his life. 'Oh my angel, my pet. Do not worry. You will not shock me.' He smiled at her impishly, thinking how adorable she looked in her pale taffeta dress that matched her eyes. She seemed to have difficulty in telling him what was the matter.

'Fabrice ... Fabrice ...'

'Yes. That is my name,' he laughed.

'Yes ... well ... you did say ... you ... you ...' She blushed and seemed intent on tearing her tiny lace handkerchief to bits.

Fabrice knelt before her. Sophie saw the devotion in his eyes and it gave her courage. She took a deep breath.

'Fabrice ... you did say you liked me?'

He threw back his head and laughed. 'I adore you. I worship you. I am madly in love with you.'

An expression of relief flooded Sophie's face. She had not for a moment believed Arabella's proclamation but she had had a moment's misgiving in case she had misread the situation. She clapped her hands together.

'Oh wonderful, wonderful.' she cried and blushed again. 'I have done something you may not like,' she stammered.

'What is it, my adorable one?' His heart went out to her in her distress. 'Please tell me. There is nothing you could say that I would not like except if you told me that you do not care for me at all. Then,' he said dramatically, but she could see he was hiding a deep seriousness beneath his theatricality, 'I would be devastated.'

'No. No, Fabrice. Quite the contrary. You see ... James has made me cross. So cross.' She frowned. 'And I told him I would marry you.' She looked at him hopefully and he smoothed away the crease from her forehead with his finger.

'*Mon amour*. You do me great honour,' he said doubtfully. He looked so serious that she was a little worried. Suppose he could not marry her? Suppose there was some hitch, some reason she could not understand? Her heart beat fast and she gazed at him anxiously.

'My darling, when you look at me so, I want to slay dragons for you, I want to do great deeds of daring for your sake,' he said.

'But all I want is to marry you,' she said simply.

'Ah, but why? Do you love me, *chérie*? Or is it that you want to get your own back on James? Is that how you say it? Is there another reason that I do not know about? It does not seem to me that you would do such a thing — marry for such a reason — but I have to ask. Why did you tell James you would marry me? What was the reason?'

She could not tell him about Fergal. She had already caused enough trouble for the poor little hunchback. She looked at Fabrice, at his handsome face and the kindness and concern in his eyes and she knew she could not tell him about the baby she was expecting. She had her hand on his arm and looked at him with pleading eyes.

'Don't ask me to answer that,' she cried. 'But believe me it has nothing to do with you. It is a family matter.' This, she thought fervently, was true. 'Please trust me,' she said softly. 'I do love you, Fabrice. I could not marry you unless I did.'

As she said it she knew that she did love him, not with the passion she felt for Red, but with a warmth and reality that promised her content.

Fabrice smiled at her. 'Oh my darling, then I dream of nothing more. Nothing else is important. Nothing else matters. Of course we must be married. The sooner the better. I love you so.'

He took her in his arms and kissed her softly on the lips and Sophie thought of the wild wanton kisses and the slim white body of another man. A tremor shook her. Fabrice felt the shiver and held her closer. Neither of them saw the cold, hate-filled face of Bella in the doorway.

Chapter

25

THE next morning it rained. The skies opened and half-drowned the countryside. Going out of doors was rendered impossible. Gale-force winds tossed the trees so that they swayed and danced and their branches creaked in the storm. June seemed vanquished and it appeared that November had returned. The sun was a memory and the weather reflected the household's mood at Usher.

James sent for the Widow. He was nervous of the interview, and this made his manner brusque. His mind was made up and he was almost relieved by Sophie's intervention, for it gave him a perfect excuse to remove from the house this blot on the Jeffries name, this slight on the House of Usher, this humiliating extension of himself, a misshapen crooked Jeffries sibling. Fergal was a constant reproach to his manhood, and the opportunity to get rid of him forever seemed to James heaven-sent.

His bargain with God, a whispered pact made in the far reaches of the night, in the dark recesses of his mind, was to have the child cared for as long as he did not become a threat to the House of Usher. And now he had. Sophie, out of her mind, it seemed, at the moment, suggested he should join the family for all the world to see. It was outrageous! Sitting at table with them, a hunchback, a deformed creature? No. No. It was insupportable. The child must go. He had been to his lawyer and disinherited him in favour of Cormac. If Fergal remained, supposing for a moment he allowed Sophie her way, acknowledgement of him would mean acceptance of him as heir to Usher. Good God, could anyone imagine such a creature as the

Knight of Usher? No. Not in a million years. He had to be discarded, put out of sight and out of mind, securing a firm place for the beloved Cormac. Sophie had given him the perfect opening. But the Widow would be difficult.

She refused to sit. She stood before him cleanching and unclenching her hands, hands that had swollen knuckles and ragged nails. They were broad peasant hands, wide-palmed and short-fingered, but they could, he knew, be sensitive as a young ladies, touching a delicate piece of embroidery, handling a baby or a child. Her eyes were anxious as she looked at him and he felt a sense of guilt and shame and was angry with himself.

'Widow, I want you today to take the child Fergal to Knockharrig over the mountain to the orphanage there and deliver him to the nuns. I have written a letter to the Mother Superior.' He tossed a missive to her across his desk. 'There. Take it. It will explain to her what is to be done. It is all quite legal. She will treat him well. Her convent is financed by our family, so all will be done correctly.' As she opened her mouth to speak he forestalled her, holding up his hand. 'I want no argument, no case from you at all. Just do as I say and do it to-day. I want you, or one of the servants, to come to me here tomorrow and tell me it has been done.'

He did not want to look at her, but in spite of himself his glance was drawn to her face and he never forgot her eyes. They were to come between him and sleep for quite some time. They were ice-cold and malevolent, black as a witch's and full of evil intent. 'My God, she would kill me happily,' he thought and dismissed her.

She picked up the envelope and went to the door in silence. There she turned her head to look at him. Again the malevolent glance.

'You'll regret this, Lord usher. It is a very foolish thing to do.' He opened his mouth to rebuke her for daring to address him so, it was outrageous for a servant to speak to her master thus, but no words came. He trembled with the surge of rage that shook his body but before he could master his thoughts she was gone.

Sophie saw the Widow pass her bedroom door. Arabella had gone downstairs without exchanging the time of day with her but Sophie was too abstracted to care. Normally the atmosphere in their rooms would have caused her acute misery and she would have pleaded with her sister to make it up and be friends again, but her mind was not on her sister. She was barely aware of her existence, behaviour which added fuel to the fire of Arabella's resentment. Her mind was on her own condition and the fact that she was with child.

She was glad she had decided to marry Fabrice. She had liked him from the beginning. He was impossible not to like. More than that, she was very attracted to him and when she was with him she loved him. She had enjoyed his gentle kisses last night, enjoyed his arms about her, and the expression in his brown eyes had thrilled and excited her. Aurora was right. She had no choice but to marry Fabrice. He suited her to perfection. He was charming, a delightful companion, and if it had not been for Red Rafferty she would have thought herself madly in love with him.

Red haunted her dreams, disturbed her sleep. There was nothing romantic about her fevered thoughts of him. Passionate longing for him tormented her and it seemed as if he had left her, not only with child but with a part of himself, a ghost-presence. He was her companion wherever she went and whatever she did. She tried to shake her memories away, to rid herself of them, but it was difficult. Only when she was with Fabrice did she feel better, did she have some peace. He diverted her, set himself out to amuse and beguile her. Then, for a brief time she could forget and laugh again. He had told her over and over that he loved her and she knew he spoke the truth. He was going to ask James for her hand and she hoped they would be married soon.

Yet all the time Fergal's eyes haunted her dreams. Her mind was in turmoil, preoccupied one moment with Red and the next with Fergal and then Fabrice. It was no wonder she had not time for Arabella. She had been sure that she could somehow persuade James to see Fergal her way. James loved her. She was his pet. She had always been able to coax him into doing what she wanted. She had been horrified at his reaction to her request. Horrified and afraid. She had not known how deeply his feelings ran and in revealing the depths of his loathing for his son he had revealed to her the extent of her caring.

She was anxious and worried about Fergal, and about the child within her. She had tried to warn the Widow, but her sister's jealous eyes followed her everywhere. Now Arabella was not around and the Widow was passing her room so Sophie called her in.

The woman came a step inside and Sophie was shocked by her face. It was haggard; pale and angry, yet at the same time bitter.

'Oh Widow, what's to do? It's all my fault. You have only me to blame.'

The Widow put her finger to her lips. She shook her head, then beckoned to Sophie. The latter followed her and they stole up the curving stone stairs to the Widow's room above.

'Close the door, my lady, and sit ye here.' The Widow indicated a stool which Sophie sat on whilst the woman sank onto the white counterpane on her narrow bed. She did not close the door, and they both forgot that it was open.

'Oh Lord, Widow Boann you don't know how I regret what I did. Please forgive me.'

'Yerra, that's not much use now, an' what's to forgive? Ye only acted out of pity in yer heart, *alanna*, an' there's nothin' to be gained now by all that. Recriminations and regrets, recriminations and regrets ... all useless.'

'But what has happened? I implore you to tell me.'

'Yer brother Lord James has commanded me to remove Fergal to the orphanage.'

Sophie let out a cry and jumped to her feet. The Widow rose and pressed her back onto her stool.

'Ach, ragin' and cryin'll not fix anythin',' she said, 'No. We've got to think.' She gazed out of the little window a moment while Sophie twisted the lace handkerchief between her fingers.

Then Sophie had an idea. 'Widow Boann, you'll not take him there? Couldn't we just keep him here? James would never know. He never comes to this wing. He would never find out. How could he?'

The Widow clicked her teeth. 'No. It would be very dangerous. Soon Fergal'll be runnin' and much too big to conceal. You've no idea how worried I've been, knowing how he'll grow, knowing how he must stay unnoticed if he is to survive.'

'But you'll not give him away? I would never rest, Widow, never, if that happened.'

'No. No. I have no intention of that. But he'll have to be kept secret. I'll take him to my sister in the valley an' he'll rest there awhile. But it's a big problem; who's to look after him and love him? He only knows me. He'll be so bewildered. I dunno'. Oh my lady I dunno'.'

Even as she spoke the impossibility of her leaving Fergal became more certain in her mind. Cormac would have an abundance of love. He would never want for attention. In fact if things proceeded as they were, the child was well on the way to spoiling. It was becoming clearer and clearer to her that she could never leave Fergal.

Sophie was speaking. 'Well, take him to your sister then. At least it's a beginning. Then something will come up, I'm sure,' she finished lamely.

'I hope you are right. *Dia's Muire duit*, I hope you are right.' Neither of them heard the light foot-falls outside in the passage-way. Arabella had come up to their bed-chamber and heard the voices, coming, unusually, from the Widow's room. For them to be together, her sister and the Widow Boann, was strange enough, but for them to be in the Widow's room was very strange indeed. She climbed up a few steps towards the top floors of the high tower and waited, listening. She went up as far as she could without casting her shadow, pressing herself against the wall. She could catch some of what was said but not all.

'Widow, there's the priest's hole, remember? I was down there and it was quite adequate to live in, I remember.'

'Yes. Miss Sophie. I know all about you and Red Rafferty ...'

Arabella heard Sophie gasp and she had to press her hands against her heart, for she thought she would faint. Red Rafferty? Who was he? And if he was in some way involved with Sophie, could not Fabrice be jealous? Fabrice wanted a wife. If it was not Sophie it would be her. She had quite made up her mind to have him by hook or by crook. She began to tremble with excitement as she stood silent and alert outside the door.

Within Sophie was becoming more and more enthusiastic as she warmed to the idea. 'The room is not uncomfortable. We could smuggle him there, tonight. Do it up a bit. Make it more liveable in. After all, it was good enough for the priest's so it will be good enough for him.'

Arabella, catching the last bit thought, 'Him? Who is he?'

The Widow shook her head. 'I dunno, m'lady. I dunno. It's dangerous and we don't want to arouse Lord James' wrath. He's angry enough as it is, God knows. At any rate, we'll see.'

'It's only for a day or two while we think of something else,' Sophie said.

The Widow dropped her voice to a whisper so that Arabella had to strain every muscle to hear her. 'I'll act tonight at any rate. Tonight. It's the deadline. He wants it all over be morning, an' Master Creagh is havin' a meeting there tonight. We best be very careful. Very careful indeed. Lord James will kill us else. Now go downstairs, m'lady, or Lord James will become suspicious and we don't want him to know anything about this, do we?'

Arabella fled down the stairs in her embroidered yellow slippers. She hurried into their bed-chamber and sat at her mirror and looked at her flushed face. She heard Sophie coming down the steps. Then suddenly making up her mind, for she wanted to compose herself before she had conversation with her sister, she quickly slipped out of the room, waving to Sophie as she passed, then hurried to the drawing-room and rang for tea.

She picked up the marmalade cat, Sian, and sitting on the window-seat, settled it on her knee. She liked the cat and the cat liked her. She stroked its soft fur and it purred under its breath. She sat and looked out at the soggy valley below. She could not see far and the mountains were veiled as mists slipped across the green faces of the high hills.

The words she had overheard buzzed in her head, exciting her. Why were the Widow Boann and her sister talking of the priest's hole? Who was Red Rafferty? If it was political and Creagh was involved, then she could make a great deal of trouble for them both. She smiled in satisfaction, and smoothed her skirt of cream brocade embroidered with little yellow flowers. She picked at the threads and when the door opened she jumped.

It was Clarie with the tea.

'Put it down there, Clarie,' she said, and waited whilst the maid poured her a cup from the silver samovar and brought it over to Arabella with a tiny linen napkin. She brought a cake-stand and stood it beside Arabella where she sat in the window. The cake-stand had four silver-plated tiers. The bottom one held bread and butter, the next had small cucumber sandwiches. Next up was a plate of fruit cake and last a group of tiny frosted angel cakes, each a light and melting mouthful.

But Arabella was not interested in cakes. She was full of

168

excited questions that she did not have an answer for. She was wondering how best to use her incomplete knowledge to her advantage, which she felt she could do. If she could align herself with James there was no knowing what she could accomplish. It might really be very easy.

She sipped her tea, stroked the marmalade cat, nibbled one of the tiny cakes and thought how she hated Creagh. If he had not interfered last night she might very well have won that round. Damn him. What had the Widow Boann said about him? If she was clever enough, she could trap them all and get Fabrice for herself.

As she ate she saw Creagh on the gravel below her. Then she saw a stranger crossing under the arbour and running up the steps of the garden until he was on a level with her brother. Both the men were drenched. Creagh was well-protected against the rain, but the stranger was not. Creagh wore gumboots and oilskins, like a peasant, a fisherman, Arabella thought disgusted. The stranger was in a light riding habit and he wore neat ankle boots. The leather, Arabella could see from where she sat, was discoloured with the rain and his trouser ends splashed with mud. His face was tanned — he was obviously from a different climate. She opened the window.

She leaned out, impervious to the rain. The men huddled beneath the overhang of the window-ledge and Arabella could just hear their voices before the wind tore the words away. At least they spoke in English. She surmised that the stranger did not understand Gaelic.

'Listen, Hank ... meeting ... tonight ... priest's hole ...' Those were the words she heard. The rain drenched her face and saturated her hair, but she was too intent to notice. He whole body was tensed in breathless concentration on what she could hear below.

'Village ... time, old buddy ...' The stranger's voice had a resonance that rendered whispering impossible.

'... night,' she heard. 'The Fenians ... be there. All of us ... in your honour.' The last words spoken by Creagh had a clarity so unexpected that she withdrew her head abruptly. The wind had died down and she could not almost hear the men breathing. The rain was sighing to a whisper, punctuated by a harder splash here and there. The leaves on the trees looked silver in the mist.

Arabella closed the window and left the room. In the hall she met Clarie and told the maid to clear up, she had finished her tea. She heard the sound of the piano tinkling, a lovely wistful melody echoing from the direction of the music room. She could also hear the voice of Fabrice and Dolly laughing as Sophie said something. Arabella shivered. Sometimes she was frightened by the magnitude of her own feelings. It seemed to her now that everyone was against her. There was absolutely no one on her side.

She hurried to her room and rang the bell. Molly came in soon after. Arabella wished she did not need Molly, but she was incapable of grooming herself and after her wetting she had no choice but to seek Molly's help.

The maid infuriated her with questions and admonitions. 'Where have you *been*, Miss Bella? You must be out of your mind to go abroad in weather like this. What would Lord James say?'

'Oh, be silent, Molly. All I did was put my head out of the window to see what kind of weather it was outside.'

Molly tutted and added innocently, 'Sure, any eejit could see it was raining, m'lady, unless you were blind as a belfry bat. You couldn't miss it — the rain, I mean. Sure, what made ye do it at all?'

'I said be quiet, Molly. If I'm as blind as a bat then you're as deaf as the post on my bed.'

Molly towelled her hair dry and Arabella pulled off her cream and yellow dress, for the rain had soaked the bodice. She went to her dressing-room and rifled through the gowns there.

'I might as well dress for dinner now,' she said, pulling a coffee-coloured satin dress trimmed with écru lace out of the closet and marching back into the bedroom.

'But m'lady, it's only six of the clock.' As she spoke the Angelus bells sounded from the chapel. 'Listen. It's the Angelus, m'lady. Sure it's a mite soon for the dressing.'

'For heaven's sake, Molly, hold your whist or I'll knock your head on the wall. You are doing it to aggravate me.'

Molly stared at her innocently. 'Doing what, m'lady?'

'Shut up and help me,' Arabella almost shrieked. 'Help me on with my dress and do my hair and be silent while you work. I will not tell you again.'

Molly blinked the tears from her eyes. She loathed Arabella,

170

hated looking after her and would have refused to do so if she could. Arabella was always so beastly to her. She would simply have persuaded Cronin, the groom's son, to run away with her had it not been for m'lady Sophie. She was passionately devoted to Sophie and rejoiced in her heart to see the French gentleman and Miss Sophie fall in love. But she kept a close eye on Arabella's activities, for she put nothing past her and feared for Sophie and Fabrice and the turn Arabella's resentment might take. Molly knew the girl was capable of harming one or the other of them with wanton cruelty.

She was perplexed about the dampness of Arabella's clothing and resolved to go at once to the Widow and confide her fears to her. Meanwhile she obeyed Miss Bella's orders and dressed and coiffeured her in total silence.

Arabella went straight to James when her toilet was complete. He was, as usual, in his study. A fire glowed in the grate and a log fell as Arabella entered the room, looking, James thought, remarkably pretty. She was smiling sweetly at him and James was relieved that she had obviously not come in to scream at him and harangue him about Fabrice. He felt quite sorry for Bella, but the boy was obviously besotted with Sophie. What Arabella imagined he could do about it he was at a loss to understand.

He smiled at her now and indicated the chair on the other side of the fireplace.

'Good-evening, sister. You seem in a better mood this day.'

'Yes, James. Thank you.' She settled herself in the chair, arranging her skirts. Her cheeks were flushed to a becoming rose and her eyes sparkled. She wrinkled her delicate nose at the smell of James' pipe, and fluttered her fan in front of her face in mute protest. James smiled. He sucked on his meerschaum with relish. This was his study, his territory, and he had no intention of laying it aside in deference to Bella's wishes. If she objected, then she could ask him to see her in the drawing-room or the music room or any of the boudoirs where smoking was not acceptable. If she was intent on seeing him here, she must do it on his terms. Still, he resolved to say nothing, for she seemed in a sweet temper and he was weary of storms.

'So. What brings you here?' he asked her.

'Well, James. I have learned some things ...'

A foretaste of trouble stirred within him and he said lightly,

171

'Well perhaps you should keep them to yourself, Arabella.'

'No, James, these are things you ought to know.'

James sighed. It had been too much to expect Bella to have changed her spots.

'Could this not wait until tomorrow? I am weary, Arabella. I have had a lot on my mind recently and I am not disposed to listen to complaints or gossip.'

Arabella's lips tightened. 'Oh, I think you will want to hear this. It concerns the safety of our home.'

James looked up, surprised. Arabella paused, choosing her words carefully, for she was not exactly sure what information she was imparting to her brother. She guessed that what Creagh was doing was against the law, but she was not sure how far her brothers would go to defend each other. She knew that James would, of a surety, be angry with his brother, but she guessed that he would protect him, and that would not suit her at all.

'James, listen to me. I will be frank with you.' As he started to protest she said firmly, 'The truth of the matter is ... Sophie and the Widow are in some kind of plot, James, and I thought you ought to know.'

'A plot? What kind of plot? Have you been reading novels again Bella?'

He thought of the child upstairs and the ultimatum he had given, and surmised that Bella had heard some remarks made about it by the Widow and Sophie. He felt a rush of temper at the thought that the two women were discussing it in spite of his orders, but he put that aside for the moment.

'I have not been reading, James. Do not mock me. I heard some things.'

James was angry now. 'What things? Tell me at once, though you know I despise listeners and tittle-tattlers, miss.'

Arabella's mouth turned down petulantly and she tapped her foot on the carpet impatiently.

'It's no use your getting in a pet with me, James. If you do, I'll tell you nothing, and then you'll be sorry tomorrow, for the rally is tonight.' She could have bitten off her tongue for she had said more than she had meant to. His face was startled and though she was gratified by his look of stark astonishment she felt a tiny quiver of panic that she had gone too far.

'What do you speak of? What rally?

'The one in your own house, James. The one in the priest's hole.'

172

James' face had lost its ruddy colour. He looked at her sharply and she squirmed beneath his gaze. But she did not let him see her discomfiture.

'Did it ever occur to you that the Widow might be a rebel? It makes sense, does it not? She is forever gossiping in Gaelic. She brought Creagh up a peasant and an Irish-lover. Much loyalty he has to Queen and Country, James.'

'Is Creagh involved in this?' James asked.

Bella shook her head. 'Oh no. No. Just the servants. Though Sophie knows about it. The Widow spoke of it tonight to her. They said there would be a rally tonight in the cellars. Just think, James. Our house will be dishonoured. You will be held responsible if it is found out. It is, you know, a criminal offence.'

James shuddered. He knew what she said was true. Arabella continued, 'Yes. You could even hang. Oh James, our name will be spat on. Everything will be taken from us. They will confiscate our home and our lands and then what will we do? I *had* to tell you. You must see that. Even if I am wrong in what I heard we cannot take the risk.'

James said sarcastically, for her motives were clear to him, 'I did not know you cared for the family honour so much, Arabella.'

She looked at him with guileless eyes and he was suddenly afraid of her. Then he pushed the thought away as silly. She was his little sister. A mean one sometimes, self-willed and spoiled, but only a girl after all.

'Very well, Arabella. I'll see what is to be done.'

'Send for the soldiers at the Curragh. Exonerate yourself by showing your loyalty to the Crown. After all, if the Widow is guilty she should be punished. And we don't know if they have been watching us, do we James? Do we?'

He hated to admit that she was right, but he knew she was. He wondered briefly if the Widow had done it to get her own back on him, then decided the thought was unworthy. He realized with irritation that after a meeting with Arabella he inevitably went around suspecting people, doubting them. She spread her poison. But this was different. Treason. That was serious.

'You may go now, Arabella'.

'But James, Sophie's part in this cannot go unpunished. She ...'

'I will take care of all that, Arabella. I bid you leave me now. I must think. Time is short. Please go.'

He watched her rise and leave. A vixen he thought disgustedly. He pondered what she had said. She was right, he knew. He must send for the soldiers, have the rebels arrested and thereby protect his family's name. It was his duty, it was where his allegiance lay, but he was loathe to do it. He hated interference. But what if the soldiers were watching them, the castle? He could never explain away his ignorance, and ignorant or no, he would be held responsible. The British Government dealt swiftly with traitors. He remembered the many times his father had had to take such a stance in foreign lands and how bitterly they had been hated by the natives of those lands for doing their honourable duty. It was one of the reasons he had not followed in his father's footsteps. He had not counted Ireland in the same category as the eastern lands. After all, the Irish, except for a few fanatics, were a loveable, gentle people. They were quite happy for the British to take the responsibility of running their country off their shoulders. They were not equipped to run it, anyhow. Everyone knew that. Besides, they spoke the same language. Everyone knew that too.

It seemed now that there was no choice but to interfere. There was one thing, though. He could face the Widow Boann with the charge. It would give her a chance to call the whole thing off. It would give her a chance too, to deny or refute the accusation. It would give her a chance, if she were guilty, to warn her fellow rebels and avert the debacle that would ensue from their arrest. It was possible, too, that Arabella mis-heard and the conversation referred to concerned Fergal. In that case the Widow would be drawn back to the task in hand and would realize that she could not hide the child in the priest's hole now that he knew of it. So she would perforce have to obey his orders.

But the Widow Boann could not be found. Dominic said she might have gone to her sister in the Valley. James was suddenly certain that Arabella's accusation were true. She had not the wit to make up something like that and 'rally' was not a word in her vocabulary. He knew too that he must send for the soldiers. He stood to lose too much if he did not.

He rang for his groom, and wrote a letter to the commander of the battalion at Bray, not far from Usher Castle. When

Dominic appeared he told him to saddle the roan, gave him the letter and the address and told him to deliver it with all speed. Less than an hour after James' conversation with Arabella, Dominic, armed with the missive was on his way through the driving rain.

James was satisfied. He had done his duty. What he did not know was that Dominic had sent a desperate warning to call the meeting off. But it was too late. Stephens' precautions for secrecy proved sadly successful in this case and the message was never delivered.

Chapter

26

DINNER that night was a tense affair. Dolly was still abed, feeling indisposed, but Old Gentleman and Angela were there, along with a lively Creagh, an excited Arabella and a curiously silent Sophie and Fabrice. James wished himself back in the time before the turbulence had invaded his home.

Angela was chattering about Singapore. He knew she was mixing it up with Burma, yet he did not set her right. He found her recollections curiously reassuring tonight. The Old Gentleman was sucking his teeth outrageously and glancing at Fabrice de Beauvillande across the table from him. He was hoping to aggravate the Frenchman into showing distaste for his noisy bad manners, a last satisfaction of old age. James was amused to see that he did not succeed. His uncle liked nothing better than to disconcert others. Evil old devil, James thought, but, here too, he found comfort in the predictable behaviour of his Uncle. He was imbibing heavily as was his wont and his head for the wine was not as strong as it use to be.

James looked at Sophie and Fabrice, who were smiling at each other across the table. The young Frenchman had tried to see him twice today but he had been busy with other matters. He would find out his intentions, which were pretty obvious, and settle the matter once and for all. He was quite fed up with the ridiculous triangular situation at Usher and resolved to sort it all out next day. The sooner Sophie was married, the sooner Arabella would get over her obsession. What a gloriously handsome couple they would make, James thought. Fabrice and Sophie were a delightful pair, and, he felt, would be very happy.

He looked at Creagh. The boy was growing up. He would

have to speak to him too, encourage him to take a bigger share of the running of the castle. He would, tactfully, have to discourage him from racketing around the countryside, leading a thoroughly disreputable life. You had only to think of that affair with the gypsy. Well, he had been lucky that time, but think of the situation with a more mercenary female. Creagh spoke the language and knew the peasants, the workers, the artisans hereabout. He could be of immense help to James with his knowledge of these people. If Creagh were at his side there would be no rebel meetings under his roof. James was suddenly furious. How dare they? he thought. What right had they to put him in this position? Creagh could have helped him so much today, but there he was, head thrown back, laughing at something Arabella said. Another oddity. Why was Arabella so friendly to her brother? He remembered her the other day, the venom in her voice, 'You'll pay for this Creagh ...' Well, he could not worry about that now, he had more important things to occupy his mind. He stood up.

'We'll have coffee in the blue drawing-room,' he said to Maitland. Then to Peadar, Dominic's second son, 'Has your father returned?'

'Yes, my lord.'

'Tell him I'll speak to him later.'

'Yes, my lord.'

Creagh turned in the hall as they went, two by two, into the drawing-room. He detached himself from his sister's side and James thought, how odd, and caught a malicious gleam in Arabella's eye as Creagh removed the arm so confidingly in his.

'Will you excuse me, brother, ladies, Fabrice?' Old Gentleman and the Dowager were too far behind to hear. 'I cannot join you.' He winked at James. 'An assignation that won't wait,' he said and James laughed while Sophie blushed and said, 'Oh, Creagh.'

'Yes,' James said, suddenly remembering his role of protector. 'Creagh, remember there are ladies present.'

Arabella, he noticed, had suddenly lost all colour, and again he was puzzled, for she did not usually show such delicacy.

But he was tired of puzzling, tired of trying to work out people's motives. It was not in his personality to be subtle or intuitive. He was a straightforward man, uncomplicated and he loathed all this involvement in plots and schemes. He longed for this evening to be over so that he could go upstairs to his rooms with Dolly. They would sit, the three of them, in perfect peace. Often he begged Dolly to unwrap Cormac's swaddling clothes so that he could gaze at the perfect little body, the tiny feet and hands of his heir. The sight filled him with pride and a curious humility. At such times he prayed, bargaining with God for the safety of this baby.

However, he knew his duty. He must remain here. He must make polite conversation with his mother and uncle, his sisters and the Frenchman, until the soldiers came. He sighed and wished life was not so complicated.

Chapter

27

THE Widow Boann made her arrangements early that day. She had no desire to find her charge taken from her and delivered by another. She wanted to find a way to protect Fergal as completely as possible. Was there anyone she could trust? She doubted it, but money was a powerful incentive and in her small room she thought about the pile of coins she had amassed over the years. It was a small pittance to be sure, her total earnings for a lifetime of devotion, about fifty pounds in all. Still, it was something, and Molly Broderick had been mooning about over Cronin Dominic, Matt Dominic's, son like a sick cow. The eyes on her popped out of her head every time she passed him and you could almost hear the starch of her apron creaking with the accelerated beating of her heart when he sat beside her, accidentally on purpose, in the kitchen. The Widow saw the way they looked at each other, the love-sick expression in their eyes, and she could almost swear that they had been experimenting with each other in a sexual way. There was something hot and feverish and knowledgeable in their glances. You could almost feel the erotic currents that passed between them. Well now, she thought, Lord James might give them permission to be wed, if they were lucky. But then again he might not. It was his prerogative. The Dominics and the Brodericks had been in service at Usher for a long time, since Bessie Broderick and Matt Dominic were youngsters. Fifty pounds would help if, as the Widow had heard, the couple hoped to abscond to America. Molly was a pretty wee colleen and she would make Cronin a good wife, though there was no way it could be done for they had not a brass farthing to rub between them.

179

She took down a draw-string bag. It was made of patchwork, the colours faded from lack of use, for when had she ever needed it before? She kept it between two sheets of tissue paper and now she laid it on her bed. In it she put a change of undergarments, a flannel nightgown and cap. In a napkin she had put some bannock cakes, some raisins and dried apricots and a tinder box. She tied up the napkin and put the bundle on top of the other things. Tenderly she took her rosary-beads, and carefully she took down the statue of the Virgin Mary and covered it with her other shawl, which she was taking in case she needed it against the bitter wind that blew these times.

She would never come back here. A tear came onto her eyes and she angrily wiped it away. This was no time for tears. She would not be able to bid farewell to Creagh, and the thought of leaving him fair broke her heart. She recalled holding him in her arms that first time and how her heart had near burst within her. She thought of love that had bloomed suddenly and unexpectedly in her cold heart. She had been amazed and warmed by the reciprocal love the child lavished on her. Now she would be leaving him without even saying goodbye. She thought of their talks together in Gaelic and of the lessons he had learned from her, the stories and tales and how he hung on her every word, standing at her knee, his head resting in the crook of her arm. Ah, those had been wondrous times and now she would never see her lamb again.

For she could never come back here, never see little Cormac either. However, that baby would survive very nicely without her. She loved the bonny little fellow, Creagh's son, but she had not had him long and her clear duty was to the helpless one.

She looked at her coins and took out forty-five. She took up her patchwork bag, glanced around the little room she had been so happy in, then bade it a silent farewell. She drew her shawl around her and went upstairs to her charges.

As she had hoped, Molly was there with Cormac. She was the only other servant allowed up here, besides herself, and that only since Cormac's arrival. It had created a bond between them. The girl had endeared herself to the Widow, for she showed no distaste for the hunchback. All she said was, 'Ah the creature. Isn't it sad for him anyhow, an' isn't it the sweetest smile he's got?' The girl held Cormac in her arms, rocking him gently and crooning to him. In his play-pen in the corner Fergal turned the pages of a book. It was an old one of Creagh's, Irish Fairy Tales, with illustrations, and the child turned the pages delicately, staring at the pictures with rapt attention.

The Widow beckoned the girl to the door. She did not know how much Fergal understood. He was a bright little boy, and she did not want to risk him hearing what she would not have him know. Molly placed the sleeping babe tenderly in his crib and tiptoed across to where the Widow stood in the doorway.

'What is it, missus?' she asked in a whisper.

'Listen, Molly, can you hold your tongue?'

The girl looked perplexed. 'Why, missus? Yes. You know I can. But not if it's wrong. Not ...' She finished lamely, her wide brown eyes looking fearfully around the room as if she expected evil spirits to leap out of the dark corners.

'Listen, Molly. It's nothin' wrong. What do ye take me for? No. There's money in it fer you if you do as I say.'

She regretted her words immediately, for the girl sidled round the Widow to the doorway, obviously trying to escape, unwilling to be embroiled in what she perceived as some sort of mischief.

'Oh Bessie Broderick, you've brought them up well,' the Widow said quietly to herself whilst Molly jabbered, 'I'm a good girl, I am, missus an' I'm not doin' anythin' that would oblige me to go runnin' to the priest in confession.'

The Widow blocked her way. She knew intuitively that Molly suspected some kind of danger for Fergal, for her eyes had flashed a panic-stricken glance in his direction. She decided to be frank with the girl.

'Listen a tic, Molly,' she said soothingly. 'Lord James, bless him, is a good man, the best.' Molly nodded piously in agreement. 'Well, as you know — who doesn't in this house? — as you know he has a blind spot about Fergal.'

The girl's body tensed and she would have escaped down the corridor if she could have got past the Widow's stout frame. The Widow put her hands on the girl's shoulders.

'Well, today he ordered me to take the poor little fellow to the orphanage over the mountains in Knockharrig where the nuns are.'

The girl cried out. It was a cry of real pity. 'Ah no. Ah no. Yerra, what a thing to do to the poor little mite an' he not guilty of any crime, Sure, how can he help the way he was born?'

'Isn't that what I'm thinkin' myself? So what I'm goin' to do is this.' She prayed as she spoke that the girl would not give her away, for if she did, all would be lost. She hoped that she had judged her aright and she could be trusted. 'I'm going to *pretend* to take the scrap to Knockharrig. I'm leaving Usher forever. I want to get the carriage out and for it to make the journey to Knockharrig *without* me and pretend to leave the child there. Everyone, especially Lord James, must think I have gone with the baby. Someone has to come back to the Master and say the job's been done and Fergal delivered. I cannot do it, for I'll be with the child in hiding somewhere else. It's best no one knows where, not even you, though I trust you, Molly. It can be said I left full of grief for my loss, for it is well known how I love the wee lad. Anyhow, my plan is this. Get your young swain Cronin Dominic to bring the carriage.' The girl blushed scarlet and would have protested, but the Widow put her fingers to the girl's lips. 'Yerra, don't bother to argue. Sure, haven't I seen you together an' don't I know what's obvious under my own nose? Now there's forty-five guineas if you get him to drive you there, a bundle in your arms. A large bundle, mind. Use one of Miss Arabella's dolls. You must go all the way. Someone might see and report. An' come back and tell Lord James exactly this. "The child is safely delivered at Knockharrig."' Understand?'

She looked at the girl, wondering if she was being rash to trust her, wondering what on earth she would do if the girl betrayed her.

Molly looked back at the Widow. 'Listen,' she said, 'I don't want yer money fer doin' this fer ye. Indeed'n I don't. Keep yer money I wouldn't have a hair on his head harmed. I've heard about that orphanage. Kept in cells, they are. Given no chance at all. Considered insane if there is anything wrong with their little bodies, so they are. An' with him, all crookedly, sure he'd wind up dead of a broken heart before the year was out. No, you can count on me, Widow, an' I'll not ask fer payment.'

Tears clouded the Widow's eyes. She gave the surprised girl a warm hug. 'Ye'll have the money nonetheless. Ye'll need it, you an' Cronin. I'd like te see you happy, so I do.'

'Well, if ye insist. I'll do it, an' be glad to. I'm grateful for the money an' it's going to make the world of difference to me an' Cronin. But I'd do it anyway. He's a sunny little fellow an' as bright as a button. I've grown fond of him over the last weeks, an' sure, isn't he one of God's creatures no matter if he's astray in his body?'

The Widow heaved a sigh of relief. Molly asked, 'How long will it take to get to Knockharrig an' back?'

'Why, let me see. It's an hour's drive. It will take a half-hour, I suppose, for you to deal with the nuns, an' then another hour back. Two and a half hours, Molly, why?'

'Well, I have to be back to dress my ladies for dinner or there'd be too much attention paid. But if that's the time it takes, sure I have plenty.'

The Widow was galvanized into sudden activity. She thrust the money into the girl's hand and told her to get Cronin to harness the horses and bring the coach to the back entrance as soon as possible.

A little later Molly could be seen leaving with a bundle in her arms. The bundle was large and wrapped in a shawl. It was raining heavily and Cronin helped the maid into the carriage. The Widow could be seen, standing in the downpour, weeping, apparently distraught. Cronin cracked the whip and clicked at the horses and the carriage swayed into the mist and around the curve of the drive until it was lost to view behind the tossing oak trees. From his window James watched it vanish out of sight, his heart full of guilt and relief.

The Widow, meantime, with Fergal in her arms and her patchwork bag over her wrist, sped quietly down the stone stairway to the girls' room. She stood silently, afraid to breath, holding Fergal's face close to her breast in case he called out or cried. She had made him promise not to make a sound. He was a bright little lad but he had never been out of the high tower before, so she was not sure how he would react. In the event he was as good as gold, keeping his promise, his small arms wound around her neck.

There was no sound of Sophie or Arabella, so she slid, silent as a shadow, down the remaining steps to the cellars below. Past the wine cellars, the saddle and carpentry rooms, the larders, the store rooms which led to the scullery adjoining the kitchen. She could hear her sister in the distance. Bessie Broderick was, as usual, scolding one of her daughters. Well, it would not be Molly who was getting the back of her tongue this day.

She looked to her right and there was the oyster sign. The priest's hole was there. The corridor led to where Mass was said in troubled times. When you reached the large cave-like room where the priest had performed the ceremony, there was a trapdoor exactly under where she hoped to shelter Fergal for a while. If the place was raided the priest must escape, for he had not only to protect his life, but also the sacred host and the wine. In this small room he could hide out, until the soldiers went away frustrated. Even so, in case of watchers, spies even, the priest had often to remain in the little room for days, weeks and in the case of one unfortunate man, months, whilst he hid from a zealous Cromwellian officer.

When the Widow saw the room she was more than content. It was comfortably appointed; a bed, a carpet, a ewer and basin in fine porcelain. There was a crucifix on the wall and the room had been used recently. Creagh probably slept here sometimes, she thought, and worried again about his foolishness using his own home for his meetings. She sighed, realizing that she was responsible for the way he felt about this country.

Well, at least it was warm and dry, protected from the elements. She settled Fergal on the bed. He gazed around the room, saying nothing, then looked at her solemnly, trustingly.

'Listen, *alanna*. You must stay here, quiet as a little mouse. Nana's got to leave you.' His face crumpled a little and his wide blue eyes filled with apprehension. 'No, no. Don't fret, my love. Nana will be back soon. Take these.' She took the bannock cakes out of her bag and left them with the raisins and an apple on the little table beside the bed. She lit the torch with the taper she carried. The lamp burned warmly in the gloom. It was never day or night here, she thought.

The child looked up at her from the bed. 'Don't leave me, Nana. Don't. I'm frightened.'

'Yerra, don't fret yourself now. Nana must go. Listen, *astore*, I have a plan. You and I are going away together. We'll have a home ...'

She knew the child did not understand. It was outside his experience. He knew no one but her and nowhere but their rooms in the high tower. Of course he knew Molly now, and he had seen Sophie and Aurora Vestrey, but she was his world, his life.

'I'll be back,' she said.

'Promise, Nana.'

'I promise. Now you must be good. You must be very quiet and Nana will come soon.'

She kissed him and left him there, small, alone, and afraid.

28

THE Widow Boann hurried to the cottage in the valley as quickly as she could. She felt as though a hundred eyes were watching her, for anyone in the castle could see her despite the driving rain. It did not matter, though, for if Molly Broderick did as she was told all would be well.

She was wet to the skin when she reached her sister's cottage, her clothes soaked, even the spare shawl in her patchwork bag was saturated and useless. However, Craw Kilty undressed her before the fire and wrapped her in a blanket while she boiled pots and kettles filled with water and poured their contents into the tin hip-bath held against such an emergency. The hip-bath was not used that often for cleanliness; it was more generally used for mustard dips and camphor steam washes for colds, or when a body was soaked in a storm.

Ronan lay asleep on his pallet. He was like a dead thing, lying there, his face as white as snow, his eyes blue-lidded, his lips parted and no sign of breath at all. The Widow thought he looked like one of the beautiful pieces of sculpture in Usher.

Craw Kilty nodded at him. 'He's out cold as a fish that's been caught. He had a great fit last night. A falling-down and such warnings of happenings I'm that eager to tell ye. 'Twill amaze ye.'

'An' wait till ye hear what I have to tell ye, sister, for ye won't believe your ears this day.'

She was excited now, greatly relieved, in fact. She could unburden herself to her sister and get rid of the hundred anxious thoughts whirling round and round in her brain. She knew that speaking of them would clarify them and she could judge whether she had acted sensibly or no. But her sister gave her no chance to speak. Hustling between the range and the hip-bath, her face flushed in the steam from the pots and kettles, she spoke non-stop and her words threw the Widow off her balance and amazed her as she sat listening, the blanket clutched around her.

'He got into great distress, he did, cryin' he was, and moanin' something shockin'. I've never seen the like. Never in all my born days. At any rate, in you go.' She did not pause in her narative but pulled the blanket from her sister and shoved her towards the steaming bath. 'In ye go. Ah, that's better, isn't it? Well, on and on he went about danger at the castle tonight. "Danger," he kept sayin', "Danger" an' "Mistress Arabella" and he shivering like you are now, *dip* yoursel' right down in the water if ye want the benefit, go *on*, I know it's hot, it's boilin', but te do ye good ye have to *immerse* yourself entirely. Where was I? Yes. "Danger from Miss Arabella" he cried an' him foamin' at the mouth an the second sight on him an' me worried outa me mind about him, for if ye saw the state he was in so would ye. I thought he'd like to die.'

She ran the back of her hand across her nose, for it and her eyes had moistened, though whether from the steam of the bath or emotion the Widow could not tell.

'He said Creagh was in danger an' the cause of that danger was my lady Bella. That was what came outa the rigmorale, for 'twasnt easy to follow and I cannot give it to you *verbatim*. But Creagh is in some kind of danger, or will be this night. An' the fit died down then and came back again shakin' him like a sapling in a storm and he cried out about the humpyback, an' anger again. "Escape," he kept calling, "or death will come. Escape or death." An' then the life went outa him an' he fell on the floor like a dead man an' I dragged him to the pallet there an' covered him with the counterpane an' he's lain there like that, just as you see him, as iffen he was a made of marble, an' never moved once.'

She banged the kettle down abruptly on the range and sat suddenly in her rocking chair. A sob caught in her throat.

'An' sister, you'll never know how glad I am to see ye. Right joyful I am, for I was at my wit's ends to know what to do, an' the relief I felt when I saw ye staggerin' down the path swept over me like a wave.' She wiped her nose with the back of her hand again and looked at her sister.

'Jasus, Mary an' Joseph, sister, what is it? What in the name o' God is the matter?' The Widow was struggling out of the hip-bath, her plump body red as a plucked turkey. 'Will ye get back in the water, for mercy's sake or are ye out of yer mind this day?'

'No. No.' The Widow moaned. 'Don't ye see? The message is for me. Oh Lord. The things that have happened beyond in the castle, an' now you've told me what Ronan said, sure I see a lot more clearly now.'

She saw in her mind's eye Arabella's cold eyes, she saw the priest's cell, obviously used in the recent past. How could she have been such a fool? She saw too, little Fergal, his trusting blue gaze as she told him to wait and promised him that she would be back.

She started to pull on her damp clothes but her sister snatched them from her. 'No. Here, take this. It's me last garment to spare, an' I'm givin' them away right, left and centre. Dry yersel' first an' put them on an' welcome.'

She gave the Widow a black alpaca dress, one she wore for funerals, wakes and Fair days and other important occasions. The Widow Boann put it on and fastened the bodice. It was a trifle tight but that could not be helped. She stuffed her wet clothes into her patchwork bag and pulled on her soggy boots. Craw Kilty owned none, she did not need the likes of boots. The Widow wrapped herself gratefully in the woollen shawl that was warm from her sister's body. She was ready to go without a plan in her head when the sisters both heard the beat of hooves thudding steadily nearer and nearer. They froze where they stood, looking wide-eyed at each other. They waited for the hoofbeats to thunder past the cottage, but they came closer and closer and eventually stopped outside their door.

Craw Kilty motioned her sister behind the door. The Widow crouched in the shadows, her heart thumping. When Craw Kilty heard the banging of the riding-crop on the door she opened the top half so abruptly that the rider found his hand before him suspended in mid-air. Craw Kilty gave a crow of relief.

'Dia's Muire duit, sure it's only Fogey Mulcahy himself. Tar istigh. Tá athas orm thú a fheiceáil. (Come inside. I'm glad to see you.) An' what brings you out on a night like this?'

'The Soldiers are comin', the soldiers are comin', the soldiers are comin' to the castle,' the boy cried breathlessly, near to tears, shivering with excitement at the importance of his message.

Craw Kilty saw her sister about to rush out of the door, the boy about the collapse on them and the Minstrel stirring to awaken.

'Hold on now, the lot of ye,' she cried in a strong voice. 'Stop runnin' around like headless chickens and sit yersel'n down for a second whilst we work this out. Now.' She was about to pour a cup of the black tea brewing in the pot on the hearth when she changed her mind. She went to the cupboard and drew out a glass bottle half-full of transparent liquid. 'I think a little poteen is called for. Widow, get the mugs and give each of us one.'

The Widow said, 'But ...' and pointed to the door.

'No. Wait, I said, and wait I meant.' Craw Kilty sid firmly, 'Sit yerself down there. *Ná bí buartha.* (Don't worry.)' she measured out a smart three inches of the drink in each person's mug and one for herself and they drank it down in one gulp.

'Ronan, you too.' She said and the Minstrel rose, naked as Apollo and as beautiful, his hair tousled and his eyes clouded from sleep. But he looked refreshed, the life had returned to his face and he pulled on his pants in a leisurely fashion and joined them around the table.

'It's obvious someone has informed on Master Creagh.' Crew Kilty spat. 'Ah the divil! Who was it, I wonder? Bad cess to them. An' we'll find out who it was an' then the Blessed Virgin help them. But whist ... first, what to do? You know the house, sister. What to do?'

'The Master sent for the soldiers after he talked to Lady Arabella,' Fogey interrupted and the two women looked at each other with dawning understanding. 'He sent Matt Dominic off in a hurry. "Hurry up," he kept sayin', "I've just been told." Well. The only other person he saw privately was you, Widow. And the Lady Arabella after you. That's what they say at the Castle. So it has to be Lady Bella, bad cess to her.'

The Widow looked grim. 'That will have to keep. I'll get back to it, never fear. I'll deal with it later. But we've more important things to think of now. The situation's urgent. Fergal is below in the priest's cell all on his own an' I'm promised to return to get him. Lord James wants to send him to the orphanage.'

'Jasus, Mary an Joseph,' Fogey spluttered. 'I've heard the lot this day.'

'An' you'll keep it to yourself, do ye hear? on the pain of death.' Craw Kilty had him by the ear and as she spoke she gave it vicious twists.

Fogey screamed at her, 'Well o' course. Why do ye think they trusted me te come here an' tell ye iffen I couldn't be trusted? Yerra, let me ear alone, ye ould witch, or ye'll have it off.'

'Who sent ye? Beggin' yer pardon.' Craw Kilty let his ear go and began then to rub it better, which proved to be equally painful for Fogey. He pulled as far away from her as he could.

''Twas Matt Dominic, sent by Lord Usher for the soldiers as sent me here. First chance he got. He told me te hurry. They won't be long. But Lord Usher is . . .'

'Nothin' you know, boyo.' The Widow was not going to listen to a tirade about her master.

'What's to do? Oh what's to do?' Craw Kilty agitated, then answered herself, 'I'll tell you. Ronan'll go to the castle an' warn them. He's like a shadow, an' he's charmed anyhow. Divil a thing can harm him. He has God and the Devil's protection. He knows the way well an' he often goes up there with Master Creagh.'

'I'm going with him an' nothin'll hold me back. I've got to get wee Fergal or he'll be out of his mind with fear.' The Widow still sounded more upset than Craw Kilty had ever heard her. She saw there was no gainsaying her; her mind was quite made up and there was no time for argument. She shrugged and accepted the inevitable.

'You'll do what ye have to do,' she said to her sister. 'Well then, off ye go.'

'But where'll we take them? This'll be the first place they'll look. You know that.'

'Ronan will take you to Dark Rosaleen in Dublin City. Lizzie Brannagan's, she's at. It's a safe house, That's the best I can think of now. It'll be a long journey, but you must shift as you can. Off wid ye now, an' God be with you.'

She took a scapular from round her neck. It was a little brown felt envelope on a long tape. It was purported to have the dust from the ashes of Saint Philomena within it. With it on another tape was a pouch of garlic to ward off evil spirits. These two she put around her sister's neck and tucked them down her bodice next her skin.

'You'll be all right now,' she said, her brown walnut face smiling reassuringly at her sister.

Ronan had put his shirt on and thrown a cloak about his shoulders. It was a good warm cloak given to him by a gentleman he had charmed with his fiddling in Donegal.

Heated by the poteen within and the warm clothes without the pair set off out into the cold wet evening. It was dark on the journey and neither knew the hour, but each supposed it was the twilight time, early now with the terrible day that was in it.

They climbed the steep side of the valley, taking the pathway gouged out of the rock that the shepherd used. The rain made visibility nil, but they kept on upwards, ever upwards, as the ditch spilled over with brown flood water and the branches of the trees slapped their faces. The wind was humming, a keening monotonous sound. They reached the woodland, their feet made swift by anxiety. Beneath the trees the ivy crawled and it tripped them and made them stumble. Ferns grew lacy and rubbery strong. They were hung with raindrops, a green filigree decorated with diamonds. Reeds were waist high, sharp-edged, rigid, a glowing emerald colour. The undergrowth was dotted with black briony and cow-parsley. Here and there a moss-covered tree-trunk lay fallen and they had to climb over it if the trees were close. The Widow Boann knew the way well. She often came here to help Craw Kilty gather her herbs and other ingredients for her brews and potions. The Widow would pick some too and bring them to the castle for Bessie Broderick to put in her stews and ragouts, and for Molly to have for her tisanes.

They had soon reached the back of the castle where the land rose steep behind them. The Widow put her finger to her lips and motioned Ronan to follow her. The two tiptoed to the entrance to the wine cellar. She would not use the other entrance, for that was the one the soldiers would come by, she knew. It was near the graveyard and the most commonly used way to penetrate the secret passages.

She unlatched the heavy door. Ronan helped her to push it open and together they went into the caves.

Chapter

29

THE soldiers' uniforms would have been conspicuous in the mountains, so for that reason, and against the rain, they wore their greatcoats. They had galloped in single file after Matt Dominic until they had reached the environs of the castle. They were just in time to conceal themselves in a circle of trees near the graveyard when they saw the lights of the procession coming up the hill to their right.

Lieutenant Andrew Clegg, leading his platoon against the rebels, knew it could do him no end of good if he were to come off well in this skirmish. He remembered his visit here a few months ago. It was the reason they had chosen him for tonight's raid: his familiarity with the territory and the fact that he had been in the house already and knew the lay-out.

He thought of the shooting in the woods and Red Rafferty's escape. He had felt at the time that the rebel had gone to earth somewhere in the vicinity of the castle, and he now felt the satisfaction of a man whose hunch has been proved right. There was a rebel in the Usher household, according to the earl. Suspicion had fallen on the Widow Boann, the servant, and it seemed she was the guilty one. There was an ancient priest's hole where all unbeknownst to the master of the house illicit meetings were held. Clegg had sent a message to Lord Usher telling him to keep away and to leave him to sort out the nest of rebels that presumed to use his premises for their treasonable pursuits. His sort were well-meaning, but usually messed the whole operation up by their amateurish interference. He hoped the earl would obey.

He saw the twinkling lights of the cottage in the valley.

'Think they can see us, Bates?' he asked his second-in-command. He was proud of his relationship with his men. He was not afraid to ask their advice if he felt it was warranted and they respected him for not being a know-all as so many of his fellow officers were. The Sergeant shook his had. 'Maybe. Maybe not. It's no matter, sir,' he said. 'Even if they do see us there's nothing they can do. They couldn't reach the castle in time. We 'ave 'em, sir.' There was a gleeful tone to his voice. His men had not been pleased at all, Lieutenant Clegg knew, to leave without their quarry the last time. Redmond Rafferty was a thorn in their sides and the sooner he was out of the way, dead or alive, the better. He irritated Bates, for the fellow seemed to be cocking a snook at the army. He had laughed at the soldiers that day they had shot him. They heard his laughter echoing through the trees. Sergeant Bates hoped with all his heart he would be in the priest's hole tonight with the rest of the rebels.

They sat on their horses, the rain spilling down their faces, blurring their vision. The blackthorn and hawthorn, field maple and ash formed a copse around them, and except for the occasional whinny or snort from the horses they could have been part of the trees about them.

Lieutenant Clegg felt a stirring of excitement as he saw the lights, tiny pinpoints in the distance but proceeding towards the castle. Tonight, if the indications of the lights were anything to go by, they would catch quite a few of the firebrands who tried to upset the applecart for everyone.

The torches shone clear in the night now, bobbing and disappearing and reappearing in front of trees and shrubs.

'Try to count them, Bates.' he ordered.

'There's at least thirty, sir.'

'That's what I reckon, too. It's more than I expected. But we'll be well able for them. Can you see any more?'

The night was now dark around them, the rain clouds above them uniformaly dense and swollen. One feeble light remained after the others; then it too vanished.

Matt Dominic had given them directions to the entrance of the priest's hole. The soldiers followed Clegg and Bates, their horses daintily picking their way along narrow pathways, steeply descending gouged out of the rock-face, to where the furthest opening was supposed to be. He had told them to look for the oyster sign. It had been used in the old days to indicate that here was where the Catholics met, the oyster sign showing that the pearl of the True Faith was within. It was clearly visible now, carved into the rock entrance.

They dismounted and tethered their horses to nearby trees and gathered behind their lieutenant. He shook the rain off his coat. Then he pushed back some ivy and dipping his head, entered the cave. The others followed. It was hardly dryer within, and it was certainly colder. The dripping walls gave off a dampness that was icy and struck a chill in their hearts. Bats scurried past them like winged mice. But they plodded on. As they turned a bend the cave narrowed into a passageway. It was very dark and they had to continue without any lights, in case they were discovered or gave themselves away. Now and then their hands contacted the slimy walls and they had to bite off a scream, the surface of the tunnel soft and cold as a toad's belly.

At last the passage curved and they saw the glimmering of a light in the distance. The sound of voices came to them faintly. The lieutenant held up his hand. He motioned Bates forward. Bates moved cautiously. He knew what he had to do. There would be a lookout, perhaps two, though he did not think they would be that careful. The rebels he had had to deal with had shown themselves reckless in the most foolhardy way.

He moved stealthily in the dark, his gun in his hand, but held by the barrel. He made no sound. The others waited behind with Lieutenant Clegg. They were tense as they watched his progress. On the one hand they had the thirty-odd men trapped like rats in a hole; on the other, if anyone saw or got behind them or gave the alarm, the tables could be turned. Then they themselves would be ignominiously routed or killed. Everything rested on the next few minutes, on their coming into the light of the big room where they had been told the rebels would be, taking them by surprise, surrounding them.

Bates moved forward with the softness and alertness of a cat. His eyes found the shadow and he knew he had been right. There was only one lookout and he no more than a boy. He blended with the rock upon which he rested, his body leaning forward towards the entrance to the room, which was a pool of light. He was trying to catch what was being said inside. Curious and intent, he sensed nothing else. That was his mistake, Bates thought triumphantly. *He* would never have allowed a watch to turn his back on where the enemy might strike. Which was where all his attention should have been. It was almost too easy. He never heard Bates creep up on him. He knew nothing until the hand, hard and unyielding, clasped itself tightly over his mouth and the butt of the gun hit him heavily on the skull, and darkness flooded over him.

Bates beckoned to the lieutenant and he and the men behind him followed through the passageway, splitting up into two lines, one on either side of the entrance. They pressed themselves against the damp and slimy walls, indifferent now to the moisture soaking through their uniforms. A rat ran over their feet and scuttled somewhere into the darkness behind them, but no one in the room beyond them turned to look.

Their faces were turned towards the raised platform that must once have been an altar, the lieutenant thought. On the platform stood three men. One of these was Creagh Jeffries; one, and the Lieutenant felt his pulses leap, was Redmond Rafferty; and the third was an American, Hank O'Reilly. The American was speaking and the flushed faces of the audience were raptly attentive.

In American, men are free men,' he was saying. 'It is written into our constitution. You don't even have a constitution. You have to obey the laws of a foreign government. Where is your identity?'

What a load of old twaddle, Bates thought. He stood on one side of the entrance, the lieutenant on the other. They looked at each other, eyes holding eyes, then the lieutenant jerked his head and they erupted into the room. The audience was taken completely by surprise. Suddenly they saw the place was full of soldiers. They were surrounded swiftly, encompassed about with guns at the ready. A tableau of frozen faces turned to the back and sides of the room, staring open-mouthed at the ring of soldiers there.

From his platform Creagh looked helplessly into the forest of guns. So. It was all over, he thought, for him, anyway.

He glanced at Red, who gave him his sweetest most reassuring smile. 'Dear God help us now,' he prayed silently as Red shouted, 'Douse the torches.'

The lieutenant shouted at the same time, 'Don't anybody move.'

There was a flurry of movement and lights began to go out. The lieutenant called, 'Fire.' Creagh saw flashes of gunshot. At last all the lights were out. At the same time there was another blast of gunfire, screams from various parts of the room and a searing pain in his breast. Then a falling, falling, falling into darkness.

Chapter

30

CRONIN Dominic sat in wrapt attention letting the oratory of the men on the platform flow over him. Words like 'freedom' and 'Erin' and 'brotherhood' and 'insurrection' inspired him. He and Molly had made the journey to Knockharrig and back without mishap. He had been excited by the sudden acquisition of wealth. On their return he had given Molly a kiss, then unharnessed and stabled the horses after he had rubbed them down. Peadar, his young brother had told him of the meeting. He had never gone to one before, but tonight he had felt a surge of excited anticipation within him, so, feeling celebratory and adventurous, he had decided he would like to go and see what the secret meetings were all about.

He did not think he was taking any chances. There had been meetings at Usher now for a long time. He was an ambitious lad and he knew there was no future for him and Molly here in Ireland. He did not want either of them to be in service. Service, he thought, was all right if you chose it. It was most definitely not all right if it was thrust upon you. And it had been thrust upon him and Molly. There was no way they could escape it in Ireland.

He had grander plans. He wanted to breed horses. He was good with horses, a brilliant judge of horseflesh. He had an eye. Lord James swore by him and often gave him *carte blanche* at the horse fair to bid and choose, and he allowed himself to be guided by Cronin. He wanted to take Molly to America. America was the land of the free. But he did not want to take her steerage, on the 'coffin-ships'. No, he wanted to do it in style. Chippy and confident of himself, he had felt sure he would find a way. Then tonight he and Molly had been given a totally unnecessary gift of forty-five pounds. Molly and he would have saved the little Fergal for nothing. But they had received the princely sum and his dream was suddenly much nearer.

He had enjoyed the meeting. He listened to the fine talk, the patriotic fervour, and he loved it all. He believed it would come, Ireland's freedom, eventually. Too late for him and Molly, though. It would not come this year, as Stephens had promised, nor next. He would have to go to America for freedom. Maybe his children could come back when they were old enough and Ireland then would be free. These men would ultimately win it for future generations, he thought. It was sad he would not see it.

He did not want to give his life, the ultimate sacrifice. He was too fond of the smell of horseflesh and the warmth of Molly's breasts against his cheeks. He loved it all; the rain on his face; the snow biting his nose; kicking the leaves; and resting and sweating in the sun. All of life was within him. He could smell and taste it. Ah no. How could these men contemplate losing the preciousness of living for so arbitary a thing as freedom? He looked about him at the faces of the men listening with awe to what Red Rafferty was saying: 'This is our country, the country that we love. The country that we would die for. She needs us. She may need our blood that our children may live in freedom. What have we got to lose? We have nothing to lose.'

Except our lives, Cronin thought, the most precious thing of all.

'You take men's souls, you make them slaves. Violence becomes their stock-in-trade. I would say to the English government, "Beware a man who has nothing to lose."'

'Yes,' Cronin thought. 'I understand you, and what you are saying is right. That is what all of you are like. You have no hope except through revolt. But I have a plan. I have seen how to escape. I know what to do and this night I have the means of doing it. We'll run away, Molly and me. I'll go to John Joe Neary in Kentucky. He'll start me off. Molly'll be with me for help and love.'

He felt the surge of hope within him, a sudden charge of excitement. The men around him leapt to their feet to cheer. He leapt up too, from the impetus of his ideas, not the fighting words of Redmond Rafferty. The men's faces were shadowy in the torch-light, their eyes were bright and their cheeks looked flushed. He thought, 'I don't belong here. I am not filled with the same fervour. Yet they are my friends and I grew up with them. We have shared a life together. But we see different ways out.'

He was wondering whether his was the wrong way, whether it was cowardly to run way and find your dream in America, when he heard the shouting. 'Don't anybody move.' 'Douse the torches.' 'Fire.'

'Oh God,' he thought. 'Oh God, help me now.'

He saw the soldiers ring the vault. Fear flooded him. He was caught like a rat in a trap. Suddenly the lights went out. All was darkness. He heard the gunfire and felt the tearing pain in the region of his heart.

'Molly . . .' he whispered.

Then there was an explosion of agony, and then nothing.

Chapter

31

THE Widow and Ronan crept down the narrow steps into the cellar. All about them the stacked wine bottles were covered with dust and cobwebs except for the pipe of port laid down recently for Cormac. A cobweb caught the Widow's face, the spider clutching its legs about the skein, desperately holding on as his carefully constructed edifice collapsed about him. The Widow did not notice, for all her senses were alert to what was happening around her. She was watching and listening. She heard Bessie Broderick's voice from the kicthen. It was a far-away sound, muffled by the closed doors between. There was normality, the warmth of food cooking, the firelight, the conversation. Here was secrecy and stealth and betrayal.

They came to the entrance and for the second time that day she chose the corridor that led to the priest's cell. When they reached it, all was as before save that the food had been eaten and the child lay asleep, his face streaked with tearstains. The Widow Boann sent up a prayer of thanks. Relief flooded over her and she rushed to him. The boy's eyes fluttered open and he saw her. He opened his mouth to call to her joyously. She quickly silenced him by putting her hand over the bottom half of his face. Gently she told him to keep still. He was very sleepy and he obeyed her, happy that she was with him again.

They could hear the men above and the Widow's heart sank as her worst fears were confirmed. Red Rafferty's voice reached them clearly, loudly proclaiming something. There was a murmur of heavy male voices assenting and then the sound of soldiers' boots on the platform above. It sounded like thunder to the group below.

198

Fergal opened his eyes and looked up, frightened out of his wits. He had had a very disturbing day, the Widow thought, as she wrapped him in the blanket from the bed, soothing him as she did so and lifting him up in her arms. Her mind was working desperately. How to help Creagh?

Then she had it. She pointed to the Minstrel. 'There. The hook. It's a trapdoor,' she whispered almost soundlessly

Just as Ronan was about to pull the ring they froze as they heard the sounds above them becoming louder and the soldiers called their commands.

'Don't anybody move.' 'Douse the torches.' This last was Red's voice.

'Fire.'

Ronan and the Widow stared at each other in the gloom, petrified momentarily. It seemed an eternity they stood there, Ronan looking to her for guidance, but it was only a second. She heard the cries, the crack of shots, the screams. She nodded her head. The Minstrel firmly pulled the hook and there was a crash as two men fell into the empty bed. Then the trapdoor flew back into it's place.

The first man was Red Rafferty. The next Creagh. The Widow let out a breath of relief. Then she saw the blood on his coat and her heart sank.

'Oh God, he's wounded,' she cried.

Red laid him on the bed. 'We'll have to get out of here, he said examining Creagh's wound. 'That bullet will have to be removed.'

'But they'll catch us,' the Widow whispered fearfully. The soljers will be everywhere.'

'We'll go by the third exit the one in the woods. I doubt if the soldiers know of that one. I'll carry Creagh.'

'But are you all right? You're bleeding too. Have ye got a carriage nearby?' the Widow asked, holding the wide-eyed Fergal close to her bosom.

Red nodded and lifted his head a second, listening. There was pandemonium above, which drowned out, the Widow hoped, the noise of Fergal's sudden wailing and the cry of pain that escaped Creagh's lips as Red lifted him into his arms. It must have been agonizing, for he fainted clean away and for a moment the Widow knew despair. But Red was as gentle as possible. He nodded to her. She could see his face was tense with anxiety and knowing that he too had been wounded she wondered how this night would end. But he gave her a reassuring look, and lifted Creagh's unconscious body over his shoulder as a shepherd does a lamb.

'Tis well ye were standing side by side,' Ronan said, indicating the senseless Creagh.

Red was not listening. He whispered, 'Come on. Follow me. We have a coach under the trees in readiness for just such an emergency.'

There was a thunderous banging above as the Widow, carrying Fergal, followed Red with Creagh, Ronan bringing up the rear. They could hear the soldiers' voices and Red beckoned them to hurry. They left the room and crept along the way Red indicated. All seemed quiet, and they met no one. They had turned to go into the wine-cellar when a burst of noise came from the other end of the corridor and the door from the kitchen burst open and there stood the buxom figure of Bessie Broderick, who stopped abruptly in mid-sentence.

'An' I'll need at least a pint of cream ...' Her mouth opened in a scream as she spied the group, dark shadows emerging from the bowels of the earth. The Widow touched the scapular and the garlic bag at her breast and whether it was the miraculous properties of the one or the pagan power of the other, or simply the fact that the cook recognized Creagh hanging bleeding over the shoulder of his companion that kept her silent was never established. It might have been the sight of her sister with the bundle in her arms. In any event the scream never materialized and the cook stood in silence, mouth and eyes wide open, arm raised, hand holding the rolling pin as they filed into the wine-cellar, hurrying down corridors the Widow never knew existed until they reached the exit, then out into the cold wet night.

They all breathed a sigh of relief to find themselves in the open air. But all was not over for them yet, the Widow knew. There would be soldiers everywhere. She longed to go to the cottage. She needed her sister. But it was impossible. The soldiers would be bound to search there, and she would be endangering all their lives, Craw Kilty's too.

Red now turned to her. He was obviously in great pain, limping badly, his face pale and drawn.

'Follow me,' he whispered. 'My carriage is below. I had to use it tonight, and thank God I did. I was sure to be recognized on horseback. It is at the Drover's Bridge.

Gratefully she followed him. She was tired of being in charge and it was good to receive orders instead of issuing them. They scrambled down the side of the mountain, brambles tearing at their faces and clothes. The wind was nearly at gale force again, and little Fergal, who had never been out in a storm in his life was scared half to death at this terrible disruption of his hitherto peaceful existence. Feet slipping in the mud, they hurried as best they could, glancing behind them to see if anyone followed. But the night was dense and black behind them, no lights anywhere, the they journeyed on slipping and sliding and cutting their hands as they grasped at branches and thorny bushes to save themselves from falling precipitately down the mountain.

At last they reached a plateau that was shielded by a clump of beeches and a little bridge which rose before them as they descended, darker than the night itself, shrouded in mist.

The Widow could see the faint outline of the bridge. It seemed to hang in the mist ahead of them. She could barely make out the group of chestnut trees at the farther end where the carriage must be hidden. It was a stone's throw from them.

Suddenly she felt her arm grabbed roughly. She turned, startled, to see Red and the Minstrel looking towards the bridge and as she followed their gaze she too saw what they saw.

Two soldiers sat, sheltering under a huge oak on the near side of the bridge. They were almost invisible. Red could not understand what they were doing there sitting motionless but he knew they could not get past them to the carriage. He put his finger to his lips and gently slid Creagh's body off his shoulder onto the ground. He indicated to the others to be still. Then, sinuous and silent as a cat, he inched forward, stealthily clinging to the shadow of the trees. The Widow and Ronan watched him with bated breath, the Minstrel keeping an eye on Creagh to see he did not moan or make a sound. But he was unconscious, and the Widow had bound Fergal to her in her shawl so that he was completely swathed, his head pressed to her heart.

As they watched, Red disappeared in the swirling mists that lay heavy in this low place. One of the soldiers yawned and the sound seemed right beside them. Ronan looked at her with startled eyes, but she had seen Red re-emerge from the shadows. He was right behind the two soldiers. Holding their breath in an agony of apprehension they saw him creep down to where the men were sitting and raising his gun high in the air he hit one of them with the butt. The soldier groaned and fell and instantly the other leapt upon Red and Ronan, unable to lie still any more and reasoning that in any event it did not matter if Creagh broke the silence now, ran to his aid. The second soldier was throwing punches and Red, wounded and weakened by loss of blood from his thigh, was defending himself as best he could and waiting and hoping for an opportunity to finish the man with his lethal upper-cut.

Ronan slipped off his boot and brought the heel down heavily from behind on the soldier's cranium. He fell limply to the ground and lay there inert. Ronan examined the other body, turning it over with his foot. 'Out cold,' he said. Then he called and beckoned 'Come on' to the Widow, and turned to Red.

'Look, Red, yer wounded bad. Ye can hardly walk. You get in the carriage an' I'll get Creagh. You've carried him far enough.'

Red stumbled to the coach and untied the horses who were grazing. He was soon joined by the Widow and Fergal, then Ronan, stumbling under the weight of the wounded Creagh.

Red looked at them apologetically. 'Can anyone drive this thing? I don't think I can quite manage.'

Ronan let Creagh's body slide from his shoulders into the carriage and he pushed Red inside after it, saying, 'I'll do it. I've never done it before, but I'll do it.'

Red said, 'Thank God.'

The Widow got in heavily after the men. When she was inside she loosened her shawl and Fergal peeped out, looking about.

'It's all right, my lamb. Everything is all right,' she soothed him.

'The Minstrel slammed the door behind them, mounted the driving seat, pulled out the whip, cracked it in the air and the horses plunged down the mountain road, galloping wildly down the slope, the carriage swaying dangerously behind them.

Chapter

32

AFTER a while the Widow's back began to ache. She had lost all count of time. They seemed to have been in the coach for an eternity. They lurched down mountains, over flooded roads, on and on through the night. Ronan, she thought wryly, was probably enjoying himself hugely, up there like God cracking his whip. The men across from her were leaning against each other, both unconscious. The coach jolted over the uneven roads. Fergal was staring through the window with wide eyes. It seemed an age, though she would never know for certain how long they travelled, when the coach slowed down and skidded to a halt.

The Minstrel's face appeared at the window. 'The horses are exhausted. I'll bet they've been on the road before this journey. So I'm stoppin' here.'

'Where is here? Are you drunk or mad or what? Aren't we in danger of our lives?'

'Ah whist, woman, I've driven across country, leaving fake trails. We're quite safe. The people here are friends. It's the blacksmith and isn't he one of us.'

'An' what does that mean? One of us? Don't you go includin' me in your shenanikins, me boyo, do ye hear?'

Fear made her brusque but the Minstrel was not upset and the Widow was relieved in spite of herself at the appearance at the window of the carriage of the apple-cheeked face of Mrs Riley.

Red had sat up as they halted. 'Are ye crazy to stop here?' he cried as Ronan opened the carriage door.

'No. No, *astore*,' Mrs Riley said. 'They've been here already.'

'Who?' the Widow asked.

'The soljers,' Mrs Riley said matter-of-factly. 'They've come an' gone. They'll not be back this night. Rampaged all over the house and forge, so they did, and found nary a mouse for their trouble. Had to apologize. Oh, we were as sweet as honey to them. Gave them tay and they went away satisfied. So yer not to worry.'

The blacksmith's wife clucked and cooed and hustled them inside her cottage. There was a warm glowing turf fire and the Widow had never been so pleased at the sight of anything as she was at that crackling, blazing welcome. Mrs Riley gave them a mug of black tea, some brown bread hot from the oven, the most delicious barm brack, moist and so full of fruit you couldn't prevent it from crumbling.

She was relieved too, when the blacksmith, a giant of a man, had carried Creagh into the back room as if he was a sack of potatoes and weighed nothing at all. She sighed to herself and thought wistfully that she would love a man exactly like that for herself.

Mrs Riley said, 'The lad'll be safe enough there be the time. Mister Riley will go for the Doctor. Yerra, now, don't fret yerself. The doctor's a sympathizer an' he'll have them right as rain in no time at all. An' you, me fine boyo,' she looked keenly at Red, 'You need a bit of attention yerself an' I'm not mistaken.'

Red's face was chalk-white. he sat in the chair beside the fire and the Widow realized for the first time how badly he was hurt. In the leaping flames she could see his trouser-leg was soaked in blood, which she had not noticed before.

'Let me help you off with yer coat,' she said, but Fergal began to cry and Mrs Riley shook her head.

'Leave him be until the doctor gets here,' she said. 'You and the morsel, the little lamb, can bed down here on the sofa beyond, in this room. Ye can put the mite on the floor on the duck-down pillow.'

'But where'll you go, mistress of the house?' the Widow Boann asked.

'Ach, I'll take a wee nap in my rockin' chair in the kitchen. Now you don't worry about me. Himself will be about the place with the doctor comin' and goin' and I'll not rest an' them needin' tay or a kittle o' water. So you bed down an' get some shut-eye, for ye don't know what's ahead of ye, God help us.'

At that moment the blacksmith put his head around the door.

'The lad has gone for the doctor. I'm afraid the slim young man is hurt bad.'

'You mean Master Creagh is . . .'

The blacksmith raised a palm as big as a hock of ham. 'I don't want to know his name. No names here, please. It's safer, missus.'

'I'm sorry.'

'Now you get some sleep an' we'll look after the lad. It's safe here. The soldiers won't come back tonight. They may be content to arrest the others the ones yon man says were caught at the meeting, an' our poor American brother won't know whether he's comin' or goin', so he wont. Oh bad cess to them. Ye never know what they'll do, but you're safe here anyhow till the morning.'

It was a fitful night for the Widow. Fergal slept peacefully enough, worn out by his experiences. She held him in the crook of her arm, but every time she dozed off, lulled by the comforting crackle of the fire and the monotonous flicker of light from it, the soft plop of the ash as it fell, she would be jerked out of her descent into unconsciousness by voices outside, or a door banging, or worst, a scream of pain from behind the wall.

The Minstrel came in as a golden dawn crept through the curtains. 'Widow. Widow. It's me.'

'Hush up. The babe's asleep still. Worn to a frazzle, the miteen.'

'The doctor has fixed Red up but he doesn't want Master Creagh moved. We can't leave him here. He'll be captured if he stays. The soldiers'll come back for certain if they don't find us. It's too much to ask of the Rileys. They'll be arrested too.'

'Oh God help us, Ronan. Yiz are right. The Rileys have been that good . . .'

'We'll have to get Master Creagh into the coach and drive to Dublin town. They'll never find him there. We can be sure of that.'

'I'm that worried about Master Creagh, Ronan.'

'Well, there's nothin' we can do. If he stays here, an' suppose by some miracle the soldiers are eejits an' never think to return you can be sure someone will inform on the Rileys. Too many stop at the blacksmith's. In fact the sooner we start this day the better. Else someone will open their gob, then it's all over for Master Creagh, Red, us *and* the Rileys. If he's to die, Widow, he can't take them with him. Us either. Think of Fergal. We have to get movin', really we must.'

'Ye know where we're goin'?'

For the first time in his life that she could remember, the Minstrel's clear eyes slid from hers.

'Oh yes, missus. It's to Rosaleen we go.' He looked up at her. 'I don't think ye'll like it, Widow, but it's all we got.'

She did not understand what he meant. She was not to understand until their journey was over and they at last cast themselves on the mercy of the gypsy.

Chapter

33

THE soldiers were everywhere. Dolly was upset and the Widow could not be found. Sophie was helping her sister-in-law with Cormac, certain that the fuss was over Fergal. She murmured *paternosters* and *Ave Marias* to herself for the little one's escape and tried to calm Dolly.

The platoon consisted of thirty men, two of whom had been dispatched back to the barracks for reinforcements, and another two sent to the junction of the main Dublin Road as look-out. The rest searched the house and grounds of Usher, trying desperately to be discreet and not managing very well. They arrested rebels who tried to escape and questioned anyone in the vicinity.

James was anxious, very anxious. But he did not show it. He was learning. He remembered Lieutenant Andrew Clegg and the episode of the rebel whom they had shot and who was supposed to be in hiding in the woods at Usher. Now the lieutenant stood opposite James once more in front of the fire in the Great Hall, attentive, suspicious, alert but scrupulously polite. He had told the lieutenant that he would find nothing in the house. The lieutenant had been courteous but adamant. The castle had to be searched.

James was angry. 'Why do you think I sent for you, Lieutenant? I'm hardly harbouring criminals. I would certainly know if anything was happening in my home,' he said with some asperity, and saying it, he realized it was not true. The castle sprawled, and was honey-combed with tiny rooms and antechambers where a fugitive could hide for weeks without being found if he had an accomplice within the household. That was the rub that made James shiver.

'With respect, my lord, you did not know what was happening in your cellars.' The lieutenant's voice was neutral.

'The cellars are deep, it is quite another matter,' James replied heatedly.' The tunnels there have not been used since Cromwellian times.'

'Again with respect, my lord, that was not what we found.' He paused, 'Every door lock was well oiled.'

The soldiers were running up and down the stairs.

'Yes, my lord,' the lieutenant continued, 'You may not have known about it, sir, but the cellars showed every sign of constant use. And, as you know, the meeting we disturbed was quite large.'

James tried to control the turbulence of his thoughts. He was silent. A terrible suspicion had entered his head and was growing in his mind.

At that moment Sophie appeared at the top of the stairs.

'James, what is going on?' she asked. 'Dolly is alarmed.'

'My dearest sister, it is nothing. Go back to Dolly. Calm her. Tell her I'll be there in a moment. It is a routine check. There is a rebel on the loose. The lieutenant is trying to catch him.'

Sophie nearly swooned. She at once thought of Red. her heart leapt within her and she ran down the stairs.

'Have they caught . . . anyone?'

'None of the leaders, Sophie. Now go to Dolly, please. Tell her I'm on my way.'

Lieutenant Clegg watched her return upstairs, a query in his mind. He looked at James.

'Tell me, my lord, where is your young brother tonight? Creagh Jeffries, is it not?'

James started guiltily. It had been of Creagh that he had been thinking. His young brother's frequent absence from home; his conversations in Gaelic; the strangely ill-assorted people that he consorted with but who never came to stay, who always scuttled away at James' approach.

He shrugged silently, not trusting himself to speak. Then he said, changing the subject, 'Have you captured most of them, Lieutenant? The rebels?'

The lieutenant nodded. 'Most of them you'll be glad to know.' He glanced at James. 'Some of them have been shot. Some wounded. Some escaped, including the leaders, except an

American. Unfortunately we could not hold him.'

'Why not?'

'It is not politic. We want to remain friends with our neighbours across the Atlantic. Unfortunately they think our Irish friends are right. However, an incident with an American citizen could cause unnecessary fuss.'

'Oh, I see.' James paused. 'And the leaders? You used the plural.'

'Yes I did, my lord. Why are you interested?'

James' lips tightened and he tried once again to control his anger. His patience was stretched to the limit.

'Let me ask you this, Lieutenant. If you found there had been secret meetings in *your* cellars, would you be interested in the leaders?'

The lieutenant smiled. '*Touché*, my lord. Though it is unlikely. Well, unfortunately we lost Redmond Rafferty again. He is a great trial to us. The man is a traitor and has led us the very devil of a dance. Slippery as an eel he is, and takes the most hair-brained risks. How we haven't caught him is a mystery to me.' He looked at James. 'He was the man we winged that afternoon. When we were here before, remember?'

James nodded. 'I remember very well,' he said dryly.

'Well, we recognized him tonight, in your cellars. Strange that. Twice in this vicinity. Almost as if he knew someone here.'

'I protest, Lieutenant. That is a monstrous insinuation.'

'I do beg your pardon, my lord. Only you must see the way my thoughts run. Well, in any event he escaped. With the third man.'

'Who was?' James could not keep the anxiety out of his voice. He could feel his heart accelerate. He was torn between wanting the lieutenant to continue and wanting him to stop.

The lieutenant was silent a moment. Then, 'We don't know. That's the damnedest thing.'

James tried to keep still, very still. To break the tension he asked, 'Would you like a drink, Lieutenant? A brandy?'

The lieutenant's face relaxed. 'It would be most welcome, my lord,' he said gratefully.

James rang for Maitland. He was trying to keep entirely unemotional. His suspicion had become a certainty and he was appalled. His thoughts were thrown into confusion as he tried to grapple with the awful realization that had been thrust upon him. And he was desperately trying to conceal the fact.

Maitland came on an instant, and anticipating the order, carried a silver salver upon which there was a decanter of brandy and one of whiskey, with glasses. He poured them both a good measure, put the tray on the table before the fire, and left.

James indicated a chair near the lieutenant, but the soldier shook his head saying he preferred to stand, then sipped his brandy appreciatively.

'Excellent vintage, my lord, excellent,' he murmured and James wondered, not for the first time, if the lieutenant was playing games with him. He longed for the soldier to volunteer more information about the third leader without James having to ask him, but he was silent, drinking his brandy. So James perforce had to broach the subject himself.

The other leader?' he asked as carelessly as he could.

'What? Oh yes, my lord. There were three on that platform. They disappeared. Into thin air.'

James smiled wryly, 'Ah yes. The trapdoor. It runs the whole width of the platform. It was constructed so that priests and servers could ... er ... vanish when discovered saying Mass. So they used that, did they?'

The lieutenant nodded. 'It's impossible to detect,' he said, watching James intently. 'We could not discover how it was worked. We guessed there must be something of the kind there — a secret doorway, some concealed exit, a hidden trapdoor — but blow me, my lord, we could not find it. It had us baffled.'

James laughed. 'That is why we were able to practise our religion, my dear sir, all the years it was forbidden,' he said. Then realizing the import of his sentence he paused and looked at the lieutenant who said softly, 'I wonder then, apart from the family, who would have known how the trapdoor worked?'

'Well, the servants ...' James blurted out.

'Ah yes. I'll want to talk to them if I may, m'lord?'

'Yes. Yes, of course. But they had nothing to do with it I'm sure. They're loyal ...'

'To whom, my lord?' the lieutenant interrupted.

'I beg your pardon?'

'To you or to their country?' the lieutenant looked at James quizzically. 'They have an odd idea of loyalty, some of them.'

'Them? Who?' James asked.

'The Irish.' The lieutenant paused to sip his brandy. Sergeant Bates came into the hall and saluted. The lieutenant went to him and they spoke together in an undertone. James could not hear what was said. After a few moments Lieutenant Clegg came over to him.

'You asked about the leaders, my lord,' he said, smiling. 'Well we saw three men. One was the American. One was Red Rafferty. The other a young man of medium height, early twenties I'd say, brown hair, wearing the clothes of a gentleman. Vanished, as I said before. But before they disappeared I'm pretty sure both of them were shot. My aim is good and Sergeant Bates' is excellent. So they won't get far. My men are searching the vicinity and I have detailed some of my best soldiers to track them down.' He was watching James closely but his face showed nothing. He paused, then added, 'All is well in your home, my lord.'

'I told you it would be,' James said coldly.

The lieutenant replied mildly, 'I'm sorry to have been such a nuisance, and I'd like to thank you for your co-operation. You did right to send for us. You should look, though, to your staff. It appears the stable lad Cronin was at the meeting.'

James looked surprised. 'Good lord, I don't believe it. The boy was only interested in horses. In any event, he was out today. He drove the coach to Knockharrig for me.'

'Well, he must have come back in time to go to the meeting, for he was certainly there. He was shot. He is dead.'

'Oh my God, no.' James was shocked. He could conceal his feelings no longer. 'But he was going to marry Molly. I was going to give them my blessing, though they did not know it. They wanted to go to America. Poor boy. Poor boy. I'm deeply sorry. And for Molly too. Does she know?' The lieutenant nodded. 'Is someone with her?' The lieutenant nodded again.

'You must not waste your sympathy on the likes of them. They were traitors, my lord.'

James turned on him, his eyes blazing. 'Silence. How dare you speak so of the dead. You did not know him. I did. He was a lovely lad, so full of life.'

The lieutenant looked at James curiously. 'Where was your brother tonight, my lord?' he asked again.

James glared at him. 'I neither know nor care, Lieutenant,'

he said icily. 'My brother has a penchant for women.' He looked at the soldier straight in the eye. 'He *will* go philandering. I have spoken to him about it many times, but you know what the young are like. They will not listen to older, wiser heads. Now, Lieutenant, will you please leave my house?'

'Not so fast, sir, not so fast. I must speak to your servants before I go. And I would like to talk to your brother on his return.'

James bowed. 'Certainly, Lieutenant. Maitland will take you to the kitchen. He will allow you to conduct your questioning in his office. Now please excuse me.'

He went to his study. His whole body was shaking. Creagh: his dearly beloved little brother who exasperated him and irritated him but whom he loved with all his heart. Creagh was a rebel. He could not be more certain than if he had seen him with his own eyes bearing a gun for the peasants. It explained so much. It was like finding the lost piece of a jig-saw puzzle and suddenly seeing the whole picture revealed before your eyes.

But Creagh had been shot, was even now running away from Usher, escaping, being pursued by soldiers. Good God, a member of his family on the wrong side of the law. He shuddered, but to his surprise he did not disapprove. He loved Creagh, and his little brother was in danger. His very life was at stake. What did appearances matter at such a time? He thought of the faces of his friends: Lord Rennett, Lord Vestry, the Blackwaters, the Gormans, the Sheas. He shook his head. None of them mattered any more. What they might think, how they might disapprove, was of no consequence. All that mattered was his little brother running for his life. He wanted to rush to his aid and but for the presence in his home of the lieutenant and his troops he would have mounted his horse and scoured the countryside for him. But that would be the worst thing he could do just now and he had perforce to sit still. He was not very good at waiting. He must go to Dolly. She would soothe him. She would allay his fears. But he wished from the bottom of his heart that he knew where Creagh was. And he knew that his sole aim was to help him.

Chapter

34

BESSIE Broderick sat down at the big kitchen table and looked at her daughter's tragic face. She felt heavy-hearted in the face of Molly's grief. Molly was sick from weeping. Her face was splodged with large red patches and her eyes were swollen.

'I asked him not to go, Ma. I asked him and asked him. It was dangerous, I said. He laughed at me. He said no soldiers would ever come here, not into the castle, not into the Queen's own territory, he said. They'd never suspect there could be anythin' amiss here, an' now he's dead. Dead, do ye hear? Oh Ma, Ma, he was my love, my love. He was also my only hope of escape from here. And I kept thinkin' of Sylvie. Where is she now?'

Bessie Broderick's face darkened. She hated to hear even the mention of her run-away daughter. She tried to console Molly, but the girl rambled on and on, her mind occupied solely with the loss of Cronin.

'We had such plans, Ma,' she sobbed, 'He was goin' to America, to Kentucky. You know how good he was with horses. They like that in Kentucky. He would have made money, I know. I believed in him, Ma. What a life we would have had. Oh, he painted such pictures, such pictures. He believed in himself. And now he's gone, gone, gone. Dead, Killed.' She sat down and buried her head in her arms, weeping.

Bessie's normally acid tongue was still. She had, as she liked to say, 'whipped her daughters into shape.' She felt she had done a good job and was proud of her girls. They were efficient, gave excellent service and the family at Usher were delighted with them and never lost an opportunity to congratulate her on their good work. All except little Sylvie, pretty Sylvie who had run off with Sean Donahue from the edge of the valley where it met the road to Arklow. His father was a tenant farmer and Sean had filled Sylvie Broderick's head with fancies. He had told her that in Dublin City you could become rich with working. 'For they want the likes of us,' he said to her, 'strong and healthy from the country.' They had run off together full of high hopes and that was the last Bessie Broderick had seen or heard of them. It changed her, for Sylvie was her secret favourite and she became waspish and bitter with her going.

It had seemed very likely that Lord James would give his consent to Molly marrying Cronin. In any event the pair were firmly set on Kentucky. Bessie knew that Cronin was indeed a genius with the horses. He knew when they had curby hocks or went too far over at the knee, or were only fit for the knacker's yard. When he advised Lord James to buy he never made a mistake. When they had spat on their hands and clapped a fistful of earth on the horse's flanks, well, you could be sure it was a prime purchase they had. It did not take a scholar to see that Cronin was bound to have a big success in America's racing country, and Bessie had visualized a grand and glorious future for her daughter; a free woman, living her own independent life, with her own money, no longer in the bondage of service. She would be an American Mrs, not a first name only, and she would have a home and husband of her own.

All such hopes were blasted now. Cronin was dead and Molly was doomed to spend the rest of her life in Usher.

'Sure, it's not such a bad life, is it? When all's said an' done?' Bessie said helplessly, knowing it was no comfort but unable to think of anything that was. 'Lord James and Lady Dolly are kind. We could be landed with much worse.'

Molly looked at her mother with fury. 'Ye don't understand. I loved him. We were goin' away. I would have had me own house, Ma. Now I'll be stuck here for the rest of my days.' She burst once more into weeping.

'Maybe you presumed too much ... got ideas above yer station. Ye liked it well enough here, before ye fell for Cronin. Then ye thought ye had something better and now yer not satisfied with the advantages ye have here. Well, I'm sorry for ye, truly I am, but there's nought ye can do about it. So cry yer fill now and then get on with yer life. It's what we all have to do.'

Mrs Maitland came into the kitchen. 'Ah, Molly, there you

are. The bell's been ringing the last ten minutes or so. Up you go to Miss Sophie and get a move on. I know you're heartsick and I'm sorry for you but duty is duty and I'm responsible for the smooth running of this house. So bathe your face now, and up you go to your lady. Bessie, Lord Usher told me to compliment you on the lamb at lunch. perhaps you could put it on the menu for Saturday. He enjoyed it so much.' Bessie Broderick smiled and bobbed her head.

'Now isn't that nice of Lord Usher to compliment me? Did ye hear that, Clarie?' she asked her other daughter who had just come downstairs, 'Lord Usher especially liked the lamb.'

Clarie puckered up her face. 'That's nice, Ma, but there's soldiers everywhere and Miss Sophie is ringing and ringing for Molly, so please can she hurry? And Lady Dolly wants tea in the blue drawing-room, please.'

'Tea? At this hour?' Annie cried, 'Whatever next?'

'Well,' said Clarie, 'it's a madhouse up there, I'm tellin' ye. An' they're comin here in a minute. I heard the Master tell the lieutenant ...'

'An' what's that to do with us?' Annie cried.

Mrs Maitland sighed. 'I'm sure I don't know. Now can we hurry up and get the tea my lady asked for?'

'The house upstairs is like a bloody barracks,' Clarie said and Bessie tutted.

'Well, it's true, Ma. An' we have all got to be interviewed. In Maitland's office. The lieutenant said.' Clarie looked triumphant. She had at last managed to get her news out.

Everyone froze and sat still staring at Clarie who was putting the Limoges cups on a tray. Bessie Broderick looked startled.

'Interviewed?' she cried. 'What for?'

Mrs Maitland looked at her with asperity. 'To see if any of you Irish knew what was going on in the underground of this house.' Being English she was sure the soldiers would believe her and her husband's innocence and realize they could not have been involved.

Clarie suddenly lost all her bravado and ran to her mother, 'Oh Mam, Mam, I'm scared. I don't like being asked things. I get muddled.'

Bessie had been scared too for a minute. She kept remembering the sight of the unearthly procession that included her sister and master Creagh lying lifeless over the stranger's shoulder.

215

She firmly put what she had seen out of her mind. She drew her vast body upright.

'Sure, we know nuthin',' she cried firmly. 'Nuthin' at all. Isn't that so, Molly? Clarie? Annie? All of yiz? We know nuthin' at all. That's all we have to say. Understand? All.' She turned to the scullery maid. 'Will ye stoke the range, girl.' she ordered, 'An Molly, get a move on.'

Molly splashed cold water on her face and dried it in a coarse cloth she found beside the sink. She felt hopeless, empty and devastated. Cronin gone! Life would go on as her mother had said but it would be without Cronin. No more laughter behind the scullery door. No more kisses in the passageway. No more courting in the heather and bracken on the mountains when the sun shone and the birds sang and it was summer. She heard the bell ring again and saw it was Miss Sophie's. She fixed her cap firmly in place and went to obey the summons.

PART TWO

Chapter

35

'THERE, out on the street you go, you slut, where you belong.'
Ignatius Callaghan slammed the door behind him and Rosaleen
picked herself up off the street where he had thrown her.
Rubbing her arms where the man's fingers had gripped her and
brushing the dirt off her gown she stood full of impotent fury.
The street was muddy and the road liberally littered with horse
manure. She pulled her bright-coloured shawl about her
shoulders and looked defiantly at the sneering, jeering crowd
that had collected to make fun of her.

'I'll put the evil eye on ye,' she cried and held up the first and
second finger of her right hand. The crowd instantly dispersed,
nervously looking away from her and crossing themselves. The
organ-grinder turned his handle and a boy with a brace of
rabbits over his shoulder stuck out his tongue at her and ran to
the servants' entrance to one of the houses on the Rathmines
Road. A child bowled a hoop along, and a Nanny tutted and
firmly held the hands of a fat little boy and girl. The boy made a
face at Rosaleen and a gentleman rode by on a chestnut roan.
Just then a carriage careered past, splashing her skirts and
causing her to jump back onto the pavement. She moved up the
street, her hips swaying, her feet bare, her face a study in anger.

As she reached the top of the street a carriage drew up beside
her and the door opened. An old roué dressed in the mode of
an earlier age called to her.

'Come along, my pretty. Take a ride with me. You'll enjoy
the soft interior of my carriage. It's well sprung and a deal better
than walking. We could have some fun together and five shillings to put in your bodice for your trouble.'

His breath smelt foul and she drew distastefully away from him.

'An' what makes ye think I'd let ye touch me with a barge-pole, ye old goat?'

Blind fury and outraged pride made her speak more hastily and with more venom than was normally her wont. He really was a pathetic creature, more deserving of pity than anger.

His leer changed to malevolence and he lowered at her, identifying her accent as regional.

'Ah, me pretty! A country cousin? Up to get work no doubt? Well you'll find it difficult, me girl an' I'd seek it now while ye have your looks for you'll lose them soon enough, and then you'll not be so lucky to find anyone who'll pay five farthings, never mind five shillings, for your favours. Drive on, Byrne.' He slammed the coach door as the horses jerked into a gallop and disappeared up the street.

She had felt she was lucky to get work in Rathmines when she arrived in Dublin. When Grattan's Parliament was dissolved and the Act of Union took place in 1801, 'society' moved to London, taking with it the wealth that would have been invested in indigenous industry. Without it Dublin faltered and died and only unskilled labour was in demand and that at best casual and intermittent. Many of the fashionable houses became slums and the monied middle classes moved to the outskirts of the city to the new residential areas like Dalkey, Pembroke and Rathmines. People there preferred to employ country labour, for they were healthier than the now ill-nourished, sickness-ridden native Dubliners who lived in the once-glorious Georgian houses that now had to shelter ten to fifteen families apiece.

These houses quickly became uninhabitable and the people survived as best they might on next to nothing. Poor diet and squalid living conditions rendered them unfit for the work required of them when they were lucky enough to find it. So Rosaleen thought herself fortunate that her first job was in Rathmines.

She had obtained the post of housemaid in the establishment of a gentleman who lived in Rathmines Road called Mr Ignatius Callaghan. Both Ignatius and his son Benedict, a chinless fish-eyed apology for a boy of eighteen, had predictably fallen for Rosaleen's opulent charms and presumed on her role as employee and dependent to try to subject her to their unwanted attentions. When one day Mrs Imelda Callaghan had come into the hall and found her maid struggling to avoid the wet seeking lips of her adored son, she had been shocked and had succumbed to a severe attack of the vapours, but she had been prevailed upon by her husband to keep the girl.

'For what is to happen to her, my dear Mrs Callaghan, if she is thrown out on the street? We must do our Christian duty, indeed we must,' Ignatius Callaghan had reasoned sanctimoniously.

So Rosaleen stayed. But when three weeks later, Imelda Callaghan had found her husband panting on top of the maid on the sofa in their drawing-room, while the girl struggled beneath him in a vain effort to escape, and he thrust his hand up her skirt, and she bit and scratched at him and cried out for help, and all this in broad daylight and before her scandalized eyes, well, a body could stand only so much! This time Imelda Callaghan did not much care what would happen to Rosaleen out in the street, so out she went. To the great distress of the Callaghan males, Ignatius and Benedict, Rosaleen's successor was a buxom wench whose face sprouted the odd hair here and there and who had large yellow teeth and looked remarkably like a horse.

The Callaghans had refused to pay Rosaleen a penny even though she had worked for them for a month. They were quite within their rights. Mr Ignatius Callaghan vindictively said he would have her arrested for immorality, which was also within his rights. Who would take her word against his?

Rosaleen was not too cast down at having lost her job. The time she had spent in the employ of the Callaghans was the most miserable she had ever endured. She hated the obsequious behaviour expected of her. She hated the permanent watchfulness she had to employ in order to avoid the wandering hands of Mr Ignatius and his son. She hated the small cluttered house in the terraced row of houses. Its dark, heavily curtained interior seemed to entomb her, and the kitchen where she spent most of her time was in the basement and gave her claustrophobia.

Besides which, she was overworked. The title maid-of-all-work meant just that, and she was run off her feet morning, noon and night, with the cleaning and the cooking, the washing and the ironing, blackening boots, cleaning shoes, shopping, stitching, sewing, mending ... Her day began at 5 a.m. and ended when she collapsed on her cot-bed in the attic at 1 a.m.

The only good thing about her time with the Callaghans was that she was always too busy or tired to give in to the sharp ache of loneliness she carried within her night and day. She missed Cormac with a physical pain as if from an amputation; a part of her seemed severed. She felt incomplete without him, even though she had had him for such a short space of time. And her body missed Creagh. He had spoiled her for other men. Her soul pined for him. She held the memory of the Arcadian Grove, of those cloudless, scented June days of lovemaking, close to her heart. Sometimes, drowsily waking at five o'clock of a morning, she lingered in those memories in her dreamlike state, and she was once again in Creagh's arms and when she opened her eyes she would find they were wet with tears.

No, she was not sorry to leave the Callaghans and now she headed towards the city centre. It was here that poverty became obvious. There were beggars in the streets just off the main thoroughfares where shops displayed goods of every description and the wealthy sauntered or rode to their coffee-houses or clubs, and women shopped for Indian cotton and Burma silks, carpets from Samarkand and brocades from China. They rubbed shoulders in these arcades of plenty, Aladdin's caves for the rich who could afford the 'Open Sesame'. But in the slum streets that radiated out in all directions the rich never came. They were overcrowded alleys, filthy and decaying, impossible to live in, impossible to escape from. Rosaleen had wanted to avoid going there. That was why Rathmines had seemed so attractive. Her parents had often told her that Dublin was no place for her. They only went there when they had to, and that was not often.

'Tis no place fer a gypsy. There is no freedom there,' Hagar said. 'You are trapped. The deer don't run there and you cannot see the wheeling swallows or hear the nightingale or look upon the kingfisher flashing its bright plumage in the dark of the river Liffey. The eagle who hovers above the moor-fowl is a stranger there. The red squirrel shuns the place as do hedge-hogs and badgers, or so it seems to me. Maybe they are about, but in that place I do not see them, I have not eyes for them. We are not looking for the beauty of nature there. Our souls

222

wither there, and we want. We are content without gold in the wildness of the land. In the city we become greedy. So much we cannot afford laid out on display before us. So much that is unnecessary. It is a trap, the biggest trap of all, for greed binds us to the place that we think might satisfy our desires. Only it never satisfies. Gold never satisfies. There is never enough. Beware of it, Rosaleen. Beware of the tentacles that will bind your heart and trap your spirit and render you always dissatisfied.'

But Hagar was not here now and she was alone in this dangerous place and the only address she knew was Lizzie Brannagan's and The Green Cock.

She came to Carlisle Bridge. Carriages drawn by clopping horses crossed the river. Barefoot children begged or played in the roadway. Fancy ladies and grand ladies strolled by and gentlemen raised their hats. She took a turn to her right down the Quays. She could see the tall ships bobbing on the grey water and her ears were full of the shrill cries of seagulls. It was said that the birds were the souls of dead sailors. Grim-faced men, shirts blowing hard against hollow chests, lounged on bollards stained green by the droppings of birds, and blew on their fingers. They looked at her indifferently. Things must have come to a pretty pass, she thought, if they could not appreciate the picture she made in her bright shawl with her thick black curls bobbing about her and she tossing her head. Ah well, maybe it was all to the good, though she pitied them, but, sure, that had been her trouble in Rathmines.

She knew about Doone Alley, Lizzie Brannagan's and The Green Cock from her parents and Craw Kilty. She had not wanted to go there but now she had no choice. She had nothing; no clothes, no money, no possessions. Mr Ignatius Callaghan had thrown her into the street in what she stood up in. She was sick of respectable folk and their hypocrisy. Whatever happened now could not be worse than that.

The sun was going down over the Liffey, and the Custom House loomed large and pale behind her across the curling water. It was a big orange ball and seemed to suck all the colour to itself, leaving everything grey. She stood awhile and smelled the salt smell of the sea and the tar, the stink of the fish and she looked at the empty faces of the men sitting still as statues and felt a chill of apprehension.

Hagar and Melba came seldom to the city but when they did they went to Doone Alley for news of what was happening legally and illegally the length and breadth of the land. The people in the Alley knew it all, and nothing happened in Ireland that Lizzie Brannagan was not aware of.

Hagar had told her of the tavern, 'The Green Cock'. It was on the corner of St George's Lane and Dimchurch Row and opposite it Doone Alley ran parallel to the Quays, a cul-de-sac. Hagar had told her to go to the tavern if needs be and ask for One-Eyed Willy who, he said, practically lived there and was a friend. Well, she needed someone now and though the place looked dark and unsavoury she pushed the little half-door open and entered. It was dirt-floored with a liberal littering of straw on the ground. There were upturned barrels for tables. The place was full of smoke. Men sucked pipes and foul-smelling cheroots bought cheap from smugglers. The beams of the ceiling were low, and she had to bend her head, and there were no windows in the place. But the atmosphere inside was welcoming. The landlord and his wife were 'friends', Milo and Maisie Malloy they were called, and they sat in the light from the tinted oil-lamps fixed to the beams above them. They sat behind the tiny horse-shoe-shaped counter and served the customers black porter and brandy to them that could afford it. Sailors came here but never the soldiers, except on duty. Smugglers came looking for the 'fences' who drank here where contact could always be made. The dealers themselves did not venture here, it was too dangerous. But there was a small army of raggedy men who were 'go-betweens' and whose lives depended on knowing who was interested in what. Guns, opium, tobacco and brandy all found their way via 'The Green Cock' to a likely buyer.

One-Eyed Willy was a friend of Breen Dubh, the organizer of the area, and Breen owed his life to Hagar and Melba. He had jumped into the caravan an' it stood stuck behind a horse-and-wagon of manure and a milk-cart. He was carrying a bag of swag over his arm and three members of the Irish Constabulary were after him. The policemen had not thought to look in the caravan after they had poked about in the manure, and seemed glad enough to give up the chase. Hagar had driven Sissy the nag right into Doone Alley, with Breen sitting in the back cool as a cucumber. They thereby consolidated an already illustrious reputation for bravado, a quality very much admired in the area. Breen, One-Eyed Willie, Lizzie and others in the Alley had good reason to be gateful to Hagar and Melba. In the laws of this particular jungle such debts were sacred, so Rosaleen felt safe where another would have run in fear of her life. For this was dangerous territory and even the soldiers thought twice about entering and never dreamed of coming here alone.

One-Eyed Willy was leather-faced with a bulbous nose and two uneasy bottom teeth left in his head. He had only one eye, which gave him his name. It was lost in a waterfront fight and it left him with a horribly scarred socket.

'Now listen to me,' he said to her, when she had introduced herself to him, for there was no mistaking him. 'Now listen to me.' He winked at her with his good eye and slurped away gummily at his porter. 'You take my advice and sell what ye have, and that's considerable. You can take my word an' I'm a connoisseur.'

'But I have nothing. Don't you understand?'

The little man leered at her, his face breaking up into a thousand wrinkles.

'Are ye stupid or what?' he asked, exasperated. 'Sell yer body. Sell yer body, if ye have te have it in words of one syllable. For iffa the men are goin' te take their pleasure offa you, ye might as well get paid fer it.'

'The men here will not take their pleasure offa me at all.' Rosaleen sounded indignant. 'I love who I choose an' no one else need come around.'

The little man threw back his head and laughed. It was a merry sound and Rosaleen wanted to join in. Then he leaned forward breathing porter fumes into her face and said, 'They'll take their pleasure widout yer consent. Ye'll have no choice. Where de ye think ye are? Dublin Castle? Gawney Mac, ye'll be raped quick as a flash. Ye can't avoid it here. I'd do it te you meself, so I would, only I always have too much drink in me te get it up, if ye see what I mean. But I'm no ordinary eejit an' so I try te keep in wid Himself.' He blessed himself piously, took a drink of porter, followed it with a mouthful of whiskey, and drew his lips back from his pair of teeth as the straight whiskey hit his gums.

One-Eyed Willy went on trying to persuade her to use her body to make her way but she would not listen.

'Don't do it in the street,' he cautioned her. 'Ye'll get knifed or beaten or even murdered. Go to No. 1, the Bordello. Lizzie Brannagan'll see you right. Though, mind you, she's not at her best just now.'

She had no intention of becoming a whore. It would be abhorrent to her. But she decided to go to Lizzie Brannagan's to see what she could see and ask for news of her parents, for Lizzie would know. One-Eyed Willy bought her a brandy, he said, for her father's sake. She drank it quickly and left.

Lizzie Brannagan lived in the biggest house in Doone Alley. It was the first house and it had a mews behind it that flanked St George's Lane. It would have done no business if it had been further down the Alley. Strangers took their lives in their hands walking down that place in the dark of the night. The smells, if they had to penetrate further, would have quite put them off the task in hand: the quenching of their lust. Though the house was smartly painted, with windows gleaming, it nevertheless had a tawdry look and few mistook it for other than it was. The red-shaded gas lighting proclaimed its business to the world and many were shocked at the brazen way Lizzie Brannagan's advertised itself.

Rosaleen shivered going down the Alley. The cobbles beneath her feet were slimy with debris and a drunk lay across the entrance to Lizzie's. She knocked at the door. It was opened by a small girl of indeterminate age with a vacant gawpy look about her. The girl asked her what she wanted through a crack in the door. Rosaleen was tired out and fed up, despondent but full of the Dutch courage the brandy she had had in the tavern had given her.

She stuck her foot in through the door and said firmly. 'I want to see Lizzie Brannagan. She knows my father and mother.'

Someone else arrived behind the stupid-looking one and Rosaleen saw a large brown eye in a full soft face peering at her.

Through the crack a golden glow seemed to illuminate a lot of red plush, but Rosaleen, though she tried, could not see much.

'Who're you?' the new voice, flat Dublin, asked, 'What de ye want?'

'Yerra, I've already said. I want to see Lizzie Brannagan.'

'Well yiz can't. She's sick.' The door was firmly closed, but it met the obstacle of her foot.

'Ouch! That hurt,' Rosaleen cried. 'You don't understand. I was sent here. One-Eyed Willy sent me.'

'Why didn't ya say so in the first place?' the brown-eyed one said and the door was flung open with such suddenness that Rosaleen nearly fell into the large entrance hall.

Inside it was over-warm, over-perfumed, over-decorated. Red plush, ceilings painted in erotic imagery by a very bad artist, which somehow rendered the frescoes lewd and vulgar and therefore in the opinion of many a customer more conducive to arousal than if they had been executed by a genius.

The small vacant-looking person was dressed as a maid in a black uniform and a white mop-cap. The other larger woman held a black peignoir together over precious little else. She shamelessly revealed vast quantities of pink flesh with a careless indifference that had Rosaleen's eyes wide with astonishment.

'Are you Lizzie Brannagan?' she asked. The big woman shook with laughter, her rosy flesh undulating with her abandoned movement. She held a cigar between her fingers and when she had finished laughing she puffed on it, looking at Rosaleen speculatively.

'Yiz are a tasty piece an' no mistake,' she said. 'No, I'm not Lizzie. Lizzie is sick. Very sick. If yiz want te see her ye'll have te go to the second floor.' She jerked her head. 'Up there.'

Rosaleen mounted the red carpeted stairs. The banisters were painted gold and there was a naked golden cherub at each landing. The scent of musk and tuber-rose was overpowering. Rosaleen came to a large door that the vacant-looking maid indicated. She knocked, wondering at the maid's attitude, for the creature had fallen back nervously and was obviously not going to announce her.

She entered, gasped, and nearly fainted at the sight that met her eyes. The thing that was propped up on red satin cushions in the vast bed was the remains of a woman. The face, horribly bloated, was covered on one side with suppurating sores. Most of her hair had fallen out and she looked toothless. She was dripping with perspiration and appeared in great pain. The eyes that searched Rosaleen's white face were full of an awful pleading.

'Ah Jasus, am I as bad as that?' she wheezed.

'No. No,' Rosaleen whispered, trying to keep her equilibrium.

227

'Don't lie to me, child. I can see it in your face. Ah, God help us,' it's worse than I thought. The others keep the mirrors away.' She had difficulty breathing, her chest seemed congested. 'Who are ye?' she asked after a pause during which both women stared at each other in the gloom. Rosaleen told her. 'God bless us. Melba and Hagar, my old friends. But they're in Spain now. Breen Dubh got it from the Minstrel.'

'I know.'

'An' why aren't you with them?'

'It's a long story, Lizzie. May I call you that?' Rosaleen was becoming acclimatized to the room and its inmate.

'O'course, dotey. O'course. What a beauty you are. Melba never told me.' She chuckled silently,' Hagar never brought you here in case you were shocked. Did you know that?'

Rosaleen shook her head. Hagar seemed very far away now. But it was good to talk of her parents to people who knew them.

'Yes. He kept you away. Gawney Mac, there's nothin' to be shocked at here. Except me, dotey. Except me.' Lizzie tried to raise herself higher in the bed but failed in her attempt. 'You're Dark Rosaleen, aren't you?' she wheezed.

Rosaleen nodded.

'Rosaleen. It's a lovely name.' Lizzie's small eyes, engulfed by rolls of flesh peered at her. 'An' what do ye want of me?' she asked.

'I wanted you to give me a job.'

'Janey, nothin' could be easier. Lookin' like you.'

'No. No.' Rosaleen was nervous. 'I want a job, but ... but not whoring. I couldn't do that.'

There was a terrible sound from the bed and Rosaleen nearly ran away. It began low, then grew in volume, gathering rumbles and whistles and a moaning sort of bellow. Rosaleen thought Lizzie Brannagan was having a fit until she realized the woman was laughing.

When at last the spasm had ceased she said, 'A girl who comes to a brothel lookin' fer work, but isn't about to whore ... Jasus, I've heard it all now.'

'I've been working in a house on the Rathmines Road. But I got thrown out,' Rosaleen said nervously.

'Why?' The woman was looking at her intently.

''Twas the father and the son. They plagued me morning, noon, and night. 'Twas the missus found first the son and then

the ould fella trying to ... to ...' Rosaleen faltered and Lizzie
Brannagan did her imitation of a landed whale again.

'Sure, you needn't go on,' she said. 'A bat could see it all. No
sane man could keep his hands offa you. The picture is as clear
as crystal without explanation.'

'Well, I made up my mind, never again. It's not the way I
plan to exist. So if it's all you've got to offer, then I'll be on my
way.' Rosaleen moved to the door.

'Hold yer horses there!' Lizzie leaned forward and called,
then exhausted fell back on the red satin pillows panting and
gasping. Rosaleen looked around the room. It was a mess and
she could not see a cloth anywhere so she took a towel from a
rack. She went over to Lizzie and gently blotted the sweat from
her face. The woman looked at her gratefully.

'Thank you, dotey. Thank you.'

When she had recovered herself somewhat she eyed Rosaleen
speculatively.

'You don't look shocked any more. Have ye got over yer
fright?'

'Yes, I have. I'm sorry it showed. I wouldn't have ... if I'd
known.'

'Ye mean those bitches down there didn't warn ye? Christ
almighty! Well. Do you find me too repulsive to be near?
Answer truthfully.'

Rosaleen shook her head. 'Oh no. I'm a woman of the roads.
Things like that don't offend me.

Lizzie looked at Rosaleen a moment. 'I believe you,' she said.
'Could you look after me, do you think? It'll not be easy. But
the others are so hell-fired nervous of comin' into the room that
I'm often in desperate need of water or clean linen. Could ye,
do ye think?'

'Is what ye have contagious?' Rosaleen asked. 'Ye see I've got
to be practical ...'

'Say no more. I'd ask the same an' I were you. No. It's not.
To you at any rate. It might be if I plied my trade again, but
there's no chanst of that.'

'Well then, I'll be glad to, Lizzie Brannagan, for eighteen
shillings a week and my board and lodging.'

When the madam of the brothel took Rosaleen's hand in
hers to seal the bargain she knew she had not made a mistake.

'What's the matter wi' ye?' Rosaleen asked.

'The sickness. It's an occupational hazard. Sure, what can ye do? The other girls help as best they can. Ye can't blame them for being afraid. I lie here and hours go by an' no one comes.' She sighed, 'Look at me now. My face is eaten away. Seven years after I got infected I was sick for a while, then I thought I was better. But no. It's bad, Rosaleen. Bad.'

'Never mind. I'll help ye now. Ye see, Lizzie, I have nowhere to turn. Nowhere to go. So I'm grateful for the chance.'

'Aren't ye from heaven itself? Look, take the room down the corridor. Elsie O'Connor, a cow of a girl, had it and she ran off with the son of the haberdasher Rourke, an' God knows where she is now. In the river Liffey no doubt. You go there an' have a rest.'

It had been a long and trying day. Rosaleen was physically and emotionally worn out. But she insisted on fixing Lizzie up before she took the promised rest. She changed her sheets for her, washed her down, and made her a cup of tea before she peeled off her clothes. She was amply rewarded by the gratitude Lizzie showed. Finally she threw herself on the unmade bed in the room Lizzie had allocated to her and fell into a deep dreamless sleep.

Chapter

36

IN the weeks that followed Lizzie talked to Rosaleen, who nursed her and looked after her briskly and efficiently. The two women grew very fond of each other. They had a lot in common. Both of them fought the world knowing they were playing against loaded dice, but they fought cheerfully and without complaint. Rosaleen knew that Lizzie had not long to live. She found out all about the sick madam and the more she learned about Lizzie the more fond of her she grew.

Lizzie Brannagan was a Manchester girl, with an Irish father and an English mother. She was a survivor who had overcome almost insurmountable odds in her thirty-five years, only to be finally and ironically struck down by her sexual illness when she, at last, had become solvent.

She had fallen in love at sixteen with an officer, a captain in the Dragoons, who took her lightly, then told her he had been transferred to Dublin. She followed him, by now pregnant, innocently assuming he would look after her. He cruelly refused to see her and sent a brother officer to state his position with brutal frankness. He did not want to see her again. She was socially inferior to him and any contact would be abhorrent to him. He felt no obligation towards her. She must do as she pleased. How did he know he was the father of the brat she was carrying? If she did not stop pestering him he would have her arrested and thrown into prison or deported, he said.

Lizzie had had her baby, a boy she called Jimmy after his father. She walked the streets trying to find work, work of any sort, but it was a hopeless task. She might have got herself a job in service, but that was out of the question with her child. There was no work for a ruined maid and no respectable house would entertain the idea of giving her and her baby a home in return for even the most arduous work. She was a 'fallen woman' and therefore outside the pale.

'They were dark days, Rosaleen,' she said. She lay propped up by the red satin pillows, covered with red satin sheets in her giant canopied four-poster. 'On a good night I could squeeze four officers into this bed, Rosa,' she confided. 'The officers were fun. All together, all young. Our bodies looked like white flowers on the crimson sheets, legs and arms, breasts and faces all tangled together in the pleasuring of ourselves. Oh, it was grand. Those were the good times.'

Rosaleen bathed the swollen raddled face and tenderly dipped the napkin in cool water or warmed oil to try to ease Lizzie's discomfort.

'Yer a good girl, Rosa. Yer not afraid of me. The other little whores are. They think they might catch it from me.' She laughed mirthlessly. 'Gawny, how stupid can you be? I asks you. Their problems come in the door and wear pants. Yerra sure, they can't help it. Stupid, most of them. Haven't the nouse to run this place. I could. I always had the will. It was my Manchester know-how. The be-Jasus has been beaten out of the Irish after all this time with the occupation and they're useless to run anything.'

Rosaleen built up the fire though it was tropically warm in the room. Lizzie kept the dark red velvet curtains drawn night and day and liked the lamps turned down low.

'I look so monstrous, dotey. Once I was lovely. So lovely. That's why my soldier fell in love with me and couldn't stay away. Until he thought I would hamper him socially. Ah, it's always the same. Power for the men. Don't they love it?

'My little lad Jimmy died, you see, of not enough food and no medicine an' a cough that would not go away an' me walking the length and breadth of Dublin looking for help or work or both. But there was none to be found. Even in the churches. The clergy scolded me and said I'd reaped my just reward for my sin, and they wouldn't tell me how to find shelter except in the workhouse. The nuns said I was a scarlet woman and not deserving of God's mercy.'

She looked at Rosaleen, her eyes full of tears, their expression helpless and miserable. It was an old story. That was the moment in Lizzie Brannagan's life when the light had gone out and all feelings of hope for a better life, of innocence and trust had left her forever.

'He died, my lamb, my pet. I swore then that they would never beat me. They could try their damnedest but they'd not break Lizzie Brannagan with their cold smiling faces, their fat bellies and their hypocrisy.

'I buried the boy in the graveyard above in Glasnevin. I did it myself.' Her coal-black eyes glittered. 'Ye wouldn't believe it, dotey. They called me a pauper and him a bastard and wanted to throw my baby in a communal grave. A pauper's grave. But I ran away and stole up to Glasnevin at night. I was near dead with grief and hunger and fatigue but I found a little plot under a yew tree. it was between a Brannagan, my name see, and someone called Martin. I dug and dug and dug with a spade I'd stolen from the hut in that place. It didn't need too much diggin', for the boy was tiny, and I wrapped the precious little body in my mother's silk shawl and covered him with earth and prayed over him a while, for if His clergy on earth are heartless and cruel I'm sure the Sweet Lord Jesus is kind, and didn't he say "Suffer the little children ..."'

There was a long pause punctuated only by Lizzie's sobs. Rosaleen let her sob herself out. She bathed the forehead, hot and sticky with sweat. She thought of Cormac and her heart swelled with gratitude. This could have been her story too. Her heart was full of tenderness for the woman who had suffered so much and yet had not given in.

For a while the only sounds in the room were the ticking of the clock, the plop of the ash in the grate and the disembodied cries of sex that came occasionally from the other regions of the house.

'It was that night I met the man who gave me this house. It was in that very place, the graveyard in Glasnevin. He was visiting the tomb of his daughter who had recently died of a fever. He liked to go in the evening when there was nobody there. He saw me hunched up and crying, half-mad with grief, and he put me in his carriage and he drove me round and round till almost dawn. He told me of his wife, a cold righteous woman' — she broke off. 'You know Rosaleen, in my life I have discovered there is nothing worse than a righteous woman. They are without pity' — 'denied him his rights as a husband.

Well I eased him on that score. By this time we had told each other everything. You see, I never felt that sex was too important. No to me it wasn't. Not after the first one deserted me. And if it meant so much to him ... well. And he was grateful. He showed me how grateful he was. It's no use *sayin'* yer grateful if you don't *do* anything about it. He did. He bought me this house. And furnished it. We did it up together. It's mine, lock, stock and barrel. Yes, he was good to me.'

'What was he like?' Rosaleen asked.

'He was an old man, more like a father to me.' A roguish look crossed her face and she smiled, revealing her empty gums. 'Though he was not like me Da in this bed. He treated me fine and put this house in the name of Lizzie Brannagan. Then he died. After ten good years with me as his mistress he died. Then all I had was this. God, Rosa, I missed him. I never realized how much he meant to me. He made me laugh, see? So I turned it into a bordello, a whore-house. It's all I know how to do an' I've done it well. Up to now. I've got good girls and I treat them fairly. The only thing was, I was hoist on my own petard. Bloody syphilis, or gonorrhoea. Ah, God, I'm not even sure. The doctor simply shakes his head. Rosaleen, yer right to keep off the men. For pleasure they're fine, but it's their world. They hold the power of life and death over us and they know it. Except for a few like my Charlie, it's they who make us what we are.'

She turned painfully this way and that and looked at Rosaleen with pleading eyes.

'What could I have done? she asked.

Rosaleen hushed her. 'Keep still and I'll change the sheets. Get you fresh ones.' She rolled Lizzie's vast bulk over and with the tenderness of a mother she stripped the body, rolled her back on an oilcloth and gently sponged her down. She replaced the sheets, one side first, then the other. She had pleaded with Lizzie to get sheets in some more practical fabric like linen or cotton but she would not hear of it, she stubbornly refused to budge.

'Me red sheets are *my* indulgence, a sign of my success,' the raddled woman said, seeing no irony in her statements. 'Ye'll not take them away until I'm dead.'

When at last Rosaleen had her as comfortable as she could be. Lizzie would ask for her opium-pipe. Rosaleen prepared the hookah for her with care and watched until she fell into an opium dream-world where she could forget her pain for a short while. She would sit with her, stitching in the lamplight, feeling peaceful and curiously content.

After her experiences of the last months — the bearing of her child, then the pain of giving it away; the misery of the time she spent in Rathmines; the fear she had known and her loneliness for Creagh and her parents — Rosaleen found the brothel in Doone Alley a refuge and a respite. She smiled at the perversity of fate, but she was glad of the comfort and security she found within its walls. And she was in a place where news of Cormac could reach her easily.

It helped that Lizzie knew Melba and Hagar. They often talked of her parents to while away the pain-filled hours and Rosaleen told of their lives and their wanderings. Lizzie told Rosaleen that she had heard via the grapevine that Melba and Hagar were in Saintes Maries-sur-Mer in the Camargue. They had been there this May to visit the burial site of their patron saint, Black Sara, and to join the gypsies who would come from every corner of the globe to take part in this 'pèlerinage des Gitans'.

'God'n it sounds grand, Rosa. Yer parents told me about it. Three Virgin Marys crossed the Mediterranean Sea with their black servant Sara. Sara is buried in a church there. For a week the gypsies dance and sing and honour her. They go to the church and kiss her in the crypt where she lies. Oh, it sounds grand. Just the sort of party I would love. Then they were headed for Spain.' She rolled up her eyes. 'Some people!' she said. 'Talk about luck!'

Rosaleen talked of Creagh but never of Cormac. That was still too painful. They became very close and Lizzie looked on Rosaleen as the daughter she never had. She told Rosaleen that she was leaving her the house to do with as she saw fit.

'It's a little gold-mine, Rosa, and you'll not want for anything, I'll be bound, as long as there are men in the world.'

'I really don't expect you to do this, Lizzie,' Rosaleen said. 'I feel ashamed, as if I was nursing you for some ulterior motive. Instead I'd do it now even if you couldn't pay me.'

'Think I don't know that? Never look a gift-horse in the mouth, Rosa. D'ye hear. Yerra, you've done more for me in the last months than anyone, apart from the ould fella who gave me all this. Charlie and you. *No*, Rosaleen, take my word for it, you'll be all right here and you deserve it. You'll not be dependent on any man at all, and we have a good arrangement with the powers that be through Breen Dubh. Watch out for him, *acushla*, for he's a wicked one.'

Rosaleen listened to Lizzie's advice. She was grateful to the woman and content as she could be in the city, enclosed and trapped as she sometimes felt herself to be. Nights she lay sleepless in her bed dreaming of cold streams, fields of poppies splashing the corn with scarlet, drifts of bluebells under the trees and the beckoning finger of the open road. But here she had the opportunity to make some money and be safe. That was what she wanted. And she was in the place to find out about Cormac. She still missed him very much and often awakened calling his name, her cheeks wet with tears.

Her bedroom was, in contrast to the other rooms in the house, simplicity itself. Her small trestle bed was covered with a white cotton counterpane and the bright-coloured shawl Craw Kilty had given her. The walls were painted white and there was nothing in the room save the bed, the wash-basin, a single chair a dressing-table, and always, whenever she could possibly get one, even if she had to steal it, a flower in a glass vase.

Rosaleen was very fond of Lizzie, but realistic enough to accept that the woman was dying and would not last that much longer. She was appalled by the ravages of the sickness, and the pain Lizzie suffered scared her. It only cemented her decision not to take up the world's oldest profession. The Minstrel came sometimes. With him she could talk of things the others did not understand, even Lizzie, who understood so much. He would sit across the kitchen table, his wide startled eyes gazing at her, his faun-like face expressing all his thoughts, running his hand through his cap of curly hair.

'I don't know how you can stay here, Rosaleen,' he would say.

'I don't know either, Ronan. But stay I must till Cormac is grown. Ah God, sometimes the heart within me weeps for a sight of the sounding sea, the lapping lake-water or the cowslip curtained about with blades of sweet green grass. I ache to smell the cows and the lambs in the frost. I want to be on my stomach in a meadow, my face in the clover and listen to the skylark. You know, Ronan, I dream even of the harshness, the cold winds that slice your face in half and the times yer feet are numb with the snow and frost on the ground. Ach, Ronan, 'tis good to see you here, bringing the memory back to me.' And she would look at the tenderness and understanding in his eyes and feel a closeness to him that she had never felt with anyone else. 'Sure, it's in our blood,' she would add, sighing.

'Then why do you stay? Why not come away with me now, back to the wild wide world?'

And Rosaleen would shake her head regretfully. 'I can't, Ronan. Don't tempt me. I have to take this time out of my life to set. To stay put. It's Cormac, you see. I must be within reach. Do you see?'

He understood. He always did. He would give her then the news from Usher. It was always the same; Dolly was overly-protective of Cormac. She guarded him night and day in her anxiety that nought bad should befall him.

'Better that than neglect and poverty and the wild,' Rosaleen would say. 'Much better too much than too little.'

But Ronan was not so sure.

Chapter

37

ROSIE Moore and Batty Macklin had been with Lizzie from the first. Batty who had opened the door for Rosaleen that first day had rabbit teeth and was not the full shilling. She was astray in her wits and her job was to open the door for the gentlemen. She knew a member of the Irish Constabulary a mile off and had an unerring nose for troublemakers. Rosie of the brown eyes, eyes a man could drown in, Lizzie said, was the prettiest and the cleverest girl in the house.

'Which wouldn't be hard, now would it?' Lizzie laughed, 'She is the most popular one with the men. She's as welcoming as a duck-feather eiderdown and as lazy as a pregnant cat '

The other girls, Rosaleen found, were stupid, or even astray in their minds. Some were mean and sulky, some resentful, some lazy beyond belief. Rosaleen took charge of the place, shouldering the responsibility of the running of the establishment. This allowed Lizzie to sink into her drugged world where she could forget the pain and escape thoughts of the inevitable horror of her death. As time went on and April slipped into May Lizzie became worse. Most of her days and nights were spent in an opium delirium. Sometimes she came to, out of her world of pain and shadows and perpetual sleep, and spoke to Rosaleen of earlier happier times.

'We went for a picnic, once, to Killiney Strand. There were seals in the bay and the sun shone. I'll never forget it, Rosaleen. I'd gone with some customers, soldiers they were. I always had a weak spot for a uniform, Rosa. I loved them all that day. We sat on the beach and ate ripe plums and drank champagne. We were like innocents, no maiden from Merrion Square could have been more modest. We laughed and played. The pebbles were polished. For hundreds of years the sea had been caressing them, one of the soldiers, a Welsh lad, said. That evening we went to the theatre. The Theatre Royal in Hawkins Street. There were girls in pink tights and bright lights. A woman sang with a harp and a clown made us laugh and cry. It was Harlequin and Colombine. I remember. The soldiers bought us some chocolates. I felt like a human being. For the first time since I left Manchester, maybe in my life, I felt like a real person. I could hold me head up. I could laugh. I'd got nothing to be ashamed of for that one day. It's sad that women have to suffer so. It's a man's world, Rosa. Remember that. They take us lightly, get their fill of us soon enough and are off and away. Like a bee they flit from flower to flower and never give a thought to what they leave behind. We are broken blossoms, Rosa, for what can we do? Where else could I end up with the babby? Or you with your looks? We are victims, Rosa. Victims.'

'I'm not going to be a victim, Lizzie. Not I.'

Lizzie shook her head feebly. 'We all say that, dotey. All of us. And we end up the same. Married if we're lucky. Obeying him, doing as we're told. Never letting him see what we think and feel. Oh, I've had them here, the husbands, grunting on top of me. All the same, they are. An' if we don't marry? No status. You'll end up a helper in the house without the dignity of being "wife" or "mother". And if there is no relative to take you in then it's service or the streets. That's a woman's lot. How can you avoid it?'

'Money,' Rosaleen said simply. 'Money.'

Lizzie tried to laugh, but it was too much for her now. It hurt. 'Maybe you're right,' she wheezed. 'Maybe. But it won't get you accepted in polite society. An' none of the men who come here will bow to you in the street. Ach, it's an unfair world I tell ye.' She fell into a troubled doze.

The days passed without much happening other than the regular business of the place. Rosaleen was mostly occupied with Lizzie and all the paraphernalia of nursing the sick. She had hardly been outside the door since the day she had arrived. She decided it was time she had a look around.

Chapter

38

A few weeks later Rosaleen sat in front of her dressing-table, the maid arranging her hair. She had piled the dark tresses on the top and back of her head and now was gently teasing the soft black ringlets into strategically seductive arrangements over her shell-like ears, and at the nape of her neck. With the silver handle of the comb she coaxed fluffy tendrils onto the milk-white forehead. Batty glanced at her in the mirror, catching her mistress's eye which gave her the signal to proceed and told her Rosaleen was satisfied. They had discovered how talented Batty was, accidentally and to their mutual satisfaction. Now, as well as opening the door, she was Rosaleen's personal maid.

She had dressed her in a wine satin gown trimmed with tassles. The bosom was cut low. It revealed the marble-white mounds of her breasts nearly to the nipples. The beads around her neck were red crystals. The gems were cut in teardrop shapes and lay on her pearly skin like drops of blood. The waist of her dress was tight and tiny, the skirts flowing down to her red slippers. Batty now fixed ruby-red pendants in her ears and Rosaleen picked up her fan.

It was not late and the sun still shone in the sky but Rosaleen was dressed for the night. She went to the window and leaned out. She had made a very short-lived excursion into the area around No. I Doone Alley and what she saw had disgusted her. She had quickly returned and had not ventured out again.

Below her, a group of boys in tattered breeches and caps, torn shirts and laceless boots was playing cards. One of them saw her and nudged the others. They sniggered and the smallest gurrier cried out an obscenity, but she did not hear. She had bathed and tended Lizzie and left her in a drugged dream, which was all that was left to her, poor sod. She would go in again to check on her before she went downstairs, and perhaps coax her to a sip of the caudle she had brewed that afternoon especially. But, for the moment she wanted to look at the first stars in the indigo sky. She did not see the filthy alley below her. She looked to where the Liffey flowed, slate grey in the fading light. She had been horrified by the little streets that radiated from the Quays, mean slums, foul with rotting rubbish and debris. The dark alleys and crime-infested tenements leaned drunkenly against each other. The houses were precarious, windows broken, stairways rotting, walls damp and slimy with neglect and the proximity of the river.

The cul-de-sac called Doone Alley was the worst, a hell-hole of pestilence, of hopelessness and despair. The gates of Hell were supposed to carry the warning, 'Abandon hope all ye who enter here'. That warning would have been very appropriate for Doone Alley. Knife fights here, and there were many, ended in death, for there was no escape. You were cornered. The dwellers said that once you were in Doone Alley you could never get out.

Slatternly women sat in the cobbled street this June day. Men lurked, furtive, shifty-eyed and listless, hoping for a coin to go to the Green Cock tavern beyond Lizzie Brannagan's, fatalistically certain it would not be forthcoming. It seldom was. The cobblestones were usually covered in excrement and dirt. Around the corner in St George's Lane were shops. Ships chandlers, trunkmakers. There was a dairy with cattle in the stalls yielding milk of doubtful cleanliness. A barber's pole overhung the footway and there were huckster shops stocked with every sort of saleable and perishable goods. They thrived on credit and barter, for the alleys around St George's Lane were squalid and grim, and there was no money there. The sun never seemed to shine there, a darkness reigned over the place and the meagre livelihood available to the pathetic inhabitants of the myriad lanes and alleyways that ran from the wharves and dockside, stunted their growth, rotted their teeth and laid them open to all the illnesses rampant there, through deprivation and neglect. Disease spread rapidly in the tenements. It was transmitted easily in overcrowded rooms. Most had a very low resistance for they were weakened by lack of proper nourishment and by the cold and damp in which they lived and the inadequate clothing which was all they had to wear.

The rats in the garbage sometimes bit. Prams made of wicker or of planks, on rickety wheels or none at all, stood outside most of the slum houses. The houses were infested with cockroaches and the halls were unsafe places full of dust and debris and decay. They smelled of stale vomit, urine and yesterday's beer. Fifty percent of the children died of tuberculosis or malnutrition.

Rosaleen knew these things, but with her inbuilt sense of survival she did not dwell on them. She was realistic enough to know there was nothing she, singlehandedly, could do in the teeming warren she had found herself in.

The tall masts of ships bobbed on the skyline and far in the distance where Rosaleen gazed now, she could just make out the mountains of Wicklow somewhere behind them, so far, far away. It was stupid to wish, to remember, to dream of the June days this time last year when she had gazed at her reflection in the pool of the Arcadian Grove, and the swans sailed majestically past. Creagh's face had joined her in its mirror clearness until he shattered the blue waters with his fingers and broke the picture in a shower of silver ripples. To remember the Arcadian Grove now was painful and a waste of time. She did not intend to remain forever in this squalid place and she was not depressed at her progress. She had done, was doing, quite well considering the fact that she had started with nothing. She felt that some of the Minstrel's charmed existence had rubbed off on her, for she had not sought to make money out of Lizzie Brannagan.

She looked at the street below her, which was cleaner than usual. The cobblestones had been washed by the torrential rain last night and shone slate-grey, wet and shiny, and now were steaming dry in the late sunshine. June had reasserted herself and the weather today was more in keeping with summer. A grey day after the storm the previous night and now, of a sudden, the sun had appeared joyously from behind the swollen purple clouds. Everyone in Doone Alley had emerged and journeyed into St George's Lane, or sallied as far as the wharves, to get a taste of its warmth. Women were hanging their washing across the street, for there had been water after the downpour. Children had tied a rope around the lamp-post and were swinging out of it. The men wore greasy caps and leaned against the walls, or lounged in the doorways of the broken-down houses. Some of them sometimes got work on the docks beyond, but the competition was fierce and the jobs were scarce. So was money, food, or anything at all you could name that would give a creature comfort in this outpost of hopelessness.

Rosaleen shivered and left the window. She touched the beads at her throat and looked at herself in the mirror with satisfaction. She looked well-fed and sleek, unlike the women she had seen below. Her dark cloud of hair was as glossy as a raven's wing and her eyes were full of starlight.

She left her room. She opened a door further down and peeped in.

'Rosie, you all right?'

The pretty woman nodded. She seemed all flesh. She was soft as a cream *gâteau* and as sweet. Her skin, and she showed most of it, was of a thick white texture and it glowed in the dim light, making you want to touch it. She wore a black satin chemise, lace trimmed, and she lay on her bed, plump knees in the air, waiting for her first customer, like dessert.

'Yerra, I'm fine, Rosaleen. An' herself?' she asked.

'She's very poorly. She won't last long, Rosie. I'm going to close the house for a few days when she goes.'

Rosie wrinkled her nose. 'The girls'll complain. Money lost, you see.'

'Well, tell them they're lucky I've decided to keep the place going. Lizzie says I can close any time. I've kept it going for their sakes. You tell them that. An' if there's any trouble I'll sell out. That ought to put the fear of God in 'em. Janey, Rosie, I'da thought they'd have been glad of a day or two off.'

She shook her head. Rosie laughed. It was a warm deep belly-laugh.

'I know. Me, I'm relieved. Them, they think like shop-keepers. Anyhow, all o' them think yer goin' to close. They're sure of it. But not yet, not yet. That's why they don't like time off. They're in a hurry. They really believe they're different. They think that one day they'll escape. They don't yet know we're all goin' to end up here.'

'I don't intend to, Rosie. Not me,' Rosaleen said firmly.

Rosie smiled ironically. 'You too, Rosaleen?' she asked. 'You too?'

Rosaleen looked angry. 'I mean it, Rosie. Not me. Not here. I'd die.'

'They all say that.' Rosie shrugged, 'But they don't realize they are all going to end up like her. Like poor old Lizzie, God help her.'

'You'll tell them, Rosie?' Rosaleen had had enough of the conversation. 'An' you'll see they don't make a fuss? I don't want any trouble. I want Lizzie to have as easy a passing as possible. An' I want her to have a fine funeral.'

'I'll tell 'em, Rosaleen. Never you fret.'

Rosaleen closed the door and went down the corridor past the other girls' rooms and up the stairs to where Lizzie's apartment and her own were situated. She went in to the invalid's room. The heat and the smell pulverized her. Lizzie seemed comatose. But when Rosaleen crossed the room she stirred and opened her eyes.

'I knew you'd come, dotey. God, you're a good girl. I knew it the minute I clapped eyes on you. I said to meself, that girl is one hundred percent, that's what I said. Sure, coming from Melba and Hagar ye'd have to be. It's a pity, though, that you wouldn't work. You'd 'a made my place famous throughout Ireland.'

'It already is, Lizzie. It is. Now be still and let me fix you up more comfortably.'

'Well, then, in the world. You're made for men, Rosaleen, and ye look it tonight. You're a man's dream come true. Why are ye dressed up so? Have ye a lover? If not it's a terrible waste.'

'No, Lizzie, I haven't a lover. I'd have told ye if I had, wouldn't I? No. But I have a feeling ... You know. A sort of premonition that something ... something is on the way.' She shook her head. 'It's silly, I suppose.'

'Never say that. Those feelings are the most accurate. Well, I'll be glad if it is a lover on his way, I'll tell ye that. It's not natural.'

'Oh hush up, Lizzie. Is the pain bad?'

'Excruciatin'. Excruciatin'. I'll go to heaven, Rosaleen, so I will, for I've had me hell on earth.'

'Of course you will, an' welcome.'

The terrible face turned to Rosaleen. 'They'll let me in, will they? In spite of what I've done? How I've lived? You know ... this place?'

244

'Of course, Lizzie. Of course. Don't fret. Sure, those girls downstairs would be dead or doing it in the streets and alley-ways and gettin' knifed for their trouble if it wasn't for you. God understands. Surely He does.'

Lizzie lay back exhausted but satisfied. 'I had no choice, Rosa. Maybe I shoulda died. Maybe God'd be better pleased if I'da died with my babby.'

'No, Lizzie, no. Then what would I have done? I'm not ready to die and you've been good to me, Lizzie. That'll get you into heaven, on the strength of that alone.'

'Listen, dotey. I have quite a bit stashed away for a rainy day, only the rainy day was sickness an' it's never goin' to get sunny. So. You must have it.' And as Rosaleen was about to protest, 'No. I'm that scared the others will get their hands on it. I need to know you have it. I haven't long to go, Rosa.'

'Ah, don't say that, Lizzie. Where there's life, y'know ...'

'Tell the truth, I'll be glad to be outa it. Look, over there. The wardrobe. Open it. There's a chamber-pot in the bottom. You'll find a stocking full of coins. It's yours. Get it now, for I'll not have it lost. You'll hide it well and make the best use of it. It makes me happy to think I'll have helped you. Maybe you'll escape after all ... maybe ...' Her voice trailed off into a mutter and she drifted into an uneasy sleep.

Rosaleen prepared the hookah. When she gave it to Lizzie the dying woman whispered, 'Get it now. Take it. You've been so good.' Her eyes filled with tears, 'Me own daughter couldn' done better. We been good to each other, eh, Rosaleen?'

Rosaleen nodded. 'Yes we have, Lizzie,' she said and the older woman turned to the solace of the drug.

Rosaleen crossed the room to the heavy wardrobe. She opened it and saw the porcelain chamber-pot decorated with pink cabbage-roses. Lizzie had put it away when she became ill and now used a white ceramic one that Rosaleen emptied for her.

The pink chamber-pot had been kept for her gentlemen customers. There was no lavatory in the house, only an outside privy, which hardly suited the gentlemen. It was at the bottom of the muddy square that passed for a garden behind the house. It leaned against the mews where the gentlemen tethered their horses or housed their carriages while they took their pleasure on the girls of No. I.

245

Now Rosaleen lifted the chamber-pot out and inside it she found the stocking. Her heart jumped with excitement. There were at least a hundred gold coins in the stocking. They winked in the candlelight in the roseate room, beguiling and seductive.

Rosaleen had never wanted money before. She had wanted Creagh with all her heart and body and Cormac with all her soul. Well, both had been taken away from her and had left a cold and empty place within her. These bright coins could assuage her loneliness and fear and fill the gap a little. She had never coveted possessions in her life, but now she was becoming aware that there were some things that soothed a broken heart, and that comforts helped and money bought such comforts.

She smiled and threw the coins on the dressing-table. They had an exciting tinkle to them like the bracelets on her ankles. She let them fall through her fingers. She could grow to love them, she thought. The light from the fire and the candles flickered and the glow from the coins danced back. She sat awhile dreaming.

Suddenly a tingling shivered up her spine, a thrill of impending danger. She had felt it this morning. Was it excitement or was it something to be feared? She didn't know. She sat up, tense. A cold chill followed the shiver, and, alert now as a deer in the forest, she frowned.

'There's danger coming,' she whispered. 'Danger.'

She knew it in the marrow of her bones. What it was or from whence it came she did not know, but it was there outside in the dark of the night. She carefully put the coins back into the stocking, replaced the stocking in the chamber-pot. She decided that the wardrobe was the safest place after all, and she had just hidden them behind a row of Lizzie's boots when there was a rapping at the front-door that made her jump.

Chapter

39

IT was a furtive rapping. Not the firm authoritative knocking their customers usually made, nor the careless rap of the gentlemen demanding entrance, nor yet the rumbustious commotion the soldiers created when they visited Lizzie Brannagan's. It was either the rapping of a green-horn or something sinister. She decided it must be the latter because of the apprehension she had felt all day.

She heard Batty go to the door. She glanced at Lizzie and saw that there was nothing further she could do for her benefactress, so she left the room. She crossed the landing in time to see Batty open the door and the Minstrel burst in, followed by the Widow Boann carrying a child in her arms. For a frozen instant Rosaleen thought the child was Cormac, but almost as soon as the shock ran through her, her reason asserted itself and she realized that the child in the Widow's arms was too big.

She ran down the stairs that led to the reception area. The Widow had sunk onto one of the plush love-seats that graced the centre of the hall. As Rosaleen reached the hall the Minstrel saw her and caught her awkwardly in his arms as he greeted her, his face anxious.

'Oh Ronan, what brings you here?' she asked.

'Ah, Rosaleen, we wouldn't have come here if we had any choice, *a grá*.'

'Never mind that, Ronan. An' where would ye go but to friends, I ask you?' She touched his pale face with her hand. 'I've missed you,' she said. It was two weeks since she had seen him. 'What happened?'

'They were betrayed at Usher. A squadron of soldiers surrounded them. Some were shot. Some escaped and no doubt some were arrested. We did not hang about to find out.'

She had turned white. 'Creagh?' she whispered. 'Creagh?'

'Oh *alanna*, he's hurt bad. Very bad. He's in the carriage in the mews. Redmond Rafferty is with him. Can we bring him here?' At that moment the rat-a-tat-tat of an early customer sounded on the door. The Widow jumped up in fear.

'*Dia's Muire duit*, don't let anyone ...'

'Don't worry, Widow. Yer safe now.'

Ronan held her arms. 'What will we do? They are looking for Redmond and Creagh, Rosaleen. What will we do?'

Rosaleen called Batty, who was cowering at the door, sensing danger, not wanting to be involved. But she adored Rosaleen and there was nothing she would not do for her.

'Open it, Batty. Tell whoever is there that the place is closed for the moment. Say Lizzie Brannagan is dying. It's true, God help us, and it suits us now to say so.'

They held their breath while Batty told the slightly intoxicated gentleman outside that the place was shut against Lizzie Brannagan's imminent death. They heard him grumble and complain to Batty and ask what he should do.

'Yerra, go home and play wi' yerself,' she replied tartly and slammed the door in his face.

When he had gone Rosaleen instructed the Minstrel to go to the back and bring the men inside. 'Get Regan to help you,' she said.

Regan was their bodyguard, their chucker-out. A red-haired giant of a man, a native of Doone Alley, he was simple-minded but loyal, strong as an ox and given to blinding red tempers terrifying to behold if any of the girls were threatened. He had loved and guarded Lizzie since the beginning, when she had opened No. I and his mere presence was usually enough to keep order in the place.

Rosaleen hurried upstairs. The girls were about in various stages of undress. They were an apathetic bunch and their faces were resigned and faintly sullen under their paint.

'Keep to your rooms tonight, girls.' she said.

They looked at her with fearful eyes. Rosie Moore had told them that Rosaleen would keep the place open and be their new mistress. They were relieved, but the habit of distrust was deeply ingrained in each and every one of them. They had dreaded the alternative: working the streets, unprotected, at the mercy of anyone stronger than they. There were a lot of sadists, lunatics and sexual perverts that they were powerless to control, out in the jungle near the waterfront. It was so easy to end up in the river. No one cared, no one worried. You were just another piece of flotsam and jetsam. Lizzie Brannagan's was a heaven to them compared with the life outside.

In a feverish desire to impress the new madam they showed a willingness that was startling in its alacrity and vanished into their rooms. For the first time in a long time, for Lizzie worked Sundays, they used their beds that night for sleep.

Rosaleen brought the little band up the backway. She settled the Widow with the child in the spare room the other end of the corridor and left her there with milk and some of the caudle she had made for Lizzie, some bread, butter and jam. Rosaleen knew who she was, remembered her from the night when she had handed over Cormac to her. How could she ever forget? She whispered to the woman the question that had burned in her brain since they had arrived.

'How is Cormac? Is he all right?'

The Widow nodded and pressed Rosaleen's hand. 'Don't worry a second over that mite. He is well looked after. He is very loved up there.' She looked into Rosaleen's eyes and added, 'Thank you for this. You'll never know how grateful . . .'

Rosaleen hushed her. 'It's all right. You would have done the same.'

She left the Widow and her charge in the room and sent Batty to her to organize a cot, or 'a small bed for the child', and to make the room as comfortable as possible for their unexpected guests.

Regan carried Creagh up to Rosaleen's bedroom and the Minstrel helped Red Rafferty to her little withdrawing room. There he put Red on the *chaise longue* and examined his thigh. The wound had reopened and was bleeding.

'We'll have to get a doctor, Rosaleen,' he called through the doors open between them. He could hear Rosaleen crying.

Red said to him, 'Go in to her, Ronan. Creagh's very bad . . . see if you can help.' He rested his leg on a cushion and gave the Minstrel a push, 'Go on. I'm all right.'

Ronan went into the bedchamber and found Rosaleen sobbing over the still form of her lover, who lay white and motion-

249

less on her bed. He comforted her as best he could and in a few moments she had herself under control.

Regan stood over her, gazing at her, waiting for instructions. She turned to him, her face streaked with tears.

'Regan, get One-Eyed Willy for me. He'll be in the "Green Cock". Tell him to get Dr Davies. Dr Davies, remember. He's a sympathizer and a saintly man. He'll know what to do. Willy knows where he is to be found.' Regan turned to leave, a great shambling awkward man, suddenly full of importance. 'And tell him to hurry, hurry, hurry.'

Rosaleen turned back to the bed. 'Bring me some water, Ronan. Help me off with his shirt. Let me tend your wounds, my darling, my love.' She spoke softly to him, murmuring endearments and she did not see the pain in the Minstrel's face.

The doctor did not arrive for an hour. Rosaleen bathed Creagh's wounded chest as best she could and plugged the hole gaping in his side. He remained inert and pale as death, though she could hear the tiny tapping of his heart. Rosie Moore came in with a cup of tea for Rosaleen and she left the girl in charge of him for a moment.

In her dressing-room she found Redmond Rafferty, blood seeping through the towel Ronan had bound his leg with. He was lying back on her chaise, his handsome face twisted in pain.

'I'm Rosaleen,' she said, holding out her hand to him.

He clasped it firmly in his own, looking into the clear troubled depths of her eyes.

'Ah. So you are Rosaleen. I've heard of you. How lovely you are. They do not do you justice, the people who sing of you.' He winced with pain. 'Forgive me. I cannot rise.'

She shook her head. The pile of dark hair pinned up at the nape of her white neck was so heavy that it tilted her head back.

'Tell me what happened,' she asked.

'We were betrayed, Rosaleen *Dubh*. Betrayed. Informed on. And I mean to find out by whom. Ah God, this country breaks your heart. It's bound to be one of our own.'

'No. Don't say that. Don't. I don't believe it.'

'Well, it's true. Stephens tried to stop the informing by making the groups independent of each other. But there is a wee rat of a man called Nagle giving information to the authorities about the Fenian organization, bad cess to him. The likes of him is our tragedy.' He shook his head. He seemed near tears, angry and frustrated.

'If aught happens to Creagh ...' There was a sob in Rosaleen's voice.

'Calm now, girl. Peace now. We'll see. We'll see. Don't cross your bridges before ye come to them.'

There was comfort in his presence, Rosaleen thought. He was a strong man, but he had a lightness of spirit that supported and gave courage. It was at this moment that the doctor arrived, a short little man with a resigned face, sad eyes and grizzled hair. While he tended Creagh, Rosaleen stood beside him, tense as a harp string. He said nothing. Then, after he bandaged Red's leg he asked Rosaleen to take him to Lizzie Brannagan.

Rosaleen waited in an agony of apprehension. Why had he said nothing? What was Creagh's condition?

'Rosaleen dear, where can we be alone? I'd like Mr Rafferty there too. Just ye both.'

'In my withdrawing room then, where he is. We'll shut the door.'

Ronan closed the doors behind them, shutting himself in with Creagh.

'Bring some brandy and three glasses,' Rosaleen asked Rosie Moore, who was back with the request in a trice and who left them alone without being asked.

They settled themselves as best they might. Rosaleen sat with Red Rafferty's feet pushed behind her on he chaise. The Doctor perched on the stool in front of the dressing-table. The doctor insisted they all have a brandy before he spoke.

'Now be brave girl. Y'hear?' He took a deep breath and Rosaleen looked at him with wide pleading eyes. She knew what he was going to say. She had known all along, yet she hoped against hope she was wrong. The doctor said, 'They'll both be dead by morning. The young man and Lizzie.'

Rosaleen uttered a cry and Red reached for her hand and held it firmly in his own.

'And you've got a problem. How are you going to get rid of him?' He jerked his head towards the other room.

Rosaleen was still trying to recover from the news that the two people she loved best apart from her son, would be lost to her this night.

The doctor continued, 'You can't take him out of here feet first in the cold light of day. The law doesn't allow for the dis-

251

posal like that of dead bodies. I'm sorry, my dear, to be so blunt, but it must be discussed.'

'I must be with them. I must go to them,' Rosaleen said, rising, and they realized she was speaking of Creagh and Lizzie.

The doctor firmly told her to sit and listen. 'I'm thinking of all your safety, an mine, I'm not ashamed to say. The bastards may have taken one life tonight, and Lizzie has to go anyhow and I think she's just as glad, but there is no need to wantonly risk the lives of the rest of us. You must see that.' Rosaleen looked at the doctor. Her face was bleak. 'You have to go on, Rosaleen,' the doctor said. 'You have to protect yourself. You have to plan. If anyone suspects you are harbouring wanted men here, rebels, you'll be as guilty in their eyes as they are. They'll shut this place down and the girls will be thrown out on the street. They're only waiting for a chance to close Lizzie Brannagan's. It's only because Lizzie has been so discreet and this place is popular with the soldiers that it's been allowed to function. But if it comes to light you've got wounded men here, well, it's prison for you, make no mistake.' Rosaleen felt her blood run cold. Prison. No gypsy could live in prison.

'You're right, Dr Davies,' Red said, one eye on Rosaleen, 'And it will be one less safe house. Our network will have to be rearranged. You've no idea how dangerous that would be. It's Creagh's life-work. Don't let him down now.'

Rosaleen sighed wearily. 'It's all ye ever think of. The Cause. The Brotherhood. God Almighty, you and Creagh both. It's all you ever care about.'

Rosaleen broke down, sobbing her heart out. 'Creagh is dying. Dying. And all you can talk about are safe houses.'

'It's what Creagh is dying *for*,' Red replied. 'His death has great purpose.'

'Well, at the moment I cannot see it,' Rosaleen sobbed. 'I simply cannot.'

The doctor interrupted. 'Let us get down to the living. Nothing is to be gained by more of us falling foul of the law. Now I suggest we wrap the young gentleman in a sheet and put him in the carriage and drive him back from whence he came.'

Rosaleen startled the doctor with her look of wild fury. 'He will not be bundled anywhere, do you hear me? He will not be wrapped in a sheet like a blasphemy. He'll be treated with love and respect. That's what he had for others, it's the least he can expect from us now.' She brushed the back of her hand across her eyes.

'All right. All right.' The doctor fell silent in thought. Then, 'Listen, girl. What I suggest is this.' She listened to him, hiccupping now and then. 'Get a coffin. Say it is for Lizzie. Then we'll say it is not big enough and we need another, larger. I'll speak to Marty O'Doherty the undertaker without letting on. I'll tell him you'll send the first one back, but you're too distressed to bother about it now. I'll make some excuse — Regan has broken it, he'll believe that. And I'll pay him for two. I'll tell him he can give the money back when the first coffin is returned. He won't want it at all, you can be sure of that. He'll hope you forget and I'll warrant that's the last you'll hear of it.'

Red Rafferty was thinking. 'Won't he want to come here and measure the body?' he asked.

'Not if I hint that what she died of is very contagious,' the doctor replied.

Rosaleen wiped her eyes. She said with determination in her voice, 'All right. It's settled then. You do that, Doctor, when the time comes and you'll have a golden coin for your trouble.'

The doctor looked outraged and started to protest.

'It's no more than you deserve, Doctor,' she added. 'We will pay you what you would get from a rich house in Merrion Square. I'll go to them now. Batty Macklin can go for the priest. It will have to be the young curate Father Flynn, for the old one and the parish priest won't darken this door. I know what I have to do. So do you, Doctor. I suggest we get on with it.'

Ronan tapped at the cross-door and entered immediately. He was uneasy in the presence of death. He looked startled and eager to escape, as if he had found himself in some sort of a trap.

'He's askin' for you, Rosaleen. He's askin' for you.'

'Will you get Batty to go for Fr Flynn, Doctor? And put a notice on the door saying Lizzie Brannagan is dying. It'll keep everyone away from this house this night.'

The doctor nodded. Red tried to stand but Rosaleen pushed him back on the chaise.

'No. You try to rest, for I'll need you later. Rest as best you can. It's not easy, I know, for the length of you is long and the chaise is meant for the size of me.' She smiled at him. She had become icy calm. She felt that all this was happening to some-one else. She simply knew she had to be brave.

Creagh's eyes were clouded with pain and the drug the doctor had given him. 'Rosaleen. Oh my love. My Dark Rosa-leen. You're here.'

'I'm here, darlin' boy. I'm here, heart of my heart. Don't fret. Don't worry. I'm close. Close. Close.'

'Oh Rosaleen, I'm fading. Fading. Dearest, I'm fading and I'm frightened.'

'Don't be, lovely man. There is nothing to fear. It is all a mystery and you'll find the grand answer and 'twill be all right.' Tears filled her eyes and a sob caught in her throat.

'And if there's none?'

'Then it does not matter at all. You'll simply sleep.'

'You're crying. I felt a tear on my face. I've never known you to cry. Don't weep for me, my love. All you ever gave me was joy.'

'I'm crying for that joy, Creagh, with gratitude. I'm crying because you made me happy. You are so dear, my love. You are so dear.'

'I never knew how much I loved you until now. Now that I'm leaving. Look after Cormac. He's James' now. And Dolly's. But you'll see to him sometimes?'

'Oh yes. I always meant to.'

'We made him together in love. Do you remember those days? The Arcadian Grove and the pool? The swans swam there and the sun shone there and we were from another time.'

She smoothed back his hair tenderly. 'You came to me there ... "Over the footbridge he came one day, a fair-haired man coming at sun-rise to light the place. He rode over the bright land against which the ocean murmurs ..."' Her tears fell on his face like rain, but he smiled, holding her hand.

'Like me,' he said. 'Like me.'

'Oh my darling, 'twas a grand time.' She felt his hand slacken in hers. She looked at him and saw he was dead. She closed his eyes and kissed his lips and crossed his hands on his breast.

There was a knock on the door and Father Flynn, young and earnest, his face red from running, hurried in. He took the situation in at a glance and asked, 'How long has he gone?'

'A few minutes only, Father.'

'Then I'll administer the last rites. Batty'll help me. I take it herself is also ... poorly?'

'She'll not last till morning, Father, if she's not gone already.'

The young priest blushed and hurried about his business.

Rosaleen left the room. She stood outside the door trying to breathe. Dry sobs rose in her throat and she felt bruised, as if someone had punched her. But she bit her lip and fought for the courage to go on. She waited for a moment, then went in to see Lizzie.

The older woman was sinking fast. It was terrible to see. Delirium had set in. The doctor was with her and shortly the priest joined them. For a moment only she regained consciousness. For a moment she recognized Rosaleen, who marvelled at the staying power of the woman. Then she recognized Dr Davies and Father Flynn. She could hardly speak but she managed to whisper, 'Doctor. Yer a good man. Make sure, Rosa, he has his pick and never pays.'

She drew a terrible rattling breath, then looked at the priest. 'Father Flynn. You're a saint, so ye are. Don't let on where ye've been or ye'll be in trouble.'

It took her a painful long time and effort to say this, Rosaleen saw, but though she held Lizzie's hand in hers and tried to hush her she needed to talk to Rosaleen.

'All the papers are there. In the bureau. All signed and in order. It's yours now, Rosa, to do with as you please. And thank you, dotey. Thank you.' There was more she wanted to say but her strength failed her.

She looked at Rosaleen with large frightened eyes and her hold on Rosaleen's hand tightened.

'Don't be frightened, Lizzie. You'll be welcome up there. The good Lord loves the likes of you. Isn't that so, Father?'

The priest nodded. 'Of course it is,' he said. 'Think of Mary Magdalen.'

'*In Nómine Patris, et Filii, et Spiritus Sancti, Amen ...*' The priest prayed, anointing Lizzie as she lay there struggling. A terrible rattle sounded. It transcended the voice of the priest as he intoned the Latin. It scared Rosaleen half to death. Lizzie Brannagan was dead. The sound of life leaving was a fearsome one, Rosaleen thought. Going away. Never coming back. She was acutely aware of the feel of her body, the warmth of it, the strong beat of her own heart. There was silence in the room.

Chapter

40

IT had been a long night. There was so much to be done, yet time went on leaden feet. Rosaleen felt as if she was acting in a dream. There was a strange sense of unreality in all she did.

She did not cry. It was not the time. She had wept sad tears when Creagh was dying but as the night wore on and fatigue enveloped her she continued to perform the myriad tasks the double death had thrown up, dry-eyed and calm.

When the old crones from the Alley came to earn a shilling by laying out the corpses, Rosaleen went to see the Widow Boann. The last and most daunting task was to tell her that Creagh was dead. The Widow cried out, one long terrible wail. The child, who lay on a mattress tucked around with soft blankets in what looked like a drawer from Lizzie's mahogany chest, opened his eyes in alarm. Rosaleen left the Widow, who sat on the floor rocking herself to and fro in anguish, and went to the boy. She looked at the flushed face and the sweet curve of the mouth, she saw the twisted shoulder and the brilliant blue eyes and her heart welled up with love. An outpouring that she had controlled and had been dammed up within her burst forth in a flood. This was the child whose place her son had taken. She lifted the boy in her arms and he wound his legs about her and clutched her thick curls between her fingers.

'Petty ... petty,' he said, and smiled, then looked anxiously around the room. 'Nana?'

The Widow's cries ceased abruptly. She hurried over to the child, but Rosaleen had already soothed him.

'It's Fergal, isn't it?' she asked, kissing the soft cheek next to hers. The Widow nodded and dried her tears on her shawl.

'How did ye know?' she asked.

'Creagh told me about him long ago. In another time,' Rosaleen replied wistfully. 'He's not wanted at the castle.' It was more a statement than a question.

The Widow shook her head. 'That he's not. Lord James sent me to take him to the orphanage at Knockharrig. I've run away with him. No one's going to put him there. Not while there's breath in my body.' She faltered. 'But ... but we've nowhere to go.'

Rosaleen cradled the child, who had fallen once more into an exhausted sleep in her arms. She looked into the Widow's eyes. 'He can stay here. I think he's meant to. You both can stay here.' She put Fergal gently into his drawer-bed and tenderly pushed his hair back from his forehead. 'I know what I have to do,' she said. 'I don't think it was an accident; you coming here tonight.' She felt there was a curious pattern in the coming of this child here, quite unplanned and unintentionally, yet to the very house where she dwelt, she who had left her son in his father's house. 'I'll need help here, now Lizzie is dead. Help and protection. I know and love your sister, Craw Kilty, and I trusted you the first moment I saw you, Widow. I remember the things Creagh told me and when I handed you Cormac I knew he would be safe with you. I'd be so relieved if you could ...' unexpectedly a sob shook her and she held out her hand ... 'help me ... I feel so helpless just now.'

The Widow put her arms about the girl. 'You're exhausted. I'll take charge from now on, whether you like it or not. It's time you laid down the load, at least until the morning, and shut your eyes.' The Widow was glad she had something to do. It gave her a purpose. The activity would help to assuage her grief and help her to feel less of a burden.

'But Widow, this is a brothel. You must know that before you decide. If you're morally offended I'll understand ye taking the little fellow and going elsewhere. Although ...' she looked at Fergal asleep and hoped with all her heart the Widow would not do what she suggested.

The Widow looked outraged. She was already feeling at home and motherly towards this girl.

'An' where would I go?' she asked simply. 'The gutter? An' as for moral outrage, since when have the likes of you an' me had time for that? I don't give a tinker's curse what this place is.

Isn't it a roof over our heads an' isn't that a miracle? The place I'm in doesn't matter to me at all, it's the people. An' you, Rosaleen, are a grand woman.' From a woman who never gave compliments, it was the height of praise. 'Now lie yourself down and take a wee rest, for there's still a lot to be done.'

Rosaleen nodded a heavy head. Her body felt leaden yet she had to go on. There was still things to find out before she could indulge in the luxury of sleep.

'Who did this?' she asked. 'I have a mind to find the betrayer. Mr Rafferty says it's an informer.'

The Widow snorted. 'Ach no. Not that. Not this time. Those men were hand-picked. Master Creagh knew them all. They'd'a died for him. And for Red, and for Stephens and the likes of O'Donovan Rossa. No. This was Mistress Arabella Jeffries herself and that's a fact.'

'Arabella? You mean his sister?' Rosaleen was incredulous. Loyalty to family was ingrained in her. It was something she took for granted. To betray one's own kind was unthinkable. 'It cannot be. You must be mistaken, Widow.'

The Widow shook her head. 'I'm not. It's the truth, God help us. Creagh showed her up in a lie. Oh I don't think she meant that he should die. Things just went further than she planned. There's nothin' but hate in her heart an' she lustin' after her sister's intended.'

'But Widow, I can't believe it. Creagh always said she was mean but I cannot credit . . .'

'Will ye believe me when I tell ye the Minstrel saw it?' The Widow interrupted triumphantly. 'He had one of his spells before it happened and he said Lady Bella would cause Master Creagh great danger. When I heard it I knew. She said she would get her own back on Master Creagh and she hates Lady Sophie. She loves to cause trouble. Yes. Ronan saw the whole thing. "Danger at the castle", he said, "caused by Lady Bella".'

She told Rosaleen the bits and pieces of the story that she knew and they fitted together enough to persuade Rosaleen that Bella was indeed the guilty party. Besides, Ronan was not to be doubted. Rosaleen took a deep breath to still her anger. This was not the time for it. There would be time for anger and for tears, but not yet.

'Ah God, what people do to each other,' she said, sighing and looking at the child asleep before her.

'What'll ye do with the body, Miss Rosaleen? For ye can't have him buried with strangers, surely? He'll needs be by his family in Usher, so he will.'

'I will take the coffin — its all arranged with Marty O'Doherty — in the carriage to Usher. A sad journey it will be. I'll tell Lord James the truth about Creagh. I'll leave Miss Arabella to him.'

The Widow said, 'Aye. He'll be hard on her, that he will. He loved his brother dear.'

'If he's not, I'll do something myself. Don't fret yerself, Widow, she'll not escape punishment.' Rosaleen's eyes glittered. The women looked at each other in understanding and nodded, then they proceeded with their sad tasks on this saddest of nights.

Chapter

41

THE next few days were difficult in both No. I Doone Alley and Usher Castle. James was in a thundering temper, at odds with himself and everyone. His family were useless to him. Angela and Old Gentleman kept to their rooms and refused to be drawn into discussions of any kind. Bella was in disgrace, and Sophie seemed worried and preoccupied. She spent most of her time with Fabrice. James could not turn to the very people who could be the most help to him; the Constabulary and the Army. He wanted desperately to send for them, to ask them to scour the countryside for Creagh, but to do that would put the boy in danger and might even result in him losing his life. James writhed in an agony of anxiety, realizing that there was nothing he could safely do to solve the problem. As time passed, and hours ticked by and Creagh did not show up, he became more and more at variance with everyone, and with himself.

He took to riding abroad morning, noon and night in a vain hope of coming across his brother. He had a totally unrealistic hope that he would turn a corner, ride around a bend and there would be Creagh sauntering along singing one of his Gaelic songs. He would smile up at James and ask why on earth he had been looking for him. James would be angry with him and resist the urge to dismount and take the lad in his arms and hug him. But deep in his heart he knew this would not happen. He did not know what he expected or where to turn.

Bella kept to herself. She was mortally afraid at the magnitude of what she had done. She knew she had stirred up a hornet's nest and she regretted it bitterly. She realized that it had gone much further than she had expected, and to her horror she found that the servants blamed her directly for Cronin's death. They seemed to know of her involvement, though how they did so was beyond her understanding. They barely took the trouble to conceal their contempt for her. She stayed in a state of feverish suspense, her brain buzzing with plans and stratagems, counter-ploys and ideas, ways of 'showing people' and 'getting herself off the hook', until it ached and ached but she was afraid to ring her bell for fear Molly might answer. She was terrified of facing her servant and suffered her migraine rather than send for her.

Sophie found Fabrice a source of solace and peace. He diverted her with tales of Paris and his life there. He set out to entertain her and lighten her mood and he succeeded. He sang her songs and insisted she play the piano for him, which she loved to do. His thoughtfulness manifested itself in a hundred different ways. She was not only worried about Creagh but also about Red. She tried not to be, but it was difficult. She knew he had escaped, the lieutenant had told them that, and it consoled her. But there was a thread of uncertainty about the whole situation that left her feeling uneasy.

Dolly was serenely untroubled by all the commotion, once the soldiers had gone. She felt sure that Creagh was on one of his silly jaunts and perhaps had been gambling and lost some money and was uneasy about facing James. She was very sorry for Molly in her loss and shocked at the news that there had been secret meetings held in the priest's hole below Usher Castle, but her mind and feelings were totally taken up with Cormac and she lavished all her attention on him. There was little left over for anyone else.

Usher Castle prepared for Cronin Dominic's funeral and at No. 1 Doone Alley similar plans were being made for Lizzie Brannagan's. Creagh's coffin was kept locked up in Rosaleen's dressing room. If the girls knew anything or divined that something was going on, they were either too stupid or had enough native commonsense to say nothing. It was in their interest to keep Rosaleen happy and this they tried to do. She was their future and they would want to be eejits to much around with that.

Chapter

42

LIZZIE Brannagan would have loved her own funeral. A sumptuous hearse with black plumes, drawn by four black horses, left Doone Alley and went grandly in solemn procession down the quays and over Carlisle Bridge to Sackville Street. It proceeded up the main thoroughfare passing the Protestant Cathedral until it reached Glasnevin. She was buried in style; a headstone commemorating her and her child was laid over her grave.

Rosaleen and Regan led the procession. Then came Batty Macklin and Rosie Moore, who wept copiously all the way. The girls followed, with sundry bodies from Doone Alley and St George's Lane. All were in black. They made a dramatic and dismal picture on the bright June day. The doctor did not come. He was happy enough to treat the women of No. I secretly, but to be seen to be associated with them in broad daylight would be foolhardy. Father Flynn was there, but he need not have looked so embarrassed, for no one, once they reached Sackville Street, knew who they were. It could have been the remains of some grand lady from Merrion Square for all anyone could tell, for Rosaleen had ordered only the best.

As they passed, the men on the streets raised their hats out of respect, and people stopped walking and waited till they passed by. Yes, Lizzie would have loved it and Rosaleen, although she knew she would miss the older woman, was glad enough her ordeal was over and she was at peace at last.

They came back to Doone Alley and Rosaleen opened a bottle and settled the girls under the watchful eye of the Widow and Regan, who had instructions not to let them get too drunk. The house was closed for business out of respect, and Rosaleen told the girls it would remain shut for a week. They were none too pleased but afraid of angering their new mistress, so they acquiesced as gracefully as they could. Lizzie had been generous with them. Full of pity for them, she understood their stupidity and their plight. They had been allowed to keep twenty-five percent of their earnings, which was magnificent. Sometimes they fiddled a little extra and she closed her eyes to that, unless it became habitual and blatant, and in that case a girl was out on the street in the clothes she stood up in, that was all. They hoped Rosaleen would be as moderate a mistress.

Rosaleen left them to their porter and climbed the stairs to her room where Creagh lay in his coffin. She looked on the face of her love for the last time. She had no tears to shed. Not yet. Not now. There was still too much to be done. She kissed his pale lips and laid a rose on his breast between his white fingers. Regan covered the coffin for her and she felt, as he did so, a pain pierce her heart and she gasped at the agony of it. Then straightening her back, she got Red and Regan to carry it down the back stairs, through the dried-up grass square of a garden and out into the mews. No one saw them.

For a while they were fearful that it would not fit into the carriage, but eventually Regan pulled out the seat at the front of the vehicle and they were able to settle it comfortably on the floor Rosaleen sat facing it on the remaining seat, her little black shoes resting on the pale wood.

Red wanted to go with her but she chided him. 'It would be too dangerous. What would Creagh think? Ah no, Red. You're needed. It has been a sad way for me to meet you, but you have been an enormous help. I hope we can meet again under happier circumstances. This will always be a safe house for you.'

'Let me at least escort you some of the way,' he pleaded, but her answer was unequivocal.

'You are needed, Red. It would be terrible an' you got caught and all because you came with me. No, stay here a while if you want, or find somewhere you feel safe. The road will be alive with soldiers looking for him.'

'Well, be careful.'

'I'll be careful, Red.'

She noticed how tired and drawn he looked. He had been a pillar of strength to them and had had precious little time to recover from his wound, which the doctor said had been serious. She was grateful to him for his support over the last troubled days.

He looked at her now as if he wanted to say something.

'What is it, Red? You can trust me.'

'If you see my Lady Sophie, say ... tell her I'm all right.' His eyes were unguarded for a moment and she realized that for all his stoic courage he too was vulnerable. Then the curtain came down again and he might have been sending a message to his tailor. 'But only if you can get an opportunity in private.'

She nodded and he took her hand in farewell. 'You're like Ireland herself, Dark Rosaleen, travelling across the land in dark mourning with a coffin at your feet.' He leaned into the carriage looking at her, his face framed in the door.

'Take care of yourself,' he added, patted her hand, smiled, and was gone. The warmth of that smile helped her through the journey with all its fears and nostalgia. For it was the first time since she had come to the city that she had returned to the country. The day was alive with bird-song. Red deer crossed their path and Regan had to stop the carriage to let them pass.

On the long slow journey to Wicklow, the carriage was stopped many times — by a division of Dragoons on the Dublin road and a company of foot soldiers in the hills. The coffin was opened twice, and each time the soldiers were appalled to discover genuine death within. Verifying that it did not contain guns or a wanted man was a great embarrassment. Simply doing their job, the soldiers were shocked at the face of death and the distress of the beautiful woman in black who sat dry-eyed in the carriage with the coffin. You had to admit, though, they said to each other, that it isn't every day you meet a corpse in a coffin on the floor of a carriage with the seat taken out, bumping across the Dublin and Wicklow roads.

They stopped at the blacksmith's for a change of horses and some light refreshment. Mrs Riley asked how everything was and skittled inside when she saw the coffin.

'You'd think Ireland was peopled with giants,' Rosaleen thought, watching Regan and Riley the blacksmith talking together. She saw Riley shake his head mournfully and Regan came back and climbed on their hearse, cracked his whip and they were off again, leaving Riley and his wife waving after them, tears streaking their cheeks.

The mountains lay on either side sleeping in the sun, a patchwork of emerald, lime, sage and moss-green. They were clothed in sycamore, oak and ash, beech and elm and poplar. Little waterfalls spilled over the sides of the mountains, streams swollen by the recent rain. They passed pools of water glittering in the golden light with willows weeping over them, drooping their delicate leaves, round-shouldered. Little lakes of navy-blue and gold looked entrancing to Rosaleen, starved for so long of a sight of the land she loved so well.

They passed the mountain behind which the Arcadian Grove nestled. It would be warm there today, Rosaleen thought, and a sob caught in her throat, hard as a bullet. It was only a year ago, and he had been so alive then, his body hard in hers, his skin soft and warm to the touch. His mouth had been as red and sweet as the berries that grew there, and his body as white as the swan's wing. She knew a pain of longing so fierce it took her breath away.

She looked out of the window. A lacework of leaves overhead had cut out the sun and she could not tell the trees that wore them for the tears in her eyes.

'I must not cry. Creagh, Creagh, help me not to cry. It is too soon.'

Her prayer was heard and answered, for the tears did not fall but vanished in the corners of her eyes and she saw that they were on the mountain pass to Usher.

The coach swung along. She could see the smoke from Craw Kilty's cottage below in the valley. She kept a fire going winter and summer and the pot would be on the hob. She would go there later, maybe stay a night or two. She trusted Widow Boann implicitly and knew things would be calm under her authority at No. 1 Doone Alley.

The horses clattered under the old stone arch, trotted up the drive and drew to a halt in front of the great entrance. The heavy door of Usher Castle stood wide open. Rosaleen did not go to the kitchen this time. A groom had come from the stables and a lad was with him. They stared at her as she descended from the carriage all in deep black on this glorious June day. They thought for a moment it might be the Dowager Lady Angela, but this one was too young, too pretty.

The giant with her beckoned Padraig, and he hurried over, glancing at Matt Dominic for permission first. The giant asked Padraig to help him with the coffin that was inside the coach.

Matt Dominic had suddenly realized what had happened. He nodded to Padraig to obey. The giant lifted one end of the coffin and indicated to Padraig to lift the other, but the lad couldn't, it was too heavy. Matt, who had been hovering about, hurried over to help.

Rosaleen, her veil blowing about her pale face, mounted the steps to the door. Her back was straight as a ramrod and she held up her black taffeta skirts in her gloved hand. She saw a hawk fly over the face of the sun and drop down like a stone to the valley below. He was after a rabbit, she thought, as she entered the Great Hall. The open reception area was cold and shadowed. She looked about the vast dark-panelled place and saw the fire burning, with logs the length of a man on it. She heard a piano playing some light trilling music from the room at the end of the hall to her right. It seemed a long way away and the sound was merry.

She stood alone a moment, uncertain. Then she saw a big red-haired man slowly descending the stairs. She recognized him as the man in the kitchen on the night she had brought Cormac here. He suddenly stopped, looking at her in amazement, and she realized that Regan and the men must have arrived with the coffin, for his jaw dropped, his face flushed and he hurried down the stairs, saying, 'What is the meaning of this? What the devil goes on?'

It was Lord Usher, she knew. He resembled Creagh in his cast of feature, his speech and manner, though at the same time they were very unalike.

She lifted her veil. The music played on, the sound like water cascading. She watched the expressions cross his face as he halted on the bottom step. He was in riding garb and carried a whip. She must have caught him just before he left the house. His boots were polished to a high gloss. He looked startled at first, because her face was familiar and he obviously could not think from where. Then realization began to dawn. He looked at the coffin. A puzzled expression crossed his face and he shook his head.

Rosaleen stood in the dusk of the hall. The coffin lay in the shaft of sunlight from the door. Motes danced about, specks moving in the blade of golden light. As Lord Usher looked from her to the coffin his face paled.

'The gypsy,' he said. 'The gypsy wench and ... and ... Creagh? Tell me it isn't true?'

She said nothing. His body seemed to sag and his eyes met hers, pleading for contradiction. The music stopped and a woman laughed.

'Not Creagh?' he whispered.

She nodded.

'Yes, my lord. Your brother Creagh.'

'Ah no. Ah no.'

He held onto the banister as if he would fall if he let go. Two women had come out of the room at the end of the hall from which the sound of music had recently come. One was fair as a snow-flake, slim as a reed in a pale pink silk gown, and carried a baby. Cormac. It must be Dolly. The other wore gentian-blue wild silk that matched her eyes exactly and she had rich gold hair fixed in soft clusters about her face. Sophie. The eyes were too warm and tender for it to be the other one.

'Yes, my lord,' she said.

Dolly ran to her husband. 'What is the matter, dear? What has happened to make you look so?' She held the child to her as if it were a treasure, Rosaleen noticed, and she pressed her hand to her heart to still its beating.

Dolly glanced apprehensively at her and then at the coffin. 'Oh what has happened, James?'

'Dolly, go to your room. This is not for women's ears. Sophie, see your sister-in-law upstairs.'

'I will stay, James. I am not a child that you can tidy away. I am an adult, whatever you may think, and you are sore distressed. That is my business, dear,' Dolly said firmly.

A servant girl came running into the hall, then halted when she saw the group. Her face was red with weeping and her eyes full of anger.

'Oh m'lady, forgive me.' Molly came to an uncertain halt. 'It's time for me to take little Cormac.'

But Dolly held the child to her heart and looked at her husband. Molly waited.

'What has happened here?' James asked. 'Tell us what has happened.'

As he spoke a girl appeared on the landing above. The movement was like a shadow slipping on the scene. She wore unadorned white and she descended a few steps, then stood, still as a statue, staring at the woman in the hall below. Bella. At last Bella. Rosaleen let out her breath, realizing that she had been holding it. They stared at each other.

Rosaleen removed her bonnet and shook out her black hair. Her head ached. She looked Lord Usher squarely in the eyes.

'It is the body of your brother Creagh, my lord, in the casket there. I was his lover and his friend and I come to you for justice. You are the Knight of Usher and Lord of these parts.' Dolly had cried out and Sophie put her arms around her but Rosaleen continued. 'The other night there was a meeting here. Creagh had organized the meeting. He was there with a man called Redmond Rafferty.' Her quick eyes caught Sophie's blush and the anxious inquiry in her eyes. 'He is all right.' There. She had done as Red asked. 'He escaped, where I know not. But those soldiers who killed your stable lad also killed your brother.'

For a moment there was silence in the hall, broken only by the ticking of the clock.

'Creagh, Oh Creagh.' James cried out, looking at the coffin. He made as if to go to it but Rosaleen held up her hand.

'I'm not finished. Have you asked yourself how the soldiers knew where to go? Have you asked yourself . . .'

'Yes!' James cried out.

'But you did not know about Creagh. Whoever told you meant to betray Creagh. Whoever told you knew about Creagh.'

She stared at the girl above them and everyone's eyes were drawn to the white figure on the stairs. She stared back at them, her eyes dilated with fear, her face white.

'I didn't know. How could I have known? It's not my fault.' But everything in her attitude revealed her guilt.

James had someone to vent his anguish on. He turned and looked at her with hate.

'You little bitch,' he shouted. The other women drew back in astonishment and shock. He was not used to speak thus. 'You traitor. You murderess. There is no word bad enough for you. Of course you knew.'

The girl shrank back.

James ran up the stairs to where she stood. He lifted his hand and struck her across the face. She screamed and backed away from him.

Sophie lifted her skirts and ran up the stairs after her brother to try to stop him and Dolly cried, 'Oh James. No.'

. But before Sophie reached him James let his arm fall. Rosaleen watched him, waiting. When at last he spoke his voice was quiet, his tone colder than the ice in the river in winter.

'You have done a terrible thing, Bella. This woman has come for justice and justice she'll get.' He looked at Rosaleen, who stood motionless. 'You, Bella, will never marry. You'll stay to the end of your days unwed.'

Bella moaned and sank to her knees on the landing. 'But James, I did not mean ... I did not mean ...'

'Your every action was malicious. Ever since Fabrice de Beauvillande came to Usher you have gone from bad to worse. You have behaved inexcusably. You are not fit to consort with civilized people. Well, Sophie will marry him *now*, do you hear me? Sophie, you will marry him now.'

'No. No, James. This is not the time to decide such things,' Sophie cried, distressed. She did not feel that this was the time for recriminations, but her brother and the strange woman in the hall seemed intent on a judgement. It was as if they were acting out some scene already written, and there was no changing it.

'Yes, Sophie. You'll do as I say. I'm master here,' James said quietly, firmly.

'But the County?' Dolly's voice sounded anxious.

'I do not care what the County say or think. Justice must be seen to be done here. Sophie will marry the Conte as soon as possible. And until then, sister,' he looked at Bella and she was stunned by the grief she saw in his eyes, 'until your sister is wed you'll stay in the High Tower. Alone. Molly will take care of you.'

Bella looked at Molly and saw the hate in her eyes and her heart turned to stone. She cried out in anguish, 'No, James. Please no.'

'Yes, Bella, yes. You'll not marry as long as I'm master here. You'll rot an old maid. You'll have fine clothes and food but never a man in your bed. Never, do you hear? Never. Here you are, Molly. See she's locked in.' He handed the maid a bunch of keys. 'Get Annie and Clarie to move my lady Sophie's things. Guard her well, Molly. Guard her well.'

'Oh I'll do that, sir. Never fear,' Molly said.

Rosaleen was satisfied. Her heart felt at rest. She knew she was going to weep, the time had come.

Lord James came to her. 'Is there anything I can do?' he asked.

She looked at him with wide sad eyes. 'No, sir. You've done enough. I am satisfied.'

'Justice?' he asked and she nodded.

'If ever you need anything . . .' he stuttered over the words.

'No, sir. I am all right now.'

She saw he was crying and he put his arms around her. She could feel his body shaking. She stayed like that awhile, then she broke free and glancing up the stairs saw Molly grab Bella's arm and pull her out of sight around the bend in the gallery. She walked out of the castle and down the stone steps to the carriage. Regan followed her. She looked back into the house and saw James kneeling over the coffin, his head touching it. On one side of him was his wife holding Cormac in her arms, and on the other his sister Sophie, her head bent.

But her eyes were filling with tears now and she could not see any more. A sob tore her body and as Regan urged the horses forward she leaned her face against the carriage window and gave herself over to her grief at last.

Chapter

43

ROSALEEN spent a week with Craw Kilty. The old witch woman tended the girl, leaving her alone to grieve. After the noise and smells, the lack of air and the enclosed life she lived in Doone Alley, the girl opened like a flower to the sun and relaxed in the peace of the valley. It was a place of golden shadows, radiant sky and quiet whispers, a place where peace dropped slowly on the daily round and entered the soul unbidden. In the warm June days Rosaleen healed and mended, drew courage again and renewed her energy.

The Minstrel joined her there. He told her that all was well in Doone Alley, that the Widow Boann had everything under control. 'Will ye go back?' he asked her.

She smiled at him, tenderly touching his face, so young under the moon. 'Of course,' she replied.

'But you hate it so.'

'Only the environment,' she said.

He was not sure he understood. 'Ye are a gypsy, Rosaleen. Don't deny the road or ye'll dry up from the lack of it,' he said.

'I know it. But I have no choice now.'

He looked at her and she could see how he loved her and wanted her. So in the lambent evenings their bodies cleaved to each other, petal-soft and passionate in the urgency of youth. It was a consolation to Rosaleen, nothing more. A fulfilment of her womanhood, an appeasement of her need. It was also a re-affirmation of life. She had lived with death for too long.

Craw Kilty talked with Rosaleen under the stars in the quiet of the evenings. The valley spread out at their feet and the mountains guarded them on either side.

'He is loosing the second sight, so he is, Ronan,' she said with a sidelong glance at Rosaleen, 'Now that he's no more a virgin, mabbe he'll lose the gift.'

Rosaleen shrugged. 'Mabbe. An' mabbe it's worth it,' she replied tartly.

Rosaleen stretched her arms in the silver light. She felt slow and comfortable in herself, for she had slaked her desire on the Minstrel's warm body in the long twilight moments before the stars came out.

'Time passes and youth grows lusty an' there's little ye can do about it,' Rosaleen told Craw tranquilly with a shrug.

Craw Kilty wiped her nose on her sleeve and said after a goodly pause, 'Ye'll look after my sister an' her charge?'

Rosaleen nodded. 'She'll look after me, more like, for she's a managing woman an' no mistake. Oh, I'll see to her, never fear. She can stay with us awhile.'

'Ye'll keep the house goin' there?'

'I've been thinking. Craw, an' I'd like to close it, and will too, sometime soon. But, well, maybe you'll understand. It's the love I felt for Creagh. He gave his life for the Cause, even if it was truly ended by that bitch above.' She looked up at the dark mass of Usher Castle above them on the mountain. The high tower pierced the dark velvet sky and you could see a light glowing from the window. She was shut up there. Rosaleen thought with satisfaction. Like a nun. And how she'd hate it, the time slipping away, slowly withering her, drying up her juices, stealing her prettiness until she was an old unloved maid. Ah yes. Vengeance of that sort was sweet. She turned her attention to the old crone once more.

'Lizzie Brannagan may have kept a bordello but she was also a patriot and the brothel was a "safe house". I loved them both, Creagh and Lizzie, an' I'd like to keep up what was important to them. I'm not risking much if I keep the house open and give shelter to the odd Fenian on the run. It's the perfect alibi. I never know who my clients are. I can always plead ignorance. But if I sell up I couldn't do it. In an ordinary house I would be caught. So I think I'll keep it goin' for a while.'

'Ah sure, Rosaleen, if ye did buy a house in a respectable neighbourhood ...'

'In Merrion Square, Fitzwilliam Square, Rathmines or Dalkey,' Rosaleen said dreamily.

'Well, those places. Wherever they are. Sure they'd never have you. You're not their sort at all. You'd be uncomfortable even if they did. But you'd be an outcast, so you would.'

Rosaleen thought of Ignatius Callaghan and his son and shuddered. She shrugged.

'Maybe you're right, Craw Kilty, and maybe you're wrong. I've discovered that people don't ask too many questions when you have money. Money opens a lot of doors in friendship.'

'Money? Since when have you talked of money, Rosaleen *Dubh*? Is that what you call friendship?'

'You'll not get a rise out of me this night, old woman. Tonight I'll sleep under the stars and breathe the sweet night air of Wicklow. Tonight I'll not be troubled by thoughts of tomorrow or yesterday, for a chapter is closed and I must rest before the next one begins.'

Chapter

44

JAMES thanked God for Dr Hegarty. he had called him in immediately after Rosaleen had left the coffin that day, and he did not beat about the bush with him. He had told him the truth.

'Creagh was involved, Doctor, with rebels and traitors. For that I am ashamed.' He saw no agreement in the doctor's eyes, so he continued, 'In consequence he was shot. I do not want this fact to be made public. It will bring our names into disrepute. I do not want the cause of death to become known. Do you understand?'

The doctor understood and although James did not know it, he was glad the shooting was not to be made public. It would entail enquiry and in all probability a heavier crackdown by the authorities on the covert activities of the rebels in these parts.

It had been the doctor's decision that the cause of death be listed as pneumonia after a chill, and James had gone along with that.

The next morning Creagh was buried in the crypt in the chapel at Usher in a sad little ceremony. Rosaleen came and stood alone. No one spoke to her, but Sophie and James both greeted her and held her hand a moment in silence. Then it was over and it was as if the whole incident had never happened.

Creagh's death left the family curiously guilty. They had been used to his absences, used to him not being there, and now when they did not miss him they felt they should. The fact that he was no longer with them caused them embarrassment when, laughing or enjoying themselves, they suddenly remembered. Their conversation would die and silence fall and uneasy glance meet uneasy glance. He had been a stranger to them and they only realized it now, James with great sadness and a sense of lost opportunity, Sophie with regret. The Dowager Lady Angela's cold nature prevented the rest of the family from knowing how deeply she felt her loss, but no one thought that she was too devastated, for she had seen her son less than anyone else.

Life resumed its even pace, if it could ever have been said to have lost it. The tragic scene in the Great Hall receded from their minds and routine helped them, all too quickly, to forget. Creagh had impinged so little on their lives, and suddenly it was as if he had never been.

Bella in the High Tower was glad enough that James had banished her there for the time being. She would have reminded the family of Creagh's death if she had been among them. She, however, was relieved to be away from them, to be separated from them at this time. She could not bear their reproaches, their condemnation, and was happy enough to spend her days in isolation. In her mind she had shifted the blame onto James' shoulders. After all, she reasoned, it was he who had sent for the soldiers. The fact that she had deceived him quite slipped her mind.

Molly said, 'You stir things, my lady, and only woe comes of it.' Molly guarded her well. Bella hated that. She did not need Molly to guard her. Where would she go? Where could she go? She sat and shivered, stewing in her own misery, biting her nails and watching from her window, and plotting revenge.

James had a visit from Lieutenant Andrew Clegg two days after Creagh's funeral. The lieutenant rode up to Usher Castle with four soldiers and asked James' permission to search the priest's hole and its environs again. James was incensed but he could not refuse.

'I fail to understand what you think to find here, sir. I'm hardly likely to be deceived a second time,' James told the lieutenant tight-lipped, not bothering to keep the impatience out of his voice.

The lieutenant was, as usual, urbane. 'Well, you never know, m'lord. Stranger things have happened.'

The soldiers had already vanished into the bowels of Usher Castle.

'Well, if that is all, Lieutenant?' James turned to go, but the lieutenant detained him.

'Lord Usher. Just a moment. I was sorry to hear of your brother's premature death.' James did not reply, he simply nodded his head. The lieutenant continued, 'It was unexpected, surely? They tell me pneumonia is the official cause of death?' He emphasized the word 'official' ever so slightly. James, however, simply nodded again. The lieutenant stared at him a long moment, but it was the lieutenant who was the first to drop his eyes. 'Quite a coincidence, isn't it?' he said.

'What, Lieutenant?' James' voice was cold and neutral.

'His death ... after the fracas here that night and our search for a man whose description bears a strikingly close resemblance to your brother. It was that very night your brother died? I find the circumstances distinctly odd. Distinctly odd.'

'That is your privilege, Lieutenant. Yes. He was saturated. I presume you remember the weather that night? James could not keep the sarcasm from his voice.' He caught a severe chill which carried him off. It turned to pneumonia. If you have any doubts about the veracity of this, you must contact Dr Hegarty. He will confirm it for you.'

The lieutenant gave a twisted smile. 'Oh I'm sure he will. They are all the same hereabouts. Close as clams when it comes to trouble. I have no doubt Dr Hegarty will verify your story. But I still find it incredible to believe that a young, strong man like your brother should be carried off like that so quickly. It is not as if he were deprived. Is that not so?'

'All I know, Lieutenant, is that my brother is dead, tragically young. That fact has only increased our sorrow. I do not know what purpose you have in asking these questions. If there are any doubts in your mind about my poor brother I think you should speak to Dr Hegarty and not to me.'

Both men knew that the other was aware that they were not speaking the whole truth. But there was nothing Lord Usher wished to do, or the lieutenant could do, to make the conversation more outspoken. Realizing that the interview was at an end Lieutenant Clegg bowed to James, then walked to the door and turned.

'We'll get him eventually, you know,' he said.

James was genuinely puzzled. 'Who?' he asked.

'Red Rafferty. We'll get him in the end. Good-day, my lord.' He turned on his heel and left, taking his soldiers with him.

James insisted that Sophie's wedding went ahead. He had

given his word and he never broke it. It was a matter of honour. Sophie made feeble attempts to reason with her brother for appearances' sake, but underneath she was relieved beyond measure. Her brother, all unknowing, accomplished for her what she had been terrified she could not accomplish for herself.

Dolly was too engrossed in Cormac to worry deeply about anything else. Besides, whatever James did was right as far as she was concerned. As wedding plans went forward she did, however, put in a plea for Bella. But James was adamant.

Dolly, brushing her pale gold hair in the lamplight, said to her husband, 'Don't be too hard on her, James. She's very young. She's never had Sophie's sweet disposition. You can hardly blame her for being jealous. I'm sure she never meant to cause Creagh's death.'

'Nevertheless she did. She has to pay for the wrong she did.'

'Well then, keep her in the tower for a while then forgive her, James. You must.'

'Never.' James shook his head. He sat in bed in his nightshirt watching his wife's rhythmic strokes and the sparks that flew out with a crackle from the long gold strands. He loved that sweet face and he would do anything to please her. But not this. he had his principles and he would never act against them.

'No, my love,' he said now in a quieter tone, 'I do not intend to talk about it with you. You are the softest creature, Dolly my dear. I only wish Bella was more like you. But there is evil in her and I do not want any more damage inflicted by her on our family. She had done a terrible thing and must be punished. If she were a man she would be put to death.'

Dolly drew in her breath sharply and pressed her hand to her fluttering heart. 'James, do not say that.'

'I would have fired the shot myself.'

'After all, she is your flesh and blood.'

'I cannot help it, Dolly. She must realize what it is to be a Jeffries. When I think of what she did, how she degraded the honour of our house ...'

'But she did not mean him to die.'

'So you said. But that is not of much use to Creagh now. To die so young in the path of a bullet. It's not to be borne.'

Dolly looked at her husband and knew it was of no use to argue with him. He sat in their big four-poster with his arm across his eyes. He had not realized how much he loved his little

277

brother until that awful day when the gypsy woman brought the coffin to Usher.

Dolly put down her brush and took off her *robe de chambre* and slipped into bed beside him. She knelt before him and pulled his arm away and kissed his eyes. Winding her arms around him she cradled him to her bosom, crooning softly to him as she did to Cormac when she held her baby to her breast. She could feel the great strong man melt within the circle of her arms.

She felt desire rise within him and she held him closer, but he tried to push away.

'No. No, my dearest. Remember what the doctor said . . .'

She slipped her lawn nightdress over her head and flung it aside. Sitting there naked, bathed in the amber firelight she smiled at him and held out her arms to him. He groaned and reached for her blindly.

'The Widow told me. It's all right now, James. The Widow said. It's safe.'

James knew it was too late to stop. He felt warm and safe and welcome in the embrace of his wife's arms and he gave himself up to the pleasure of his love.

Some people were shocked at the announcement of Sophie's wedding, coming as it did so soon after Creagh's funeral. They nudged and nodded knowingly to each other and examined Sophie's waistline with gimlet eyes.

'Oh my darling, do not concern yourself about it,' Fabrice told her in the arbour. He was fanning her, for the weather was warm and sunny. He was like a child who loved to play, she thought fondly, as he waved the fan over her face and she could feel her hair lift from her damp forehead and flutter in the breeze it created. It was very pleasant.

'James is very correct,' he continued, resting a moment. 'He is a man of his word. And he gave his promise.' He laid the fan down beside Sophie on the stone bench.

Sophie glanced down at her hands. 'But I don't want our wedding to be fixed simply to teach Bella a lesson,' she said, grimacing.

Fabrice shrugged. 'What does it matter, *ma chérie*, as long as we both want to get married?' He took her hand and raised it to his lips.

'Your brother, Sophie, tries so hard to do the right thing. He is a kind man and very often wise. He solved that problem ...' He hesitated, then continued, 'How he punished Bella, saw that justice was done, was very fitting. I admired him for it. I was only sorry I was not there, perhaps, to help.'

'Oh Fabrice, there was nothing you could have done.' Sophie smiled at him.

He shrugged. 'Perhaps not. My presence might have made things worse, who knows? But it was fitting. Bella has behaved wickedly and I was part of the cause, however unwitting. For that I am profoundly sorry. So. James wants us married, thereby removing Bella's ... how you say? Obsession?'

Sophie nodded, 'And he tells her she will never marry. It is what she wants most of all.' Sophie said, agreeing with him. Then she sighed. 'But it's hard.' she added.

'You must remember she has deprived her maid of her chance ever to wed. And Creagh of his life. I think it is wise of your James.' Fabrice had plucked a rose and was carefully snapping off the thorns. 'You do not mind, *chérie*? That your brother wishes us to marry soon? It does not cause you any ... panic?' His voice was anxious.

'Oh no, Fabrice. Oh no. I'm so happy to obey him in this matter.' She had a wild desire to laugh. That Fabrice and James were both rushing her, and that to them she seemed the reluctant one, was ironical. She looked into the clear loving eyes of her betrothed and felt a shiver of fear and one of shame. What was she doing to him? There was no malice in his charming face. He was without an unkind bone in his body. And he loved her. Was she being fair? It was not a question she could afford to ask. She quickly pushed these feelings aside and smiled at him. He tucked the rose behind her ear in a tender possessive gesture.

'Is the butterfly-netting party still as arranged?' he asked.

Sophie nodded. 'James said it was too late to cancel.' She stood up and took Fabrice's arm. They walked under the trees' dappled shade, the dogs yapping at their heels.

'What is it? Butterfly-netting?' he asked, puzzled.

'Well, we catch butterflies and then we put them in books or under glass,' she replied.

'Oh how cruel. Poor butterflies. They have such a short life anyway.'

Sophie looked up at him, 'I had not thought of that before,' she said, and stopped. 'Do you think it is wrong?'

'I do not thing it is very kind to the poor little butterflies,' he said.

Sophie glanced again at his handsome profile. 'Well then, I will not catch any more, ever again.' He smiled and dropped a gentle kiss on her cheek. They walked out into the sun.

'I wish I'd known him better.' Sophie said softly. One of the satisfactory things about Fabrice was his intuitive knowledge of what she was talking about.

'Creagh,' he said. 'We feel that about anyone who dies. When I shot Armand ...' He frowned. 'The remorse was terrible.'

'Oh my darling, I know.' Sophie pressed his arm.

'But when I left Paris in so much of a hurry I came here, and all I could think of were the things I had forgotten to say to everyone, most of all to my *Maman*. There was so much left unsaid, but living life daily we feel that there is always tomorrow.' He looked at her sadly. 'But sometimes, my darling, it is too late and there is no tomorrow.'

He put a firm arm around her shoulders. She could feel such solace from his presence beside her and she suddenly had an enormous conviction that everything would be all right.

The day of the butterfly-netting party at Usher, Sophie and Aurora Vestry sat in the arbour beneath the High Tower. They had broken away from the other girls because they wanted to talk, and also because Sophie had promised Fabrice she would not catch any more butterflies. The sun shone and birds fluttered around the stone Flora chirping loudly. The roses were in bloom, nodding their heads and filling the air with their sweet scents. The girls sat in the apple-green shadows in flowing sprigged-muslin dresses light as gossamer, their heads and faces shaded by their Leghorn hats, gossiping in the shade of the weeping pear tree. The clematis, pink and purple, climbed up the old stone walls and wound itself around the tree. The stone bench on which they sat was warm from the sun.

'It's lucky for you that James intends to keep his word by hook or by crook and marry you off within the month, Sophie.' Aurora said. 'It would not do to wait much longer.'

Sophie nodded. 'It's awful, Aurora. People stare and stare and I know exactly what they are thinking and it does not help one little bit to know that they are right.'

But Aurora was practical. 'Oh, let them talk. They are just jealous. They'll have forgotten by the time the baby is born.'

'Some of them. But some of them will have counted every single hour, and they will be as smug as buttermilk when it is premature.'

'Does it matter? Of course not, dear one. You'll be safely married to Fabrice. And he is not ...' she blushed and stammered to a halt. 'Oh Sophie I did not mean ...'

Sophie laughed. 'Fabrice will not think about it at all. He is the most amiable man, always considerate.'

There was a pause, then Aurora asked, 'Are you sure, dear Sophie, you want to marry him?'

Sophie took her friend's hand. 'What choice have I got?' she asked. 'And he is a dear,' she sighed. 'He's the gentlest, sweetest person imaginable and he loves me as much as he could love anyone. He is fun to be with and he sees life as a party. No, it could be a great deal worse, Aurora.' She thought of her sister above in the high tower and shivered. The disgrace of bearing an illegitimate child would be as abhorrent to James as the death of a brother, she thought. No. She was, indeed, very lucky.

The girls looked out over the valley. They could see the shepherd with his flock of sheep on the side of the mountain and the spiral of smoke coming from a charcoal-burner's fire. A haze of shimmering gold mantled the world.

Sophie sighed again and Aurora kissed her cheek.

'Do not worry, Sophie. Everything will be all right,' she said.

Sophie believed it would be. But there were compromises to make. She accepted them with the best grace she could muster. Craw Kilty came to see her, ostensibly about the wedding, promising a love philtre to ensure her lasting happiness. Lord Usher, who liked to keep the tenants happy, encouraged this sort of thing. She told Sophie that Fergal was safe and assured her that she need not worry on that score. She sent greetings from the Widow. Sophie asked her tentatively about Red, but a shuttered look came over the old wan's face and she pleaded complete ignorance. So Sophie put it all out of her mind, together with the tragedy of her brother's death, and decided that life was for the living and she must make the best of her lot.

Chapter

45

BELLA in her tower looked down on the gardens below. She could just see Sophie in her wedding-dress, white silk organza overlaid with Brussels lace. She carried a huge bouquet of orange-blossom, carnations, and rosebuds white and pink, and she hung on her new husband's arm and gazed into his eyes. Bella shivered in hate. It was like a dream below, a dream she had visualized herself in, dressed in white and holding onto Fabrice de Beauvillande. Until the very last moment she had believed it might happen. Some accident would befall Sophie, Fabrice might come to his senses and suddenly realize it was she he really loved — oh, anything. But it hadn't and the wedding had proceeded as planned. Her sister Sophie was now the Contesse de Beauvillande.

Fabrice's blond hair was ruffled in the breeze and he looked splendid and handsome in pearl-grey. James had not weakened, despite Dolly's pleas, and Bella was forbidden to take part in the celebrations. Aurora Vestry was the chief bridesmaid instead of her and she held the train, with six little girls to help her. They all wore pink, dresses so pretty that Bella would cheerfully have killed to have possessed one.

The bridesmaids moved about on the different levels of the garden below her and leaned on the parapet overlooking the valley. They had flowers in their hair and the young men flirted with them. Bella moaned. She saw Sophie laughing up at her husband and she wanted to murder her. It all looked so pretty below and everyone seemed so happy. But the worst moment for Bella had been when Sophie had first appeared, coming from the chapel just after she had been married. She had glowed with a joy Bella could see from the high tower and the bells had rung out over the valley and Bella knew that she had lost.

James had refused even to see her. She had sent messages imploring him for just five minutes of his time but he did not even deign to reply. Then she had written him apologies, begging him to forgive her. She received nothing but silence for her pains.

Someone was singing below and they were drinking champagne. You could hear the clink of glasses. A couple of silly girls were squealing delightedly as that stupid Donal Fitzroy tried to kiss their cheeks. Angel was bounding about yapping and Darcy Blackwater and Barth Gorman were flirting with Aurora Vestry.

Sophie had come to the high tower to see her, but she told her to go away. Molly had said she could talk to her, but Bella would not speak to her sister. Sophie said she wanted them to be friends and for there to be peace between them, but it choked Bella even to have to think about Sophie, let alone see her. Molly guarded her like a dragon, and Bella often laughed mirthlessly to herself as she thought how much they had in common: a burning hatred and an implacable desire for revenge.

Every day Molly took her down the stone stairs for a walk in the arbour at the bottom of the tower where the statue of Flora stood gazing through time at the valley and the mountains. She had thought of running away from Molly, finding James and throwing herself on his mercy. But she had soon realized she had no chance at all of evading her guardian's vigilance. Molly would never forgive Bella for causing her lover's death. James had chosen well.

Molly liked to tell her all that was going on in the house, each piece of information guaranteed to annoy her.

'Cormac has smiled at Lady Dolly and Lord Usher has given him a golden bracelet for his chubby little arm. Lady Dolly looks so well these days and she has ordered some gowns from Paris, and shoes and a fan from London. Lord Usher will take her on a visit there in the autumn. Miss Sophie and her husband will live here for a while at Usher until the unrest is over in Paris and then there is the business of the duel. The Conte says France is impossible for a while. Lord Usher agrees. He does not want to be parted too soon from his dear sister. He has given them Master Creagh's rooms. They have been newly decorated for the bride and groom, but they have not seen the apartment yet. It is to be a surprise when they return from their honeymoon. Lord Usher could not bear to leave the rooms as they were. It broke his heart, he said. Creagh's death has hit him hard, an' the manner of it. Miss Sophie and her husband will go with them to London for the season in the autumn. They'll go to balls and assemblies and buy a lot of new clothes.

She went on and on in a light stilted voice, feigning normality, turning the knife all the time.

Bella saw that a crowd of tenants had come up the driveway. The couple were honeymooning at Lough Erne and the tenants would pull the carriage containing the young couple down the driveway and through the woods, where, a few miles away, four greys waited to be hitched to the carriage. It was decorated with garlands of flowers and Bella watched the merry throng laughing and singing bawdy songs in Gaelic till the bridal pair disappeared between the trees.

Below, an orchestra struck up and she could hear the stamp of feet as the dancing started. A waltz. Now an eight-hand-reel, now a cotillion. The music sounded sweet on the air and the laughter drifted to her on the breeze. It made her feel isolated, shut out. Tears of rage and frustration filled her eyes and she knelt in an agony of fury.

'Let me find a way. Please God, let me find a way to destroy ... to destroy ... to destroy.' She laid her burning forehead on the cold stone as she heard Molly enter her chamber.

'Oh dear dear, Miss Bella. On your knees? Praying for forgiveness, are we? There are those who'll never forgive. But for you I'd have had a weddin' too. Not as grand as Miss Sophie below, but a weddin' nonetheless. But you took my lover away from me, you did. You caused him to be killed. I hope God forgives you, m'lady, for I canna.'

The maid laid a tray on the table beside the window. 'There's some food for ye. An' weddin' cake. It's me Mam's best recipe. Not that you'll enjoy it, will ye? Well, I'm goin' downstairs, though my heart's fair broke in half this day thinkin' of what I've lost.'

She left the room and Bella was left alone to gaze from the high window on the festivities below.

Sophie enjoyed her wedding day enormously. The sun shone

and she looked pretty and felt wonderful. She was starting a whole new life and she could put the past behind her. The morning-sickness that had been part of her daily life and the dreadful apprehension and sleeplessness had vanished and she felt and looked radient.

Aurora Vestry was a great support, especially in the most practical ways, helping Clarie, who had been promoted, since Molly was now exclusively concerned with Bella. She was now Sophie's personal maid and she took her duties very seriously. Aurora helped the maid to arrange the bride's head-dress of orange-blossom and to do up the hundreds of little pearl buttons at the back of her dress, for Clarie became all fingers and thumbs through nerves and couldn't seem to manage the minute fastenings. Aurora pressed her hand and gave her encouragement and reassuring glances every so often during the ceremony.

As the day went on Sophie felt as if she had replied to the same questions over and over again. Yes, they would live in Usher for the moment. Yes, she hoped to live in France eventually. No, her mother-in-law was not here, she was too frail to make such an arduous journey. And on and on. She did not say that they had asked Fabrice's mother to come to the wedding, but had received no reply from her directly. The Reverend Mother of the Convent in Chartres had written a note on her behalf saying that she did not want any communication with her son. Fabrice was dreadfully upset, but he was an optimist and consoled himself by saying to Sophie, 'It is only temporary, my darling. She'll soon come round.'

When at last Sophie repaired to her room to change, it was afternoon and her legs were tired from standing.

Aurora had come in to help her. 'Oh Sophie are you wild with excitement?' she whispered, a soft blush colouring her cheeks.

'I don't know what you mean, Aurora.' Sophie was trying to remove her veil which was tangled with her hair.

'Oh yes you do. Don't be obtuse.' Then Aurora realized what she had said and put her hands to her mouth in consternation. 'Oh the saints preserve us. You know. You already know. Oh Sophie, I'm so sorry, I . . .'

Sophie was spared the necessity of replying for Clarie came in with Sophie's pale blue moiré dress trimmed with braid and a fringe in the same colour. She was soon changed, giggling and laughing all the time.

Aurora tied the bonnet under her chin, and pushed the bow to one side. 'There, that looks much more coquettish,' she laughed.

'You are quite shameless, Aururra,' Sophie replied. 'Why on earth should I want to look coquettish? Really!'

Dolly came in looking for the bride, saying Fabrice said to hurry for they did not want to reach Dublin late.

Sophie kissed everyone, and threw her bouquet. Aurora caught it, then laughed back at her friend in delighted surprise.

'You'll be next.' Sophie called.

When they got to the Shelbourne Hotel in Dublin where they were to spend their first night together, Sophie was pleased to find everything in readiness for them, and having dined off fresh salmon and lamb and eaten a pineapple imported from the South Seas, the height of luxury, they had laughed a lot and drunk a lot of champagne and gone to bed relaxed and light-headed.

Fabrice was experienced with women and to Sophie's delight he was a wonderful lover. Her experience with Red had been intense and overwhelming. But it had also been very confusing. She had never truly sorted out her feelings about what exactly had happened. Nothing had prepared her for the fun and excitement that permeated her lovemaking with Fabrice.

When the little clock on the mantlepiece struck 3.a.m they fell asleep at last, well pleased with each other.

Their honeymoon continued on a very agreeable note. Nothing marred their pleasure. The weather was fine. The house on the edge of Lough Erne was delightfully appointed and James' friends who had lent it together with their servants to the young honeymoon couple had left detailed instructions for their comfort, the most important of which was to leave them alone.

'Like the fairy tale where everything is done by unseen hands.' Sophie said ecstatically to Fabrice.

'But it is you who are a fairy tale, my darling,' Fabrice replied, 'for you are like the princess in one of them.'

He said such pretty things to her. It made her feel wanted and loved. They whiled away the long sunny days, idling, loving, enjoying themselves with no thought for the morrow. It was so easy to do that with Fabrice.

He took her boating on the lake and they picnicked under a willow tree on the edge and Sophie peeled off her stockings and pulled up her skirts and her petticoats to her knees and wiggled her toes in the sun. They ate roast chicken legs from red-checked napkins, dipped the strawberries into the white wine they drank, then covered their faces with their straw hats and went to sleep. They awakened in the golden sunset, the water turned dark midnight blue, and dusty and dishevelled, they cleaved a glittering pathway home across the lake and arrived in time to bathe and dress for dinner.

When Sophie stung her bare legs on nettles and cried out at the discomfort, Fabrice pulled dock-leaves and wrapped her legs tenderly in them till they cooled and the stinging abated. They slept under a linen sheet and held each other's bodies through the long silver nights. Fabrice taught Sophie to understand her body's pleasure and how best to please him, and they took it all lightly and joyously, giving themselves up to the satisfaction of the moment.

In July they returned to Usher Castle. When their carriage rumbled up the driveway Dolly and James came running down the steps to greet them, with Maitland hard on their heels to help unstrap their luggage.

'Sophie, you look absolutely wonderful.' James kissed her joyful face. She glowed with radiant health and happiness, he thought. Her cheeks were rosy, her eyes sparkling. 'Fabrice, you are obviously good for my sister. And she has put on weight.'

'Yes, you have filled out. You were too thin before. Congratulations, Fabrice.' Dolly hugged her sister-in-law while James greeted Fabrice.

It when James had turned to go into the house that Sophie, glancing about reassuring herself that nothing had changed at Usher, caught sight of her sister standing in the open window of the high tower. Even from that distance Sophie could sense the malignance that seemed to emanate from the motionless white-clad form. She turned away quickly.

Dolly was saying, 'I hope you like your apartments. They are the very pink of fashion.' She shrugged. 'Well, I mean, compared to the rest of the castle they are the very pink.'

'I know I'll love them,' Sophie said.

'Well, I thought it would please Fabrice, being in the French style. I do hope you like it.'

Dolly looked so nervous, so anxious to please that Sophie hugged her. 'Dearest Dolly, it is quite lovely. I personally am enchanted.' Then she looked quizzically at Fabrice. 'Darling?'

He spread his hands and shrugged his shoulders. 'It is adorable. I am mad about it. What you have done, Dolly, is perfection. Now if you will excuse me, I will leave you ladies to gossip the afternoon away. I have to write to my Mama.' He kissed his wife, then bowed and left them.

'He still hopes she will forgive him,' Sophie said pulling off her gloves. 'Oh Dolly, I sometimes get so fed up with family honour. So much unhappiness is caused by it. Surely loving each other and forgiving is more important?'

'Don't let your brother James hear you saying that,' Dolly replied, ringing the bell for the servants.

Clarie answered it and Dolly ordered tea for them both. 'Tell Annie I am with the Countess.' Sophie blushed and giggled. She was not used to her new title. When Charles left she sat beside her sister-in-law and hugged her.

'I forget when I'm here that I'm not James' little sister and I have to remind myself that I'm really a married woman.'

Dolly looked at her shyly. 'Are you . . . are you happy? Do you enjoy being . . . being married?'

Sophie burst out laughing, and as she saw a delicate blush mount Dolly's neck and face she gave her another hug. 'Oh darling Dolly I *love* being married and all that goes with it. I do know what you mean, so don't blush so. It's wonderful.'

To her surprise Dolly's eyes filled with tears and she said, 'Oh I'm so glad, Sophie. So glad. I thought I was . . . well . . . shameful. Wanton. I love James and, and, well, all my friends hate it so, you know, that part of marriage, and I thought, I thought I must be distinctly odd.'

'Darling Dolly, then so am I. So don't you worry about what *they* say. Most of their husbands lack, shall we say, finesse. It's a word Fabrice uses a lot. Finesse.'

Dolly giggled. 'Yes,' she said. 'When you think of some of their husbands . . . I never thought of that before. It, well, it can't be much fun.'

'Well, Dolly, from now on you just count your lucky stars that we have such beautiful husbands.'

'And what's this you say about Fabrice's mother?'

'She stays in her convent and no one knows what she thinks.

She says that she'll never forgive him. That does not sound a very Christian thing to me. Poor Fabrice did not mean to kill Armand. She never replies to his letters, but he, dutiful son, always writes to her and tells her how he is and what is happening.

Clarie came in with a silver salver and the tea-things. She poured, and gave each of them a cup. The French windows were wide open and a cool breeze blew in off the mountains. Sophie thought how pleasant it was to be home, and how delightful her new apartments were. The birds sang outside the window and the two women sat tranquilly sipping tea.

At last Dolly sighed and rose, shaking out the folds of her primrose voile skirt.

'I must go to Cormac. You will be delighted with your godson, Sophie. He is quite the most delightful child and so pretty. James and I dote on him.'

'I'll rest awhile, Dolly. Then I'll visit your rooms and see my remarkable godson. Oh, and thank you again for our suite. It is lovely. And you. You look so well. You have lost that pinched and tired look you had which worried me.'

'And I can return the compliment, Sophie. As I said, you've put on weight and it suits you.'

She kissed her sister-in-law and left the room, leaving Sophie to wonder how soon she could tell her husband she was *enceinte*. She realized how happy she was with Fabrice, and felt a moment's guilt over how quickly she had forgotten Red. She knew she still loved him with a passion that frightened her when she thought of him. But it was too big a problem to worry about now and she found day-to-day living with Fabrice a joy and a delight.

Chapter

46

SOPHIE settled down in the new apartments, feeling very contented with life. She could not have chosen a husband more suited to her than Fabrice. Aurora had been right, she thought, they were made for each other. Creagh's rooms had been decorated in the Empire style in soft shades of pink, moss-green and gilded bronze. The walls had been hung with old-rose damask, and Sophie loved the pink brocaded chairs and *chaises longues* which Dolly said she had ordered for Sophie. 'I thought you would like the style particularly,' she said. Fabrice's rooms were Empire green and there were miniature sculptures in black marble scattered about in niches here and there.

All that summer the roses bloomed riotously. Salmon and white, blush-pink and scarlet, wine and crimson. There were moss-roses and tea-roses, Bourbon roses and damask-roses. The arbour and the gardens were festooned with nodding fragrant heads, cream, red, white and yellow. The lilac hung in heavy mauve masses and the laburnum tree dripped yellow clusters and later scattered poison pods all over the grass, that Dolly was at great pains to keep little Cormac away from. Rambling roses climbed over the grey stone shot with silver that constituted the walls of the high tower, and everywhere there were trees, casting shade from the heat of the sun and draping the mountains in a mantle of green.

It was a hot summer, but cool here in the mountains. Long days slid contentedly into each other and the household at Usher dwelt in peace. Except for the solitary woman in the tower. She watched alone as July shed her rose-petals and August arrived and Usher Castle slept in the sun. In the long days of golden light there were parties, and croquet was played in leisurely fashion. There were picnics in the woods under the cathedral canopy of birch and oak, beech and chestnut. Dolly and Sophie read poetry to each other under their parasols. They swayed in hammocks beneath the trees and talked about babies and birthing. Sophie grew and swelled and bloomed. Her skin was like the peaches that they cut with silver knives and ate off delicate Chinese porcelain under their straw hats in the sun.

The geraniums scattered colour over the leveled lawns and they often drank tea on the loggia overlooking the valley, or took their coffee there of an evening after dinner and watched the sun set and the stars prick the blue velvet of the sky with pinpoints of shining silver light.

Clarie made Sophie tisanes of camomile to sooth her and she drank fresh milk from Craw Kilty's goat, sent by the crone to the castle especially for her. She felt loved and protected and cossetted.

Fabrice often talked about his past to her over the summer days, and they grew very close, dear friends as well as lovers. He talked about Ornella and the duel, and how he had killed Armand and left France in disgrace.

'I regret it all, my darling, so deeply, but I did not know you then. I planned to marry and go back to Ornella. How naive I was. Now you are so much a part of my life that I cannot think how I can have loved someone like Ornella. Oh she was beautiful, yes, but a courtesan after all. I have written to Maman and told her how I feel. I have also told her about the baby. It will be her grandson, the next Conte de Beauvillande. I feel sure she will forgive me now at last.'

But though he told Sophie all about his past she did not confide in him. She knew that, close as they were, their marriage could not sustain her having had a lover. It was different for men. They could make mistakes. Fabrice could tell her of his affair with Ornella, and it would be unreasonable of her not to forgive him. But such behaviour was not appropriate in the 'gentler sex'. Sophie felt it was all very unfair, but she was not prepared to risk the delightful relationship they had. She knew Fabrice was irresponsible. He expected to be looked after and with his charming personality and mild temperament he would always find someone to take care of him when funds were low so he did not need to worry on that score — and he didn't.

When his Maman forgave, and Paris pardoned him, he could return to France and his chateau and his Paris house and take charge of his money, titles, and lands, but until then he would have to live off the Ushers and his wife. It caused him no qualms, troubled him not at all. He felt sure it was only temporary and he could repay their kindness soon. When Sophie asked him once, did he not mind? he replied by shrugging his shoulders and turning down the corners of his mouth and saying, 'But what can I do? C'est la vie!'

This attitude sometimes irritated Sophie and she felt she had married a charming boy, a toy she liked to play with, a sweetheart she was delighted with, but one with no serious side. No depth. He was not grown-up. Unlike Red.

When she thought of Red, and she tried not to, she shivered with desire and excitement. Here was a man, an adult, living out his life of danger, fulfilling his ideals and having the courage of his convictions. Here was a man in whose arms she felt overwhelmed, whose kisses shook her to the foundations of her being and whose lovemaking had thrown her body into such an exquisite concord of sensations and feelings that whenever she thought about it she could not breathe, and had to press her hands over her heart to still its beating.

But she was happy with Fabrice. They were like a pair of kittens, heedless and unselfconscious, utterly given over to the pleasure of the moment.

He was pleased about the child, delighted. It would really force his Maman to forgive him, he said, and to petition for his pardon. When she told him, he put her feet up on the chaise, though she said she felt fine, and fed her sugar comfits though she said she preferred grapes.

James was happy with him in the castle. There was peace in the house and content, singing and laughter. After all they had been through, he was more than grateful to Fabrice for the joy he had brought to Sophie and indirectly to Dolly.

September followed August and the leaves turned to amber and gold, yellow and bronze. The men went hunting. Bessie Broderick made jams and preserves for the next year and the farms brought in the harvest. The lanes were often impassable with carts of hay rumbling by, top-heavy, and many a horseman chose a quick route across a forbidden field rather than get stuck behind one. James took Dolly to London while Sophie and Fabrice stayed home and looked forward to the coming of the child.

Winter brought with it icy winds and darker days and finally the snow. The family clung close to the fires. The women put aside the gossamer dresses of summer and swathed themselves protectively in furs and velvets. And at last Sophie's time came. Fabrice was told his wife was in premature labour, and who would tell him otherwise?

Chapter

47

DR Hegarty could not but be reminded of the last time a baby had been born at Usher. He urged his horse forward in the wildness and dark of the night. He knew too that there was something wrong with the dates of conception and expected birth that the young Contesse de Beauvillande had given him, so he was not at all surprised when he received a call to say that his young patient had gone into labour weeks too soon. However, he was not going to show any surprise at all, whatever might happen. Matt Dominic had roused him to come to the castle, and his head in a whirl, the doctor obeyed. The couple had been married in June. He had been a guest himself. But who was he to upset Lord Usher and the Conte de Beauvillande, who, rumour had it, was very apt to use a gun on the slightest of provocations? He might break Miss Sophie's heart by saying that the child could not have been conceived in wedlock. He loved Sophie and would not have her hurt. Perhaps it was the Conte's and the young couple had anticipated the wedding, and perhaps it was not the Conte's and Sophie had done what girls since the dawn of time had done, and married de Beauvillande to give the child a father. Whichever it was, the good doctor had no intention of upsetting the apple-cart. His mind was firmly made up. Nevertheless, it was with his usual feeling of apprehension that he rode through the wind and the rain to Sophie's bedside.

He need not have worried, for Sophie de Beauvillande lay in her pink and gold bedchamber and pushed and struggled, putting her whole effort into her labour, and after a scant four hours, and quite the easiest time imagineable, a beautiful black-haired boy was born.

Dolly was quite amazed. 'Oh my dearest Sophie, how much more competent you are than I. I made such a to-do and had everyone so upset.'

But Sophie would not hear her. 'Now Dolly, it simply means I'm made like a peasant, is that not so, Doctor? So you must not talk like that.'

Fabrice insisted on calling the baby Armand after the boy he had killed in the duel, and he made his mother cognisant of that fact in a letter to the convent. He appeared not to notice anything strange about his wife producing such a large baby so prematurely, or that the child was so dark. He seemed ecstatic, his mind not on those things at all. He went his way as usual, joyous and carefree.

James noticed, but said nothing either. It was almost as if he feared what he would find out, and indeed all he desired was for Dolly and himself, Fabrice and Sophie, to bring up their children in an atmosphere of good-will and peace.

Sophie was besotted with Armand, and the two young mothers became absorbed in talk of babies habits, stools, teething, wind, nursing, almost to the exclusion of all else.

'We are becoming quite boring,' Dolly said one day, and Fabrice yawning in the window seat remarked, 'What we should do is have a party, a celebration.'

Sophie clapped her hands. 'What a wonderful idea. Oh do let's. Dolly and I sound like our wet-nurses. We are becoming drears. Dolly, ask James if we may. Do you think he'll agree?'

Dolly laughed. 'All he wants is for us to be happy as we are. Of a certainty he'll say yes.'

'Why not a masked ball? Fancy dress? Everyone in black and white? It's winter. Look, it's snowing outside. It would look so pretty.'

'Oh that's a wonderful idea, Fabrice. Trust you to think of something like that,' Dolly cried. 'How romantic it will be.'

The proposition was laid before James and in his mood of content and his obsessive desire to maintain the household's happiness he gladly gave his consent.

Usher was forthwith thrown into the turmoil of preparation and the dinner-table conversation changed from babies to costumes. Mrs Maitland said the flowers and decorations would be black and white in so far as was humanly possible and Bessie Broderick promised a wonderful feast.

'Plum puddin's, m'lady, and pork, brandy-snaps and ginger tarts.' All was hustle and bustle, excitement and delighted anticipation. Wicklow and Dublin society accepted and the affair promised to be a crush and quite the party of the year.

Sophie, encouraged by her husband, wore a very daring white gown. It was *à la Josephine de Beauharnais* and cut in Grecian style, very Empire, very revealing and suited Sophie's pale prettiness remarkably well. Fabrice dressed very dramatically all in black, with Beau Brummel in mind. They would be a stunning couple, Dolly said. She had tried to persuade James into a pierrot costume but he refused adamantly. He would wear his black evening clothes and a plain mask.

'I'm the host, Dolly my love, and that gives me some rights.' he said with finality.

Bella spent most of her time in her apartments in the High Tower. Once Sophie's wedding was over she had been allowed out, but she shunned the family and did not return to the rooms she and Sophie had shared before the latter got married. She became more and more of a recluse. Pride hemmed her in. She had sometimes joined the family when the young couple returned from their honeymoon, but she found their evident happiness too painful. Like her mother she drew apart from everyone. She did not like people and she desired Fabrice too much. So she retreated further and further into a world of shadowy hatreds and imagined persecution. When Sophie's baby was born the young mothers pleasantly asked her to join them, but she thought they were mocking her. When they tried to make conversation with her she found insults lurking in every phrase. So when James asked her quite kindly what she would wear to the ball she was certain he was laughing at her. She said sarcastically that she would come as a ghost, that would be appropriate, but no one laughed and she left the room, leaving behind, as was her wont, an uncomfortable silence.

In the High Tower she made up her mind. Her idea had been a good one. She *would* go to the party as a ghost she decided smiling silently to herself.

Old Gentleman and the Dowager Countess had no problems. They both would come as they usually dressed, Old Gentleman in a black smoking jacket and Angela in her deep mourning.

When the evening finally arrived Sophie sat in front of her elegant little Georgian dressing-table, looking at her reflection in the oval mirror. She was perfectly happy with what she saw, and she marvelled that having a baby had made so little difference to her looks. If anything she looked prettier than before. Dolly had looked haggard and worn out for months afterwards, and here she was, a scant eight weeks later, face smooth as a rose-petal, pink and bright-eyed, feeling full of sparkle and energy.

Clarie, who was a treasure now that she had overcome her initial nerves, dressed her hair, carefully placing a shimmering tiara on her golden locks.

Fabrice came in looking remarkable beautiful in his black. He kissed her and together they went down the wide staircase to join the party. It looked very elegant, everyone in black or white. The music wafted down over the snow-carpeted valley and the shepherd on the hill, the charcoal-burners, Craw Kilty and the Minstrel in the valley, heard it and gazed at the windows of the castle lit up, shining in the dark and at the black and white figures that drifted out into the night air, laughing, or leaning over the balconies, or waltzing in the grand ballroom.

There were pierrots galore, Dolly teased James, for, she said, he was more at odds with the company in his evening clothes than he would have been as a pierrot. There were angels and Neros, (the fat Vestry Uncle) Julius Ceasars and Greek ladies (the Gormans and the O'Sheas). There were black and white clowns and a frightening figure of death who was really only Darcy Blackwater. There were skeletons and Celtic warriors and an Irish Queen decked in a long white tunic bordered in Celtic design. There was an all-in-white Marie Antoinette. And there was a ghost.

The festivities lasted until dawn. In the banqueting hall tables groaned with food; boars' heads, sticky with honey coating; suckling pigs; mounds of fruit imported from sunnier climes; trifles and comfits and cakes; flagons of wine and brandy in crystal decanters. An orchestra played waltzes, reels, and polkas, and the cotillion, and James had a mime especially booked from the Royalty Theatre in Dublin, whose eloquent, silent mastery of his art moved them to tears and laughter.

Dolly and James had opened the ball with a waltz and Fabrice, holding his wife in his arms, whispered to her that she was the most beautiful woman in the room. It was certainly true. Sophie had the bloom of happiness upon her and her eyes sparkled behind her mask and were brighter than her tiara.

They danced most of the time together, she and Fabrice, and it had grown late and she was talking to Dolly and nibbling on a candied fruit, when the stranger came and took her hand for a polka. She thought he was a stranger, for she could not place him as she had most of the others. You could tell the Vestries by their red hair and the Gormans by their height. Others she recognized by a gesture, a tilt of the head or a revealing mannerism. The stranger she could not place, yet he was familiar. She had seen him somewhere before and for some reason the thought troubled her.

As soon as he touched her hand she knew who he was. She caught her breath and felt her heart pound as he led her into the merry dance.

'Red,' she whispered, 'Red.'

She looked around in an agony of confusion. 'Are you mad?' she said. Where was Fabrice? James was near her. Suppose he found out who danced with her? It was so dangerous. He must be crazy to come here. But she was glad that he had. Her knees felt weak; her bones had turned to water.

Red was not in fancy dress, although he could have been mistaken for a highwayman. He wore black trousers, a loose white shirt and a black double-caped cloak. His only concession to the party was a plain black mask that hid his face.

He led her onto the balcony, then down the steps and into the arbour. The snow-capped world was silent and a million stars thickly jewelled the velvet night sky. It was bitterly cold.

He did not speak but encompassed her in his embrace and kissed her lips with a passion that shook her to the core and made her hungry for more.

'Oh my God, I've missed you,' he said softly to her. 'I've ached for you in the long and lonely reaches of the night.' She leant softly moaning against his breast. Her legs would have given way under her if he had not held her so fiercely.

'Oh my beautiful one, you crept into my heart and made your home there. Try as I will I cannot get you out.'

'We must not. You must not. It is not right, now,' she protested weakly, but he kissed her again and again, and helpless she returned his embrace with a fervour that denied her words.

'I know. I know. I have nothing to give you but death. Oh my darling, ours is a foolish passion,' he cried.

Sophie clung to him. 'I know. It is foolish, we cannot help it.

But you are mad. You have risked your life to come here. You risk it every moment you are with me in this house. Oh my love, go. Please go. If anyone recognizes you ...' The thought was too frightening for her to put into words. She stared at him with anguished eyes.

'Listen. I came to you for forgiveness and to tell you I am always at your service if you need me.'

She touched his face with her fingertips and her hands were cold so he enclosed her within his cloak, near to the warmth of his body.

'Forgiveness?' she asked, 'What for?'

'Creagh,' he answered. 'Creagh. If there was any way I could have saved him you must know I would have.'

She put her fingers to his lips. 'Shsh, my darling, my love. You are not to blame for that. I know.'

She shivered and he held her closer. A cloud passed over the face of the full moon that hung in a silver disc over their heads, bathing the valley and the mountains in a sheen of cold silver, making the white snow all around them sparkle with a thousand diamond lights. They did not see above them the appearance of a ghost, a white shadow leaning out of the window of the high tower. Listening. Listening.

'You know it is impossible for us.' Sophie pleaded.

'I know.'

Their faces melted together, blending in shadow, becoming one.

He asked, 'Are you happy? Oh my darling, I hope you are happy?'

She nodded and put her head on his breast and snuggled into the warmth of his cloak. 'I am. As much as I can be, and more indeed. My husband is kind and tender. He treats me well. But he is not you. He is not you.'

'I am glad that he is good to you. I would not wish you to be unhappy. I love you too much.'

'And you?' she asked. 'You, my darling? Are you happy?'

'There is no time for happiness or unhappiness in my life. It is run on different perameters, my love. Stephens was arrested and spent two weeks in Richmond Jail. I helped him escape. It was a great victory. Creagh would have been elated. The morale of the Fenians is high. But the reality is that there is little organization and a terrible scarcity of armaments. That is my job. We can hardly take on the British Army with pikes and knives, now can we?'

He saw the bewildered look on her face.

'Red, Red, I don't understand you when you talk like that. I don't understand.'

'Oh my love, I must not talk thus to you. How could you understand what I'm talking about? You are protected by a castle, an allegiance to a Queen, a grand army and a great culture. It is not your fault that you see nothing strange in the colonization of our land by our neighbours against our will. Ach, no, do not speak. How could you understand?' he asked gently, not expecting a reply. She looked at him with wide cornflower-blue eyes, the colour of his own. There was incomprehension in hers and compassion in his.

'I hear tell,' he said, 'I hear tell your husband has hair the colour of corn?'

She nodded, aware suddenly of where the conversation might go.

'And I hear tell you have a son, born prematurely, with hair the colour of a raven's wing?'

Once more she nodded, wide-eyed, gazing at him unblinking.

'I hear tell from the gypsies this is unlikely, not to say impossible.'

Once more she nodded.

'I wanted to know that. I wanted to assure myself that you and he were well and there was no animosity?'

'There is none. Fabrice . . .'

'Hush.' He stopped her. 'Do not tell me. You would feel badly if you did and for me there is too much pain in it all. There is naught I can do about it. Unless of course that you were greatly unhappy or punished in some way.'

'I am not,' she said. 'No one knows. James guesses, I think, but he'll never say anything.'

'What is his name? The child?'

'Armand.'

'Ah yes. Armand. French of course, for you are the Contesse de Beauvillande, are you not? Still, it's better than an English name. I shall call him . . . Patrick. Guard him well, Sophie, and if ever you need me, or there is danger or sadness, send for me here.'

Into her hand he pressed a piece of paper. Afterwards she saw written on it,

Rosaleen *Dubh*
Lizzie Brannagan's,
No. I Doone Alley,
Dublin.

'Goodbye, my love, my heart of hearts, my darling. I'll hold you always in my thoughts. *Slán leat*,' he said.

She held him to her, knowing their time was up, that Fabrice and James would notice her absence and set up a search if she did not return soon. She kissed him and replaced her mask and left the warm shelter of his cloak. She felt the hot tears seep beneath her mask, which absorbed them. She fled back over the snow to where the black and white figures spun round and round in an endless waltz.

Redmond Rafferty stood still and tall in the shadowed arbour, his face raised to the moon, and the girl above him marvelled at its beauty and drew back in case she was seen. Her thoughts were a mixture of bitterness and exultation. Sophie's baby was not de Beauvillande's. There was power in that knowledge. It was a useful piece of information. She had a secret now. But how she could use it she did not know. If she sent a note to Fabrice he would ignore her. They would not believe her. Creagh had branded her a liar and they all knew she would say anything, do anything, to get out of her predicament, prove that she had not been at fault.

Ah well. Perhaps some day. Her time must come.

In the meantime, and her heart withered within her at the thought, Sophie not only had a husband and that husband Fabrice, who Bella still coveted, dreamed about, but a handsome lover as well. The little scene below brought gall to her heart and filled her with poisonous hate.

For long moments they both stood, the dark stranger, cloaked against the night, staring at the moon, the slight figure of the girl in her white ghost-robes above him in the high window.

Then the silence of the night was broken by a laugh as a drunken jester in chequered silk, and a shepherdess came running out into the garden. The girl in the tower glanced towards them, envying them the fun of their game and when she looked back the stranger was gone. She sighed and closed her window against the cold night air and decided not to rejoin the party. She had too much to think about and for the first time since Creagh's death a ray of hope had entered her life.

Chapter

48

SYLVIE Donahue nèe Broderick raised herself feebly on her elbow. She reached for the rag to wipe the sweat from her body. She had a constant fever these days. She coughed, and in the strength of the coughing brought up blood which made a dark stain on the already dirty rag. She wrinkled her nose in distaste. Sean was a long time gone, she thought. Maybe, with luck, he had a job on the docks for the day's unloading. That would be great. Jobs were so few and far between, but her Sean never stopped trying.

The babby set up a wail. She lay on the mattress beside her. There was no furniture in the room where they lived. Once they possessed a table and chairs, but they had to be pawned for bread a while back.

They lived at the end of Doone Alley. You came into the house by a hall-way with a black and rotten floor. There were gaps in the floorboards, which were damp and decayed, and through them you could see the cellars below. The hall was filthy and there was only one privy in the back-yard, which was ankle-deep in human excrement and filth. There was no sewer at the end of the alley, which curved around and had another row of houses opposite, a horse-shoe of houses trapped in their own filth. There was one water-tap for all the houses, in the middle of the courtyard, but Sylvie was too weak to get to it. She put the babby to the empty breast to hush it and fell back on the mattress, exhausted.

The doctor said she had enteric fever and tuberculosis. They could not afford the doctor, but he had looked in to see her when old Mrs Wiggs above had died when the roof fell in on her. It had not been repaired since. It was always damp and cold in the Donahue's room.

Sylvie coughed and held onto the babby and wondered what in the name of God and his blessed Mother was going to happen to them. Even if she was healthy, the strain of living in this place took its toll. All the houses were in the same condition and that applied to over two thousand houses in Dublin. Sean had heard a rabble-rouser, a member of the *Fianna*, the Brotherhood, tell them at a meeting, one of the forbidden ones, that there were twenty thousand families in tenements in Dublin and of those, seven thousand lived crowded into rooms much too small to house them. Houses sheltered five or six families. Acts of Parliament were passed to rectify the situation, but lack of proximity, for the seat of Parliament was in London, and lack of profit from the outcome, saw to it that the laws were never implemented.

There was on average one toilet to thirty people in Doone Alley, and all the water for cooking, washing and cleaning had to be carried from that one tap in the courtyard, winter and summer. Sometimes in winter it was frozen. Then you had to do without.

How could anyone survive and make a home under those conditions? Sylvie wondered. They had tried when they came here first from Wicklow, but they soon gave up. It needed superhuman effort, and Sylvie was constantly sick. She was a slip of a girl with red-gold hair, who had once been full of light and music and laughter but the dank, dark alley they found themselves in oppressed her very soul. She lost her dancing ways and sank into grey depression and sickness. She had put up a good fight. She had promised herself when they had come here first that she would not sink into apathy as the rest of the women here seemed to have done. Sean would work. They would save. She would polish and clean and cook. It was what she was best at. She had been brought up in service and hadn't a lazy bone in her body. But there had been no work, or very little. She had watched the hope die out in Sean's eyes and despair take its place. You cannot cook and clean when you have nothing to do it with, nothing to do it on. Rags were valuable. Food was scarce. She was soon sick, and illness sapped her vitality. She was not unusual. Many of the women in the slums looked fifty years old and they only half that age. The battle for mere existence was too exhausting, too unremitting.

Sylvie looked at the walls unseeing. A damp and slimy fungus grew there, seeped and oozed and let off a smell that caught her nose and throat. She felt the babby tug at her breast. Tears slid down her cheeks unheeded. She had not known that people could live like this until it was too late, and she and Sean were caught in the trap. No work, sickness, no escape, no doctor, no recovery, no hope.

She would have gone home and thrown herself on her mother's mercy and the kindness of Lord Usher, but Sean was too proud and they didn't have the strength or the wherewithal to get there. Sean was losing his dignity day by day as failure bowed his shoulders, and furrowed his brow. It is a terrible thing to see the eyes of the man you love become haggard with worry, hunger and fear. She had had miscarriages over the years. The pain in her body and in her soul after she had lost a child was appalling. Normally you could not identify the bloody mass as a babby and it was thrown away with the garbage, but her body knew. Lost in her own gloom, she left Sean isolated and lost.

Then little Maeve had been born. Here on the filthy bundle of rags that passed for a bed she had sweated and screamed and fainted in agony and only Ma Wiggs to aid her. Sean had sat whimpering all through, suffering near as much as she, frightened out of his wits, inadequate and scared.

She did not think they had too long to live, herself and the babby. She thought it would be a good thing really. She knew she was useless, no help to Sean at all, and without the encumbrance of a sick wife and babby he still might make a go of things. She took out her rosary and let the beads slip gently through her fingers. Aves and Pater Nosters. The slow rhythmic monotony of the prayers comforted her.

'Dear God, dear blessed Virgin in Heaven, can you hear me? Are you there? Help me to be strong. Help me to be brave. Dear Jesus, why have you let this happen to us? What have me and Sean ever done to offend you? I know I haven't been to Mass, but sure, I haven't the strength, ye must see that. Dear God, if it's goin' to go on like this please let me die. Let little Maeve die now if she cannot have a decent life.'

She suddenly cried out, 'Oh Mary, blessed Mary, I didn't mean it. I know it's a sin to say that an' I can't bear to think I'm headed for Hell for entertain' the thought. Oh Mary, blessed Mother, help me and forgive me.'

She heard the shrieking in the street. Ragged children, calling to each other. She heard the sound of a drunken woman, singing. She was terrified of having another child, but in the night, close to Sean whom she loved with all her heart, she gave herself to him, for that was all she had to offer, the only thing that could make him feel a man again for five minutes.

She remembered the kitchen at Usher. The long table, the copper pans and the range. The warmth there, the smell of the food. The stuff they gave the pigs and the chickens and geese in one day at Usher would feed Sean and herself and Maeve for a week. And some over. And she would not turn up her nose at it.

Her chest hurt. Every movement was painful. Her body ached for the feel of fresh sheets smelling of lavender and she remembered bitterly how she had thought her little cell at Usher was not worthy of her and reckoned she could do better in the big city. If only she had known. She would dream at night in her fitful sleep of that little white-washed room with it comfortable bed and clean linen, its ewer and basin always full of fresh clear spring water. She remembered the white counter-pane and the bowl of flowers, lilac or roses, sweet-peas or forget-me-nots, that stood under the crucifix on the wall. To wake in the morning to the rattle of pots and pans and the sound of the cocks' crow and the smell of new-baked bread and bacon sizzling on the pan.

She groaned and pushed back her saturated hair and saw that little Maeve had given up her sucking and fallen into a death-like sleep on her shoulder. She looked at the small pinched face of her child. The blue lids shielded dark green eyes and there were hollows beneath them. Her mouth was open and she looked lifeless as a doll.

'Oh I love you, but what is going to become of you?'

When Sean came home that night he thought they were both dead. He had been lucky. A day's work unloading the 'Queen of the Sea' had paid him three shillings. He had stopped in the 'Green Cock' for a penny pint and a bit of warmth and cheer on the way home. He felt guilty as hell doing this and knew he should hurry back to his sick wife and child but he ached for a tiny respite after his back-breaking work and made a pint last as long as he could before turning into Doone Alley and home.

Home. Such a word to describe the place. He kicked a tin

can the children had left, not noticing the filth and the dirt in the street around him. At first it had horrified and disquieted him, but time had passed and now he was used to it. Besides, he had other more urgent things on his mind, like whether there was work or not, and so, whether they would eat or not. It all boiled down to that.

He took the bucket from outside the door. Weasel (so called because he looked exactly like one) Wiggs pushed past him from the house. He had the back room since the roof had fallen in on his mother. He was astray in his head and spent the day wandering the streets of Dublin, cursing loudly and taking the Lord's name in vain. He used words that gentlewomen had no knowledge of, but knew, just the same, that they were blasphemous. He walked down the courtyard, suddenly stopped at the door to No. 1, the brothel, and screamed a tirade of four-letter words at the softly red-lighted house.

Sean filled the bucket at the tap in the courtyard. He pulled off his shirt and splashed the icy water over his head and chest and let it flow over his hands in a vain effort to rid himself of the stink of fish. Putting on his shirt, he picked up the bucket and walked gingerly over the rotting floorboards into his home.

The one room hit him again in its bleakness, its dirt and its squalor. There was nothing there except the pile of rags and the bodies of his wife and child lying on them. He knew a moment's irritation with Sylvie for being so weak, so sick, so unable to cope, then realizing how unfair that was, he crept over to her.

She slept motionless, the child in her arms. Her face was gaunt, her breathing harsh and when he touched her she was burning. He lit a candle and pinned up the piece of sacking they used to cover the window. He felt his heart plummet and all the cheer the porter had instilled in him left him abruptly. He sank to his knees and gathering Sylvie and Maeve into his arms wept hopelessly for the desolation they had found themselves in.

Sylvie's eyes fluttered open. 'Ah darlin', there you are. I been so poorly. I'm sorry. If ye could get me a drop of water?'

'I got it an' more. Bread there is and tay an' a pot o' jam.'

But Sylvie shook her head. 'I could'na. Just the water, Sean.' She coughed all the time she was speaking. It seemed to Sean that she would choke to death before his very eyes.

'Here's the water.' He held the cracked cup to her lips. She drank greedily and fell back on the filthy rags. 'I'll get you some bread an' jam.'

'No, no, Sean. I couldn't. I just don't feel like it.'

'You *must*. You've got to keep your strength up. Think of little Maeve.' His voice had an hysterical edge. He felt impotent and defeated. He had done his day's work. He had brought home the food, yet now she refused it.

'Ah, God help her. Much of a heritage she has, poor wee mite. All right, Sean. Bring me a drop o' tay first an' maybe it'll whet my appetite.'

He was immediately satisfied and felt useful again. He bustled about, lighting the fire with a few planks from above, for when Mrs Wiggs died Sean could not resist the temptation to steal upstairs and take a plank or two or a beam from the collapsed roof to make a fire and a bit of comfort for themselves down below.

'It's pullin' the roof in on top o' you, if ever I heard,' One-Eyed Willy said to Breen Dubh in the Green Cock. 'An' if the landlord finds out, sure poor Sean'll be clapped in jail.'

Breen said, 'Never mind jail. I'll see that doesn't happen, never fear. Me an' Regan from Brannagan's 'll sort out anyone lays a finger on the Alley.'

Breen was a hunk of a man with a pugilist's face and an acute sense of rough justice. He was a vigilante. Many went in fear of him, for his violence was unrestrained when aroused. He had been a student at the university until his parents had died in a tragic accident in a runaway coach. His father's estate was sold to pay debts and there was nothing left for Breen. His education was cut short, his friends deserted him, and disillusioned he was cast forth on the city of Dublin, penniless and ill-equipped to fend for himself. But he was a huge lad and full of fury. They put him in the ring and he made his living fighting for a while. He soon realized it was a fool's game and left it and settled in Doone Alley. Originally he helped the inhabitants thereabouts with letters and correspondence, for a fee — few could read or write. Then as time went by the help took more practical forms. They turned to Breen in the Alley when all else failed. Breen always knew a way out. His subject had been law.

His love for the law had turned to contempt and he had developed a passionate desire to make the well-to-do authorities, whether Irish or English, suffer and pay for their indifference to the plight of the poor in Dublin and more particularly in Doone Alley. He resented the rich and carried a chip on his shoulder which gave him the rights, in his own estimation, of judge, jury and executioner.

The Alley was his territory. He had lived there for ten years now. He seldom left it and it did nothing for his humour when he went as far as the Quays and to Sackville Street. There he could see the fine ladies and gentlemen in their furs and velvets, their bonnets and cloaks, with their grand carriages and matched horses, and he growled under his breath, almost like Weasel Wiggs, and he cursed, and woe betide anyone who crossed his path on his return.

He protected the people in the Alley. He settled scores, guarded them against eviction and ran his minor business with aggressive fervour. He suffered from constant irritability, but he had a soft spot for anyone who was clearly out of their depth. The Donahues fell into this category.

Most of the inhabitants of the Alley were born and bred into it. They had, despite appalling conditions, developed a chippy sense of humour, a resilience to the terrible life they led. Knowing nothing else, they had no comparisons. There was a camaraderie, a sense of kinship in misfortune, there, and they helped each other out whenever they could. They were tough, and laughed often to hide their desperation. They bred like rabbits, and the women were worn out by the age of thirty. The children survived as best they could. The worst that could happen was when a tag was slipped over a little one's head, or attached to a cutdown jacket, announcing the child was for sale. Children often went off two-by-two, holding each other's hands, unaccompanied into the city, looking for work, and their mother, if she still lived, would pray that they were given a hole somewhere to sleep and enough food to subsist on, for that was the very best that could befall them. Otherwise it was starvation, child prostitution, cruelty and exploitation on a scale no mother dared to dwell on.

They worked, the lucky ones whose parents still had a room. They slept six, seven, eight or more on a filthy pile of rags. They worked as chimney-sweeps, or waded in the mud-banks of the river at low tide searching for bits of iron or rubbish to sell to the rag-and-bone man. Little girls and boys who hoped to make a penny or a half-penny went to Sackville or Grafton Street and there would rush to sweep the road clean for a lady or a gentleman wishing to cross the muddy highway. They were rewarded with a tip. They ran errands, were messengers, held horses outside shops and clubs and coffee-houses, then swept up the manure the horse had deposited in the street and sold it for fertiliser. Breen Dubh felt swamped by the sheer numbers that were helpless in the tidal-wave of poverty. Sylvie and Sean were not the worst. Many families had no homes at all. They slept under the barrows in St George's Lane. They searched the dust-bins for food and begged in Sackville Street or Grafton Street or on the steps of the Cathedral. They were not allowed in the environs of Fitzwilliam or Merrion Squares.

The lanes and courts and alleys around Doone Alley were crowded with beggars and thieves, sellers of rags and old clothes. There were knife grinders, chair-menders, mat-menders, rat-catchers, shoe-blacks and chimney sweeps. There were shoe-translators who made over old shoes and adapted them for a larger or smaller foot. Poverty bred its own requirements.

Breen Dubh knew that Sean and Sylvie did not belong among this hodge-podge of humanity. He had bumped into the tall young man staring at the clipper ships, the schooners, the East Indiamen in the docks. They had their sails furled, their masts tall, bobbing against the grey sky.

'It's no use lookin', man. There's no escape that way.'

He had seen the ache in the young man's eyes and guessed he was from the country. They were all the same. They came to the city thinking the streets were paved with gold, and they lived to regret it. It needed a special kind of apprenticeship to adjust to Doone Alley. These country folk got the work at first, for they were fit and looked it. But they were also the first to fold. No stamina. The scrawny Dublin slum-dweller had more staying-power.

The young fool wanted work as a labourer. Pride stood in his way, so he would not stoop to rag-picking or thievery. He could not bring himself to live by his wits. But was the only way to survive.

'Yer into a mug's game, for they'll destroy ye. You'll work for a day here, a day there, then nothing. Nothing. And the wait-ing. The heart'll go out of ye entirely,' Breen told him.

Breen Dubh was right, Sean thought now. The heart had gone out of him. He stood, day after day, in line, waiting, wait-ing. Waiting with others, silent, hoping, yearning to be picked. A few times, like today, he was chosen. Most times he was not. He felt a failure as a man, a failure as a husband. He needed to produce something for Maeve. He needed to give Sylvie what she deserved: a little home that was clean and enough food to exist. It wasn't much to ask, but he might as well have asked for a pot of gold and Usher Castle itself, so far out of reach it seemed.

He supported his wife in the crook of his arm. The plank of wood burned merrily in the grate. He fed Sylvie her small pieces of bread and jam with the tea. She enjoyed the tea and looked at him out of black-ringed saucer eyes full of gratitude. It twisted the heart within him and made him want to cry out at the unfairness of life. To be grateful for this little was heart-rending, and he felt full of impotent fury.

Breen Dubh had said that if ever he wanted to 'cross over', Breen's word for joining the fraternity of the Alley as apart from trying to make an honest living as a labourer, he should come and see him. It was Sylvie's look of gratitude and her trembling words, 'You're so good to me, Sean,' as she sucked the jammy bread and drank the hot tea, that decided him to throw his lot in with these dregs of humanity.

'For we're one with them now,' he said to himself as he fed little Maeve. The three of them huddled close to the tiny fire in the gloom of the damp little room. The child pointed to the flickering shadows on the walls and said, 'Dada,' and his last reservation slipped away. He caught the minute hand in his and kissed the little fingers. What did honesty matter in this situation? When they took away your pride, your self-esteem, when they left you without hope, with starvation and death staring you in the face, did honesty matter then? He knew the priests would tell him yes. Well, the priests were not starving. Even Father Flynn, compassionate as he was, could not understand. Didn't he have bacon and eggs every morning, washed down with a pint of porter, up at the presbytery?

Sylvie had fallen into a troubled sleep. Her breathing and the fever were always worse at night. He put the chamber-pot where she could see it, for he didn't want her going out into the yard in the night with her sweating and weakness for she would surely fall in the filth. Sometimes women or men, drunk or sick, fell and couldn't get up and died out there in the dirt. He sighed. He had reached the end of his tether. He had made up his mind. He leaned over and kissed his wife's pale face. He tenderly touched his daughter's cheek with his finger. Then he put another bit of wood on the fire and left the house.

Chapter

49

SEAN nearly fell over Boney Best's scavenger cart, emptied now for the night. It was placed in the middle of the courtyard right in his pathway. Every evening Boney brought all the stuff he had collected during the day into his basement room, which looked more and more like the city's rubbish dump, the more he piled into it. He lived in the house next to the Donahues.

There were three little gurriers, two boys and a girl, huddled together on sacking beneath it and Sean shuddered, new purpose entering his step as he thought of Maeve.

The red lights of Lizzie Brannagan's glowed in the dark. They still called it Lizzie Brannagan's even though she was dead and gone, poor bitch, this many a moon. He could see shadows cross the windows and heard the faint sound of music from within. He thought how warm and inviting it looked and how wonderful it would be to be able to afford to go there. Not for sex, though that would make him feel a 'boyo' again and no mistake, but for the warmth of a feather bed and the comfort of a plump body next to yours. He made the sign of the cross. It was blasphemous to think such a thing. It was not fair to Sylvie, he thought, and despised himself for even entertaining the idea.

Jangles McMahon's barrel-organ, stolen from a foreign Eyetalian man who had died of cold, sat further down in the courtyard. It had one wheel missing and Jangles had to practically carry it when he went out of a morning to the Carlisle Bridge where he had his spot, winter and summer. It was a passport to a kind of security. There was rarely a night Jangles could not afford his penny pint and maybe more.

Sean knew that Breen was very likely to be in the 'Green Cock'. He usually sat there of an evening in the curve of the tavern where the one plush seat followed the line of the street outside as it went around the corner. Sean pushed open the door. The blast of warm air and smoke from pipes and cigars filled him with gratitude. He still had some coins in his pocket and he could afford the price of a drink.

He procured his glass from Milo behind the counter and took a swig. He saw Breen Dubh across the bar and wandered over to him. Breen was flanked by One-Eyed Willy and Jangles McMahon. Jangles was a war veteran. A member of the 34th Regiment, he had been wounded in '55 in the Crimea. His chest and shoulder-blade were broken away and his arm and his leg had been shot off. He had twinkling watery eyes and trouble with his sinuses. He had arthritis and a huge walrus moustache rigid with beer. Despite everything he managed to be cheery and active and pull in the few pennies, enough, he was fond of saying, to keep the wolf from the door. There was also a rumour about that he was an informer.

'Sit down, boyo, sit down and join us.' Breen slapped the seat beside him pushing Jangles further down and making room for Sean. Jangles and One-Eyed Willy watched him with bright eyes and alert faces.

'I could tell by the cut of you when ye came into the place that ye were on yer way to see me,' Breen said. He slung his arm over Sean's shoulder.

'Yea. We could see that,' the other two said in unison.

'Jangles, get the boyo another drink.' Breen gave Jangles a couple of coins. Jangles nodded several times and went to the counter. He thought he'd get himself another at Breen's expense. His foot was wet, his boot leaked, and another would go down a treat and maybe Breen wouldn't notice.

But he did. 'Yer generous with me money, aren't you, Jangles? If you try to treat me like an eejit I'll make algebra of yer leg and arm.'

'I'm sorry, Breen. I'm sorry. I misunderstood entirely. Completely. I'll pay ye back.'

'An so ye will. Right now. Up ye go to Milo and get another porter.'

'But I've no money. What d' ye expect me to do?'

'Put it on the slate an' pay tomorrow,' Breen said with equanimity.

Jangles went to the counter again, shuffling through the

sawdust with his crutch and Breen turned to Sean.

'So. Well. What can I do fer you?'

Sean looked confused. He didn't know what to say, how to phrase what he had in mind.

Breen helped him out. He shook his bullet-head at Sean and said, 'It's all too much? That way? Their way?' Sean nodded. 'Then we'll have to find you a handle.'

'A handle?'

'Yea. An occupation. Something ye can pursue, and nick a bit at the same time.'

'Ye mean steal?'

The men around the upturned wine-cask burst out laughing. Willy thwacked his knee over and over and Jangles took his pipe out of his mouth and wheezed as if he would have a fit.

Breen did not laugh. He fixed Sean firmly with his dark eyes and nodded. 'Steal,' he said. 'Or purloin. Take what's rightfully yours. Did ye knew that people like us, starving people across the sea in France, rose up and killed their King and Queen for the way they were treated and the poverty they were kept in?'

'God, we'd have a hard time tryin' to kill Victoria, God Bless her, an' she across the sea in a palace.'

Breen gave Jangles a withering glance. 'There was a rebellion,' he said. 'All the peasants in France rebelled. They had no bread. Like us they could not live.'

'Well, an' are they better off now? That's what I'd like to know.'

Breen looked irritably at One-Eyed Willy. 'For God's sake, man, o'course they are. Not much. But a little is better than nuthin''

'Well, it's my experience that those revolutions don't work. Things like that never work except for the people at the top. The likes of us are always left behind, no matter what.' One-Eyed Willy wiped the froth away and Jangles snorted.

'In your experience ... In your experience ... For God's sake, *what* experience, man? The way ye talk ye think ye'd been in the thick of a hundred revolutions.'

Suddenly Sean realized that the men around the barrel were looking at the door. The brilliant cerise tip of Willy's nose twitched and Breen cursed under his breath. Sean followed the direction of their eyes and saw in the doorway a tall dark-haired man in a cloak. Everyone looked at him and a hush had fallen over the whole place. He looked out of place there. His clothes had the cut and style of a gentleman, and the cloth of his cloak was rich. He looked too well-cared for, fed and rested. You could tell he was not from the neighbourhood by the patina of his skin and the full set of white teeth in his head. He looked around as if searching for someone. Everyone watched him. Then his blue eyes rested on Breen and he nodded and strode across the room, people automatically scuttling out of his way.

He held out his hand and Breen clasped it between both his own and wrung it.

'Ah, Red. It's good to see you. But are ye drunk or mad or what, that ye come here of an evening bold as brass.'

'Since when, Breen, have the military or the constabulary dared to penetrate the Green Cock? Or Doone Alley for that matter?'

'They come in peril of their lives,' Breen replied and Red threw his head back and laughed in a way that made all the others in the tavern look uneasy and pull their jackets or their shawls closer about themselves.

'An' you're the one who complains about informers,' Breen said.

'Don't worry. I don't intend to stay long. And thanks to you, the constabulary and the soldiers don't like to come here at all. They are very reluctant, or didn't you know?' He smiled at Breen, his eyes twinkling. 'Listen, Breen, and understand. I can't spend all my life hiding. I have to walk the streets and ride across this land or I'll get nothing accomplished. There are informers and dishonest men everywhere. I can skulk behind closed curtains in a little room and never see the light of day and still be betrayed. Don't ye see, man? If I'm to be informed on, it will happen, come what may. And it will. I'll die, sooner or later. It's all the one. But while I live, sure I'll take precautions, I'm not a fool, but I'll hold my head high. I'm a free man and I'll not make my own jail and put myself in it.'

Breen chuckled. 'Ye love risks, Red Rafferty. Ye'd have made a great burglar.'

'Ah now, Breen, there I draw the line.'

'Anyhow, there's few here 'ud sing on ye,' Breen said, then raising his voice so that all assembled could hear him, he said loudly, 'If any of ye here think to say who ye saw here this night, ye'll rue the day ye opened yer gobs, do ye hear?' He fixed his gaze on a dumpy little woman, Flossie Mulcahy, who was leaving the place. Caught, she pulled her black shawl tighter around her and stared defiantly back at him. 'I'll personally beat the bejasus outa them an' they'll have bad luck for the rest of their days.' He included Jangles in his orbit. Jangles was looking distinctly furtive and edgy in his movements. 'It's asking a lot of them, Red,' Breen said. 'You're putting a terrible strain on them. A hundred pounds would see them right for the rest of their days.'

Red's face grew serious. 'They'd have to catch me first. But you know I wouldn't be here if I didn't have to be, Breen. I won't be long. I need your help.'

But Breen was still preoccupied. 'You could have sent for me to come to Lizzie Brannagan's. I mean Rosaleen's.'

'There is no time. And there's money in it for anyone willing.'

'Who's paying?' Breen asked.

'Me,' Red Rafferty replied.

Sean pricked up his ears. He felt completely out of his depth. They spoke a language he did not understand. He still found the swift Dublin dialect impossible to keep up with, but this was infinitely worse. He could understand the words, but he could not comprehend the meaning of the sentences.

Red sat down and looked around. The red perspiring faces in the crowded tavern turned back to their preoccupation, the drink, and lost interest in him. Someone started to sing an Irish patriotic song and a little leprechaun of a man by the name of Brefni O'Sullivan in a shredding tweed suit with a wild head of white hair on him gave Red a large wink and sang out through his nose and banged the floor with his blackthorn in time to the words.

Red turned to Breen, speaking softly, 'There's a schooner run aground off the coast of Wicklow. It's full of guns and ammunition for us. No one has seen it yet, but by morning it will be common knowledge. I need some strong lads immediately to unload. It must be done before dawn.'

Sean gripped the man's arm. 'I've done no good for me and my family being righteous and honourable. How much is in it?'

Red's eyes raked the gaunt face. The lad was in his early twenties but he saw the marks of malnutrition there. He took in the threadbare patched jacket and the trousers that had been turned many times.

'Five pounds,' he said.

The boy was overwhelmed. 'Five pounds? Five whole pounds?' He sounded jubilant. The others hushed him. 'When do we start?' he asked.

'As soon as we get another five like you.'

'Well, count me in,' One-Eyed Willy said. 'I don't look up to

315

much but I'm a divil when I try, an' Dark Rosaleen 'ud never forgive me if I didn't go.'

Red said to Sean, 'It's dangerous, boy. You don't get money like that for nothing. It's dangerous.'

Sean nodded, his face flushed with excitement and the unaccustomed second pint. 'It's money, isn't it? Me life's not worth much.'

'I can't do it because of me chest an' shoulder an' because I have only one arm,' Jangles said, his voice reeking with pathos.

Breen grabbed him by the top of his grey and collarless shirt and jerked him up off his feet so that they dangled a few inches off the ground. 'An' if you go near a constabulary or a red-coat I'll murder you myself, so I will. The other arm'll be turned to jelly an' that barrel-organ of yours 'll never sing again.'

Jangles choked and spluttered his innocent intent. Breen dropped him and watched him collapse onto the plush seat and draw himself together as if he wanted to disappear into himself.

'I'd have got the lads in Wicklow with Fogey, but since Creagh died last year everyone in that circle has dispersed,' Red said quietly.

Breen interrupted. 'Ye said you were in a hurry. Well, give me a jiffy. I'll be back in a trice with five more.'

One-Eyed Willy said sharply, 'Four. Ye only need four,' and the two left the tavern.

The dark man looked at Sean. 'Are ye sure, lad?' he asked. His were blue eyes mild and kind, so Sean took his courage in both hands and said, 'Can I go home, sir, an' see my wife? She's expectin' me. She doesn't know I'm out. If she wakes in the dark an' I'm not there she'll be frightened. She's alone with the babby an' she's very sick. I need to tell her I'll be gone awhile.'

Red nodded. 'Get going, then. Here, take the five pounds to her. It might help her to sleep better. Hurry. We'll have to cut along very soon.' He gave the boy a kindly nod, pressed the money into his hand and gave him a push out of the place.

Red sighed and ordered a brandy, then looked mildly at Jangles sitting beside him. Jangles stared back at him, his face riddled with guilt and nerves.

'It's all right, Jangles. I believe you. I know you wouldn't do anything so ... so unpopular, now would you?' Jangles gave him a sickly smile, the struggle visible on his face. 'After all, you have to live here,' Red added. He smiled at the old soldier, and tossed off his drink. Then he too went out into the night.

Chapter

50

SEAN found Sylvie awake and restless. Her skin burned and he bathed her forehead with the rag.

'Listen, darling', I gotta job tonight. It's brought five pounds. Here. See?'

Her face lit up. 'Five pounds? Oh God, Sean, that's a fortune.'

Then she doubled up, coughing. He held the basin for her and soon the cracked grey enamel was spattered with blood. When she lay back exhausted he said, 'Do ye think you'll be all right alone in the night?' A sudden look of fear came into her eyes as she clutched his lapel. 'In the night? What will ye do in the night? It's not somethin' wrong? Oh Sean, I can't bear it if ye do somethin' bad for my sake.

'Now hush, *alanna*, hush. There, there.' He tenderly pushed back the sopping hair and kissed the hot dry mouth. She clung to him anxious and exhausted. 'It's nothin' like that. A message for a gentleman. All the way to Wicklow.' He kissed her again. 'We'll get the doctor tomorrow.'

She became calm again and a look of hope crossed her face.

'Oh Sean, Sean, it's maybe the end of all our troubles. Oh I said the rosary today. Maybe my prayer is answered and the good days are comin'. We have been patient.'

He smiled at her. 'I've got to go now. You lie still and try to sleep. We'll make it, my darling. I'll look after you and little Maeve. I haven't been much of a husband up till now ...'

She cried out in pain. 'Oh how can you say that? No one could be kinder, more loving. Oh it's not your fault. Oh my love don't say that.'

'Well, it will be better from now on. It will be.' He squeezed his eyes tightly together and murmured, 'It *must* be.'

'Look after yourself, my darlin'. Hurry back to me.' She fell back on the pile of rags.

He kissed her for the last time. 'Goodbye, my love. I'll be careful. I promise.'

He went to the door. He looked at his wife and baby lying on the filthy bundle on the floor. He saw the fungus on the walls and the corner of the ceiling where the rain seeped through. He saw the piece of sacking over the window and the empty grate, the plank burned to ashes. Her pale anxious face looked back at him. There was still hope in her eyes and his heart contracted within him and he left the room, closing the door behind him. With the five pounds they could get a bed off Boney Best, some old blankets too, and a table. It would be riches. And he'd pay one guinea to Dr Davies for a visit to Sylvie. They would have maybe a crubeen in the broth and some vegetables tomorrow. And Breen maybe would find more work for him, and now he didn't care at what. This was only the beginning.

Chapter

51

THEY could see the outline of the ship in the water, the hull looking like a landed whale. It was cold and the clouds raced across the face of the moon and the bitter wind from the sea cut to the bone. There were seven of them: Red and One-Eyed Willy, Sean and Fogey, and three others, lads who looked no more than thirteen or fourteen years of age. They sheltered behind rocks, shivering, and the wind raged and moaned around them, whipping their hair back from their faces and turning their noses red. It penetrated their threadbare clothes and chilled every nook and cranny of their bodies. Sean's teeth rattled in his head and he prayed that they could get on with the job quickly and he could go back to Doone Alley and Sylvie and Maeve.

As he looked, two men came onto the beach, a boat upside down on each head. You could see them silhouetted against the sky.

'Come on,' Red whispered and wrapped his cloak around him and pushed his broad-brimmed hat low over his forehead. They stood up cautiously and scrambled over the rocks to the pebbly beach. It was slippery with seaweed and Sean fell and picked himself up, and did it again trying to keep up with Red. He had no shoes, while Red wore boots that aided him.

They were in a little cove and the ship, listing badly, was just outside it. The men had tipped their craft onto the beach at the edge of the water, which was black and calm in the arms of the bay. When they reached the boats Red pulled two of the boys with him in one and One-Eyed Will took Sean and two others in the second. The men who had brought the boats pushed them out. They were tall thin silent men in thick jerseys and gum-boots. Sean thought they were probably fishermen.

The sea tossed them as if they were corks when they got outside the bay and Sean knew a moment of panic. He was not used to water and felt helpless on the black waves.

They got to the boat and Red showed them where the guns were located. It was quite easy, really, so easy that Sean laughed aloud. The wind whipped Red's hat away and tore at his black hair and he shook his head at Sean and frowned.

The ship had beached on her starboard side and the guns had been stowed in the hull below decks. The rocks had pierced her just where the crates lay and all that Red and his little band had to do was stack the crates of guns in the small tenders. It started to rain. Red lay on his stomach and dragged out the boxes. He passed them to Sean who passed them to the next boy down the chain and so on, till it came to One-Eyed Willy in one boat and Fogey in the other. They stacked them up, dividing them equally. When Willy's boat was as full as he wanted it he rowed manfully to shore where two men waited to help him unload. Then Fogey rowed back with the other one, and while he was doing this Red was loading the first boat once again.

They could hear the ship groan beneath them its creaking blending with the wailing of the wind. Barnacles grazed Sean's hand and he could smell the salt of the sea and the iodine of the weeds.

At last they had managed all they safely could. Red nodded to let them know it was all over. One-Eyed Willy waved triumphantly at them from his boat, which bobbed and curtsied a little way out. Sean felt a jubilant lift to his spirits. Five pounds. For this. It had been easy. He forgot where he was and put up his hand to wave back to One-Eyed Willy, and as he did so he slipped. He felt the side of the ship tear away his clothes, the thin fabric of his suit shredding in his rough descent. He slid, trying to grasp something, but there was nothing there to grasp. He screamed as he hit the icy water.

Red saw him fall. He pulled off his cloak and dived into the water. He saw Sean rise, spluttering, mouth open, hand outstretched. Red swam to him and for one second he held the boy in his arms. But the lad was struggling, pushing at him. He had panicked and he floundered, screaming, not saving his breath, taking great draughts of water into his lungs. In his panic he kept pushing Red away. He was there one moment and the next he was gone, swallowed up, leaving no trace.

Red searched, diving and treading water, but it was no use. Eventually they had to return to shore.

Chapter

52

Chapter

52

WHEN Sylvie awakened next morning she felt happy and she did not know why. When she saw Sean was not at her side, however, a dagger of fear stabbed at her guts. Then she remembered why Sean was not there. He had got a job. There was money. Five pounds. She sat up and lifted Maeve into her arms. The child made a feeble mewling sound and Sylvie said, 'Don't worry, little one. Dada will bring home food today and we'll make broth and you'll like that.'

When the door opened suddenly, for there were no locks in Doone Alley, she thought it was Sean and her face lit up. But it was a stranger. He stood in the doorway and she struggled to her feet, holding the babby in the crook of her arm. She knew something terrible had happened. She cried out, 'Sean', and in the split second before he answered her she could see his eyes take in the condition of the room and she felt for a moment vulnerable and apologetic, as if it were all her fault, the dirt, the damp, the poverty. She wanted to explain that they had tried but could not manage without any help. He had kind eyes and he looked at her with compassion.

'Sean?' she asked, a whimper of fear in her voice.

'Dead,' the stranger said.

She stood still as a statue and whispered, 'Dead?'

Of course he was dead. She should have known. How could it be otherwise? They were not meant to be happy, to live a normal life. She had not complained, just prayed and hoped and now the man she loved was gone, gone, gone. A great desolation swept over her, her eyes lost their focus. She saw behind the stranger the bulk of a huge woman. She looked wildly at the window covered with sacking as if for escape. But there was no escape from this. Sean was dead. She moaned, turning her head to and fro. Then she threw back her head and screamed. And fainted.

The Widow Boann hurried forward to help her and save the child. She stopped, suddenly stunned.

'It's Sylvie,' she said. 'It's me niece Sylvie, Bessie's child. Quick, hurry, get her out of here.'

'I had been told that it was bad,' Red said, looking around, 'but I never dreamed it was as bad as this. Let's get her out of here, Widow.'

'Where to?' the Widow asked.

'To Rosaleen's,' he said. 'I don't think she's going to care much when she comes round. This place is foul ... not fit for pigs.'

'All the places round here are the same. Half Dublin's like this. Here, you carry her. I'll take the babby. Ah, poor little miteen. God help it, the wee thing's almost dead by the looks.'

Breen met them as they crossed the courtyard to Lizzie's.

'God, Red, what are you doin' here? I told ye to get away an' not stretch the patience of the people too far. There's a hundred pounds on yer head man, don't ye remember? An' these people are starving.'

Red was holding Sylvie's limp body in his arms.

'The boy died,' he said. 'Drowned. Like a fool. It was his own fault, poor devil. But I had to come back and tell her. It was the least I could do. She's in a pig-sty over there. I couldn't leave her.'

Breen looked at him quizzically. 'We all live like that, boyo. What did ye think the Alley was ... Dublin Castle? Get on, will ye, Red,' Breen's voice held a note of panic. 'I'm uneasy, so I am. Get on, for God's sake.'

At that moment Fogey, Red's trusty friend who had been keeping watch, came charging around the corner from St George's Lane. He skidded to a halt in front of Breen and Red. The Widow had disappeared into Lizzie Brannagan's with the baby.

'The soldiers is comin'. The soldiers is comin'. The soldiers is marchin' down the Quays.'

'Jasus, gimme her.' Breen grabbed the inert body of Sylvie. He pushed Red with his free hand. Sylvie was as light as a feather. 'Get ye gone. Go through the lane to the mews. Hide there. We'll give them a merry tune, so we will, an' they'll rue the day they entered here. You get away now ...'

But Red was vaulting over a wall and he vanished down the tiny passage-way that led to the mews from the Alley.

The Widow had come back out of Lizzie's. She hurried over and stood squarely in the centre of the courtyard beside Breen. The soldiers marched into the Alley, a fine spruce body of men, smart uniforms and polished boots and buttons. Many of them could be seen to wrinkle up their noses behind the captain's back.

'An' what would you be wantin' now, disturbing the peace of this place wid yer trampin' and yer crashin'?'

Breen stood with the body of Sylvie limp in his arms, staring at them defiantly. Sylvie had started to moan softly.

The captain said, 'We have reason to believe a wanted man is hiding here. A Redmond Rafferty by name.'

Breen gave a shout of derisive laughter. 'Ye won't find anyone of that name here. All you'll find is poverty. Poverty and dirt.'

'Out of our way. My men have got to search.'

'Our pleasure, Captain. They'll learn something here today, an' everyone knows that knowledge is a fine thing.'

A crowd had gathered in the courtyard. Everyone watched, hostility in their eyes. These were Her Gracious Majesty's troops enforcing a foreign rule in their land. They did not like the soldiers.

The captain barked an order and the men split up, fanned out, and entered the houses in the crescent of the Alley.

'Who's that?' The Captain pointed to Sylvie. 'What's the matter with her?'

'She's no one important, sir. A woman dying of malnutrition and tuberculosis.'

The captain took a step back. Two soldiers had come out of Flossie Mulcahy's shaking their heads. 'Nothing here sir.' The captain's face reddened. A young soldier marched up to him pointing to where Boney Best, the rag-and-bone man, stored his stinking pile of loot. The captain called him over.

'What the hell's the matter with you?' he roared.

The boy stammered, 'It's filthy, sir ... it's filthy ... there are rats there big as rabbits.'

324

There was a roar from the interior of One-Eyed Willy's room. 'Get outa my home. De'ye hear? Get outa my home.'

He emerged into the yard, his brush sweeping two young soldiers before him. One of the soldiers fell over the shafts of a cart lying in front of Willy's door and he sprawled into the thick layer of filth that covered the cobblestones. The crowd behind Breen moved forward. They had started to mutter, a low rumbling like thunder. Weasel Wiggs erupted from the back of Sylvie's house, screaming. A soldier had disturbed him and he had become very agitated. He poured forth a stream of obscenities that brought a blush to even the captain's cheeks, uttered as they were in the presence of women.

The captain moved forward, recognizing Breen as some kind of a leader. 'Look here. We are just obeying orders. We have got to do out duty.'

'Careful. She's contagious,' Breen said, smiling at him. They both knew he referred to Sylvie who had started to come round.

Breen held her tenderly. 'Don't worry, love. We'll get you in soon. As soon as this scum have gone.'

The captain nearly lost his temper, but he realized in time that it would do no good. He looked around. His men were either scuttling out of the hovels being battered round the head by harridan women or incensed old bags of bones, or they were slipping and sliding and falling over in the dirt and debris of the place. The cobbles were wet and slimy, and the entrances shaky under their feet, and the hostility of the people throwing things at them made their job difficult to say the least.

The captain struggled to maintain their dignity. He insisted the men search every nook and cranny and so they did. But it became obvious that there were so many entrances and exits that anyone could move about from house to house without much difficulty. Eventually he had to be satisfied that Red was not there.

'The place is a warren, sir. It's impossible to keep every exit covered. He could be playing ducks and drakes with us and laughing at us just like Lieutenant Clegg says he does,' the sergeant said.

'Well, there's nothing more we can do.' The captain was glad to call a halt to the search and quit the place. At his command the men gratefully fell in and were marched swiftly away down the Alley and St George's Lane, and down the Quays to the

Barracks. There they were ordered to clean up forthwith and repair the damage to their uniforms.

Breen let out a roar as they disappeared. 'Wait till I find that little gob-shite Jangles. Just wait till I lay my hands on him.'

The Widow pulled Breen's arm. 'She's going blue,' she cried. 'Get her in quickly.'

They hurried across the Alley to the entrance of Lizzie Brannagan's. Rosaleen was waiting for them.

'Take her to Suzette's room,' she said.

'An' where'll I go?'

'I've told you, Suzette, to go to Lizzie's room for tonight.'

Suzette puckered up her face and started to cry. 'I'll not go there, an' her after dyin' in it. I'll never.'

'Don't be silly, Suzette.' Rosaleen tried to keep her voice even. 'That was a long time ago. The room has been stripped and redecorated since then.'

The Widow Boann turned on the stairs and looked at Suzette fiercely. 'Go to Lizzie's room at once, as your mistress tells you,' she said icily. Suzette scuttled past her, instantly obedient.

When they got Sylvie to the room they peeled off the pathetic garment she was wearing. Under her clothes she was skeletal and Rosaleen and the Widow looked at each other, appalled. Her bones stuck out everywhere and she was blue-lipped and lifeless. Rosaleen sent for Dr Davies and asked Batty to heat up some water.

'She'll be dead before morning,' Rosaleen said and wondered where she had heard those words before. Then she remembered. She shivered.

'Get Suzette to warm some milk for the baby,' she told Batty when she had filled the hip-bath with steaming water.

They put some eucalyptus in and herbs of the Widow's choice. They gently lowered the comatose girl into the hot water. She felt light as a child. She came to with a start and the women soothed and calmed her. She seemed not to hear them and looked about her, wide-eyed. She suddenly jumped naked from the bath and ran to the window, plucking at the fastening as if she would open it. She tried to fight the Widow and Rosaleen but there was no strength in her and they got her dry and into bed without too much trouble.

The doctor gave her some laudanum and shook his head over her. 'It's too late, I'm afraid. She is suffering from the disease of poverty and this place. How could she have any recuperative powers in this filthy hole? Oh, I don't mean your house, Rosaleen, you keep this place a little oasis of comfort in a sea of filth. Disease and poverty and filthy conditions, a prescription for death. It's a losing battle. She had no reserves. She's in shock. You tell me . . .' He shook his head sadly.

'Her husband died.'

The doctor nodded. 'Well, there's little I can do. You must expect the worst.'

'Poor little orphan,' he said when he saw the baby. 'She might survive if she got the best treatment. She just might. But for what? It's almost as well if she slipped away,' he added, echoing Sylvie's own thoughts. 'It's a terrible place she's been born into. She does not stand a chance.' He shook his head again and left.

There was a feeble cry from the bed. Rosaleen went to her quickly. Sylvie Donahue looked at her with pleading eyes. For the moment she seemed quite rational.

'Maeve? Where is she?' she asked.

'Who?'

'My baby. Maeve.'

Rosaleen soothed her. 'She's sleeping. She's had some warm milk and now she is resting. She is fine, Sylvie. That's your name, isn't it? She is fine.'

Sylvie smiled at her. 'You're so good,' she said. 'They say you're a bad woman because you live in a brothel but they're wrong. Mebbe the priests are wrong too. Sean was good. He tried to get things honestly. He tried so hard.' Her eyes filled with tears. 'I loved him so. But we had no life together really. It all went . . . so quickly.'

'There now. Don't distress yourself. You'll see him soon enough.' Rosaleen had sent for Father Flynn. It was becoming a habit in this house, she thought, but the Alley was a place where death was very much at home. She remembered the night, aeons ago it seemed now, when she carried her baby in her arms to Usher and heard the banshee wailing.

The woman in the bed was plucking at her sleeve, then she started coughing. Rosaleen waited until the paroxysm was over.

'Will you take care of her? Maeve?' Sylvie whispered. Her eyes were feverish again and there was foam on her lips flecked with blood. 'Will you promise?'

'I promise,' Rosaleen answered without thinking.

But Sylvie sensed that her reply was perfunctory and insisted, 'No. No. It is my last wish. Please, missus.' She looked up at the Widow Boann. 'Widow, I'm yer niece. Mam won't want to know Maeve, you know that. I have no chance except with you.' The light from the candles seemed to hurt her eyes. 'You hear. You're a witness. She promised. Look after Maeve an' don't let me Mam know. Any of this. Promise?' She seemed to be exhausting her last strength.

Rosaleen said quickly, 'I promised. I will. Now rest. Rest and be at peace.'

'I'm getting used to this, Rosaleen thought. Here it's a usual thing. Long ago, out in the world, roaming, travelling, death was a stranger, but here he stalked the mean foul streets reaping a grim and plentiful harvest.

As she kept vigil that night she became more sick of soul than she had been for a long time.

'It's the disease and death. It's everywhere here,' she said to the Widow when that good body asked Rosaleen what was the matter, 'There's no escape. This is a cursed land. I know now that Creagh was right. Freedom is a sweet thing. An essential thing.' She turned and took the Widow's hand. It felt coarse and rough in her soft fingers. 'Widow, will ye think badly of me if I run away to the valley at Usher? Just for a while? I need to catch a look at Cormac and be in the green country and smell the flowers and see the light change. It's nearly spring. Can I leave you in charge and go? I need the fresh breeze on my cheeks and the wind in my hair and to hear the call of the blackbird.'

She spoke quietly, as if to herself, and the Widow saw that she was crying. Tears slid from the bright blue eyes down her soft cheeks. They clung to her spiky eyelashes.

She put her arms around the weeping girl. 'Ach no, *alanna*. Go. Go. 'Twill do ye good. You go and don't fret. I'll be here. I'll tend to my charges, look after Fergal and little Maeve. Never you fear. You go and refresh yerself. I'll lick these girls into shape here, as me sister Bessie used to say, an' look after the little ones. Never you fret.'

Rosaleen saw the sympathetic tears on the Widow's cheeks. 'Ah, Widow, what would I do without you? You've been a boon and a blessing. It's a hard world here.'

'It's a hard world everywhere. She was me niece. I saw her dancing through the poppy-fields of Wicklow when she was a bonny wee girl an' no cares on her at all. Ah, God help us, yer right. It's a hard old world.'

Sylvie was dead by the morning. She simply never recovered consciousness. Rosaleen brought her back to Bessie Broderick next day. But she kept her word to Sylvie and said nothing of Maeve. Then she went down to the valley in time for spring.

Chapter

53

ROSALEEN went to Usher leaving the Widow in charge. She was grateful that she could escape to the valley, unlike the others who were trapped in Doone Alley.

Spring was coming and the cuckoo and the woodpecker could be heard in the woods. It was late when she came in sight of the valley. She could hear the lowing of the cattle who were homeward bound at dusk. She was weary when she reached the trout stream and she limped over the hump-backed bridge in the crystal evening light. Peace flooded her soul and she leant her elbows on the bridge and breathed in the cool air. It was fresh and sweet and brought to her nostrils the pungent smell of roasting meat. It came from the cottage, and forgetting her aches and pains she pulled her shawl about her and, fleet of foot, ran through the blue twilight.

A little later she sat in the saffron glow of the lamplight, her feet in a basin of water and vinegar, Craw Kilty sawing a slice of bread for her guest to quench her immediate hunger.

'For,' she said, 'There's a fat goose cookin''.

'I know. I smelled it across the valley on the bridge.' Rosaleen laughed, then grimaced. 'I'm outa the habit of walkin',' she said, wiggling her toes. 'I'm covered in blisters an' cuts, so I am. It makes me sad an' I don't know why.'

'Rosaleen!' the Minstrel cried from the doorway. He had come home silently and they had not heard him. 'Rosaleen, me darlin'.'

He held out his arms and she ran to him despite her wet feet. He held her tightly and they laughed and cried together.

'Come back an' sit down, ye fool,' Craw Kilty cried. 'Yer

makin' puddles on the floor. Put yer feet back in the basin. Ronan, it's good to see ye.'

Ronan lifted Rosaleen, swinging her around laughing and carried her back to the chair by the fire. He put her feet in the basin and bathed them gently.

'They're not tough any more, *alanna*. They're soft as a lady's,' he said regretfully, holding the pale foot in his hand and kissing it. He saw where the stones had cut her. 'Mam, where's the salve?'

Craw Kilty looked up enquiringly. 'The salve? Let me see.' She looked at Rosaleen's feet. 'Yes. She does need somethin'. Iodine for the blisters. It'll dry them up. Salve for the cuts. Ah God bless us, ye shoulda taken the coach.'

Rosaleen looked at Ronan who was patting her feet dry. She could see he was sad.

'Ah yes. A coach she'll take, no doubt. Soon she'll never go any other way. Walkin's too good for her now.' He shook his head.

Craw Kilty put her hands on her hips. 'An' why not, pray? Tell me that? What's the use of walkin' when ye can ride?'

''Cause walkin' ye can see the stars, Mam, in the heavens, and the moon winkin' at ye from the puddles in the road. An' ye can smell the earth an' ye can taste the world.' Ronan was holding Rosaleen's foot tightly. She looked down at him squatting before her and she laid her hand gently on his head.

'Ah, Minstrel, do ye truly think I'll ever prefer a carriage to the roads? Don't say so. Never say so.'

He looked up at her in the dim yellow lamplight and she thought how good it was to be with him.

'Just because my feet hurt an' I haven't walked without shoes for a wee while does not mean I don't want to. An' you know why, Ronan. Doone Alley is no place for bare feet.'

He smiled. 'No. It's not. An' I don't suppose ye'll change. I'm sometimes afraid ye'll get to be a grand lady an' leave us.'

Rosaleen tousled his hair and laughed. 'Can ye see me? All la-de-da an' not biddin' ye the time o' day?' She wrinkled her nose.

He laughed with her. 'No. Never, Rosaleen.' He had dried her feet and she stood now squarely before him. She looked over her shoulder at Craw.

'Oh Craw, that smell is makin' my teeth water. It smells like manna from the Gods or a feast at Emain Macha with the High Kings of Ireland.'

'We're suppin well tonight. Ye'd think I knew ye were both comin'.' She cackled with laughter. 'A goose an' taties an' a ginger syllabub. That's what yer havin'.'

'Ah, Craw, it's good to be here. I need to forget.' Rosaleen sighed.

Ronan picked up his fiddle. 'I'll play a song an' you'll dance for me, girl.'

He scraped on the instrument that was an extension of his soul and Rosaleen danced, her eyes half-closed. She hardly moved but swayed to the rhythm. The music was bitter-sweet and faintly Eastern.

Craw Kilty bustled about the room preparing supper and when it was ready she called them to the table. The goose was succulent, the skin of it crisped and brown. They ate it while it was still too hot, pulling the meat from the carcase and blowing to cool it and laughing all the while. The syllabub was rich and Rosaleen, unused as she was to walking the world, was exhausted and fell into a doze before the fire.

'Let her sleep in my bed tonight, Mam,' Ronan whispered. 'She's brought the weight of the world with her. Let her drop it there.'

They half-carried her across to the mattress that was the Minstrel's resting place. They covered her, tucking her in, and Ronan lifted her hair from her neck and spread it out so it would not irritate her in the night. He kissed her cheek and saw that in her sleep she was smiling.

Chapter

54

MOLLY stood in the doorway of the high tower with Bella's lunch on a tray. She looked at her mistress with calm dispassionate eyes. Bella's prettiness was passing, she thought, whereas m'lady Sophie was lovelier than ever before, an' she expecting another child any moment.

It was a day in April and the room where Bella had chosen to spend the best part of the last two years was full of light. The wind was driving fragile groups of clouds across the sky, lightening or darkening the valley below, revealing or concealing as they travelled the yellow of the furze-blossom and flag, the purple of the heather. Held in those clouds were all the colours of the rainbow, filtering through into the rooms at the top of the tower. Bella's tapestry stood in one corner. The books she read were on a table near the window. The room had rich carpets from the Orient on the floor and an elegant Sheraton chaise positioned where Bella liked to recline while doing her needlework. Her work had improved over the years and her stitches were now neat and even.

The bloom had gone, Molly thought, looking at her. Her mouth was drawn and turned downwards at the edges. There were lines of discontent curving from nostrils to jaw and her eyes and hair had faded in colour. You could hardly blame her, Molly felt, with the endless days of stitching and looking through the window, endless hours of thinking. Endless nights of unfulfilled dreams and longings, of fevered imaginings and the frustration of unrequited love. She preferred to be alone except for Molly and the bird. All the time alone. She liked her maid's company and she spoke only with Molly and the fat little yellow canary who lived in a white cage by the window.

Molly often wondered what went on in the girl's head as the days passed into months and the months into years and she kept to herself shunning the outside world. The servant knew that Bella still planned revenge, though how she was going to manage that was a mystery. She was totally dependent on James. She had no money and, Molly thought, Miss Bella was no fool. Everyone knew the only place a penniless lady could end up was the streets. She had pinned all her hopes on marriage and Lord Usher had condemned her to a lifetime of spinsterhood. Well, thought Molly, it served her right after what she had done. Not only Creagh had died, but her Cronin, her sweetheart too. And others, other people's brothers, fathers, cousins and uncles.

Molly had another suitor now, a fat tenant farmer who wanted to wed her, but he was a brutish man and desired her only for a servant, slave and fancy-woman, never mind he called it wife. Molly ruminated on her choices and it seemed to her that she was far better off at Usher than down over the hill in that little houseen, condemned to pass her days scrubbing and cleaning and cutting the corn and milking the cows and digging the potatoes. Her nights would be spent servicing that great tub of lard. The years would be spent bearing his brats until she grew too old. One a year, every year. Then tending them too. And all for nothing. No love words. No tenderness. No civility. It seemed to her a bad bargain.

Besides, here she was in an important position, the chatelaine of the High Tower as Widow Boann had been before her. It was extraordinary, Molly thought, how fond Bella had become of her, and in a strange way Molly too was drawn to her mistress. They had become inter-dependent. Life had ended for them both that night that Creagh was shot, and Molly understood how her mistress felt. She too had lost everything and was condemned to live without the man she loved. She knew the hate-filled thoughts that circled forever in her brain. She felt the same sort of resentment herself, but she did think my lady Bella carried it too far. Each of them was at odds with the life of the castle; Bella from the joyous progress in Cormac's and Armand's nursery and Molly from the laughter, tears and pulsating life of the kitchen. They were set apart, and oddly remote from the daily dramas, by what had happened to them and though they hated each other they fed off each other too, and chose each other's company for preference. Bella, isolating herself in the High Tower, treated Molly as her *confidante*. Bella told Molly her thoughts. She forgot that Molly was the enemy.

On this April day Molly had brought in her lunch on a silver salver as usual. She placed the tray on the table and removed the covers. There was a plate of beef, a fine cut of turbot, some custards and fruit and a carafe of wine.

'There, Miss Bella. Lunch. I'll bring tea later as usual. Anything else you want?'

Bella picked up her napkin and shook it out. 'No, thank you, Molly. That will be all.' Molly shrugged. As she turned to go they heard the sound of horse hooves clopping to the entrance.

Bella jumped up from the table and ran to the window that overlooked the entrance to Usher Castle. She liked to hang out of her window and watch the world come and go below. And listen.

'Molly. Molly. Don't go. Come here and tell me who is that?'

Molly went over and joined her charge. She could see the young man leap off his chestnut and throw the reigns to Matt Dominic.

'That's the doctor for Lady Sophie. She must have started labour.' Molly clapped her hands together in excitement. Bella thought fleetingly of the evening, all those years ago it seemed, when she had cried for Dolly to stop screaming in her labour; and she wished suddenly that she could turn the clock back. She believed there was still hope. That if she waited long enough, was patient, her chance would come and Fabrice would be hers. She thought of him night and day. He was with her every waking and sleeping moment of her life. When she joined the family for meals she studied him covertly; aching to see one look that would tell her her love had come. Perhaps if he had never desired her, then, maybe she would have given up. But he had. She knew he had. For those hours, those few enchanted hours that day, the day of Cormac's christening, he had fallen for her, found her attractive. She held onto that memory, living those moments over and over. Fabrice smiling at her, looking into her eyes, feeding her strawberries, dancing with her, his arm about her waist, his breath on her cheek. Until Sophie came and snatched it all away. Well, she would get him back. She would find a way.

'What of Dr Hegarty?' she asked mildly.

'Dr Hegarty had a stroke, God help him. He's below in the house beyond the valley, stuck to his bed, an' this is his son who's been trained in London.'

'Oh. I didn't know the doctor was married.'

'Ach, she died a long time ago, Miss. Now eat your lunch or it'll go cold. I'll go now an' see if I can help Lady Sophie. The Conte is really pleased about the baby. Overjoyed, I'd say,' she said brightly.

Bella bit her lip. 'If he knew. If only he knew,' she whispered to herself.

'What's that, Miss? Did ye say somethin'?' Molly asked.

'No. No. Go away and leave me alone.'

'Of course,' Molly said and left.

She hurried down from the High Tower to Sophie's rooms. There was bustle and fuss in the corridors. Clarie and Annie were rushing to and fro with basins of hot water. Molly too remembered that night when Bella had cried out that she wished Dolly would stop screaming and they heard the banshee. Well, the three deaths had occurred in the house. Dolly's baby, Creagh and Cronin. The bad luck seemed to be over, the evil spell broken. This was a far happier time.

The maids laughed as they ran backward and forward and the young Conte puffed a cigar and fussed about anxiously. He would hand the cigar to Clarie and hurry into his wife, then, unable to watch her struggles, he would rush out again and recommence puffing. James and Dolly kept coming and going from their apartments, hovering near Sophie's room and imploring Fabrice to join them in the withdrawing room, but he insisted on staying near his wife. There was joyousness in the atmosphere, excitement and optimism in the air. Sophie had a girl. Young Dr Hegarty kept the room aired during her short labour. He spoke of the importance of hygiene and the advisability of leaving infant limbs free and unswaddled. 'In order to allow the baby to stretch and grow.' he said.

Dolly was scandalized. 'For,' she said, 'everyone knows how prone an infant is to chills if not kept wrapped up tightly for at least a year.'

Sophie was not so sure, but discreetly she said nothing. She decided to take the young energetic doctor's advice and she got a girl from the village that the doctor recommended. Her little girl they named Madelaine, Minou for short, and they started a new regime that worried her sister-in-law to death. On the doctor's advice she fed the baby herself, deriving great satisfaction from it.

Dolly was worried. 'It's not quite the thing, Sophie. Ladies shouldn't. You know that. Our milk is thinner because we have bluer blood, and that is not good for the baby.'

Sophie held her peace and went her own way and found she was enjoying herself much more with Minou than she had with Armand, whom she had handed over to his wet-nurse and whom she had hardly seen naked until he was a year old. She loved to sit on the floor of their bedroom, Minou lying naked on a soft sheet in front of the fire waving her pink little arms and legs about aimlessly, cooing and giggling.

Fabrice was as enchanted as she. He was content to leave everything to do with their children to her. He would shrug if he found himself between Dolly and Sophie in an argument. 'Whatever Sophie does, I am content,' was all he would say.

Often they drank tea together and played with their children all afternoon. It was equally pleasant as time passed and the hot weather came, to put Minou on her back under the apple-trees and watch her crowing with delight at the patterns made by the shivering leaves, Fabrice would laugh with her as they watched Armand toddling and falling and chuckling with them. It was a merry game and life was wonderful.

Except for the silence from Fabrice's mother. He wrote to her again, telling her about the birth of her second grandchild, but time passed and there was no communication from her. Months passed and summer was upon them again, Dolly and Sophie gave themselves up to the joys of motherhood. It was an enchanted time for the two young matrons. Armand and Cormac had taken their first steps, played their first games, cut their first teeth and said their first words. The mothers suffered and laughed through it all and were grateful for each other's presence and support.

'Oh Sophie, what will I do when you and Fabrice go to France? I simply do not know how I shall manage without you. You are such a solace to me. Without you I swear I would be nervous as a cricket.'

'Well, don't let's talk of it, dear Dolly, for, when, if ever, it will happen I do not know.'

Dolly jumped as Sophie a moment later raised her voice and called out to Armand. 'Mon petit, don't run too fast on the gravel. If you fall you'll graze your knee, and I shall be cross.'

'All right, Mama.' Armand's voice came back to them from just beyond the arbour.

How could she, Dolly thought? She sounded so firm. She was quite sure she could never sound like that. Dolly sighed. She knew she was weak where Cormac was concerned. She had waited so very long for a child of her own, and she found she was unable to be cross with him, she loved him so.

From the very beginning Sophie was quite strict with Armand. She was constantly admonishing him, albeit in the gentlest of tones. 'No, no, my darling, you must not go near the edge, you will fall and hurt yourself' or, 'No, Armand, you must not put anything like that into your mouth. You will be sick. Remember how much you disliked having to stay in bed all day? Be a good boy now and do as Maman tells you.'

Dolly did not like to hear Sophie being so firm with such a little child, and she was shocked when her sister-in-law spanked the small boy when he disobeyed her.

'Oh Sophie, how could you?' she cried reproachfully, unable to bear the yowls, of fury rather than pain, that came from her outraged nephew.

'It is the only way to bring him up to know right from wrong. He must not think he can have and do anything he wants,' Sophie said tartly, not in the least abashed.

'I know I could not smack Cormac, indeed I could not. And I'm sure a happier child you never saw.'

Sophie closed her mouth firmly. Then after a moment's thought she said, 'Perhaps it's kinder to teach him now that he cannot always have his own way.'

Dolly frowned. She could see no wrong in Cormac and truthfully did not think that he was ever badly behaved. Sophie, however, knew better and had often said to Fabrice that Cormac, at some point, would have to find out that he did not own the world.

'He's a winning child and means no harm, but he takes all Armand's toys. He cannot bear to lend any of his own things and makes a fuss if he does not always get his own way,' Sophie told Fabrice. 'I don't mind, for Armand is like you, my dear, he is so good-natured. But Cormac is going to suffer some day if Dolly is not careful.'

Fabrice smiled at her. 'Forgive me, my dear, if I do not worry about Cormac's future. I am much too happy with my own little family. If only Maman ...' And sighing he would leave the sentence unfinished.

A heat mist lay on the mountains and the sun slanted its rays through the trees in spars of gold. They sat in the rose-filled arbour. Blooms clustered on the wall of the High Tower in a riot of white and pink. Big open-faced ragged blossoms shook their velvet petals on the grass and the scent was seductive and heavy. Dolly fanned herself and Sophie, who was nursing little Minou, rocked herself to and fro in the rocking chair she liked to sit in whilst she had her baby at her breast. She dabbed her forehead with a handkerchief drenched with lavender water and flicked a bluebottle away at the same time. They spoke lightly and were often silent, for the heat rendered them monosyllabic.

Cormac and Armand were on a rug at their feet. Cormac was systematically destroying a little cart that was Armand's favourite. Armand did not protest. Cormac was older than he and he adored his cousin, so he would not cry. The women did not see what was happening. They sat in a soporofic trance, heat-dazed and content.

The peace was broken by Fabrice bursting into the arbour waving a letter.

'Ecoutez-moi ... Ma mère m'a pardoné ... La lettre est arrivée ... Oh, pardon ... Maman ... a letter ... Oh Sophie, Sophie, I am so happy.' He was breathless with excitement and Sophie and Dolly both laughed, for his happiness was contagious. 'Maman has written. She has forgiven me. Oh what a happy day.'

'My darling, how wonderful. I confess I had quite given up hope of us ever hearing from her.' Sophie hugged him. 'Do read to me what she says.'

Fabrice grimaced. 'Not much. But it is a start. You read it for yourself. You must not mind all she says.' He looked embarrassed and Sophie took the letter from him. It was a tentative letter asking him how he was, and begging him to pay her respects to his wife and kiss the two little ones.

Then Sophie gave a shriek of mock anger and cried, 'Dolly,

Dolly, listen. Oh heavens, listen. She asks ... Oh no, I cannot say it ... she asks ...'

Dolly pulled at Sophie's sleeve and Fabrice tried to retrieve the letter from his wife.

'What, pray?' Dolly begged. 'Oh what, Sophie? Do tell.'

'Oh Dolly, Dolly, I am distraught,' Sophie cried dramatically, rolling her eyes and holding the letter aloft. 'Oh my dear one, listen. She asks whether he is surviving in the barbaric wilds of Ireland. Can you believe it?'

Dolly pretended to be outraged. 'Heavens, Fabrice. What does your Maman think of us? Does she imagine we are a horde of savages with paint on our faces?'

Fabrice flung himself down on his knees before the two ladies. 'Oh forgive me. I deserve your scorn. Oh I am desolate. I cannot be blamed for my Maman's ignorance,' he cried, just like the actor in 'Hamlet' at the Royalty Theatre. The girls were helpless with merriment and James came into the arbour, drawn by the laughter. The pleasant sound delighted him and he called for tea to be served there with his family.

They shared the joke with him and it was a happy meal. Fabrice's joy was complete. Both he and Sophie wrote to the Contesse, but a little time elapsed before they heard from her again. However, Sophie and Fabrice had patience. They could wait. They had learned how.

It was autumn, when the trees had turned to gold and the mountain across the valley wore a bronze cloak, that eventually the second letter came. It was much more outspoken than the first. In page after page his Maman poured out her love for her son, her forgiveness and her great desire to make the acquaintance of his wife and their two children.

'I was ill dear Fabrice and became aware that I am not immortal. Time is passing. I long to see them, to kiss them and love them, for you cannot imagine how lonely I have been. I am going to petition the Duc de Mandeville to forgive you, for your only fault was that you were young and hot-headed. I am sure he knows that you had never held a gun before, and that his son was the more experienced of you and his death a tragic accident. He must see reason and know that you have suffered enough. Then you can come home to me. I embrace you and Sophie, whom you love so much and the children I long to meet.'

The castle brimmed over with Fabrice's joy. He could not contain it. Sophie shared his happiness and the house echoed with laughter. The servants went about their tasks smiling and the whole house caught Fabrice's mood. It penetrated even into Bella's preoccupation.

Molly did not like her stillness and she told her mother, 'She's up to some mischief. Mark my words. The divil of it is I don't know what it could be an' indeedn' I can't think.'

'I think that wan was a changeling,' Bessie Broderick replied cryptically. 'That's what I think. The evil ones.' She blessed herelf, and her daughters followed suit, crossing themselves, as did all in the kitchen, where all were listening avidly.

'Oh Mam, don't say that, an' Molly has to go an' look after her,' Clarie said.

Molly shrugged. 'I don't mind at all. Sure it adds a bit of excitement to the day.' She was jealous for the moment of Clarie, who had found herself a suitor in the new man-servant Fabrice had brought from Paris. Maurice was attractive and he and Clarie were walking out together.

Fabrice had received a letter from his mother's solicitors, informing him that an allowance was now on deposit in a bank in London for his use. Fabrice had at once begun, despite anything James could say, to contribute to the household.

Now Molly said to Bessie, 'I told her. I said to her that the Conte and Contesse will go to France. But they have to wait until his Maman gets ... oh something, from some Duc ... oh I don't know. And she sat as still as a statue. She didn't move. Like she was turned to stone. Oh Janey, Mam, she sometimes puts the heart across me.'

Bella had not heard the second part of Molly's sentence. All she heard was that Fabrice was going. Leaving. She could not bear it. Although she hardly saw him these days she knew he was there, and her ever-present hope was that something would happen and at last he would be hers. But now that could never happen. She would be left here to rot. A spinster. An old maid. Now James' punishment would be effective forever. She decided it was time to act.

Chapter
55

THE dining room at Usher was full of bowls of chrysanthemums that day. Sophie was never able to tolerate the smell of that particular flower in a room again. They sat on the sideboard, they graced the centre of the table, they blazed in riotous amber and gold, bronze and yellow beneath the portrait of Old Gentleman as a boy holding onto his mama's skirts. They were the centrepiece on the table half-way down the panelled wall behind the long table. Through the windows opposite a day of fitful breezes and driving rain rattled the casements and at either end of the room log fires burned.

Everyone was in high good humour, particularly Fabrice. Even Bella seemed oddly excited. They were used to her silent presence at meals and had got into the habit of ignoring her. However today Sophie noted the side-long glance Bella had given Fabrice as he politely held her chair for her before she sat. James had asked Dolly to sit at his right at lunch and Fabrice was put at the bottom of the table with Sophie on his left. The Dowager Lady Angela and Old Gentleman sat beside her and that left Bella alone on the other side, facing her sister and sister-in-law. The conversation was general and genial. They spoke of Cormac and Armand and little Minou. Fabrice waxed eloquent about his daughter's cherubic face and angelic disposition and they all laughed gently at his besotted love for his 'petit chou'.

Maitland and Padraig served them, and they all did justice to the side of beef, the medallions of lobster in pepper sauce. However, when the apple crumble and clotted cream was consumed and the cheese and fruit was on the table James called for silence and raised his glass.

'I would like to propose a toast,' he said. He looked around the table at the happy flushed faces, and for a moment sentiment overcame him and tears sprang to his eyes.

'Dear family,' he said, 'I propose a toast.' He cleared his throat. 'You are all very precious to me and life has been wonderful these last years.' He had forgotten Bella. He tended to overlook her presence, for usually she was so quiet and withdrawn when she was in their company. Now he did not notice her or perhaps he would have been warned. He did not see the insane light in her eyes or notice her mouth working wordlessly as she watched like a cat ready to pounce. She saw Fabrice cover his wife's hand with his own and look to her, a frank expression of love on his face.

'Fabrice,' James continued, 'you have brought such happiness to my sister, to my wife and the whole family. We will miss you sorely when you have gone.' He raised his glass. 'To Fabrice. And to life, which has been so good to us.' James brought his glass to his lips.

Bella felt something snap in her head. It was a click that sent the blood surging in her temples and she jumped to her feet. She threw her glass against the wall and the glass shattered. They all stared transfixed, as the wine slowly stained the pale silk covering, and ran downwards in little scarlet rivulets to the floor.

'Not to me it hasn't,' she said softly and they all looked at her in horror. 'Oh no. Not to me.' James started to rise, but she said, 'No, James. It is of no use to run away. You have always run away. Your trouble is that you do not like problems and you tend to sweep them under the carpet. Like your son Fergal.'

James threw his napkin on the table, his face white with rage. 'How dare you, miss,' he cried hardly able to get the words out. 'Leave this room immediately.'

Dolly was weeping softly. 'Dear Bella, don't spoil everything. Please, James was trying . . .'

Bella tried to calm herself, but it was no use. Deprived of an outlet for so long her hate had now burst forth and could not be stopped. She had waited so long for this, so very long. Now it was all coming out too fast. She saw the white face of her sister-in-law and Sophie's shocked look as she blinked her cornflower-blue eyes. She looked so pretty, so very tranquil in her pale blue merino wool dress with the mother-of-pearl broach pinned to the lace at her throat, her golden curls held up by a tortoiseshell comb. It was the beauty of her face, the sweetness and goodness in her eyes, and Dolly, flaxen-haired and serene, that pushed her over the edge. She hated them, these pretty fulfilled women, married with children. Well, she would destroy them.

Her voice stopped James in his tracks. 'You see no matter what you may think I'm not a villainess. Oh dear me, no. My darling sister is not the saint, James, that you and Fabrice think her. I would not say this, Fabrice, only I know you loved me first and will again when you know the truth about your precious wife.'

Fabrice was looking at her as if she were mad.

'Sophie has been carrying on a love affair under your nose, Fabrice.' She paused then said loudly. 'Armand is not your son.' The words fell like stones in the shocked silence. 'You would want to be a fool not to believe me, for his hair is dark as night and you and my sister ...' She shrugged. 'Well, it is obvious. When you see the truth of it you will come back to me, for I would never betray you.'

The silence lengthened when she had finished. She stood there, her hands gripping the back of her chair, looking triumphantly from shocked immobile face to shocked immobile face.

James was trembling. He nodded to Maitland and the servant left the room with Padraig. A log fell in the grate and Sophie gave a heart-breaking sob and buried her face in her hands.

All heads turned as Fabrice rose and calmly put down his napkin. Bella's eyes filled with all the yearning of her soul as she looked at him.

'Oh my darling,' she said.

She fully expected him to put his arm around her and leave the room with her immediately. Instead he looked at her with loathing and her soul shrivelled within her.

'You are beneath contempt,' he said. 'Do you think I did not know? Do you think I am such a fool? I am not an imbecile. But I love my wife with all my heart and I trust her. It is beyond your comprehension. She is worth more to me, even if she loved another, than ten of you. She is honourable, something you would not understand. You disgust me. What you have done is wantonly cruel. You have said the unsayable and shattered peace. *Mère de Dieu*, I doubt if I can forgive you.' He took

344

Sophie's arm. 'Come, my dearest. Let us go to our children, Armand and Minou. Dry your tears, Sophie. I will take you to Paris. It will be all right, you will see. We cannot remain here any longer. You, Bella, have made that impossible.'

He kissed his wife gently on the lips and she rose and together they left the room.

James said softly, 'Get out of my sight before I kill you.'

She fled. She ran as if her feet had wings, through the banqueting hall, the servants staring at her. They had been listening, she surmised. She ran into the big hall, down to the door to the High Tower and up the steps to her rooms. She flung herself on her bed and sobbed and sobbed. Then she went to the window and sat in the embrasure, gazing out over the soggy countryside, weeping. Soon it would be winter, the branches of the trees bare and barren as she.

Where had she gone wrong? She had planned it all so carefully. In her dream Fabrice had looked upon Sophie with the loathing he had accorded her. It was not right. Fabrice still loved Sophie after she had told him the truth. She banged her fists against the stone walls until they bled.

There was no hope for her now. She had botched it. She could feel the hope that had kept her buoyed up dribbling away. She had always been sure that one day she would get Fabrice back; now she knew she wouldn't.

No one came that evening. Molly did not bring her tea. Or her supper and she could not join the family after what she had done. Her shoulders drooped and she let her body grow slack as she gazed with unseeing eyes at the streaming grey rain outside.

Chapter

56

IF Bella found it difficult to accept the turn of events, Sophie was thrown into total confusion. Seeing her husband in this completely new light, she could not but admire him. She felt bewildered by the fact that she could have so misunderstood him, and a strange feeling around her heart informed her that she was falling in love with him. It startled and delighted her. She had thought she had known Fabrice completely, but she had been wrong. There were depths to him that she had not begun to comprehend and the thought thrilled her. In her fevered fancy she had often daydreamed of Red Rafferty, and her limbs would disolve in desire for him. She realized now that that fantasy of hers was as unrealistic and inappropriate as Bella's desire for and fantasy about Fabrice. She had been playing with fire, when Fabrice was becoming part of the very fabric of her life, and if she had not been jerked out of her dream world she might have missed the fact that she had found a pearl of great price. Her day-to-day peace of mind rested safely in her husband's hands.

His value suddenly became incalculable to her. She had taken it all for granted. She thought how nearly she had missed appreciating how much love lay in their marriage. She thought of how she had allowed Red Rafferty to obscure Fabrice's qualities from her. He was a wildness in her blood, unfairly advantaged in his guise of adventurer and freedom-fighter. He had not been at her side, as Fabrice had been, during the birth of his son. He had not held her when she was sick or upset about something. He had not beguiled the time away when it was her time of the month and she was cross and in pain. He had played the nerve-ends of her body in an ecstatic melody, but she could not cling to him in the night, every night, year in, year out and rest assured of comfort and gentleness, passion and love. And, not least, stability. She had been blind and now her eyes were opened.

'Do you think I didn't know?' To love so much! To accept so much! She felt grateful to poor Bella, but she knew now that Fabrice was right and they would have to go to France. There was only one way to affect that safely, and that required her meeting Red Rafferty again, for the last time.

She told Fabrice her plan. 'I know how much I love you now,' she said. 'Will you forgive me? You are my true love, my darling, and I did not know it.'

Fabrice laughed and said with confidence, '*Chérie*, do not speak of it. But I knew you loved me. I never doubted it for a moment. After all, I am irresistible, am I not?' and in his eyes she saw his plea for her love and she held him to her heart.

'But you are right, we must go away,' she told him. 'I do not want to stay here now, near to such malignity. It makes me uncomfortable. Bella's love for you is evil. And who knows what she might tell the children? I feel, too, that if we stay, someone, perhaps unwittingly, may hurt the children. I would rather Armand never found out that ...'

She fell silent, but he said, 'No. Of course not. I think of him as mine. I feel he is. There is absolutely no necessity he should know.'

She looked at him, her face so full of love that he felt tears prick the back of his eyes.

'I want to meet your mother and I want her to meet her grandchildren.'

He laughed in his usual way and she realized for the first time how much his gaiety concealed his true feelings.

'You don't know how I long to see Maman. Yes. It is time. But you have to know, *ma petite*, I may end up in prison.'

'That is why I must see ... a friend of mine. Will you trust me? He spends a lot of time in Paris and he knows many people and if anyone can arrange things for you, my darling, he can.'

'But of course I trust you. Oh, you look adorable like that. Come here to me, wife, right now.'

'But Fabrice, it is the middle of the afternoon.'

'And what better time for passion?'

Laughing together, their bodies interwined and they made love. Sophie felt a great freedom, a total giving of herself to Fabrice. There were no reservations, no ghosts. Fabrice said to her, 'You will never know, *mon ange*, how much I love you,' and as their passion mounted and she matched his in a way she had never done before, she understood what complete love was all about.

Chapter

57

ROSALEEN had redecorated Lizzie Brannagan's room in shades of old gold, bronze and cream. She had ordered new drapes of chocolate brown with a long gold fringe and filled the room with green plants in brass holders. When Red came to Ireland now from Paris, he stayed at Rosaleen's, in Lizzie's room. At first it had been mainly in the dark of the mews, hiding there on a damp trestle bed. But as time passed and the political tension lessened, Rosaleen prevailed upon him to stay in the house. She had felt close to him ever since Creagh's death and she liked his company. She adored the children and watched their development with avid interest but it was not enough.

For a long time she denied the messages her heart and body sent her mind. She found that she would eagerly anticipate Red's arrival from France. She did not know when he would come but she kept everything ready for his return. She polished and hummed as she dusted, knowing in her secret heart that she was doing it for one person. She would jump when someone knocked at the door, and often at night when she heard a sound her heart would leap and she would sit up in the dark, his name on her lips. She bathed in perfumed water and rubbed her body with scented oils. But all to no avail. Red did not seem to see her as a woman. He talked of politics all the time and treated her as a valued and trusted friend and amusing companion, which was fine but not what she really wanted.

She knew he had loved someone else and she guessed it was Sophie. She had heard things, and knew of messages sent. But Sophie was married and Rosaleen had judged her correctly on their brief meeting. She guessed her to be a woman of integrity, and one look at that open enchanting face revealed that she was incapable of leading a double life. So Rosaleen waited patiently, for Red could not forever love a woman, however beautiful, who was outside his grasp. Besides, he too was an honourable man. Meanwhile, she tried to still the excessive beating of her heart when he was near, the blushes that suffused her cheeks when he looked at her, and the loneliness that overcame her when he left.

There was not a lot happening at the moment. The movement was licking its wounds. The Fenian uprising had ended in débâcle. The Fenian troops were ill-trained and ill-equipped and they were betrayed. Informers abounded. The Irish-American General Massey was military commander in the field. Alighting from the train at Limerick Junction to take up his command he was arrested before he could even begin, betrayed by the informer Corydon together with all the Fenian plans.

After this the Fenians dispersed and lay low. They had to, there was little they could do save try to rally their dispirited members and re-group the tattered remnants of their brotherhood. There were a lot of defections. Apathy set in again. After betrayal and failure it was difficult to keep interest at fever pitch.

Inevitably in the face of all this the British relaxed their vigilance and Red found it easier to move about. He spent most of his time in Paris, raising money and guns for the Irish cause while Rosaleen waited hopefully for him to return. The French were very helpful. They had always hated England and espoused the lifting of Ireland's yoke as much from their loathing of Britain as from sympathy with the oppressed country. Nevertheless, it was an exhausting and daunting task to maintain their interest. He often became very homesick and felt it was well worth the risk to travel back to his native land for a while, to see the colours of the air and the magical light at dusk, to draw his cloak about him and breathe the clear moist breezes off the sea.

When he had arrived this time he had been followed by two suspicious members of the Royal Irish Constabulary who thought they recognized him, and he had to shake them off, doubling back and forth in the alleys until he felt he had safely lost them. They had not been too happy penetrating some of the filthy lanes and by-passes he had deliberately led them down and were glad enough to give up.

When he at last reached Lizzie Brannagan's he had flung

himself indoors, hoping his entrance had not been remarked by any of the Alley dwellers, for not a few of them would sell their own mothers for half the price that was on his head.

He had tip-toed up the stairs and when he had ascertained that there was no one on the first floor, he crept up the second flight. Then suddenly he beheld Rosaleen unconscious of his presence, quite naked in her room. His heart pounded and he stood quite still, an expression of shock on his face.

Up to now in this house his mind had been full of Ireland, and plots and plans, guns and the smuggling in of ammunition. When he thought of women at all, he thought of Sophie, pale-gold Sophie, of dimples and maidenly modesty and blushes. Now here before him was a woman, a dark woman, voluptuous and cool, a tumble of blue-black hair down her back. Her legs were sturdy, round and smooth, her waist sloped into the curves of her buttocks and her breasts were heavy and marble-white, dark umber-tipped. There was a richness about her, a reality, a basis in the earth. Her movements were languid as she sat in front of her mirror idly fiddling with the curling tendrils on her milk-white forehead.

He stood entranced, beguiled by the golden glow in the room falling on her soft round curves and casting shadows of mystery into the angles of her body. It was delightful to look at her, and he watched transfixed, unable to move.

She became aware of her watcher and her eyes focused, searched for him in the shadows and found him through her mirror. For a long moment they stared at each other. Red tried to quell his growing excitement, tried to speak but found his mouth was dry as a tongue-tied lad's. She turned her head and her hair fell back over her shoulder. She stretched out her hand to him. He stumbled into the room and over to her and fell on his knees before her. She drew his face to her breasts and held him to her, covering his head in her long tresses. His nostrils were full of the scent of her hair and her body. She unbuttoned his shirt slowly and he said in wonder, 'I never saw you before. Never really looked.'

She laughed and kissed him. He had never before been kissed by a woman. He had done the kissing, they had received. He was taken aback by the fierceness of her embrace and his body melted in desire.

'An' how could you, for your head was full of someone else

351

an' there was no room for me,' she said.

'How did you know that?'

'Stupid. A woman always knows. At least a gypsy woman does.' She twined her white arms around him and wrapped her white legs about his long length.

'You're a wanton, Dark Rosaleen.'

She grinned, 'Indeed'n I am. Come into me. Fill me, and taste my delights. I want you, my dark man, I want you with all my heart.'

He looked into her eyes and saw they were full of desire and he took her with him on a tide of passion until soon, too soon, they both cried out. They lay a moment quiet and she looked at him. He grinned at her and she turned him over on his back and lay on top of him.

'Now once more,' she said. 'Slowly.'

She became essential to him. The more they enjoyed each other the more they wanted each other. Life took on the quality of a dream. They spent long days in bed, eating chicken off a tray, drinking wine and biting an apple as often as they bit an ear or a shoulder in passion. They lived in a world of their own, in Lizzie Brannagan's big soft canopied bed, teasing each other, laughing uproariously, making love and talking, talking, talking. Like Creagh before him he was amazed at the breadth of her knowledge of Irish mythology and folk-lore. She entertained him like Scharazad with her tales of olden times. Often they fell asleep in each other's arms to wake in the slanting sunlight, for they had forgotten to draw the curtains. They would make love, drowning in each other's arms. Then he would say, 'And what happened to Lou of the Long Arm an' he throwing the ...' And she would continue the story, her hair a dark halo about her head. They would sleep once again and they did not know or care if it was day or night.

Then the letter came. That it was written by a lady was obvious to Rosaleen. The notepaper was fine and smelled of crushed violets. She felt her heart grow cold within her and her face paled and a shiver of fear ran through her body.

He leaped out of bed and started to dress.

'I have to go,' he said. 'Do not worry, my love. I will not be gone long.'

How could she not worry? She paced the room in her chemise, then dressed, but did not know what to do. The

Widow Boann told her he had left by the front door, bold as brass for anyone to see him.

'He saddled Tyler an' off wi' him down the Quays. Fool that he is.' The Widow shook her head. She had been very pleased with the turn of events. Craw Kilty kept her abreast of what was happening in Usher, for she had it from her sister or one of the girls. The Widow went to see Craw Kilty on a Sunday after Mass by train except on the weekends that Rosaleen went. The Widow hoped and prayed that Red would stay from the Contesse, but now, it seemed, at the first call he went haring after her like a slave. Dear God, you'd think he'd be satisfied with the beauty of Rosaleen, the true woman that she was.

'She's an enchantress,' the Widow said to herself as she bathed Maeve and Fergal at bed-time that night and listened to Rosaleen pacing to and fro, to and fro, to and fro, up and down in the room she had been so happy in.

Chapter

58

SOPHIE saw Red in the arbour. The breeze scattered the golden leaves before it, making sport with the amber and bronze carpet and sending little flurries hither and thither like cascades of umber confetti. The sun was a huge orange ball in the grey sky and the mountains were edged with crimson light.

Sophie was wrapped up against the chill in a midnight-blue velvet cloak, trimmed with fox-fur. She sat very still on the bench and when she saw Red her face flamed in confusion.

He strode towards her, tall and dark and when he reached her he knelt before her.

'What is wrong little dove?' he asked.

She shook her head. 'Oh no. You must not call me that,' she said, 'Oh Red, you must never call me that again.'

He asked her, 'Why?'

She bit her lip. 'Red, Fabrice knows about us. About Armand.' She heard him mutter something under his breath and she cried, 'No. Listen. Sit down beside me. I will tell you all.'

She watched the changing expressions on his face as she told him everything that had occurred. She wondered now what it was she felt for this man. The excitement she always felt in his presence was still there. The thrill of his touch scurried up her body when he held her wrist and kissed her hand. She felt faint at the pressure of his lips on her skin. Yet she knew it was Fabrice she really loved, Fabrice she wanted to spend the rest of her life with. When she had finished her explanation she turned to Red and clasped his hands in hers.

'Oh Red. Bella is dangerous and I fear for Armand's future

here. People will talk. It is too dangerous to stay. We must go away. We must go to France, to Paris. Yet we cannot until Fabrice is pardoned. Please. I know it is a lot to ask of you, but for the love we once had for each other and the sake of my well-being and the happiness of our child, please, go to Paris and see what you can do. Try to see Fabrice's mother. The father of the man he killed. His mistress. Anyone who can help. Here is her address. Please, for me?' She smiled at him tremulously. 'Do it for me and ... Armand.'

'Armand,' he echoed, 'Oh my love, you know I'll do anything to protect him. To protect you.'

He had heard her words, 'the love we once had for each other', and he had understood. He felt a moment of deep regret. He was sad that it was over. Yet he was relieved. He knew now that he wanted Rosaleen. With his gypsy there was no room for another.

'Of course I'll do it for you. I am due to leave next week anyway. But,' he shrugged, 'I'll go at once, my lady. I will move heaven and earth to grant your wish.'

'Listen, Red. Fabrice is delighted to accept Armand as his son and heir. It has something to do with the boy he killed and also with his love for me. It is difficult with Fabrice to know. He hides so much under an air of frivolity, yet his feelings go deep, I know that now. I love my son and cannot bear to be parted from him. The point is, can you? Can you be unselfish enough to leave him with us? Renounce all right to him? I want you to leave him with us as ours. Completely.'

Red walked away from her. He had asked himself these questions and until now he had not known the answer. He looked at the slow descent of the leaves, blown by the slightest breeze, and thought that human lives were equally at the mercy of whim and accident. He thought of Sean and Sylvie.

He came back and placed his hands on her shoulders. 'Yes, Sophie. I can. I must. I have nothing to offer him. I am an outlaw dedicated to a cause. A hopeless cause. Of course I must set him free. What kind of a father would I be if I didn't?'

'Thank God,' she said, relief flooding her, 'Thank God.'

'May I see him once in a while?' he asked.

She nodded. 'Of course. You know that.'

'And if things ever change between you and Fabrice ...'

'I doubt it, Red. I really do. I love him so much. We love

each other. You see?'

'I am so pleased for you, Sophie. Rest assured I will do my best for you both. I will send word when all is well.'

He bowed low, kissed her hand and left her in the golden dusk.

Chapter

59

ORNELLA Duvall took the small piece of bloody meat between her finger and thumb and held it out to her black eagle. He snatched it from her, his beak, sharp as a dagger, just missing her finger by inches. The bird was caged in gilt and could see his own reflection in the enormous mirror over the black marble fireplace. Did the bird remember its freedom? Red wondered as he watched Ornella feed him. Did he remember his eyrie high in the mountain fastness, its wing-span and the sheer joy of falling like a thunderbolt to catch its quarry? How did the noble bird feel, wings clipped, caged, the pet of a lady of easy virtue in her gilded boudoir?

Ornella was dressed in the very latest fashion, and looked stunning. Cloth of gold overlaid with black lace falling near her body, almost revealing her remarkable breasts. He thought of her practised caresses, the skill of her love-making adapted to a man's pleasure, the courtesan's technique geared to excite and promote physical ecstacy. There was no one more practised in the art of seduction than Ornella. But not love.

He thought of Sophie and wondered how Fabrice could have loved this woman at all. Desired her, yes. He could understand that. He looked at her standing there feeding the bird, tall, her long bronze hair hanging loose down her back, thick and gleaming in the candle-light. Her perfect body would smell of jasmine oil. She was massaged with it every morning by her black maid. He had been told that sometimes, if it suited Ornella, she would let her current lovers watch the ritual. It drove men mad with lust to look on, as the pearly body, quite naked, lay on a white sheet and was pressed and rubbed by the ebony hands that slid up and down the satiny skin, now oiled and gleaming, and the room filled with the heady scent of the perfume.

Now she glanced at Red sideways under her long lashes. 'Fabrice de Beauvillande sends greetings? How charming of him to remember me.'

The room was hot and over-perfumed. Ornella glanced at the man before her again. She would have given anything to see him naked on her black satin sheets. He had a beautiful build and was handsome as sin, but he did not desire her, she could see that. It was plain. Perhaps he had the English preference for boys? No. She thought not. He was a man with other things than women on his mind, a man with ideals, a man who gave himself to no woman. He did not dally to enjoy the many casual pleasures that awaited voluptuaries of taste and discernment.

'Heigh-ho,' she said and yawned and stretched, smiling at him. 'What do you want here? You do not want me.'

Ornella was twenty-seven and a realist. She knew men inside out and she did not waste time. Time was money or pleasure and the tall beautiful man in front of her promised neither.

Red looked around him at the magnificently appointed room. They were in her reception room and the heavy velvets on the walls and the frescoes on the ceiling were similar only in fact to Lizzie Brannagan's, for the materials here were of the finest quality in the world and the paintings of such exquisite workmanship as rendered them works of art. There were two tall gilded candelabra holding a myriad of candles in their branches. There was a vase full of lilies on an inlaid table and their scent lay heavy on the air. The drapes over the windows were drawn, though it was mid-day.

'You know, I believe, the Duc de Mandeville?' Red asked.

Ornella threw back her head and laughed. Her throat was like a marble column and her hair tumbled, a bronze banner, behind her.

'Ah. I see your drift,' she said. 'Fabrice wants to come home?'

He looked surprised and she laughed again and he could see her small sharp teeth.

'How did you guess?'

'It was easy. Fabrice's greetings out of the blue after all these years. Then an inquiry about the father of the boy he killed.

358

Armand . . .' Her voice had changed and he looked at her in surprise. He saw an expression of stark grief cross her beautiful face.

She caught his eye and shrugged, smiling wryly. 'Even I have a heart, *Monsieur*. I loved that boy. It was folly. It would not have lasted. Perhaps . . . who knows? But no. I am too greedy. Too fond of the pleasures of this life. So! I see what is your purpose. What else but that Fabrice wants to come to Paris?'

'He is married.'

'So I heard.'

'Can I prevail upon you to introduce me to the Duc de Mandeville?'

She shrugged, 'I do not know why I should *M'sieur*, but then again I do not see why I should not. Fabrice gave me a great deal of pleasure in the past.' She paused then looked up at him again. 'What is she like?' she asked. He knew exactly what she meant. She wanted to know about Sophie.

He said, 'Pretty more than beautiful, you would say. Soft as butter and delicious as spring. Enchanting, really.'

She looked at him, surprised. 'You are in love with her?'

He said, 'I was.'

'There is someone else?'

She saw his eyes darken. 'Oh yes,' he said. 'Oh yes.'

'She is lucky, *M'sieur*. Very lucky.' She thought a moment then said, 'Come to me here, in the evening, on Sunday. It is,' she smiled, 'my day off. It is my own day. It is my habit to give a party. We assemble about nine or ten o'clock. We eat, we drink, we make merry. You will meet the Duc de Mandeville then. I will make sure he comes. If he is in town.'

'Oh he is.'

'Then I took forward to seeing you, *M'sieur*.'

'Why are you doing this? It is so very kind.'

'And my sort are not kind? Say I am doing it because Fabrice de Beauvillande made me laugh so often and that is precious. Say it is because you are a very handsome man and this is my only way of pleasing you.'

Red smiled at her. She swept past him, the scent of her perfume trailing behind her. She walked, the golden skirts floating out behind her, to the double doors at the end of the room. She opened them with both hands. As they flew back he could see a canopied bed on a raised dais in the room behind her. The sheets and pillows were black satin, the lights were amber-coloured. The whole effect was intensely seductive, and, as she curtsied mockingly to him and he bowed, he wondered if he were quite sane. But even as the idea occurred to him he brushed the temptation away. It would be folly, he thought, a sport more suited to a dilettante society than to him. He remembered where he came from, and taking his hat and cloak from Suki in the hall he left.

The apartment was in the Rue de Lille and he mounted his horse and trotted down the street then rode briskly to the Bois du Boulogne. He needed fresh air to blow away the heaviness of Ornella's rooms. He thought of Rosaleen and threw back his head and laughed with joy at the delight he felt. The mere idea of her pleased him and filled him with excitement.

Time hung heavy on his hands until Sunday. He had completed his professional visits and he ached to go home to the house in Doone Alley. He longed for his lover. But he knew where his duty lay, and he knew too, that his son Armand needed his efforts now. He might never need his father again. He had faced up to that problem with his usual clearsightedness. He had renounced any claim to his son's happiness, for Armand's best interests lay elsewhere. But whenever he needed Red's help he would get it.

Sunday arrived and Red hoped that he could get the matter settled as soon as possible so that he could return to Dublin. The party was peopled with old roués, ageing members of the aristocracy and ladies of the night.

Ornella met him, saying, 'I have done my best, M'sieur. He will be here, I promise.'

Red wandered around, an outsider, slightly uncomfortable in the ornate high-ceilinged rooms. A small orchestra played and many a perfumed fille de soir tried to arouse his interest with no success. He kept an impatient eye on Ornella's movements and at last saw her curtsying to an aristocratic-looking man who he guessed was the Duc de Mandeville, for he seemed as out of place there as Red felt. His expression was austere and he looked with distaste on the motley throng before him.

Ornella signalled with her eyes and Red excused himself to the plump courtesan he was in conversation with and hurried over to his hostess.

'This is the Duc de Mandeville. Sir. May I present Monsieur

Rafferty? Redmond, this is the gentleman you wished to meet.'

The Duc bowed to Red stiffly, his eyes piercingly keen. He was obviously not a man to play games with, and Red felt a moment's apprehension at the magnitude of his task. He mentally castigated himself on his faint heart, when he heard Ornella say, 'You may use my small drawing-room for privacy if you so desire. Suki will show you the way and serve you some wine or champagne. Whatever you wish, gentlemen.' She curtsied again. 'Now if you will excuse me I must return to my guests.' They followed Suki to the quiet room.

The Duc refused any refreshment and stood looking at Red.

'You do not seem a part of this ... this ...' He waved his hand to the door, his voice dripping contempt.

Red shook his head. 'You must forgive me for requesting to see you. I did not know where to ask you to meet me and Mademoiselle Duvall agreed ...'

The Duc held up his hand, 'Please M'sieur. Let us cut out formalities. You knew no one in Paris who could introduce me to you. Ornella has been ... so you came to her. I have agreed to see you, for you said your visit had some connection with my dead son.'

Red nodded. He could see how difficult it was going to be. He decided on a forthright approach.

'Sir, I beg you to be patient. Listen to me. I am a friend of the young Conte de Beauvillande.'

The older man gasped and turned white. 'M'sieur, how dare you speak of him in my presence.'

'I dare. I dare because your son's death is breaking up three families. Fabrice de Beauvillande was very young and foolish at the time. It was not deliberate. He did not set out to murder your son. You are a fair man and you know that. It was, I have been told, a grim accident. Your son was an expert shot, not Fabrice. Consider, sir, his mother. She has not seen her son now for many years. She has spent these years in a convent praying for your son and hers. Consider also, sir, this young man has married. She is the daughter of a noble Anglo-Irish family. His young wife is blameless. Her husband has told her all his shameful past and she has forgiven him. But he cannot bring her home to France. They have a son, and a daughter. The boy is called Armand, he has been called so after your son, M'sieur.'

As the Duc began to rise Red said, 'Please listen. This young wife, her son and daugher, are innocent. They have done nothing wrong. Neither has his grieving mother. All Fabrice wishes to do is to crave your pardon. He does not expect you to forgive him but he implores your generosity in allowing him to return to France without fear of arrest.'

The Duc was deeply moved, Red could see, but whether at the remembrance of the past or his words he had no way of knowing. He waited while the older man collected himself. He walked to the piano and stood idly looking at the black and ivory keys. The silence lengthened and when he turned around he found he was alone.

Red passed a restless night. His impatience to leave Paris grew. He must be getting old, he thought, aching for hearth and home and a woman he loved. When had he last thought of Erin? I am infected with the same disease as the rest of Ireland, he thought, apathy. We go on from year to year when we are comfortable, doing nothing, sliding from day to day, not achieving anything at all in the cause of freedom. Even an attempt that ends in failure is better than inactivity. Oh Ireland, Ireland, I have betrayed you for a gypsy wench that I love and cannot do without. She is cloaked in starlight and mystery as you are, but she warms my bed at night and you do not. She is not as greedy as you, for you try to possess all of me and give me precious little in return. He hastily crossed himself as if he had uttered blasphemy and tried to sleep wondering what on earth he should do now. Try to see the Duc again? It seemed pointless.

He ordered breakfast and the housemaid brought a note with it. To his surprise he saw it was from the Duc. Opening it with hasty fingers he read,

My dear sir,

You must have thought my departure yesterday precipitate in the extreme. I beg you to understand that the whole subject is very distressing for me. However, I have given much thought to what you said and I have to admit you were fair and logical. So after deep reflection on the matter I have decided the right and proper thing to do is to forgive Fabrice de Beauvillande. Do not expect me to meet him in person. I am fair and just, I hope, but alas, not a saint. However, rest assured that I will have a word with the correct authorities and the Conte de Beauvillande will have no trouble entering

France and living here. There will, I assure you, be no threat to his safety.

It has been, my dear sir, a great pleasure and privilege to meet you, for you have in fact removed the burden of hatred that I have carried for so long on my old and weary shoulders. It is a burden I am glad to shed and for this I am grateful.

The letter was ended with the usual civilities. Red whooped with joy and the colour of his day spectacularly changed. He called for servants and his carriage and made ready to depart post-haste for Dublin.

Chapter

60

AS James had feared the family at Usher Castle was rent apart. After much preparation, farewell parties, visits and sad good-byes, Fabrice and Sophie set sail for France taking Armand, Minou, Clarie and Maurice, who had wed quietly before they left. Bessie Broderick had insisted upon it. Dolly was left with the Dowager Lady Angela, drifting about in her other world, and Old Gentleman, who became more and more fuddled with time. Without Sophie's cheerful companionship and positive support she became nervous and fretful again. She stopped having guests at Usher. She became obsessed with Cormac. She clung to him as a drowning woman clings to a straw. Even James began to suffer. Cormac was the light of her life. The sun, moon and stars shone out of him, Bessie Broderick told Craw Kilty on a rare visit to her sister.

'She'll destroy him, so she will,' she said, rocking in front of the fire, her skirts up over her knees, her legs toasting brick-red. 'He's becoming a proper little Mama's boy, so he is. Wilful he is. Goes blue if he doesn't get his own way. He'll turn into a nasty piece of work if he's allowed to go on the way my Lady Dolly lets him at the moment.'

Craw Kilty told Ronan, who told Rosaleen, who did not believe the tales, thinking them exaggerations. In her happiness she did not even notice the Minstrel's pain at her loss of interest.

'I'm going, Rosaleen,' he said and she touched his dark hair absentmindedly. 'Rosaleen,' he added, 'the roads are beckoning. Don't you feel it? I can hear the wind's siren call and feel the urge in my legs to get walkin'. Have you forgotten? Don't you remember at all?' He sounded wistful.

She looked into his eyes and saw there his love for her and his love too for the highways and the woods, the lakes and the mountains of Ireland. 'I love Red, Minstrel,' she said, 'I must be with him.'

'Red talks about Ireland,' he said, 'but with him it's all ideals. It's in his brain. With you and me, Rosaleen it's in our blood. You'll never be truly at peace till you are on the roads again, sleeping under the stars.' She looked at him angrily, but he continued, 'Ach, it's no use scowlin' at me like that. I know you love him, but it's impossible, don't ye see? He's a wild man, a man who chases after death. A bullet will get him one fine day.'

He heard her draw in her breath sharply and he saw the pain in her eyes. 'Ah, Rosaleen, it's true. He's a marked man. Death sits on his shoulder. He flirts with it. But you and I are life itself. We are part of the green grass and the running waters. The flowers are part of us, the rain and the wind too. How long will you deny this in you?'

He kissed her forehead and she clung to him and said, 'Listen, Ronan. Never think that. Don't say it. It causes me such pain. Do you know the kind of love that denies all that is in one's self? He is my blood, my sinew, the very nerves of my body, my heart. Without him I cannot be free. I need him too much. You must understand.'

'I must go,' he said. 'If ever you need me you know how to reach me.' He turned at the door. 'One day you'll come back to us. One day,' he said and smiled his sweet smile and was gone, leaving her heavy-hearted and lonely.

He was away for a long time. Craw Kilty said he had gone over the hump-backed bridge and away, his fiddle on his back, his flute in his pocket. 'He'll come home in winter,' she said.

Rosaleen came to the cottage one day in each month. She got news of Hagar and Melba from Craw and sent her news back.

'They're in the land of myrtle and tamarisk,' she told Rosaleen as they were picking herbs in the woods one afternoon. 'They need the sun now, they say. The sun is gentle on old bones.' She sighed and grimaced as she straightened up, for there was the beginning of an ache in her back in spite of the soaking in linseed and vinegar she had given herself, and sometimes her fingers throbbed. 'A caravan stopped in the valley three days ago. A bad-tempered man was in it an' his wife an' babby. His hair grew low on his forehead an' I was glad to get shot of him, I can tell you. But he had seen Hagar and Melba in Sounion an' said they were well an' sent greetings.'

The news made Rosaleen sad and she did not know why. These days she was either ecstatically happy or deep in gloom. Her mood depended entirely on Red. When he was home she was like a candle that was alight, and when he was away about Ireland's business it was as if the light had been put out.

She knew that part of him was always beyond her reach, even when he was with her. When he was away anxiety gnawed. She was terrified that he would return to her shot, wounded, maimed, or, worse still, that he would not return at all. Sometimes he made jokes about prison, but she could not bear to listen, thinking that kind of humour unfunny. He had spent a spell there, and escaped, and when he told her of it her face paled and she knew fear. Red was elusive and she accepted that, but it did not make life easy for her.

'I'm on tenterhooks most of the time,' she confided now to Craw Kilty. 'When he's with me I'm waitin' for him to go an' when he's away I worry all the time about his safety.'

Craw nodded her head sagely and sighed. 'Ah, men,' she said. 'They always bring a deal of trouble. You can depend on that.'

They had come into a clearing in the woods and the sunlight spilled through the branches dusting the green with gold. Rosaleen stopped and gasped and grabbed Craw Kilty's arm as she saw a boy sitting on a mossy log reading a book. His face was serious and his hair soft brown and tousled. When he looked up and saw her, he gave a smile so like Creagh's that her heart slipped a beat. She knew that this was her son and she stood a moment in the shade of a crooked silver tree, leaning against it, weak.

'Who are you?' the boy asked, brightly inquisitive.

'They call me Dark Rosaleen.'

'I see,' he said. 'It's as well you are with Craw Kilty. Otherwise you would be trespassing.' His bright eyes glanced at them. 'It's all mine, you know. All of it. I'm from Usher Castle. My father is the Knight of Usher. I shall be the next Knight. Like this book.' He held it out and Rosaleen, coming towards him timidly, took it from him.

'Why do you stare at me?' the boy asked, for Rosaleen was scrutinizing the curves and outline, the colour and texture of the small face raised to her. 'Look at the book,' he commanded, pointing.

She saw it was a volume by Alfred, Lord Tennyson. 'Morte d'Arthur' it was entitled, a poem. It seemed, about mediaeval knights; Arthur, Lancelot, Bors and Percival and Queen Guinevere. The knights wore armour and the queen looked tragic.

'I have a sword, see?' He brandished a wooden dummy in the air and whooped about the clearing, fighting imaginary enemies. Rosaleen sat on the fallen tree trunk and watched him. She was filled with conflicting emotions: she wanted to hug and kiss him, but she wanted too to temper his prideful boasting.

He came after a moment or two and took the book from her hands.

'It is mine,' he said matter-of-factly. Then looking at her he asked, 'Why are you sad?'

'I'm not,' Rosaleen said, and smiled at him.

'You're just like my mother,' he said.

'What do you mean?' Rosaleen queried, startled.

'She looks at me all the time as if I was going to disappear. She looks so sad. And when I ask her why, she says, like you, that she is not sad and she smiles. Just as you did. Why do grown-ups never tell the truth?'

Rosaleen shook her head. 'We do. But sometimes things are not what they seem. Although I look sad I am still happy. Sometimes it is the same thing. It is confusing, I know, but I am happy to have met you. What is your name?'

'Cormac Usher, fourteenth ...' he frowned. '... I think, Earl of Usher and Knight of same,' he finished proudly. 'And now I must go. Mama does not like me to be out long. She likes me near her. Goodbye.' And he was gone, running away through the trees, leaving Rosaleen in a turmoil of confusion.

'Oh Craw, what are they doing to him up there?' she cried.

Craw Kilty squatted beside her. She took Rosaleen's hands in hers.

'Now listen, girl,' the ould wan said. 'You must not start to fret yourself about the young Lord. He is not yours any more. You gave him up. The gentry have a different way than the likes of us. You leave him to them. You made a decision a long time

367

ago and you canna fret yourseln' now. It would be unreasonable of you. Leave him to them. They surely know what they are doing.'

'Do they? Do they, Craw?' Rosaleen asked.

Craw nodded sadly. 'Ye have to believe they do. An' Maeve an' Fergal are much more yer childer than yonder boy.'

Rosaleen nodded again. It was true. Fergal and Maeve. She had squandered her love on them and received it back a hundred-fold. It was a day-by-day thing, she thought. Did it really matter who your parents were? What mattered much more were the ones who brought you up. The ones who held you in your arms when you were sad, who nursed you when you were sick, who guided your first footsteps and taught you your first words. The ones you turned to for comfort and who gave you love and were always there.

Suddenly she wanted to return quickly to Doone Alley. Red was not there but her children, Fergal and Maeve, were. For the first time she realized how much she loved them.

PART THREE

'ALL of it is yours.' He got used to hearing them say it right from the beginning. 'All of it belongs to you. From the highest purple peak beyond the valley to the last reaches of the forest behind, it is all yours, Cormac.'

'The castle is yours, all the beautiful objects in it. Carpets, Buddhas, vases, jade, the paintings, the furniture, the servants, all, all yours. The farms over the valley, the tenants are yours. The trees, sycamores, ash, elm, oak, willow, beech, and chest-nut, are yours. The roses in the arbour, the iris, the geraniums, the carpets of lily-of-the-valley, the daffodils, the poppies splashing scarlet on the fields. The fruit, orchards of apple and cherry, the golden and purple plums, the pears, all belong to you, young man. The nuts that the squirrel buried in the autumn and the squirrels themselves, the foxes, the deer, and the rabbits all, all are yours. Yours the bees and the honey they made. Yours the birds of the air that nested on your property. For that is what it is,' they told him, 'your property. Yours.'

His mother and father adored him. He could do no wrong in their eyes. They told him of his heritage, of his inheritance and he looked about and he loved it all, took it for granted. It was his. He was monarch of all he surveyed.

There were a lot of things he did not like. He decided that when he grew up he would not allow nasty things to happen to him. He was not entirely sure how he could manage that but he certainly meant to try.

He had not liked Aunt Sophie going away to France. He would have made her stay. He loved her presence in the castle. She brought laughter and gaiety. Without her his mother fussed over him too much. After Aunt Sophie went his mother never let him out of her sight. 'I want you no further than an arm's length away,' she would say, playing with his dark curls. She held him, apparently lightly, but it was a grip of steel. She would put her arm loosely about his waist as they sat in the drawing-room after lunch or dinner, and at tea-time while she fed him little cakes iced in pink or blue, or strawberries in season, or sugar almonds, and he felt the hold was very tight. He could feel her eyes following him everywhere. Often riding back to the house with his father he saw her at her window, watching, waiting. He tried not to find it irksome but he did not succeed.

His mother missed Aunt Sophie too, he could see that. She was not as relaxed any more and she did not laugh, hardly at all. She seemed over-anxious and tense.

With his father he was awkward and constrained. He felt that something was expected of him but he did not know what it was. His father taught him everything he knew. He loved his father but felt that he did not live up to what his father wanted him to be.

He did not like riding. Horses frightened him and Matt Dominic was old and shaky and his grip was not firm. Cormac felt insecure. His father could not understand his feelings. He was impatient with Cormac and exasperated by his son's refusal to ride except when absolutely necessary. For God's sake, everyone rode, James told him, barely restraining his anger. Cormac could see it, his father's anger, though his father tried to hide it, and it frightened him.

He had no playmates. His father and mother did not wish him to associate with the children of the servants or tenants. He was the young lord and they must not get too familiar. The other big houses in the neighbourhood had no children of his own age. So he was a solitary child and grew up not sure how to treat people.

Behind his parents' backs he tended to bully the servants and employees. He did not mean to be nasty but the release from the tension of his parents' presence provoked him to unkind behaviour. He never bullied any of the Brodericks, though. There was something sacrosanct about them and they always looked at him as if they knew something he didn't.

His earliest memory of nasty things was the de Beauvillande family going to France. They took all the light and the fun from

Usher. Aunt Sophie and Uncle Fabrice were such jolly relaxed people. They did not pay too much attention to you, and never scolded if you slid down the banisters, or worried that your skull would crack open when you landed at the bottom. They hugged you without giving you the feeling that you were being smothered. Uncle Fabrice never told you to be 'a little man' but rather advised a good cry in Aunt Sophie's lap.

Aunt Sophie could be strict but he did not mind that. You knew where you were with her. She looked you straight in the eye and told you you must not do something when you knew you would be punished if you did. It was much better than not knowing what the rules were. Papa and Mama never told him the rules, yet he knew they expected a certain standard of behaviour from him and were disappointed in him when he failed.

He missed his uncle and aunt very much. He also missed Armand and Minou. Although the latter had been too small to participate in the activities of her brother and his cousin, nevertheless the house seemed very quiet without them. The sense of importance they gave him by their mere presence as juniors was taken from him with their departure.

He felt lonely and isolated. That made him fretful and bad-tempered and that made his mother fuss more. It was a vicious circle. As he grew he fell back more and more on himself and what he would one day be; The Knight of Usher, Earl Usher. Owning everything.

His mother's refusal to allow him to play with the peasants' or the servants' children made him a solitary child. He did not like hunting. His experience of being blooded made him throw up and embarrassed his father and although he did not scold him Cormac heard him make the strangest remark afterwards to his mother. Something about it being 'typical of Creagh'. He knew his Uncle Creagh had died a hero for some Irish cause so he was obviously not a coward. He wondered what his father had meant.

He didn't like his crazy Aunt Bella in the high tower. Once or twice he had crept up to see her, out of curiosity. She sat at the window, her hair grey like a witch. And she muttered to herself all the time. Molly, her old maid, said she never stopped. She had upset Cormac though he had never told anyone about it. She said he was not his father's son. She said, and he hated her for this, she said that his father had another son called Fergal. She said that Fergal was heir to Usher. She said it and her breath smelled and he screamed at Molly to let him out. It was not true, of course. Molly said she always tried to make trouble. Molly said it was because of her that Aunt Sophie and Uncle Fabrice had left and gone to France. She told lies and he didn't like her, so when he became Knight of Usher he'd get rid of her. He did not know how just at present. But he would.

They got him a tutor, a learned man from Oxford University in England, and the castle became a battleground. Young Cormac refused to learn, the professor said, and he told them his pupil was shamming. At the end of a year, fed up with Cormac's tantrums, Professor Wilson left. He was followed by a succession of worthy men who came, tried hard, but inevitably went away defeated and considerably shaken. They might have coped with Cormac, but not with his mother. She refused to allow them to lay a hand on Cormac. She countermanded their punishments and gave the boy sweetmeats if they made him cry.

James and Dolly were at their wits' end to find someone suitable for their angel when Samuel Potter arrived fresh from Cambridge and to the worried parents' delight peace reigned once more at Usher. They could not know that Samuel drank and that Cormac, discovering that his teacher was fuddled by eleven o'clock each morning, left him alone to soak himself in alcohol and simply went his own way without anyone knowing a thing about it.

Cormac was extremely attractive, having Rosaleen's dark hair and Creagh's finely-boned face so reminiscent of Sophie. There was a prettiness about him and a waywardness that he cloaked with charm. He could entice the birds off the trees with his winning ways and few saw the shallowness and selfishness beneath. After their meeting in the wood he spent a lot of time with Craw Kilty. She showed him how and where to find a badger's set, how to tickle a trout and where the deer mated. She taught him the names of the trees and ferns and plants. She showed him the swan's nest, for they permitted her near them when she whispered to them in Gaelic and ran her finger over the crown of their heads and down the backs of their long white necks. She showed him where the salmon leapt and the hiding places of the 'magic mushroom'.

And she too said, 'It all belongs to you, Cormac. All of it.'

He spent much of his time from home, paying no attention to his mother's worried face on his return. He roamed the woods and the mountainside and there was elastic in his step, for as he circumnavigated his domain his heart cried joyfully within him, 'It's mine. It's all mine. It's all mine.'

Chapter

62

THEN the worst thing that had happened to him in his life occurred. His mother died. Suddenly she was gone. Emptiness was all that was left. He had struggled against her possessiveness, he had felt the yoke of her excessive love for him and he thought he had always chafed under it. Instead, with her loss he found he needed her more than he ever could have realized. She was the one person in the world who saw him as perfect. She was always on his side. She was his champion. As long as she was there he was immensely valuable. Now she had gone and he was alone.

Dolly had grown careless. The method suggested by the Widow Boann had worked so well that bit by bit she had forgotten that there was a need for it at all. She got pregnant. At first she was frightened. Then she persuaded herself and James that really everything was going to be all right. It was not. During pregnancy she became weaker and weaker and no one was surprised when she went into premature labour in the seventh month. She did not survive. She passed away and left behind her desolation. Dolly had always been a shadowy person, taking her colour from the more forceful characters around her. She was their foil, and she was James' mainstay. Without her the house became a cold and unfriendly place.

It was a dark day in December when she died. Around the bed the servants bowed their heads and young Dr Hegarty said she never really stood a chance. James did not look at Cormac. He did not hear him weeping. He did not see the boy come to his side nor feel his gentle touch. He did not notice him go. He was too full of his own grief.

He bowed his head over his wife's small pale lifeless hands and wept. He wept for his own culpability for he blamed himself for getting her pregnant. He wept for the past when that exhausted face on the pillow, blue-shadowed, fragile, had looked at him in love and passion. He wept for the laughter-filled days that had gone, when Sophie and Fabrice were at Usher and all the world seemed young.

He realized sadly that he had never felt close to Cormac. He was the heir to Usher, a necessary member of the family and as such James trained him and instructed him in what was required. Cormac was not very good at paying attention and when it came to learning about the administration of the estate he was hopeless. James felt no tenderness towards him. It was a lack he could not help. He had tried to instil in himself a spontaneous love for Cormac, but he was too honest a man to be able to conceal his true feelings. He was always just and kind, but he could not make himself show a warmth he did not feel.

Cormac was distraught. He was a tactile person and used to his mother's caresses. The coldness now at Usher devastated him and he could not understand it.

After the funeral James, overwhelmed by the loss, became irritable and morose. He did not seem to want to see Cormac — the sight of the boy distressed him. Cormac was stung by his rejection. James had always seen Dolly and Cormac together and now whenever the boy came near him he searched for his beloved wife and could not bear her absence. He kept asking himself why? Why had Creagh died? Why had Dolly gone? And with his searching came the realization that directly or indirectly he had been to blame. He had been wrong. His judgement had failed him.

With this realization came the first tiny impulse to see Fergal, Dolly's child, the fruit of her womb. It was a small voice deep within him that wondered what he would be like now. But he squashed the voice, cursing himself for a fool.

He became prematurely aged, a serious man who seldom laughed. Old Gentleman and the Dowager Lady Angela followed Dolly to the crypt in the chapel at Usher, James hardly noticed. Now at the long table in the dining-room there were only two; himself and Cormac. They were a monosyllabic pair, moody and bad-tempered. Bessie Broderick was heard to remark that the castle was a sad and sorry place to work these times, nothing was appreciated any more and standards had slipped. Servants uncomplimented showed no enthusiasm and when they were not criticized for sloppy work they made no effort to improve it.

Cormac found himself arrogantly disagreeing with his father, exchanging harsh words with him, yet desperately desiring to please him. Life was intolerable and Cormac often went into Dublin to alleviate his tensions in a bout of hectic merrymaking and drinking. He could not bear the coldness of the life he led. He did not know how to give or receive love. He had never been taught. So he journeyed into Dublin where he frequented taverns of unsavoury reputation and wenched and drank until he was helpless. He was often returned to Usher in a sorry state. His father's displeasure did not improve him, rather it added fuel to the flame and impelled him to behave ever more irresponsibly.

When he was alive, Old Gentleman had sung the praises of 'the Green Cock' and Lizzie Brannagan's, and the young man made every effort to find them. So far he had not succeeded, for when he was articulate he was still with people of enough respectability not to know its whereabouts, and when he got drunk he made no sense at all and the company he was in did not know what he was talking about. Still, every so often, he inquired. He had been many times on the other side of the Quays opposite Klein's the pawnbroker, in a tavern called the 'Green Parrot', but there was no Lizzie Brannagan's there. It became a kind of crusade. Where his great uncle had enjoyed himself and had remembered with such enthusiasm after such a long time, he wanted to go. Perhaps, he sometimes thought, it was no longer in existence, but every time he was about to give up on his search, someone would have heard of it, or been there. They would be hazy concerning its location. Few frequented Lizzie Brannagan's sober.

Cormac promised himself that one day he would find it. One day soon.

Chapter

63

'LEAVE him alone. Leave him alone or I'll *kill* ye. I'll murder ye so I will. I'll . . . I'll . . .'.

The seventeen-year-old danced about on her toes in the Alley. Her little leather boots were split and her pantaloons were soggy with filth. The hem of her dress, soft green-and-white striped cotton, and her frilly petticoats were splashed with mud and worse and she hopped about like a flea, agitated and full of frustration that she was not a man.

'Fergal, Fergal, hit them, hit them, bash their heads in,' she screamed, and one of the melée of boys who were pounding the hunchback brutally broke away and shoved her into the gutter again, giving her a kick as she fell.

'Shut yer gob, ye little bitch, or I'll shut it for ye.'

Enraged, she jumped up again and leaping on the back of the boy who had pushed her, she laid into him, pounding him fiercely with all her strength. He shook her off easily and turned to hit her, but she raked her nails down his face and watched triumphantly as it started to bleed. The boy let out a bellow like a bull and his mates let fall the now inert body of Fergal and turned in a group to face the little red-head who paled and bit her lip.

At that moment the razor-sharp voice of the Widow Boann sawed the air and sent the group scuttling into the warren of slum streets that radiated off the wharves.

'Get outa here, or I'll make jam outa yiz,' the Widow hollered and the place reverted to normal. Dogs barked; the sun shone but could find no entry into the alleys. Jangles pushed his barrel-organ home muttering curses under his breath. He now sported a broken jaw where years ago Breen Dubh had smashed it.

'Ye'd think after me losin' me arm an' me leg he'd leave me jaw,' he confided in One-Eyed Willy who tartly told him he was a disgrace of a man to sell his friends, and he, for one, did not want to sit beside him in the shebeen.

'For,' he said, 'yer a contamination, that's what ye are. A contamination. An' they didn't even give ye the hundred quid, for they never got him, no thanks to you.' Then he added the sentence that haunted Jangles and rendered him sleepless for nights, 'If Red Rafferty ever finds out who squealed, one of his friends'll slit ye from gullet to navel, so they will.'

Boney Best pulled his cart into the yard by its one handle, scratched himself and started to unload its burden. As he began to carry it into his room Flossie McMahon reeled out of the 'Green Cock' and staggered across the Alley, singing tipsily to herself. The Widow half pulled, half carried Fergal into Lizzie Brannagan's. It was still known as that in the locality, even after all these years and the brothel closed. Maeve followed, brushing down her skirts.

'Get in wid' ye, ye pair of spalpeens. Get in an' let me get a tub going for ye.'

Maeve blushed. 'Not together, Widow. Please, I'm too old for that now.'

The Widow looked surprised. She had not thought about it but they were growing up. The boy was big, that was certain. He limped and his shoulder was higher on his left side. Otherwise, she now thought wryly, he was very lovely to look at. He had abundant soft brown hair and gentle brown eyes, the eyes of a deer. They were large and clear and innocent, but wary. His skin was soft to touch and he was tall, gentle as a lamb, full of a tender concern for all living things. And, the Widow thought, clever but without a streak of commonsense, for he refused to meet violence with violence. It irritated her that he was such a gentle creature an' him the size of an ox. He never defended himself against the bullying attacks he was subjected to day after day after day. He could have annihilated those bullies quite easily, but he refused to. The hooligans in the neighbourhood had heard about his refusal to fight and they converged on Doone Alley every day and ritually beat him up. His body was always covered in bruises and cuts. Nothing that the Widow or

Maeve or Rosaleen could do would induce him to fight back. It infuriated Maeve to think that one blow from his great fist could fell them all.

He loved all living things and would not harm any one of them. The spider spinning transparent webs of gossamer and the tiny city sparrow in its nest were part of creation, and, in Fergal's mind had a right to exist equal to his and Maeve's. The bullies were bullies because of some flaw in them that he did not understand and to hurt them would bring him down to their level. Regan had tried to teach him simply to defend himself but he was stubborn as a mule and refused to learn.

'You are giving me an ability that if I had I might be tempted to use. Then I am no better than they. Maeve, don't you see? Regan, listen,' he said in exasperation. 'They do not really hurt me. They hurt themselves.'

Maeve would shake her head. 'You look pretty hurt to me,' she would say. 'How much blood does it take?'

Fergal patiently continued to try to make them understand. 'It's a paradox. Each time they beat me up I become stronger and they become weaker, don't you see? Don't you understand?'

But Regan did not understand. He thought that Fergal must be a little odd. Someone had told him that hunchbacks, like fools and drunks, were very near to God, so he shrugged and did not argue. Maeve loved him, so she too said nothing, but her heart was sore within her at the punishment he took.

Rats McMahon, Flossie's oldest, was the leader of the gang. A rodent-faced vicious little bully, he terrified the old, the weak and the stupid.

The Widow tried to beat it into Fergal's head that he was foolish to allow himself to be thus victimized. They sat in the kitchen of No. 1 and clucked over him — the Widow, Maeve and Rosaleen — while they bathed the grit out of his wounds and patched up his scratches and ladled out advice and admonitions in the gentle voices of concern. He loved the sound of it. He had been surrounded by these pleasant sounds all his life. Sometimes he thought it was worth being beaten up just to have them fuss over him so. How they scolded and clucked. He knew they loved him and the gratitude in his heart overflowed sometimes and he had to go to his room to cry a little because he was so lucky to have so much love.

The bullying did not trouble him. He knew how he looked and what a figure of fun he cut as he loped about the district. He was the natural bait for frustrated and angry men, and there were a lot of those about. They had to take their anger out on someone and he being out of the ordinary was a handy scapegoat. He had a very sensitive awareness of life and he could see how, in the Alley and St George's Lane and Dimchurch Row and all about the Quays, he was different. Not just by his appearance but the fact that he lived with Rosaleen in a house with a reputation. Also he was better off, rich in fact, when compared with the other inhabitants.

No one teased or resented Maeve. No one ever bullied her unless she was defending Fergal. No one took it out on her that she was better dressed and better fed. She was too pretty; her disposition was too sunny, her charm too beguiling. She danced through life with a gaiety that was contagious. Everyone loved her. Not so Fergal. He attracted violence; he attracted prejudice. So she went everywhere with him when she could, and from her first awareness of him, loved him with all her heart.

'I can't take my eyes off you for a minute,' she would scold him, in fair imitation of the Widow. 'If I do, yer up to yer neck in trouble.' She would tut-tut and shake her head.

The district got used to the small pretty girl hand-in-hand with the hunchback. Breen Dubh dubbed them 'Beauty and the Beast'. They played near the tall ships in the Docks and wandered about the streets seeing a strange kind of life unfold. Their friends were Jangles and Boney Best, Breen Dubh and One-Eyed Willy. The Widow gave them what education they had. They learned of Ireland when she was young, when cities stood on green plains and the walls of castles were clothed in singing shields studded with rubies like carbuncles. They heard the grand stories of the early times when the hosts of Maeve saw their Queen crowned above them in her chariot, her apparel white, crimson and gold and the brazen-beaming blade of her great spear shone like a flame. They tried to imagine the Queen sitting on her white steed, all around her her chariot-guard and, as far as the eyes could see, in a shining tide, wave after glittering wave, flowed the countless armies of the Tain. It said in the books that the blackbirds sat on her chariot and fluted melodiously. She faced Cuchulain across the plains of Erin and the hunchback and his dainty companion, namesake of the great

Queen, listened spellbound to the tales of Ireland's glorious Celtic past.

Sometimes they went up the north side to Clontarf to dig for cockles in the sand. The tide, when out, left miles and miles of tan beach furrowed with wavy lines which they loved to explore. The north of the city was flat. You could see no mountains from its stretches of brown strand. Only the Hill of Howth raised its lovely breast to the intermittent sun.

Barefoot, Fergal with trouser legs rolled up, Maeve with skirts tucked into her waist-band, sank their feet in the saturated grey sand at the margin of the sea, allowed the dark water to freeze them. She held his hand. Always she held onto him. Often they did not speak for hours. Their thoughts intertwined without speech.

Until recently she had thought of him as a brother. He had always been at her side. Lately she had come to see clearly that for her he was much more. But she knew, in her wisdom, that he would have to be persuaded of this fact. He saw her as a goddess and he had chosen for himself, without rancour, the role of servant.

He was never servile. To serve, to Fergal, meant to care for, to tend, to nurture. He felt he was her caretaker until the Prince came along. She would have somehow to convince him that he *was* her Prince, that she, like Beauty had fallen in love with worth, that his true goodness was what had seduced her.

'Look, Maeve, look. Across the sands galloped the steeds of another era. Warriors. Men following your great ancestor, Queen Maeve. Ah, they would come over the world to pledge their fealty to their milk-white Queen. They would be willing to die for her. And so would I.'

She would laugh at his ardour, but gently, for she would never hurt him.

Once they went to the Park and heard a band play on a summer's day. Ladies moved about like bells in silks and bright colours. They wore shoes and carried parasols, and Maeve stared at them, trying to grasp the fact that there was a world out there quite unlike hers. The ladies wore bonnets and their skin was clear and their teeth were white and even and strong. They smelled like flowers when they pased and listened to the music and smiled gently and spoke softly. Maeve's head was full of questions after that and she persuaded Fergal to venture further and further from the Alley. They discovered the beautiful University in College Green. They found in Grafton Street and Dawson Street shirt-makers and furriers, jewellers and dress-shops, fabrics from all parts of the world. They dodged the wheels of the carriages and avoided the horse manure, the gentlemen on horseback and the beggars, and, scuttling up and down, pressed their noses to the glass fronts. They ran when the owners, aggravated by the marks they left with their grubby fingers on the shining shop-fronts, came out brandishing a fist or shouting. They found the sun in the green squares and the strands and lifted their faces towards it gratefully.

Maeve reached conclusions she shared only with Fergal. She loved the Widow and adored Rosaleen and thought her the most beautiful woman in the world.

When the scolding was over and Fergal had been bathed and bandaged they all had a cup of tea in front of the kitchen fire. Suzette's legs were bare under her petticoat and they became mottled red and brown with her toasting them too near the flames.

'It's as well ye gave up the business Suzette. No man would look at ye, the mess yer in, ye slovenly creature,' the Widow said.

Suzette smiled, not one whit perturbed, and Rosaleen said, 'Hush,' and looked warningly at Maeve.

'Oh Rosa, why? Why do you always say hush? Just when things are getting interesting?' Maeve inquired. She knew perfectly well that her house had been called Lizzie Brannagan's and had been a house of ill-repute, though she was not exactly sure what that meant, nor did she care.

The Widow had told Maeve of her past. It was a slightly romanticized version of the truth. 'Yer Da was a patriot. He died for his country, so he did, on a dark night at sea gettin' the guns fer the Fenians with Redmond Rafferty. But ye must never say. It's a secret. He's buried above in Glasnevin wid yer Mam.'

This tallied with what Red Rafferty told her. 'Ah Maeve, me darling, he gave his life for Ireland. He was with me and he died a hero's death in a stormy sea getting the guns for Erin's freedom.'

Her mother was more difficult. The Widow said, 'She died of a broken heart, *alanna*,' and Rosaleen cried a little and wiped a tear away, 'She was a poor sick woman, Maeve. She had no strength. God, this place is hard on the poor.'

Together, Maeve and Fergal asked again and again about Fergal but no one would tell them about his past.

'You know about your Mam and Da,' he said to Maeve. 'Yer lucky. All the Widow'll tell me is she found me abandoned. I don't believe her. Not because I don't think that could be true — I can't imagine anyone wanting to keep me when they saw how misshapen my shoulder was.'

There was no self-pity in his voice. He sounded matter-of-fact, and Maeve knew it to be his unemotional opinion. She hugged him and kissed his cheek.

'Oh, don't say that, Ferg.'

'It's all right really, Maeve, really. But the Widow is lying when she tells me that. I always know when she is. I wonder why she is afraid to tell me the truth?'

'Well, ask her.'

'I do and she denies it. But one day I'll find out. One day she'll tell me. Besides, I remember things. I remember being in a high tower. You could see all the countryside from it. All laid out below. It was magical. Fields and the mountains. It's like a dream. The Widow says it is. But I don't think so, Maeve. It is too clear. I remember once a golden-haired lady came. No, there were two, I think. One cried and the Widow got angry. The golden lady said she would come again. But she never did. Then we left there. It was frightening. It was dark and there were men who were wounded. One was bleeding. When I remind her she gets angry and says I make it up, but I don't, Maeve. Really I don't.'

Maeve looked at him tenderly. 'I know you, Fergal. I know you wouldn't. One day you'll find out.'

He had dreams, though, as well as the memories. Dreams of shining vistas he had seen from the window in that high tower he remembered. He did not tell Rosaleen or the Widow, but he told Maeve. The others would not take him seriously if he told them that he wanted some day to go there, to that magic place. They did not listen to what he said. They nodded their heads at him when he told them his ideas but he knew they did not hear. They were not being unkind. He did the same himself. He often watched Maeve as she spoke, not listening to a word she was saying, watching the expressions play across her face, the shadowed curve of her eyelids, the curtain of her lashes veiling her jewel-green eyes. He forgot everything she was trying to tell him when she sat resting her head against a chair and her hair spread out cloudy copper-gold in the lamplight. She was beautiful to look at, lovely to atch, her movements relaxed and graceful. How could he concentrate on what she was saying?

She listened to him. She understood him. 'I want some day to go to the country, Maeve. To the land. Can you imagine what the world must have been like before there were cities? Before people clustered together in a muddle and created all this dirt and filth? Can you imagine fields and meadows, valleys and rivers? All around you? Oh Maeve, I think I would die of happiness.' He looked at her with shining eyes.

We could go there, Fergal,' she said softly.

'Someday,' he said. 'Someday.'

Maeve listened to his voice. She loved the sound of it as she loved everything about him. But most of all she loved what he said. There was poetry in his mind and beauty in his thoughts. 'There are places, Maeve. I've read it all. Nooks and crannies of Ireland would take your breath away. Where the fallow doe calls to her fawn in the waist-high grass and the red kite nests in the beeches. I read that the dragon-fly leaves a blue trail in the green water and the red squirrel buries its nuts and the jay looks for berries in the autumn. Here in the city there is nothing to mark the changes of the seasons. Oh I long, Maeve, to see those things.' And sometimes when his spirits were low he would say, 'Perhaps it is all a dream. Perhaps there is no such place. Perhaps there is only desolation.'

Maeve would take his hand and smile at him. 'An' all the books are lies? Ah no. We'll go someday, Ferg. Someday we'll go.'

And together they would stand hand in hand at the window and look out over the black and rotting rooftops of the Alley.

When Red Rafferty came they had to pretend he wasn't there. It was very exciting. Maeve liked secrets and she loved Red. She thought him handsome and elegant. She liked the feel of his cambric shirt and his smiling blue eyes and white teeth. Red was for her a King. 'The Ard-Ri,' she told him. 'You are the Ard-Ri, like Cormac Mac Airt.' And Rosaleen let fall the vase she held, and that was curious, for she was sure-handed and never broke anything.

'Flossie McMahon is goin' te kill herself some night an' she in the drink,' Widow Boann said now, shaking her head.

Suzette nodded. 'She'll be on the blanket soon. She'll be confined, so she will.'

Rosaleen smiled. 'Well, an' who's to blame her wi' the life she has, God help her? Himself beats her an' the children are thieves. Who's to blame them for that? But Rats ... that's another thing. A meaner specimen would be hard to find.'

Maeve signalled to Fergal and they left the three women deep in gossip. They went to her room. Maeve threw herself on the bed. She gave Fergal a hand-mirror Rosaleen had given her on her thirteenth birthday.

'Sit on that stool, Ferg. Now hold it so ... yes. "Mirror, Mirror in Fergal's hand, who's the prettiest in the land?"'

'Oh Maeve. That's the part of the Wicked Queen,' Fergal said. 'You'd be Snow White, an' not her.'

Maeve looked thoughtful. 'I don't know. I don't want to be too good. My mother was, and she died, That's life, Fergal. Not fairy tales. The Queens of Ireland were not feeble. If they wanted something, they went after it. I think I would never be nasty to anyone, but I think, too, that if I don't try to get what I want no one will give it to me.'

'I don't know, Maeve.'

'Oh you're hopeless, Ferg. You get walked on. You let people beat you and revile you and you don't do a thing. I think it's daft myself.'

'I can't, Maeve. I just can't. Something stops me.'

'The voice of God within you,' Maeve said wryly, 'That's what Father Flynn said when I told him. He said people like you are close to God.' She gently touched his cheek, stroking it as one would stroke a cat. 'But I'm not like that, Ferg. I'm closer to the devil, I sometimes think.'

The room was warm and the fire cast shadows on the walls and ceiling.

'Do you think I'm pretty, Fergal?'

'Oh Maeve. You are more beautiful than the stars, more graceful than the trees,' he replied softly.

'Fergal. Fergal, never leave me. Never.'

She put her arms around him, clinging to him and he sat very still in her embrace. Eventually he stood up and limped to the door. His side hurt him where he had been kicked but not as much as his heart, which ached within him.

'Ah Maeve. You'll leave me long, long before I leave you,' he said sadly and left her alone.

Chapter

64

ROSALEEN had let the custom die out in Lizzie Brannagan's. She had money now. She had saved enough for their wants and she was frugal. She did not fancy the business she found herself running. It was not on moral grounds; but Dark Rosaleen had never been any man's plaything and she hated to see the whining, whimpering girls subject themselves to the degradation necessary in their profession. It made her feel unclean and she remembered how Lizzie died and knew the price was disproportionate to the fragile security it gave. She knew too that the alternative was often Sylvie Donahue's fate, and that in fact she sometimes protected girls of her sort; ignorant through no fault of their own, stupid and desperate. Yet she felt ill-at-ease in the 'house of Lust', as Canon Connolly called it from the pulpit in the Cathedral and while she had little time for his sort her lack of enthusiasm and the fact of the children in the house had frightened away both the buyers of flesh and the sellers. 'The heart has gone out of Lizzie Brannagan's,' they said, and went elsewhere. So she had gradually closed the brothel. A new one had opened in St George's Lane and most of the girls had drifted over there. Rosaleen never put any of the girls out of the house. They could stay as long as they liked, and Rosie and Batty and Suzette chose to remain forever. Suzette appointed herself as cook, a job she excelled in and at which none of the others had any talent, least of all Rosaleen.

The gilt chipped, the scarlet plush developed bald patches and the frescoes filmed over with age and dust and became blurred and indistinct. The house echoed with the sound of children's laughter and the curtains were looped back to let in the light. Maeve and Fergal grew up privileged in a world of dirt and poverty. There was always plenty of food and warm clothes, and, wonder of wonders, shoes and boots to wear. No one else in Doone Alley had shoes. Not proper ones, bought new.

Rosaleen had added significantly to the pile of coins Lizzie had left her, and although they lived modestly Rosaleen still had enough in the rose-patterned chamber-pot to ensure that for some time ahead they would not want. They did not have enough to escape from the Alley altogether but enough to ensure that they were moderately comfortable. 'Until the children have grown,' she told herself, 'Fergal and Maeve'. Her greatest consolation was the presence of Fergal and Maeve. 'And Cormac.' She had not seen her son since that day long ago in the woods. She would stay put until she and Red resolved things. She felt she was waiting, for what she was not sure. Each time he came home, Rosaleen, weak with gratitude at his safe return, forgot her promises to herself to ask him how they meant to spend the rest of their lives. Was hers to be spent waiting for him? Yet she knew too that that was unfair. He did not ask her to wait. If he realized how anxious she was he would be shocked. Each time she awakened to find herself alone she determined to sort things out between them, although what exactly she could resolve she did not know. When he did return she was so overjoyed to see him that she forgot.

Then one night in the golden lamplight he lay by her, her dark head on his shoulder, and he asked her to marry him. 'I love you, Rosaleen, and I want you to be my wife.'

She was nonplussed, he had taken her breath away, yet she found herself rejecting the idea.

'An' why would that be necessary? We are together all the time you have. I'm gypsy. Never forget that, Red. I don't want to possess you, to tie you down. Or be possessed and tied down. Besides, where would we marry? Who would marry us? Certainly no priest would. I have no name. You're a wanted man. Can ye see the banns? And the rush to the Constabulary for the reward? Sure, you'd never get up the aisle an' I'd be a widow or at best a prison-wife. Ach no. Leave it as it is. We're easy together.' And she realized it was true.

'Easy, woman? We're aflame. There's passion in us that will never be quenched.'

She felt better after that and she was not sure why. Then

another worry entered her life which made nonsense of all she had said to Red about not wanting to possess him. Craw Kilty told her that Sophie was in Paris. So now not only did she fear for his safety, but she became anxious lest Sophie might regain her hold on his heart. Castigating herself for a fool, for she really believed that she trusted Red and wanted him to be free, she tossed and turned when he was away and could not sleep.

Red told her nothing of Fabrice's return and his reunion with his Maman, of the family settling into the chateau and their house in Paris. It never occurred to him to do so. He was delighted that the de Beauvillande family were so happy. Sophie was expecting again and she bloomed. He went to see them and to see Armand, though more and more, as he said to Sophie, he felt he should leave the boy to the de Beauvillandes.

'For he does not know who I am. I am a stranger that comes to call. I find that painful. I do not wish him to query my place in the scheme of things. I want him secure and untroubled.'

Sophie was grateful, always solicitous of his happiness; she seemed to him now like a loving sister who is too absorbed in her own life to give much thought to her brother.

But he did not tell Rosaleen this. She did not know what the position was and she worried. He understood her concern when he was on business for the Cause, when he slipped in and out like a shadow and strange men came to No. 1 and there were secret meetings where she was not welcome.

'I do not want to involve you in this,' he would say. 'It's too dangerous.'

When he was there with her, in her arms, she knew then that he loved her. Every breath they breathed, every beat of their hearts, every time he kissed her and held her she knew the depth of his love. Then she was content. Then she was at peace.

But sometimes in the cold light of dawn, when Red was not at her side and when her resistance was low, she felt trapped, bound by her love to this dark forsaken spot. Doone Alley. She longed to be able to walk the road once more and sample again the free delights of the natural world. Then, sad and sighing, she turned her face to the window and tried to catch a glimpse of the moon.

Rosaleen heard the Minstrel was singing his way across Ireland. In Cahirciveen, Craw Kilty told her, watching her sideways, a malicious gleam in her eye, a young lady had gone mad for him. She had kept him with her all the summer long, decking his hair with flowers and kissing his lips, until her father found out and threatened to kill them both. Rosaleen was jealous, and angry with herself for being so.

'Ah, 'twill all come right in the end,' Craw Kilty said, smiling to herself as she snapped off a thread with her teeth.

Chapter

65

TWO years later when Mary Chappell from No. 4 came to the Widow in Lizzie Brannagan's, it was the first time anyone from the Alley had done such a thing. No one ever visited No. 1 Doone Alley. Originally the house, being a brothel, was shunned, and then the habit was hard to break. Besides, Rosaleen gave them little encouragement. Totally absorbed with the children and in her love affair with Red, she kept her distance from her neighbours. In any event, Doone Alley was not conducive to visiting.

Mary Chappell came because she was frightened and she did not know where else to go. The Widow was looked up to and respected by everyone. People turned naturally to her in a crisis. When little Alice Chappell had complained that she ached all over and her head hurt and when Mary, feeling her forehead, found it burning, she decided her only hope was to ask the Widow's advice. Naturally the Chappell's had no money. Michael Chappell begged in Sackville Street, his cap in his hand, swallowing his pride. There was not much work on the docks now and he had to earn a few pennies for food in the only way left to him.

The Widow went to the room on the ground floor of No. 4, one of the tenements in the cul-de-sac. It was in a foul state; the floor was bare, the broken windows covered with brown paper, the piles of rags the family lay on unquestionably dirty. There were eight living in that room. There was no toilet, no water — both of which were only available outside.

'I know it's a mess, Widow.' Mary Chappell's eyes took in the room as it must look to the Widow. 'There's nuthin' I can do.' Her face looked indescribably tired. 'Michael tries his best, but it's hopeless, hopeless. Dear God, life's not worth a straw here, but ye have to try, don't ye?'

The Widow nodded and bent over the children. She put her shawl across her nose and looked at the sick child on the rags. She was surrounded by five other children who stared at her unblinking with huge eyes set in small pinched faces.

She knew what it was right away. There was no mistaking the appalling signs of the disease. The child's chest had had a rash of tiny pink spots which had faded, and she was in a coma. She was muttering to herself, reaching out for something that was not there, plucking feebly at the rags that covered her. The Widow clicked her tongue. She had seen it before during the Great Famine. It came, she thought, from contaminated food or water and she was pretty sure that here it was the water. If the inmates of Doone Alley were not all to succumb to the disease, then they would have to stop drinking the water from the pump outside in the courtyard. But how could they do that when there was no alternative? She shook her head and asked if she could see the other children's chests. Three of them bore the tell-tale decoration of a group of tiny, almost invisible, little pink spots.

Mary Chappell looked at her with scared eyes. 'What is it, Widow?' she asked fearfully. 'Oh Janey, what is it? I'm that worried,' she added.

'Mrs Chappell, who else lives here?' the Widow asked.

'Insiden the house, ye mean?'

The Widow nodded. 'It's contagious, Mrs Chappell. Very contagious. I ought to see . . .'

Mary Chappell's face crumbled. Tears rolled down her face. 'It's bad then?' she said. The Widow nodded. 'Ah. God what can I do? I've not the strength.'

'We'll help you. But I must go to the others in the house.'

'I don't think they'll welcome you. The McMahons are above and Danny Muldoon and his son and the O'Briens and the Shaughnessys above that again.' She was gazing at her children, a despairing expression on her face, as she stood in the middle of the room, her shoulders drooping, one hand plucking her skirt.

The Widow left her there. The corridor was dark and dank and the stairs looked very unsound. The Widow doubted they

394

could sustain her weight. Still, if Flossie McMahon managed it home each night, then they were probably stronger than they looked.

She went up to the next landing and opened the door in front of her. Flossie was out but her husband sat in front of an empty fireplace in a rocking chair. It creaked as it swung back and forth, back and forth. It was the only piece of furniture in the room. A group of small children lay like a litter of puppies on the floor under a torn grey blanket. They looked very ill indeed to the Widow's sharp glance.

Nick McMahon had a big ugly head and she could see at once where Rats inherited his weasel eyes and pointed nose from.

'What ye bloody want?'

'I came to see the children, Mr McMahon.'

'An' who assed ye? Tell me that?'

'The Chappells downstairs are very sick, Mr McMahon. It's contagious, so it is. I'm trying' te see how far it's spread.'

'Well, ye won't do it here. Get out or I'll throw ye down the stairs meself.'

The Widow put her hands on her hips. 'It'll be as well if ye let me look, Mister,' she said firmly, standing her ground. 'If ye don't, I'll inform the authorities an' they'll put ye out on the street for not co-operatin'. How'll Flossie like that?'

It was all nonsense. The authorities couldn't care less, she knew. But he didn't know that and a more faint-hearted gormless man than Nick McMahon would be hard to find.

She was right in her estimation. He backed down before her firm purpose and watched suspicously as she examined the children. They were all infected. She thought of Rats and his beating up of Fergal and her heart sank within her.

She left the McMahons, checked up on the Shaughnessys, a childless couple, she found, but the old grandmother who lived with them was extremely ill. The O'Briens, a widow and her seven children, were all infected. Danny Muldoon and his son were out. Her spirits drooped and she was overwhelmed by a wave of disgust and horror at the conditions she found herself in. She had never had much but she took cleanliness and the basic amenities of a roof over one's head and enough bread to live on for granted. The squalor of Doone Alley brought home to her for the first time how rich her life had been. She understood now the rage Red Rafferty felt at the oppression of the people, living in terrible poverty, without hope.

She sighed and made her way downstairs again. She looked in on Mary Chappell who stood exactly as she had left her.

'I'll be back in a tick, Mrs Chappell,' she called, but the woman stood as if turned to stone and did not seem to hear.

The Widow rushed back to No. 1. 'Rosaleen, Rosaleen,' she shouted and Maeve and Fergal came out on the landing from their rooms, for she sounded hysterical.

'What is it, Widow? What on earth's the matter?'

Rosaleen appeared and stopped dead in her tracks when she saw the state the Widow was in. Renowned for her calm in the face of any crisis, they were taken aback at the sight of her standing in the hall, dishevelled and out of breath.

'It's the sickness. The sickness. The Chappells are riddled with it and the McMahons and all the families in No. 4. And if they are, there are others too. Oh Rosaleen, it's a killer. Send Fergal and Maeve from here, I beg you. And go yourself. It's like a forest fire, it destroys everything in its path. So get them outa here, woman, as fast as you can.'

Rosaleen came down the stairs. 'Calm yourself, Widow, and let's talk before we jump to any hasty conclusions.'

But the Widow was distraught, and it was only when they got her into the kitchen and Suzette brought her a cup of tea that some semblance of the Widow's usual stoicism was restored.

'Now tell me what causes this illness?' Rosaleen asked.

'Well, it's thought to be contaminated water an' that well out there and its tap. God knows, are dirty, filthy. I always think there's sewage mixed up in it somewhere. It's been gettin' worse.'

'Then they must use our water,' Rosaleen said decidedly. 'From the taps. We'll pass buckets of it out to them ... the stricken families, that is.'

The Widow nodded. 'That is good,' she said, 'as far as it goes. But I'm afraid everyone will have to have it.'

'But Widow, aren't ye being a bit ahead of yerself? It's only the families in No. 4 so far.'

'It will spread, *acushla*. You mark my words. You send the children away.'

'The children can stay here. They have not drunk the water from the well. We won't let them, and we'll stop them associating with anyone in the Alley,' Rosaleen said, and added, 'Where in God's name could I send them anyway, Widow?'

'I wish Red were here to help us,' the Widow said feebly. 'It's goin' to be the bejasus of a time.'

'Well, I'm very glad he is not. It wouldn't do at all, for poor Red would catch it at once. You know how big strong men go first. You know it's true, Widow.'

The Widow bestirred herself. 'Will ye send them to Craw Kilty, then?' she pleaded. 'Please? An' anythin' happened to them I couldn't bear it.'

'Will ye shut yer gob, woman?' Rosaleen said harshly. 'I can't do that an' you know why. Now whist an' let us work out a plan.' She thought a moment. 'I'll keep the young ones in.'

'We're not children, Rosaleen. I'm seventeen and Fergal is ...' Maeve rolled her eyes and the Widow said automatically, 'Twenty. That's what he is. Twenty.'

'If you found me, how do you know for certain?' Fergal said.

The Widow looked at him sharply. 'I guessed,' she said. 'It's easy to tell wi' a little bairn. Now whist, you two.'

'They can stay indoors with me.' Rosaleen sounded pleased with her decision. 'We'll let the families have the water, them as wants it. For you'll find, Widow, as there are those who'll prefer the well even though they're told it's dangerous.'

The Widow had been gradually regaining her equilibrium. She nodded vigorously. 'Don't I know it.'

'Now I don't know about you, Widow, but I don't feel I can sit here an' do nothing. I never was one for that. So, I'm sorry children, up to your rooms and not out of them till we say. Suzette will bring you food and give you nothing that isn't boiled. Maybe it'll all be over in a day or two, for the Widow may yet be wrong.'

But the Widow was not wrong. The disease spread like wildfire. In the twenty houses around the Alley lived approximately a hundred people. At least fifty were ill by the week's end. Rosaleen sent for Dr Davies and together the three of them worked around the clock. The good doctor got in touch with the authorities and promises were made, pledges were given, some even in writing, but both parties knew it was all a sham. The inhabitants of Doone Alley were on their own in their extremity. The doctor did what he could and it was not much. The contamination was ingrained; to counteract it was well-nigh impossible. Some of the people, as the Widow had predicted, refused to break the habit of a lifetime and continued to use the tap in the courtyard.

The Widow and Rosaleen were on their feet morning, noon, and night. They bathed the fever victims helped mothers with their children and, when the children died, and little Alice Chappell went first, swiftly followed by all her brothers and sisters one after the other, they helped the husbands with the wives. Mothers seemed to be able to hold the disease at bay until their children died, then, relieved of the responsibility, they succumbed to the disease and usually followed their offspring to the grave. Husbands fared no better, in fact, if anything, having caught the illness, they perished more swiftly. Rosaleen had been right. Big frames, badly nourished, put up little resistance. Mary Chappell helped them to nurse the others in the Alley before she too became ill, and sadly weakened, not least by her children's deaths, died within days.

The state of the hovels shocked Rosaleen. In all the years she had lived there she had never penetrated any of the homes before. The dirt, the squalor, was distressing; the people heart-breaking in their tattered dignity.

'Forgive us, missus,' Maisie Agnew said. 'Please forgive us, but Peadar has been out of work these six months an' we had to sell the bed an' the table. But have a cup o' tea.'

Rosaleen knew the small measure of tea was all the Agnews had, yet they were ready to share. Somehow Rosaleen had to find ways of refusing this kind of touching offering and not offend.

They were so grateful to her even when the children died, and usually they did. Some, though did recover and Rosaleen made broth and, holding them propped up in her arm, fed them.

The Widow remonstrated with her but to no avail. 'Ye'll catch it, Rosaleen, for God's sake think of yerself.'

The tragedy was at its height when it came to burial time. Most of the casualties were whisked away by the city's Sanitation Company and dumped in pauper's graves. Mary Chappell had seen all her little ones treated thus and Rosaleen found it difficult to look into Mr Chappell's defeated face, eyes swollen and red from weeping. When Mary died, he disappeared and was never seen again in those parts.

The people had a horror of a pauper's grave. Some of them

had gone without food in order to save enough for a proper funeral, but whereas they could just about manage one, now whole families were being buried by a survivor. It was impossible to afford funerals for them all.

The fever raged on. It rampaged around the Alley and took Rats McMahon and his brothers and their father. Flossie survived. Her neighbours said that she was immunized by the alcohol that flowed through her veins.

'Boney Best snuffed it tonight,' the Widow told an exhausted Rosaleen one evening a fortnight later. They had filled two tubs in front of the kitchen fire with hot water. They had put eucalyptus leaves in it. They wearily stripped off their clothes and put them into a huge urn full of boiling water that stood by the stove. Every night they scalded every stitch they wore. Then they stepped into their steaming baths, drawing in their breath at the heat, scrubbing themselves with carbolic. They settled down as usual for a chat.

Rosaleen was thinking how tired the Widow looked and how slow her movements had bcome when the Widow said again, 'Boney Best snuffed it tonight.'

'Poor old fellow. Poor old man. Though who'll clear out the mess he's left behind, God alone knows. I know I'd hate to make a start on the piles of vermin-ridden rubbish he has in that room of his.'

There was silence when Rosaleen finished speaking. It was a very pregnant silence and Rosaleen could almost feel the atmosphere in the room, an atmosphere full of the shock of discovery. Rosaleen was instantly alert. She jumped out of the bath, scattering water hither and yon and pulling a towel about her as she ran to the Widow.

'What is it?' she asked.

The Widow's face was ghastly. 'Get away from me,' she screamed at Rosaleen who took a few steps backwards. Then she said softly, 'Get away. I've got it, Rosaleen. God help us, I've got it.' She stood up shakily and would have fallen only that Rosaleen caught her arm and helped her. The Widow tried to get away but she was weak and Rosaleen was strong.

'You're just tired, Widow. You've worked like a labourer since the start of this an' now yer poor old body's given out, that's all.'

'No, girl, no. I thought like you did an' the pains in me head and body an' I been coughing and the fever coulda been lack of sleep. It's funny how you believe it'll never get you. But I have the rash, *alanna*. An' now if ye love me ye'll leave me be in my room. For I'd die easy in my bed knowin' ye were all right. Not else.'

Rosaleen wrapped the towel round the Widow. 'An' now, old friend, what kind of woman d'ye think I am that would leave ye to be sick alone? An' who's talking of dying? Now up ye go to yer room an' I'll look after ye.'

At that moment Maisy Cluny came knocking at the door for some clean water, for her Jake was tossing in the fever she said, and didn't know night from day and kept searching the bed for something.

'An' I don't know what it is, missus, indeedn' I don't, for wouldn't I give it him if I did?'

The Widow sighed. 'It's a sign of the illness,' she said.

The whole burden of Doone Alley now fell on Rosaleen's shoulders. Death seemed in a hurry; the harvest was good for he was not selective.

Maeve and Fergal, isolated from the Alley and the other occupants of No. 1, crept in and out of each other's rooms. They lived in their own dream world, sufficient to each other, content in each other's company.

They spoke mainly about the myths of Erin, the history of the land; tales told to them by Red and Rosaleen. But most of all they talked of the country, that strange seductive place where they had never been.

They poured over pictures in the books Rosaleen had given them, pictures of lanes like the aisle in the cathedral, vaulted but green, so much green, a density of green they could not envisage. It was created, this depth of green, by the trees that formed the arch, their branches interlacing above. They wondered what it would be like to walk beneath the trees in the cool emerald world of leaves. They looked fascinated at the frozen print of a brook rushing and curling over blue-veined stones, and ached to know what it was like in motion. They stared at the pictures of the mountains laced with tiny pathways that disappeared over the horizon veiled in a misty mauve haze.

'Where does it lead, I wonder?' Fergal asked.

Maeve stared at the picture, bewitched. 'Into the land of Tir na nOige, mebbe,' she said dreamily. 'Oh think of being there,

Ferg. Just us two in that magic place. We could find out then what lies behind each hill and dale. D'ye know, Fergal, Red told me they have meetin's there. Men creepin' in the dark to the secret caves, plottin' an' plannin' and plannin'.' Her eyes were huge as she thought about the excitement of it, and Fergal thought her eyes were the colour of the tree-bordered lanes in the pictures. Then she would smile at him and he would return her smile.

She saw him always at her side. She knew he would protect her. He would walk through the beautiful countryside and care for her. She would always be safe with him. She had not been frightened all through the epidemic, in isolation with Fergal. She knew terrifying things were happening outside, that disease and death had come to stalk the Alley. She had heard through the open window the weeping and wailing outside; heard the screams of agony as people died, heard the sobbing of the bereft, the hopeless sounds of women mourning unbearable loss. She had glimpsed Rosaleen and the Widow and their drawn exhausted faces were scary.

But she had felt secure with Fergal. As long as he was with her nothing bad could happen to her. She clung to him like a vine to a frame and she often fell asleep with her head on his knee. 'Oh Fergal, I love you so,' she would whisper sleepily and he would leave off piping his flute and gaze unseeing out of the window over the rooftops.

His head was full of the knowledge of books. He knew the prince came to take the beautiful maiden away and marry her, or just be with her and have her love. Like Rosaleen and Red. Red Rafferty was exactly what a prince should be. He was courageous. He fought his enemies, did not avoid them as Fergal did. And, above all, he was handsome, tall and graceful. That was what a prince should be. Perhaps younger, for Maeve.

Fergal knew what he looked like. Even the Beast in the fairy tale changed into a handsome prince, or Beauty could not suitably have married him. It was, Fergal felt, against the laws of nature. Maeve would meet someone like Red. She said she loved him but she did not expect a prince to come. Fergal knew that one day a wonderful hero would come out of the West and when she saw him she would forget all about Fergal. One day someone would ride up to her door and claim her. He too would be brave and tall and graceful. Fergal knew then his heart would break. But it would be the right thing. He loved Maeve with all his heart and soul. He loved her more than he loved life. But he could never claim her. He was too misshapen and ugly he thought. He put his flute to his lips and played a melancholy tune that the Minstrel had taught him many moons ago. It was full of the lilting sadness that obsessed his soul whenever he thought of losing Maeve.

One evening when they had fallen asleep, arms intertwined, her head on his breast, Fergal was pulled out of his deep slumber by the urgent sound of calling. He listened, then lifted Maeve's head gently to slip out without disturbing her, but she felt him leave her and became instantly awake.

'What is it?' she whispered.

'Shush. Listen.'

They both listened and, sure enough, heard it again.

'Fergal. Fergal.'

'It's the Widow. She wants me. Come on.'

They knew the Widow was very ill. Suzette said she was dying. When they got to her door she called out, 'Don't come in. I'll not have ye come in.' So they stood at the open door. They could not see her; she was in pitch darkness. The candles caught her hands in their light. The hands were gnarled as oak branches and they plucked the counterpane but the rest of her remained in the shadow.

'I want to tell ye somethin' Fergal *alanna*.' Her voice sounded frail, not at all her usual commanding tone, and this frightened them, more than the shadows, more than the plucking fingers. Maeve's hand groped for Fergal's, found it and held it tight.

'I know this illness, children. I know the next phase. I've nursed enough to know what happens now. I'll go into a coma and then I won't be in my right mind at all until either I get better or pass away entirely.'

Maeve choked back a sob. 'Ah, don't say that Widow. Please don't say that.'

'An' why not? Isn't it the truth? An' why should ye be sorry for me? Didn't I have the grand life, an' always with a child I loved? Wasn't that wonderful?' She coughed and was silent. All they were aware of were the spot-lit hands. 'Ah, but don't let me wear myself out. Talkin' like this. Rosaleen is out. I don't want her to know, but I couldn't die peaceful without tellin' Fergal the facts.'

Fergal felt a surge of excitement flow through his veins. At last he was to know the truth.

'There is a castle. Usher Castle. The Earl of Usher owns it. You, Fergal, are the eldest son, the only true heir.' Fergal let his breath out. He had been right all along. It was not a dream. The tower, the vistas, meadows and mountains, the golden-haired ladies, the flight that still brought him nightmares, all, all was real. He felt Maeve squeeze his hand.

The Widow struggled on. 'Lord Usher is your father. His brother had a son who is now the heir, but you are the legitimate one. He disowned you, your father did, for the way you were born with a hump on your back. He told me to give you to the orphanage. Ach, child, I hate to tell you cruelly like this, but it's a cruel story and there is no other way to tell it. But I protected you from that, from the Institution. I loved you more than you'll ever know. What you do with this information is your business. You may do nothing, ye may do everthing. What I've heard from Usher, your father may need you. I'm very weak now. It took all me strength ... Leave me now. I loved you, remember that.'

Her hands had become still and her voice softened and she began to ramble. Maeve stood outside the door holding Fergal's hand. Everything went very quiet and all she could hear was the Widow's mumblings. She put her arms around Fergal and laid her cheek on his.

Chapter

66

JAMES sat looking at Cormac who paced the small study restlessly. A fire burned in the grate and James leaned down to scratch Angel's ear, but it was force of habit for the dog was not there. Angel had died and though her offspring bounded about the castle none of the younger dogs had taken her place in his heart.

'Sit down, Cormac, for heaven's sake,' he said gruffly. 'How can I talk to you when you will not be still?'

'But Father, you never listen.'

'I'm listening. Now say what you have to say, then leave me in peace.'

Cormac looked at his father and took a deep breath. 'I want to go to America,' he said.

For a moment there was silence in James' study. Then James looked up.

'I beg your pardon?' he said incredulously. 'I don't think I heard aright.'

'You did father. You heard exactly what I said. I want to go to America.'

James banged his fist on the arm of his chair. 'For Christ's sake, Cormac what kind of nonsense is this?' He looked at Cormac in irritated incomprehension. 'Why the hell do you want to go there?'

'I don't know, Father. I just know that I do. All the time I feel restless. It's something I don't understand. I want to go. To get out of this trap. I feel trapped here.'

'Trap? You think you are in a trap? You think of Usher as a trap?' James stared at Cormac in disbelief, as if he were a stranger. He was handsome, James thought dispassionately, even though his face was creased in exasperation. A soft wing of dark hair fell over his forehead and he pushed it back impatiently.

'I can't explain, Father, I really can't. All my life I've been told that this is all mine. I just don't think I can settle down here without seeing somewhere else first.'

'Dear Lord, Cormac, I've been everywhere. Travelled east, west, north, south. It's all the same really. There's nowhere in the world like Usher. I can tell you that.'

'I don't want to be *told*. I want to find out.'

'Good God, Cormac, you are the next Knight of Usher. You will be in a year or two. I'll hand it over to you. This is your home.' James did not know what more to say. He looked again at Cormac as if he were seeing him for the first time. The good-looking face was restless, like an animal at bay. His eyes glanced constantly around as if looking for a way out. It was a habit James had notied in Cormac before, but he had never associated it with a desire actually to escape.

James shook his head. 'I don't understand you. You leave me speechless.' And sad, he thought. I wonder if you know what you are doing to me? You are making my whole life meaningless.

'I simply want to go,' Cormac said. 'To America. It's a big place. Wide. There's space there. I want to go there, Father. Will you give me the money?'

James stared at the boy. 'You are like your mother,' he said. 'No. No, Cormac. I will not give you the money.'

'Please, Father. It's my sanity. I feel I'll burst if I cannot escape.' Cormac sounded desperate.

James sighed. There was that word again. Escape. As if he was in a cage.

'I'm sorry. But I cannot allow you to go. You simply have to face up to your responsibilities. As I did. I don't want to discuss it any more. You may go.'

Cormac slammed the door behind him. James' body twitched as the sound of it shattered the silence.

He had said that by mistake; that Cormac was so like his mother. Cormac thought he meant Dolly and would not understand. But James remembered the girl who stood in the moonlight at the kitchen door, her babe in her arms. And the same woman in black in the Great Hall, a coffin at her feet. She stood always on the balls of her feet as if she would take flight at any moment. He had noticed that without being aware of it. Cormac had that habit too. They both had thick dark hair and wild blue eyes and a smile that lit up the room.

What did Fergal look like now? The thought came unbidden. James squirmed. He did not like to think about what he had done to Fergal.

He sat sunk in gloom. 'Oh Dolly, Dolly, why did you leave me?' he whispered. 'I need you, my darling. So much. I think I have made a terrible mistake.' He buried his face in his hands. He did not hear Cormac ride away from Usher.

Chapter

67

FERGAL did not know what to do with the information the Widow had given him. At first he and Maeve were too busy worrying about the severity of her illness, praying for her and helping Rosaleen. The plague had raged fiercely and now was over, leaving eighty bereft families. Widows, orphans and widowers picked themselves up wearily, broken-hearted, but with spirit and against insurmountable odds somehow carried on. Why, they did not know. They took a deep breath and went on. It was the Dublin tradition, after all. A bitter smile, a joke to cover a broken heart, and a determination to show *them* that they were not licked.

Breen Dubh had recovered. So had Milo Malloy at the 'Green Cock', but Milo's wife Maisie had slipped away very quickly and their children had put up no struggle at all.

The Widow Boann died. Rosaleen was far more upset than she had ever imagined she could be. Lizzie Brannagan's demise had shown her the face of death, had familiarized her with its horrors, its finality, had also given her a measure of acceptance. Creagh's death showed her the unfairness of the grim harvester who reaped whether the corn was ripe or no. She had had a strong premonition that the Widow was going to die but was surprised in the event. She felt a deep sense of loss. She realized for the first time how much she had relied on the Widow's strength and support, how much the Widow had given her in the way of company and companionship. Without saying too much she had always been there, encouraging, tactfully helping out, and Rosaleen felt her loss sorely.

She felt it even more so in the face of the Alley's attitude after the epidemic was over. They closed their doors, not rudely, not unkindly, but firmly, suggesting to her that she was not needed any more. She had held them in her arms while they wept, she had tended the bodies of their dead, she had nursed their children and now they had become politely formal, they had erected a barrier between them and her, and she felt doubly bereaved.

'They are proud,' Dr Davies told her. 'They took from you when they had no alternative. Now they would be beholden to you if they took more.'

'But that is silly. Surely there would be no harm to just visit? We shared so much together and somehow it's important, for it links me with the Widow. It makes her death more relevant. I simply wanted to give Shelagh O'Brien some comfort ...'

'It would have meant giving you tea and she has none to offer,' the doctor said. 'For her it would be a terrible loss of face. You must let them keep what dignity they imagine they have.'

She nodded. Life had to go on and it appeared soon as though the sickness had never been. The Alley was as dirty as ever, as foul as ever. New faces came. The City Authorities also came, and cleaned the well out and went away, promising more help. But it never arrived. Some of those who lived on the streets moved into the rooms vacated by the dead. The faces seemed interchangeable to Rosaleen, pinched, hungry, hopeless. It was depressing and she yearned for Red to come home to her. She longed for the comfort of his arms and she longed to laugh again. She was still young and beautiful and somewhere out there there were fields and trees, birds and flowers. Her soul shrank from her surroundings and she remembered the Minstrel's words. She belonged in that world. But she could not go, could not leave, even though Fergal and Maeve did not really need her any more. They were quite old enough to take care of themselves.

She was a prisoner in Doone Alley because she loved Red Rafferty. She could no more leave an' there was a chance of his return. Oh these homecomings. They made her life a beautiful thing. Waiting for him was nothing when he arrived. She forgot the lonely hours, the constant feeling of anxiety. He was home. Then it was the time for golden days and nights in bed, days of laughter and love.

Sometimes she thought of moving. She spoke of it to Red but

he explained how he might not be able to see so much of her then and that was unbearable to her. No. 1 was a place he and his friends could come. It was safe. The soldiers did not frequent the Alley, the Constabulary shunned it. It had many exits from her house, ways of escape. Also she knew it would be difficult to sell it. No one wanted a building situated in such a neighbourhood and with such a reputation.

She had heard tell of the brothel, very grand and fashionable, started by her old friend Rosie Moore. Lizzie Brannagan's had ceased to function now for so long that few customers ever came to the door nowadays. Those that did had to be turned away unfulfilled. But prospective buyers would not know that.

Spring came to Doone Alley. Not that you would know. There were no buds to see, for there were no trees. No flowers bloomed there and how the inhabitants knew it was spring was hard to tell. Mood perhaps. People felt the sweet warm breeze that blew from the river and a restlessness invaded their souls. The sap rose and the young ones, girls and boys, felt a yearning for something, anything. Emotions ran high, tempers flared, love affairs started most unsuitably and youngsters were threatened by their parents and the Canon. Sermons became severe, warning against sins of the flesh. Women with six or seven children became pregnant and husbands got drunk more often. There was no room for the poetry of spring in Doone Alley.

Maeve was drifting in a dream world that alarmed Rosaleen and as she had no idea of the cause, and at the time was too preoccupied with her own worries to pay much attention, she left her alone. She had not seen or heard from Red in weeks and she was very anxious.

Fergal gave Maeve a bunch of violets he found in Sackville Street. They must have fallen from a lady's lap and only two were crushed. Maeve kissed his cheek and thanked him sweetly. Her kiss was soft as the touch of a butterfly's wings. She curled her hand in his and pressed the damp velvety flowers to her face.

'Oh, they're beautiful, Fergal. So beautiful. I'll put them in a little vase.'

When he turned to look at her he saw tears on her cheeks.

'Oh Maeve, what is it?' he asked, alarmed. It was seldom she cried, a laugh or a song sat more easily on her lips. He pushed back the soft red curls from her forehead and wiped the tears from her cheeks. She was looking at him intently, very seriously for her. The tears trembled on her lashes and there was a tiny quiver around her soft coral-coloured lips.

'I love you, Fergal. I love you so much. You know that. I show you in a thousand little ways. You reveal your love for me a million times a day. What are we waiting for?'

Pain creased his brow and darkened his eyes. 'Don't talk like that, Maeve. Ye can't know what yer sayin'.'

'Oh but I do. I do. I've thought it out so well. But ye must ask. Ye must.' She pulled his sleeve anxiously.

'I'll never ask ye that. Ye deserve a prince. A prince ye'll get.'

'An' what would I do with a prince? You tell me.' Two bright spots of colour appeared on her cheeks. 'I don't want a prince, Fergal, I want you. It's all I ever wanted, all I've ever desired. What do I have to do to make you believe me?'

'There's nuthin' ye can do. Just wait for yer prince,' he said with conviction.

'Oh Fergal, ye'll drive me mad, so ye will, with yer talk of princes an' the like.'

'He'll come. You'll see.'

Chapter

68

HE did. With his charming smile, his devil-may-care grin, his polished boots and his impeccably tailored suit, his cloak flowing about him, sitting atop his great white stallion. He rode into the Alley one June night every inch a prince. He had enquired yet again for the 'Green Cock' and this time he had been directed correctly. He had every intention of finding Lizzie Brannagan's as well. His jaded palate required titillation, his boredom needed alleviation. He remembered Old Gentleman's expression when he told him of the place.

'Nights of passion you'll have there, m'boy. You'll learn a trick or two there. Enjoy it, m'boy, while ye may. You'll be old like me soon enough.'

Cormac came to the Alley, rode up to the house, and saw Maeve sitting in her window and the hunchback behind her. It was a trembling dusk. It concealed the depravity of the Alley and the new moon softened the light and smudged the shadows. The scene was painted with the soft colours of romance.

When he looked up at the window and saw her, he wanted her. The tumble of her red-gold hair, the curve of her cheek in the glow of the lamp contrasting with the silhouette of the man behind her his misshapen shoulder exagerated by the darkness, looming and menacing. He stared at them a long time.

He had never been in love, truly in love, in his life. He was awkward in the company of females. There had been no woman in Usher since his mother had died. His relationship with the fair sex had been, up to now, purely a matter of self-gratification. Maeve aroused his lust more than his love, and he determined to have her. What would happen after that was a question that never troubled him. Why should it? He had not been taught to curb his desires. He had been brought up to believe that as lord of the castle he was entitled to anything he fancied and he had so far never met a girl who was not willing, grateful even, for his favours and he left the wenches he consorted with well recompensed.

He went to the door and knocked. He heard the sound reverberate through the house. A plump woman, strangely respectable, answered.

'What d'ye want?' Batty asked.

'This is Lizzie Brannagan's?' he asked.

'Not any more. Yerra, if it's *that* yer lookin' for, you'll have to go to Rosie Moore's down Wellington Street.'

'But I was told . . .'

'Well, whoever told ye must have wan foot in the grave, so he must. Yiv come to the wrong place.' The door was shut in his face.

He stood back and looked up. She was still in the window an aureole of light about her, and she was laughing. He wanted to reach her, to touch her, to climb up the house and break the glass between them.

He had tethered his horse and he crossed to the 'Green Cock'. Perhaps they could enlighten him there as to how he could gain access to her.

As he went into the tavern all conversation ceased. They looked at him with unblinking eyes and wondered what he wanted from them. Within the hour they had found out it was Maeve Donahue that he wanted but they had no advice to give him as to how he could achieve his desire. Jangles, a free drink in him and one to follow, gripped his arm and set him down in the curved seat beside him, out of earshot of the others.

'Yiv no chance while the hunchback is around an' he's around all the time.'

Cormac nearly choked on the foul clouds of tobacco that billowed from the little man's pipe. 'Well, what can I do then?' he asked.

Jangles rubbed his fingers together and Cormac took out a sovereign. Jangles' mouth watered in anticipation of spending it. He plucked the stranger's cloak again.

'Listen. I'll think of a way. Just gimme a day. It's all I ask.' Cormac shrugged. He put the coin back in his pocket and

Jangles looked as if he might have a heart-attack.

'Somehow then,' the stranger said. 'I know of a certainty if I could speak to her ...'

'Couldn't ye let me have a little on account?' Jangles licked his lips greedily. The stranger shook his head.

'Cash on delivery,' he said and smiled his charming smile. And left. He went to the Shelbourne Hotel on St Stephen's Green and did not sleep much that night. He drank enough brandy to send him drunk but it was not as effective as usual. All he could think of was Maeve sitting in the window. He wanted her and he was used to getting what he wanted.

The next morning he was in front of No. 1 Doone Alley as dawn broke over the city. He did not notice the dirt of the place. His nose was indifferent to smells. There was no room in his mind for anything but thoughts of the girl he had seen in the window. He stood cloaked and motionless, waiting. Eyes watched him from every window and door and he was unaware. Life was stilled in the Alley because of his presence there. The mere sight of him, well-dressed and handsome, so alien in their midst, caused them to suspend all normal activity and stand and gawp.

Cormac's patience was eventually rewarded as Maeve appeared at the door. She wore a sprigged muslin dress and a white wool shawl was wrapped over her shoulders. She looked more beautiful than ever, fresh as spring itself. She had a radiance about her that struck awe in the beholder.

Yet she was innocent, he could see that. She wore her purity like a flower, and the lumbering hunchback at her side only contrasted with her delicacy.

He followed them through the streets of Dublin. He was their shadow while they paid a penny to a beggar and looked in shop-windows. The hunchback bought a pie off a tray and they dodged carriages and skirted the crowds, the limping man always protecting her, always holding her hand. Cormac watched jealously as she laughed up into his face and he became certain that the misshapen boy was very well aware of his presence. Sometimes he glanced over his crooked shoulder as if to check that he was still following, though why this should be, Cormac could not work out. He did not seem to mind Cormac's presence always one step behind them.

Cormac did not know whether the girl was aware of him. He

413

followed them until they returned to Doone Alley and he went to check his horse in the stables. Then he went to the 'Green Cock' to keep his date with Jangles.

Fergal said to her, 'Look at him. There's your prince. He has come for you.'

She tossed her hair back with irritation. 'Oh Fergal, when will you believe me? When? I'm not waiting for a prince. Certainly not him.'

Jangles did not keep his appointment. Red Rafferty arriving home in the night had caught him skulking around No. 1 and grabbed him by the throat.

'You little bastard. If you are spying or informing I'll kill you, do you hear me? Scum like you should be shot.' His fingers tightened on the stringy throat and he shook the little man until his cap fell off.

Jangles scampered away trying to swallow. He sobbed with fury at the thought of the shiny gold coin, but his fear of Red Rafferty was greater than his greed. He was fairly sure too that the stranger would not get to see Maeve without his help. Red Rafferty, Rosaleen or Fergal, he reasoned, were unlikely to affect an introduction. He sat in his hovel drinking black tea, chewing his knuckles and watching the entrance to the 'Green Cock'. The cobbled street was foggy and shone slimily under the moon. He saw the stanger go into the tavern and come out later, turning his footsteps towards the Quays. Ah well. All he could hope for was that the man would return on the morrow.

'It is a powerful desire he is under, to see Maeve Donahue,' he thought to himself. 'A very powerful urge. But with the likes of him, urges waxes and wanes, so they do, waxes and wanes. Still, it is very powerful.' Jangles went asleep in his chair. He always slept there, for his bones pained him dreadfully and the only ease he got was tucking himself up in an old rug that he draped around himself and putting his feet up on a stool before the fire. He nodded off with Spot, his dog, on his lap, partly for company and partly for warmth. He was restless that night, and when he awakened the next morning, he pushed the dog off his stiff knee and hurried to the window.

Yes, the stranger was there, standing like a shadow, gazing up at the window of Lizzie Brannagan's. Jangles hugged himelf with glee. The tea was still on the hob and he poured a cup and smacked his lips as he drank the tepid black liquid. He rubbed his hands together. There was still a chance to make that money, a good chance.

Red Rafferty was home. Jangles snorted bawdily to himself. That would take up all Dark Rosaleen's time and energy, he felt sure. You only had to glance at them, the lusty look of them both, the energy of their movements. That wan had been itchy for her man the last months and Red last night had been jumpy as a cat. Well, he'd be more relaxed now, Jangles was sure. It'd take a lot to disturb that pair this morning.

He knew Maeve's window. He had seen her often enough, brushing her hair with long smooth strokes, her back visible to the street.

He ran out into the courtyard and beckoned the stranger. 'C'mere. C'mere an' listen. There's no way she'll come down an' you standin' there. She'll come to help me. Hide down the passageway there an' I'll ast her to help me with the barrel-organ. She loves the barrel-organ, so she does. I got it offa a Eyetalian who died of a bad chest. Couldn't take the climate here, so he couldn't. Now ye be nice to Miss Maeve, d'ye hear?'

The stranger nodded and did as he was told. He felt hot and excited and full of an intense energy. The waiting had only increased his desire for the red-haired waif he coveted. He saw Jangles throw some stones at the window where he had first seen the girl. The day before yesterday — was it such a short space of time? He had not been free of the thought of her for five minutes since he had first glimpsed her. He saw Jangles beckoning and heard him shout something at the window. Then he waited. It seemed hours before she suddenly appeared at the end of the tiny passageway where he was hiding. 'Calm now. Calm now,' he told himself, feeling excitement rise within him and his heart pounding.

She was bending over the barrel-organ, wearing the same light pretty dress as the day before, when he crept up behind her and pulled her into the passage. She started to scream but he covered her mouth with his hand. He could feel the texture of her skin like silk and the flutter of her eyelashes, like birds' wings. The jade of her eyes was startling in her pale face. They were wide with fear and anger.

'Hush. I mean you no harm. I just want to talk. Promise you won't run away if I let you go?'

She nodded. He released his grip and she rubbed her mouth

with the back of her hand and stood trembling, looking at him.

'Listen. Since I've seen you in your window. I haven't been able to get you out of my mind.'

He could not keep the excitement out of his voice. She sensed his eagerness and backed away from him, wary as a wild animal.

'What do you want of me, sir?'

'I want you.'

She smiled. 'That's not possible, sir.'

'Good God, girl, I'm offering you so much. You don't understand. I'll buy you an apartment, anywhere you like.' He heard himself make the offer, and was surprised by his own words. What made him so generous? he wondered briefly, and knew the answer at once. He had to have her. At whatever cost. Seeing her close, being near her, had inflamed his desire for her. She smelt of flowers, her skin was milk and honey and the wild tumble of her red-gold hair caused him to gasp for a moment in the immediacy of his lust.

'I'll give you pretty dresses made of the finest silks. You can have anything your heart desires. And I'll get you out of here. Out of this foul place. It is no setting for a jewel as precious as you.'

She looked at him. 'I don't want to get out of here. Not yet.' Her face was innocent of coquetry, open and trusting.

'Well, I'll give you whatever you want. Jewels. Beautiful things.'

She shook her head. 'An' what would I have to give you for it? All those things?'

He looked at her quickly and saw she was sincere. He could not believe that anyone who live in Doone Alley could be so innocent, yet she was. He wanted her more than he had ever wanted anything and her desirability increased all the time.

'You'll give me yourself. I'll be gentle. I'll give you pleasure.'

'Oh, is that so? Well, I'm sorry, sir, but it is not possible.'

'And why not, pray?'

'Because I belong to another. I love someone else.'

'Who? Who? There is no one you could belong to here. I saw no one. Who?'

'Fergal, of course.' She said it simply and it took him a few moments to realize who she meant. His expression changed. She saw the anger on his face, the look of incomprehension

416

change to one of contempt.

'That cripple? I do not believe it. It is not possible.'

'Take care, sir. You are not to say anything unkind about someone I love.' Her voice held a warning.

'You could prefer him to me? You could choose him? When I offer you myself?'

'I love him, sir. I do not love you.'

He looked at her in astonishment then advanced towards her. The passageway was dark. He had manoeuvred her until her back was against the hard brick wall. The wall sweated a slimy grey ooze that caused Maeve to wrinkle her face with distaste. She was not too alarmed. She thought that this was a gentleman and obviously he would behave as such. Nevertheless her heart fluttered within her and her knees felt weak.

She said defiantly, 'I love that cripple, as you call him. All the sweetness of the world is in his soul. So leave me be, sir. I could never be yours. Please. Leave me be.'

He felt the anger rise within him. He knew he was losing his temper, but then he had never tried to curb it.

'That kind of scum has no soul. How dare you prefer him to me? How dare you? He is a peasant ... worse, he is a slum-dweller, a coarse ...'

'He is not.' She was nearly in tears. How dare this man insult her beloved so? Well, she would show him. 'He is not. He is the first-born son of The Earl of Usher Castle. So there. Not that it would matter to me if he were not. Now. Let me go.'

Cormac towered over her, unable to believe his ears. She tried to get away, frightened she had said too much, terrified in case she had got Fergal into trouble. She was scared now when she saw the stranger's face in the shadows.

He had caught her wrists and was holding them back against the wall, her hands above her head. He had come close to her, so close that she could smell his breath and see the pores of his skin and the fine film of sweat over his lip.

'What did you say?' he whispered hoarsely. He heard another voice in his head, the voice of his mad Aunt Bella. 'Your father has another son, older than you. His name is Fergal. Fergal is heir to Usher.' The blood was pounding in his ears. He wanted to scream, or wound or both. A terrible aggression took hold of him.

'Nothing, sir. Nothing. Please let me go.' Now his hands

417

were hurting her wrists and she cried out in pain.

'What did you say' he asked again. 'Tell me.'

'I said Fergal was the first-born son of Lord Usher of Usher Castle,' she whispered.

'How do you know?'

'The Widow Boann told us before she died. She brought up Lord Usher's brother Creagh and her sister Bessie Broderick works there. She is the cook. The Widow said Lord Usher gave Fergal to the orphanage because he was . . .well, malformed. But she brought him here and he stayed with us all his life.' She was sobbing now.

'So you thought to benefit from this, my fine young lady, did you? You knew who I was all the time? So blackmail is your pretty game, is it? Well, we'll see about that.' He grabbed her arm and she screamed again and Jangles heard her and jumped on his one leg in an agony of doubt. He wanted that coin so much. If he interfered he would have lost it, of that he was certain. He would wait a moment or two before he sounded any alarm.

The stranger stared at Maeve in horror. 'Oh God,' he said, 'Oh God. Oh my God.' He threw her aside with such force that she fell in the dark cobbled alley, hitting her head on the slimy wall. She was crying now, her head bleeding, and Flossie McMahon, who was passing, saw what was happening and shouted to the top of her lungs.

'Take your hands offa her, ye bastard. Help. Help. He's killin her.'

But the stanger had not even paid the fallen girl any attention. He pushed past Jangles and ran out. Jangles cried after him, 'Me sovereign. Me sovereign.' But the stranger disappeared into the 'Green Cock'.

Jangles followed him, out of breath. 'Me sovereign. Me sovereign. Ye promised, sir. Ye promised.'

The stranger shook his head and snarled at him, 'Leave me. Leave me, man. You'll get no money from me. Brandy, landlord.'

Jangles near died of disappointment. He looked with fury on the stranger. 'Ye bastard. Ye promised. Ye . . .'

The stranger pushed him away with such force that he fell on the sawdust-covered floor. He felt the pain shooting through his body as he hit the dirt. He scrambled upright and went out into the Alley to wait. To watch. Somehow he was going to get his own back on this gobster who built a man up with false promises then let him down.

Cormac drank his brandy. When he had finished he went out into the Alley to find it full of people. There was a mob facing him. They stared at him silent and hostile and his blood ran cold.

Rosaleen had awakened in her lover's arms, her face rosy from sleep, her eyes cloudy with desire. They had spent the night making love and now he held her softly in his arms, cradling her, kissing her as if he could never have enough.

'Oh me darlin', me sweet, sweet woman, yer the light of my life, the love of my heart.'

Rosaleen's eyes held sadness and laughter and she said. 'Ye'll leave me, though, Red Rafferty, an' go again. Yer like the wind that no one can catch.'

'You've caught me, *alanna*. Let me tell you I'm giving up. I'm getting out now. I've run my last gun. This time 'twas a big batch fresh from the armoury in Paris and they little knew it was my final trip. The soldiers were out last night after me. I'm getting too old for the nights at sea, the waiting on the hillside, the rain-soakings and the danger. No more. I'm taking you from this country, from the secrecy I force you into. We'll go to Paris and we'll marry. I'm quite decided. I'll make an honest woman of you, my Dark Rosaleen. Does that suit you in every particular, my love?'

She thought fleetingly of Ireland, her mists, her magical changing light, the mountains and the lakes, and how she would miss them. But he would too. No one loved Ireland more than Red Rafferty.

She sighed and smiled into his eyes, a smile of great content. 'Oh my darling ...'

They heard the banging on the door. Rosaleen pushed Red away and grabbed her robe.

'They mustn't find you here,' she said and rushed to the window.

'It's Jangles,' she cried. 'And ... Oh God ... it's Maeve ...' She fled to the door and was down the stairs in a flash, Red following. Something in her voice told him that it was serious.

They stood, shocked at the sight that met their eyes. Jangles was supporting Maeve, a bloodied dishevelled Maeve, her head cut and bleeding.

'Maeve, Maeve my love, what happened?' Rosaleen took the girl in her arms.

'Mister Rafferty I'm all right really. It was him ... the stranger ...' Flossie McMahon had set up a hue and cry. The people had seen Maeve and Jangles. They had emerged to find out what had happened. One-Eyed Willy and Breen Dubh forced their way to the front of the crowd. They stared at the door of the 'Green Cock' as Jangles pointed.

'Him. In there.'

As they looked the door opened and the gentleman they had seen lurking about the place emerged. They had hated him before he had touched Maeve. They had hated his clothes, the money he had, the conviction he had that they would help him.

He had found Maeve. They saw that now. Indeed he had found her.

'It was him,' Jangles cried and they stood watching, anger and resentment emanating from them. Jangles ran out of the alley onto the Quays. The light in his eyes had been rekindled. He had found a way to make a hundred times as much as the stranger had offered him.

Fergal had come down the stairs having heard the commotion, but not knowing what had happened. When he saw Maeve he stopped as if struck.

'Oh Jasus, what's been done to you, love?' he cried and as he went to take her in his arms to carry her upstairs she was brutally pushed aside by the stranger who grabbed him by the shirt-front and pulled him out of the doorway. There was no time to defend himself, if indeed Fergal would have tried. The stranger who had hurt Maeve was intent on killing the hunchback, Red saw. Why, he did not know. He watched, unable to believe the attack. All the inmates of Doone Alley watched, open-mouthed. The man seemed possessed of a demon. He was beating the life out of Fergal, calling out, they thought, meaninglessly, 'It's mine. All mine. It's mine.'

Fegal's face was bleeding and Red realized he would be killed if someone did not stop the beating. He ran into the courtyard and tried to pull the stranger off Fergal. Breen Dubh had gone to the other side and together then sought to separate the two, but the man's strength was phenomenal. Red and Breen were strong men but they could not seem to make any headway. The stranger kept up his concentrated attack and it looked as if he

420

would leave the hunchback lifeless.

There was a sudden rush of feet. Red felt a surge of relief. Someone was coming to help him get this madman off Fergal. Then he heard Rosaleen scream. It was a cry of such deep despair that he turned to look at her. The stranger heard the scream too, and also turned. She called out something to him and pointed. Red shook his head and moved to her, thinking briefly how much he loved her, how infinitely precious she was to him. He heard someone call 'Halt', but he did not think it had anything to do with him. He moved nearer to her, unable to understand the look of horror on her face. He wanted to hold her in his arms and soothe her pain, stop the dreadful cry on her lips.

He did not feel the shots at first and went on walking. He said, 'It's all right my love,' and then the pain hit him. He spun around and faced them. The Army. With Jangles.

Always a bloody informer, he thought and fell like a stone.

Chapter

69

THE walk this time was in June and the weather gentle and mild. No harsh wind whipped the trees. No cold froze their bones, no rain soaked their clothes. The sun shone and all the world was green. Sage and lime, the trees shook their sweet and tender leaves. The mountains were purple and gold with heather and flag. The sky was blue and they could hear the song of the birds.

They walked, each engrossed in their own thoughts. Rosaleen led, head held high, her hair over her shoulders, her shawl held loosely around her waist, her red skirt swishing about her as she walked, her ankle bracelets jangling.

Red was dead. She had grieved. She had wept. He had been laid to rest and she had mourned. In the largeness of her heart there was room too for loss. Death was part of life. All one could do was accept it and recover. Cormac had gone to America. James had given him the money to go. She had listened to him while he explained what he had felt when Maeve had told him he was not who he thought he was.

'It was all I had to hang onto,' he said, looking at her with eyes so like her own.' There has been no reality for me except who I was. I was the next Knight of Usher. And I did not feel it. I felt restless. A wanderer. I was brought up to believe all of Usher was mine. I kept saying it because I was frightened.'

She looked at him, the son she had given up. She felt the tug at her heart, for she could see Creagh and herself in his face.

'When I heard I was not the person I thought I was I went mad, I didn't mean to hurt Meave. You know I wouldn't hurt her or Fergal. Now I'm glad I'm not the Knight of Usher and he is. I am free. I can go to America and make my own way. I'll go to the West. They say a man can be free there. And wander.'

There was strangeness between them. 'I cannot call you mother,' he said shamefaced. 'Not yet. Dolly was my mother. I never really got over her death. I behaved like a spoiled brat. My only excuse is that no one told me.' He added 'I'm going to change.'

Rosaleen had smiled. 'You'll have to if you want to get on out there,' she said.

He nodded. 'I'm sorry for the damage I've done,' he said.

'It's all been for the best,' Rosaleen told him. 'It's not your fault about Red. He always knew that was the way he'd go. It was inevitable. He died just as he was giving it all up. But I think he would not have been happy. Inactivity would have bored him to death and I couldn't have borne that. He would have withered leaving Ireland forever. It would have broken his heart. No,' she sighed, 'better this. At least, I have to tell myself that. Life is for the living. The rest ... well, that has been all good. God bless you, Cormac.'

She kissed his forehead and he left. She did not know whether she would ever see him again. That is life, she thought. People come to you for a while, they stay, then they go. It is life.

Now the time for mourning and weeping was over. All that was left for her to do was to deliver James' son to him and then she could join the Minstrel on the grassy billows and the waving high fields over the land. It was where her heart lay, where it had always lain. It awaited her patiently, and she simply marked time until she returned to it. She had no illusions; it was a harsh and demanding life, she knew that. Red had kept her from it long enough.

She would never love any man the way she loved Red. He had been her passion and her weakness. He was dead, and weeping over her loss would not return him to her side. She was too much a woman to be alone. She wanted a man at her side and the Minstrel was her soulmate, he always had been. He was bone of her bone, flesh of her flesh. He knew all the ways they would go and he loved her.

She loved him too. Not as she loved Red. Red was the caviar, the champagne of life, Ronan the bread and water, and when all was said and done, in the end bread and water were the most valuable because they were essential. She would be at one with him, at peace. She had had enough excitement, and lifting up her head to smell the breeze, her heart sang within her, for the future with the Minstrel seemed to her bright and right and wonderful.

Behind her, hand-in-hand, Fergal and Maeve walked, gravely silent. Their gravity was caused by the sights and smells about them. Amazement gripped their souls.

'It's like the pictures come to life,' Maeve whispered, awe-struck.

'But much, much more beautiful,' Fergal said to her and pinched himself to make sure that he was not dreaming.

Around them the sweet breeze was full of the scent of flowers and the bees hung on the hollyhocks as if they were drunk. At the roadside Fuchsia splashed the green of the hedgerows with crimson. Every so often they came upon pools winking madonna-blue in the sunshine, hiding in circles of beech and willow. There was wonder in their eyes as they walked behind Rosaleen, who could not help thinking how pure and shining a thing their love was.

James had seen them for the first time at the dockside as he waved farewell to Cormac. James had grown old, Rosaleen thought, and wondered if she too had aged. She had no inclination to worry over how she looked, those days were over. Not that she ever had, and the Minstrel saw her as always young. She was in his eyes the girl he had first taken in love, down in the valley below Usher.

James had come to her and begged to have his son back.

'You gave me a substitute son, Dark Rosaleen. Now be even more generous and give me my own. I do not deserve him, but I beg you to please let me try to win his love.'

'Only if you also take his wife,' she said.

He bowed. 'It will be an honour,' he replied.

'They are sweet innocents. I'll know if you betray my trust,' she told him.

He nodded and said, 'You need not threaten me, Rosaleen. I will take such care of them.'

'She is the daughter of Sylvie Donahue, Bessie Broderick's daughter who ran away.' Rosaleen thought that Sylvie would not mind her breaking that confidence now.

James' eyes widened. Then he smiled. 'Bessie will be well pleased. She has retired to Craw Kilty's cottage in the valley.

Her grandchild has won my heart, Rosaleen,' he said. 'I will be proud to have her as my daughter.'

He sighed. 'I long for youth and laughter in Usher again. But you can be sure I will be good to them.'

'And they will be good for you.'

When he had seen Fergal for the first time his heart had ceased its steady beat for an instant, a breathless second, and then it started pounding nineteen to the dozen. For it was Dolly he saw. Dolly's smile lit the sweet face of the hunchback. The blue of his eyes was the exact colour of his dearly loved dead wife. The way his mouth curved to the right in a little half-moon, was Dolly, and the expression in those blue eyes of innocence and trust was hers, all hers. It was as if a hand had squeezed his heart and he had great difficulty in controlling his emotions.

There was no condemnation in those eyes. He had dreaded to meet them, but he need not have worried. There was no blame there, no accusation and he knew then that Fergal had inherited Dolly's lovely nature.

He was struck too by the flame-like beauty of the girl beside his son. She looked at Fergal with such overwhelming love. She watched warily as they embraced and he realized that she would guard Fergal and protect him from any hurt.

He said, 'I will take care of you both.' Then added, 'If you will let me.'

The sun was warm on Rosaleen's back and the clean air blew through her hair and brought the roses to her cheeks. Ah God, it was good to be alive, to be walking the road. She was free again. She felt the stirring of excitement in her breast and her steps became lighter. She had no shoes on and though the road was hard on her softened feet she did not care. Joyfully she quickened her pace.

There was Usher. It seemed such a short time since she had come here with Cormac in her arms. She had been so sure she was fulfilling his destiny. Well, perhaps all that had happened had been necessary. Each time she had come here she had brought something. Cormac, the dead Creagh, and now Fergal. And Maeve. Sweet lovely Maeve. Craw Kilty said that the castle was a place of gloom these days. Well, Maeve would change all that. She would light up a graveyard and bring a smile to a dead man's face.

Fergal and Maeve. Their love shone like a beacon. It overwhelmed you to look at them. They would have babbies. Usher would echo to the sound of children's laughter and James would be happy again.

He had looked into his son's eyes and liked what he saw. He looked back on the man he had been and that he did not like. He had been so quick to judge, looking down loftily from Olympian heights and deciding the fate of others. Deciding to banish someone, his own son, because he was not perfect. Like some despot king of old. Well, he had not done well. He had made the wrong choice. Perhaps, he prayed, he would be given a second chance.

They walked up the drive. The castle loomed in the sun and James waited on the steps. Fergal and Maeve stared up in astonishment. It was a castle out of their dreams.

Rosaleen stopped, curling her bare toes around the pink and white gravel. She motioned the young couple to continue without her. She had said goodbye to them properly in Doone Alley. Now they walked bravely forward, their faces lifted to the castle in wonderment. They moved slowly, hesitantly. Then Rosaleen saw that James had run eagerly down the steps to meet them. She watched as his restraint broke, and he gathered them both up into his arms, kissing them and weeping.

She turned away. The last remnants of her burden fell from her as she saw the Minstrel waiting for her at the arched entrance, one brown foot resting on the other, his flute in his hand. He leaned gracefully against the old stone that marked the homestead, the place of belonging, the enclosure. He did not like to come any further, she knew, for he did not want to be trapped. He had always said that if you went into those grand places they beguiled you away from the open roads and he could not bear for that to happen. He smiled at her now, for he could hear the bracelets on her ankle jingle-jangle as she moved.

Rosaleen walked towards him and away from Usher Castle forever. The roads called to her. And her man. And they were one. All she had to do was follow. She took a deep breath and held out her hand as she reached him. They smiled at each other and together they went away from Usher out over the world.